KARMIC TIES

A Novel of Modern Asia

Stephen Long

Medicine Bear Publishing
P.O. Box 1075
Blue Hill, ME 04614

Cover design by John Long
Cover photograph by Dave Shank

Printed in the United States

ISBN# 0-9651546-1-0

Library of Congress CCN# 96-080076
Fiction - Social Consciousness - Modern Asia

First Printing - 1999

Those whom the gods wish to disappoint they first make charming.

Gore Vidal
Empire

For my parents.
Also for Beth, Mary and Tang.

Dedicated to the memory of
Nana Veary,
who still watches over my shoulder with love,
just as she promised.

ACKNOWLEDGMENTS

My unending gratitude goes to Jonathon Ray Spinney and Robert Stein, who believed in this book from the beginning, and saw it through its many stages of evolution to this final form.

I also offer my sincere thanks to each of the following people who provided support and encouragement in one form or another during the long process: Jaya Bear, Susan Lee Cohen, Elizabeth Danysh, Ken Edwardsen, Mary & Olivia Gamble, Pauline Hansen, Darlene Hutchinson, Jeffrey Jackson, Karla Kral, David & Judy Long, Douglas, David, & Stephen Luchetti, Greg Mabry, Michele Manafy, Jennifer Metcalf, Dennis Moss, Frank & Kathy Perry, Zola Purnell, Rick & Sarah Rand, Mike and Yumiko Sayama, John Williams, Phra Bodhipalo, Phra Krupalad, Dan and Diana Borasch, Ernest and Marie Hara, Annell Potter, Claire McAdams, Luc Hovan, Raymond and Sonya Miyashiro, Marshall and Yuko Hung, Kuulei Takenouchi, Gregory Rand, and Claudia Woods.

I would also like to acknowledge the gentle people of Thailand, from whom I learned so much. God bless them every one.

Prologue

This was the biggest night of all his big nights, and he was certainly one who had enjoyed more than his share of those. He knew that if he won this election he will have shown the whole country that it was possible to overcome not only the disadvantage of a humble birth, but even a vague, clouded background if one had one; *he* certainly did. This victory would be the crowning achievement of his career so far: a spectacular, but unlikely, journey that had begun over twelve years before in a seedy bar off Silom Road in the heart of Bangkok, Thailand.

Pompam was pleased with himself. He stood quietly apart for a moment and looked out at the noisy hotel ballroom where family members, friends and followers had gathered to await the final tallies. He absently fondled three large Buddha amulets that had been blessed by holy monks; they dangled from thick chains of burnt-orange, twenty-four-carat gold that hung around his slender, handsome neck: his posture perfect, his mind wandering in and out of present time.

Vivid flashbacks of memory assaulted him, many of them full of intense joy and triumph: his amazing good luck, his startling ascent, his loves, his family, and his many and varied pleasures that he had allowed himself without restraint. But some memories were dark, difficult, and intensely painful to recall; over time his mind had drawn a thick, protective cloak around itself, obscuring certain things he had done to others — and other things that had been done to him.

He promised himself that if he won this election he would do his best to make amends for past deeds he had buried so deeply: actions that over the years eventually led him to this unforeseen earthly pinnacle. He silently vowed that he would return steadfastly to the Lord Buddha's teachings, make merit often, demonstrate compassion for the poor, and work diligently to eradicate the social and economic inequities that still prevailed — in spite of his country's new wealth and role-model status, the envy of its international neighbors. He firmly believed, however, that regardless of what he had done in the past, he was still, by nature, a good person; to this day he remained secure in the knowledge that his karma was good: otherwise he knew he would never have been so blessed by fortune.

Pompam, the nickname given to him by his mother when he was born, was a "buffalo boy" from Buriram Province in Isan, Thailand's driest and poorest region. His real name, Vichai Polcharoen, next to photographs of his well-known face, was prominently displayed on colorful campaign posters scattered around the opulent, gilded room. It was sometimes hard for him to accept the reality that the lively, brown-skinned country boy who went naked until he was five — and didn't own his first pair of shoes until he was eighteen — was one and the same person as the strikingly good-looking candidate on the glossy placards.

His elegant and beautiful wife of nine years, Rattana, was there — dressed, groomed, and bejeweled befitting Pompam's noble status in the material hierarchy. His two older children were by her side: Prakart, his first-born son aged eight, and his daughter, Somporn, six. His youngest, Surapong, a son of three, was asleep at home in the care of his nanny. How ironic it all was, he thought to himself, remembering the impoverished days of his village courtship, and the eventual births of those three innocent children to whom he had given so little of his time.

Most of his brothers were there that night, too. But not the one who mattered the most, he reflected bitterly, and then realized he was close to tears.

Kittipong, his campaign manager and closest friend since child-hood, was circulating about the room greeting friends, supporters, well-wishers, and the nervously-smiling, obsequious ones who hoped to benefit in some personally-enriching way from Pompam's election to Parliament. Kitti, as he was called, had been drinking Black Label Scotch since late that morning, but still held his own among the many business leaders, military officers, and royally-decorated ladies who had come that evening to show support for their golden boy, sampling a taste of his glory.

Pompam, back in his body again, paused another moment before returning to his guests, indulging himself in one last sweeping gaze over the assortment of high-ranking personages in the room; he felt validated that such people had become familiar, first-name participants in his not unglamorous, very public life.

Volunteer campaign workers, as well as bureaucrats invited by the Party bosses, were among the hundred-or-so well-heeled guests, and at least for that evening they all felt at-one and equal, pulling for the same man.

It was a scene much like election night parties in many places all over the free world. The difference in this instance, perhaps, was that there had been a great deal of "insurance" taken out beforehand to make sure that Pompam secured his seat without fail. If not completely happy, at that moment Pompam was sublimely confident of himself, as usual, and he stepped forward into the room with a radiant, charismatic smile.

PART 1
The Boy From Buriram

Chapter 1

It was at the end of the second year of a devastating drought in the plains of Isan that the impoverished parents of four hungry children finally came to the conclusion that there were just too many mouths to feed. Precautions had to be taken to make sure the family could survive. The previous year there weren't enough rains to bring to harvest but a fourth of their forty-acre rice field. The other three-quarters had been parched in hard-packed, cracking clay under the merciless white sun. Ochre dust choked the entire village. All of the other families surrounding them for many miles were in the same hopeless situation. The one-quarter harvest — plus the remaining rice saved from the previous year — had gotten them through so far, but with very little rain this season they could expect the same results, only perhaps worse.

Without the monsoon rains there were no fish in the ponds, nor were there frogs or water bugs in the arid fields that could be preserved as a fermented paste to flavor their rations of rice and provide some much-needed protein. They had already sold one of their two buffalo in order to raise cash for staple foods to last them through the end of the drought, even though they knew that to sell a buffalo was almost the same as selling land: no land, no rice. They desperately needed the buffalo to provide rich fertilizer for the fields and to plow the furrows for future rice; but this year their sacrifice couldn't be avoided.

"Paw," the father, told "Maa," the mother, that he had spoken to the Abbot of the village temple, and he had agreed to take the oldest boy in as a *"nene,"* or novice monk. Pompam was ten, and the next son, Nuu, was only five. Paw needed the labor of his oldest boy when harvest time came (hopefully they would have a harvest), but he knew that the Abbot would let him help out, in spite of his duties at the *"wat,"* or temple. At least the boy would be assured of one meal a day while living in the *wat*, reasoned Paw. He knew that Pompam would eat food left over after the monks had eaten; food the monks and *nenes* had begged for that morning from villagers who daily "made merit" by

1

giving what they could spare. Every morning the monks — as well as the *nenes* — would rise at 4:30 a.m. for chants and prayers; and then at 6:00, enveloped in a cocoon of saffron-colored cotton, shaved heads bowed, they would silently walk barefoot through the dirt alleyways of the village, accepting alms offered by the poorest people in Thailand.

Paw felt that with the oldest boy taken care of at the *wat*, the younger three boys — the last only an infant of one year — had a better chance to make it to adulthood. Much to Maa's regret, they had no daughters to help her in the home. Their second child, a girl, born two years after Pompam, had died at the age of three, a victim of diphtheria. In spite of the family's extreme poverty, four more boys would be born into the Polcharoen family within the next eleven years to make a total of eight sons.

Such are the ways of poor Isan, nearly one-third of Thailand's total land mass and population. Isan, in the Northeast, is bordered to the south by war-torn Cambodia and to the east by sleepy Laos. To the west are Thailand's fertile Central plains, drained by the mighty *Chao Phya*, Siam's "River of Kings." The Isan people are considered a race apart, and are of predominantly Lao origin. Many of Isan's inhabitants only speak their native dialect as did Pompam's parents, and have no comprehension of the Central Thai language which is the *lingua franca* of the country. Isan people, particularly in the region of Korat and its neighboring provinces, are considered by some to be the "original" Thais. They are known for their good hearts, gentle natures, beautiful smiles, and their devout Buddhist faith which is intermixed with local forms of animism, belief in ghosts and nature spirits — and other super-stitions that vary from province to province. Their dark skin places them lower in status in the eyes of their fairer countrymen from the Central and Northern regions.

With the Vietnam war and the rapid economic development of the late 1960's, 70's and 80's, the demand for labor grew enormously in the capital city of *Khrung Thep*, or Bangkok. The people of Isan flocked to the big city to be the factory and construction laborers, taxi drivers, hotel service personnel, maids, and workers in the sex industry. During these growth years many male and female members of Pompam's vil-lage left their native lands behind for Bangkok in search of work; when they found it they would faithfully send money home to their families for survival. Some returned home every year to plant and then again to harvest the rice. Others remained in the capital in full-time pursuit of a money supply for their loved ones back on the farms.

Paw, Pompam's father, didn't feel right about leaving his young family in the village and go to Bangkok to work; he and Maa had never even been to the capital. He tried his best to supplement the family's minuscule farming income by weaving Isan-style wicker baskets and selling them through a vendor in the local market in Nong Ki, the District's main town, about five miles from their village. The baskets brought in only a few *baht* a month, but it was still a help in keeping the family one step away from starvation. Maa also contributed to the family coffers by raising silkworms, spinning their fibers, and weaving traditional brightly-colored Isan-patterned textiles — also sold at the market.

Maa and Paw considered their decision for Pompam to be raised at the *wat* as their only choice for his future. The temple was only a ten-minute walk from their home and they could still see the boy every day. With so many children in the village from families in similar circumstances they felt lucky the Abbot had agreed to look after their oldest son. In addition to food, the boy would also get a temple education (such as it was) and perhaps the opportunity to go on to higher learning in Buddhist schools in other parts of the country. They knew that if their son could get an education there would be a chance that he could one day earn enough money to help them stay alive. Young Pompam, anxious and a bit afraid, had never spent a night away from his parents in his entire life; but he knew he had to go for the good of his family, so he kept his feelings to himself.

The appointed day for Pompam's ordination as a *nene* had arrived. The family walked together to the temple: Maa and Paw dressed in their finest, the young children barefoot and in their normal ragged hand-me-downs, scrubbed clean for the occasion. Maa's best consisted of a white lace, waist-length blouse with collar, and a *sarong* of silk she had woven herself; her thick black hair was pulled tightly into a bun, emphasizing her strong, high cheekbones. Paw, unshaven and deeply creased by the sun, wore his only decent shirt and baggy short pants. Around his waist he tied his "*pakomah*," a useful, multi-purpose piece of cloth, woven in a colorful Isan plaid. They carried with them the newly-purchased yellow robes their son would wear as a *nene*, incense, flowers, and offerings of fruit from their garden for the Buddha image and the Abbot.

"Ow! Paw, you're hurting me! Take off my hair but please leave me some skin!" Pompam cried as his father attempted to shave his head with an ancient, dull safety razor. Pompam's scalp was nicked and covered in bloody scratches when it was finished. The white of his head contrasted dramatically with the dark, suntanned skin on the rest of his body. His eyebrows were also shaved off as was the custom, leaving fierce red welts in their place. Maa suppressed a tear as she said, "You look like a baby frog from the well..."

Pompam dutifully sat before the Abbot and repeated the first part of his vows, concentrating hard so he wouldn't make a mistake. He made the proscribed three bows each to the Buddha image and then to the Abbot; afterwards he went outside with Paw to change into his new robes. It would take him a good month or two to learn how to tie them on correctly by himself. More than once he would be mortally embarrassed by having them fall to the ground, by regulation wearing nothing underneath to hide his scrawny nakedness.

The boy returned to the altar in his robes to kneel once again before the Abbot and complete his ordination. When the ceremony was over Pompam and Maa had to suppress urges to run to each other's arms for a comforting hug. This they could not do as the newly-ordained *nene* belonged to the Lord Buddha now, and even though he wasn't old enough to be a real monk, he still had to observe the rule of no bodily contact with any female — even his own mother.

Later on, after the ceremony, the Abbot, whose name was *Phra* Prateep, called Pompam over to him. Pompam knelt respectfully in the Thai style with his legs and feet tucked off to one side, hands raised together in a prayer-like "*wai*," the correct position of respect for receiving words from a monk. He was careful to keep the joined tips of his fingers near his lips, his head slightly bowed, and his eyes half-closed like the Buddha's.

Phra Prateep asked him when his birthday was. Pompam, frowning, turned to his mother and said, "Maa, I forgot when I was born." Maa told him the date and also answered the next questions:

what day of the week it had been, and at what time of day. *Phra* Prateep picked up a note pad and started writing down numbers, adding and subtracting, counting on his fingers. Then he examined Pompam's left and right palms very closely, dirt mixed with sweat making the lines more pronounced, occasionally looking up so he could see the boy's face over his bifocals.

Phra Prateep then exclaimed, "Vichai (he would never call him by his nickname, Pompam) you, like all people, have the makings for good and evil. But I can see that you are clever beyond the point of what is good for you. You must learn the teachings of the Lord Buddha thoroughly, practice meditation daily, and make merit often. These things will help you to balance your perhaps-dangerous cleverness. It would be best if you were to remain a monk all your life, but I know that this is not your fate." He paused after these words, adjusted the well-worn robe on his bony shoulder, and looked at his figures again. After a few moments he said, "Be careful, Vichai. You can have all from the world that you want, but you and many others will suffer. Never forget that you are human too, and that everyone is subject to the same basic law of karma. Also, all human beings may become Buddhas in a future lifetime, so you must treat them as such in this one."

Pompam nodded his hairless pate and acted as if he fully understood, even though he didn't. But *Phra* Prateep's serious words resonated loudly in Pompam's young soul, and he felt an uneasy stirring in the back of his head — from somewhere deep in his unconscious mind.

The following morning, after a seemingly never-ending night of unusually vivid dreams, Pompam rose with the other monks, *nenes*, and "*wat dek*s," or temple boys, and joined them in their routine of bathing, chants, and meditation. When they left the *wat* to beg for food Pompam walked by the side of the Abbot (who had a bad leg and used a cane) and carried his dented, much-used, aluminum alms bowl.

The memory of that first morning, when he passed his parents' house, never left him all his life. He found his mother waiting by the side of the road, kneeling, eyes looking down with her hands raised in a *wai*. Pompam presented the Abbot's bowl, averted his eyes, and waited while his mother put in two scoops of "*khao nio*," or sticky rice, some pungent *"nam prik batou,"* a spicy chili paste with fish which was wrapped in a banana leaf, and two small papayas. He dearly loved his mother and the burning urge to touch her was overwhelming; but he knew that he must resist, and with *Phra* Prateep passed on to the next house.

He glanced back only briefly to see his sad, barefoot Maa sitting in the dust beside the road, silently weeping into her callused, over-worked hands. She had realized with regret and certainty that her oldest son had left her care forever, but she prayed that he would grow to be a man who would have both the money and the good heart to look after her in her old age. At that same moment Pompam, also very sad, suddenly felt the all-powerful hand of fate grab hold of him and take control of his life. The realization startled him, especially since he knew not where that hand would lead him; it did little to relieve his sadness.

Later on, as the monks and young *nenes* made their way back to the village temple, Pompam decided not to resist the leading, silently resigned himself to his destiny, and surrendered his heart to the Lord Buddha. He figured it was the only thing he could do.

Thus began the cycle that would repeat itself every day for the next five years without much variation. Pompam, for the most part, was obedient and stayed out of trouble. From the Abbot he learned to speak and read Thai, and he dutifully practiced his meditation and did his temple chores, which were usually related to being the personal servant of the aging Abbot. He was always polite, never complained, and discovered not a small amount of satisfaction in the routine of his tiny monastic world.

Perhaps the only blemish on the landscape of these mostly-happy years originated, oddly enough, from the modest bronze (but to Pompam it looked like gold) Buddha image on the temple altar that had been as familiar to the boy as his own parents. It had sat there in plain view, its face radiating an almost seductive warmth, for as long as the child could remember. Although it had usually inspired innocent spiritual longings in his child-mind, shortly after his ordination as a *nene* it somehow started to make him feel greatly disturbed.

After living in the temple only a very short while he noticed himself becoming increasingly more uneasy each time he looked up at the statue; then before too long a larger, highly-animated version of this "Golden Buddha," as Pompam began to think of it, would appear in his dreams — oftentimes dancing and laughing wildly. One night the Golden Buddha even appeared with a phallus in full erection, arousing Pompam, causing him to wake up in a cold sweat.

This unpleasant dream recurred from time to time and it bothered the impressionable young boy; sometimes he lay awake at night, not wanting to go to sleep, fearing another encounter with the dreaded Golden Buddha. He wanted so much to tell *Phra* Prateep about his blasphemous dreams and find the answer to what was causing them, but he felt ashamed and kept it to himself, not daring to risk angering the old Abbot. He feared that *Phra* Prateep would think some *"pee,"* or evil ghost, was possessing him; perhaps he would be forced to disrobe as a *nene* and shame himself and his family. So he endured his nightmares alone.

Despite his troubled and secret dream-life, which he continued to share with no one, Pompam's natural charm, strong brow, radiant smile with straight white teeth, and sparks of nascent talents had their magnetic effects on almost all who came into contact with him. He was popular with the other monks and *nenes* — and he was always the center of attention during Buddhist holidays, merit-making ceremonies, and village festivities that periodically worked their way through the calendar. The other village children were instinctively drawn to him, and he never tired of helping them learn their lessons or playing football with them in the temple yard. By the time he was fourteen the young girls of the village were already spending more time than necessary around him, and seemed to make excuses to come often to the temple. Although these attractions were obvious to the old Abbot, succumbing to female attention was not yet on Pompam's agenda.

That same fourteenth year the Abbot was called to make a journey to Bangkok where he would attend a meeting of the *Sangha* Council, the governing body of the clergy; he would represent the temples of Nong Ki District of Buriram. "Vichai, you will go with me to Bangkok and serve me. You will stay by my side except when I am in the *Sangha*. When you are not by my side you will be mindful and remember who you are."

He was surprised to be the one chosen to attend the Abbot during this important event, and there was some resentment felt by the senior monks that Pompam would be going instead of one of them. They all knew, though, that *Phra* Prateep had grown to love Pompam like his own son; and since each of them loved him as well, their resentment was very short-lived.

When the morning of their departure finally arrived, Pompam's entire family came to the temple to say good-bye. The village "*tambon*," or headman, who owned one of the only motor vehicles in the village, was to drive the Abbot and Pompam to the train station in Buriram's main town, about forty-five miles away.

The *tambon*, *Khun* Direk, arrived at the temple with his wife and daughter who were going along for the ride. Of his five children, Direk's oldest two were boys in their mid-twenties: they worked in construction in Bangkok. The next two were daughters: one was already married to the owner of an auto repair shop in Nong Ki, and the other was still a student at the local high school. The youngest child, Rattana, was his precious baby and he allowed her to tag along with him wherever he went, following him like a faithful pet. She was an intelligent and beautiful child with wide round eyes, and she wore her hair in the blunt-cut style of a school girl, falling just below her ears.

After all the good-byes were said, *Khun* Direk and the Abbot got into the cab of the pick-up. Pompam, Rattana and *Khun* Direk's wife climbed into the open back of the truck for the ride into town. Ten-year-old Rattana and her mother were careful to maintain the proper distance from Pompam, and took precautions against bumping into him on the winding dirt road into Nong Ki and Buriram, clouds of yellow dust rising in their wake.

None of the three spoke a single word all the way to the station, but sensitive Pompam felt uncomfortable being the focus of the steady, dark-eyed gaze of the little girl. Once, for a fraction of a second, he imagined he saw the demented Golden Buddha dancing in the dust whorls just above her head. He quickly glanced away from young Rattana and the bizarre image disappeared, leaving the boy breathless and puzzled.

When they reached the train station, *Khun* Direk went at once to purchase third-class tickets for what would be a six hour journey on wooden bench seats. His wife gave Pompam and *Phra* Prateep a small basket of food to snack on before they began their noon fast. After about a thirty-minute wait, the train pulled into the station and Pompam could hardly contain his excitement; unconsciously he started jumping up and down, whistling, until he caught the Abbot's disapproving frown and stopped.

This would be his first trip to Bangkok — his first trip outside of Buriram for that matter — and his first train ride. Surely I am a lucky boy, he thought to himself, trying to imagine what the rich capital would look like. Television hadn't yet come to their remote village so he had no clear mental image of the city, or any idea at all of what to expect. He only knew that Bangkok was where the money was, and that money was something very important; sometimes it was even life or death.

Young Rattana and her mother *waied* very low to the Abbot and then to Pompam, muttering "*Chok dee ca,*" or "good luck." Then they waited on the platform while *Khun* Direk escorted the monk and the *nene* onto the train and found them suitable seats in the back of one of the un-air conditioned cars. He pressed an envelope containing five-hundred *baht* for expenses into the Abbot's hands, *waied*, wished them "*Chok dee cap,*" and left them on the train.

A few moments later he and *Phra* Prateep waved good-bye to their friends on the platform, and it wasn't too long before the Abbot began to snooze. Pompam, mesmerized, gazed through the open window at the passing landscape of poor villages like his own, seemingly endless fields of rice, and countless water buffalo lazing in the heat of noon. He day-dreamed about Bangkok and a future that he sensed waited for him there one day.

Phra Prateep eventually woke up from his nap, and for over an hour he silently kept his eyes on his young friend and aide-de-camp. In his reverie *Phra* Prateep, once again, began to intuit something about Pompam, Bangkok and money: something powerful, passionate and fateful.

Chapter 2

They arrived at the bustling Hua Lampong station in downtown Bangkok late in the afternoon. Pompam was at once stunned and overwhelmed, as he had never before seen so many people in one place. There were perhaps thousands of intent-looking travelers scurrying to and from the crowded platforms — many of them having to step over the migrant, homeless Thais sprawled out sleeping near the walls, and the "*farang,*" or foreign, tourists — most of them young with backpacks — waiting for trains that would take them out to the exotic Thai provinces. The *farangs* were quietly sitting about, reading their guidebooks, many of them munching on Thai fruit and sweets purchased from street vendors outside. All of these scenes swiftly caught Pompam's attention, one after the other.

"Vichai," the Abbot called out sharply as the young novice was about to get lost in the crowded terminal, "I told you to stay next to me. If we get separated you might never find me again — or ever see your mother in Buriram." Young Pompam silently apologized with his eyes and thereafter did his best to keep up with the old, but robust Abbot, who managed to walk quite quickly in spite of his limp. They fought their way through the masses and finally made it out to the taxi stand where they could hire a three-wheeled open taxi called "*tuk-tuk*" for their journey to *Wat* Mahathat near Sanam Luang.

Pompam's head was on a swivel as they made their way in the careening *tuk-tuk* through Chinatown towards Rattanakosin Island, the original, two-hundred-year-old royal city of Bangkok. He held on tight to the *tuk-tuk* hand-rail as they swung onto Ratchdomnoen Avenue past the Democracy Monument, the scene of a violent student up-rising in 1973. Cars, trucks, *tuk-tuk*s and motorcycles were jammed together in clouds of exhaust, inching their way down this grandest avenue in Thailand, built by King Rama V in the latter part of the 19th century, his very own Champs Elysses.

When they got to the end of Ratchdomnoen they made a left

turn at Sanam Luang, the vast royal park where the King presides over the annual plowing ceremony, and where kite competitions and Buddhist celebrations are often held. From there Pompam got his first glimpse of the glittering Grand Palace and *Wat* Prakaew at the far end. *Wat* Prakaew, or the Temple of the Emerald Buddha, is the most sacred place in the entire Kingdom, and every Thai holds it in his heart with the highest reverence. The site of its tall golden spires reflecting the sun's last rays in millions of multi-faceted colored mirrors caused Pompam to fall silent in awe, and offer a *wai* with his hands.

"I will take you to *Wat* Prakaew tomorrow morning, Vichai. In the meantime, keep yourself mindful." "Mindfulness" is one of the most important virtues in the Buddhist religion, and *Phra* Prateep never tired of preaching about it to his young attendant.

Even though Pompam knew he couldn't have anything to eat (as it was already way past noon) the variety of tantalizing smells coming from dozens of braziers and food stalls lining the street made him almost unbearably hungry. He thought of the following morning, and if the Abbot was in a good mood there might be a chance to sample some of these tempting delicacies, most of which he had never seen in his native Buriram.

The *tuk-tuk* stopped at the west entrance to *Wat* Mahathat, the Abbot paid the driver, and they entered the gates of the famous royal temple that supposedly contained a relic of the Lord Buddha himself. The *Sangha* Council was to meet at *Wat* Mahathat because the Abbot there was also the Supreme Patriarch of the Buddhist religion in Thailand — similar to the Pope in Rome.

Inside the temple compound Pompam was astonished to see so many monks. The vast courtyard looked like a saffron sea, shaved heads bobbing up and down like whitecaps. In spite of the fact that he was carrying both of their bags, their two umbrellas, and the Abbot's ceremonial fan, Pompam managed not to stray more than one foot behind *Phra* Prateep, thinking it would be far easier to get lost in the *wat* than at the train station.

Phra Prateep smiled and politely greeted other monks as he led the way to a registration area where he signed his name to a roster. Standing nearby was a group of resident monks who welcomed each arrival and assigned them to billetings in the monastery. *Phra* Prateep

11

and Pompam found out they were to stay in Section III in the *"kuti,"* or room, of a resident monk from India named *Phra* Asoka.

The Indian had been in Thailand for only three years at the time, but he had the singular status of having been brought to *Wat* Mahathat by the Supreme Patriarch himself, after he met him during a pilgrimage to the holy places of Buddhist India. Before coming to Thailand and being ordained a monk, *Phra* Asoka had been a professor of chemistry and physics. He had long suspected the links between the physical sciences and Buddhism, and ultimately made the decision to enter the monkhood for life. It was his long-term goal to help spread this advanced religion in his native India once he had established his base in Thailand. He was given the Buddhist name "Asoka" by the Supreme Patriarch, who named him after Emperor Asoka, the third century BC Indian monarch who converted to Buddhism and spent the rest of his life spreading the *"dhamma,"* or teachings of Buddha, throughout his kingdom.

Pompam knelt before the *"ajarn,"* or professor, *Phra* Asoka, and *waied* three times touching his head to the ground. When Pompam looked up he felt warmed by the kind, gentle eyes on the darkly handsome face of the Indian, who appeared to be in his late thirties. Even at the age of fourteen Pompam was already sensitive enough to recognize an authentic holy man when he saw one.

Abbot Prateep didn't kneel to *Ajarn* Asoka, but Pompam could see in their eyes a kind of spiritual recognition pass between the two men when they introduced themselves. There were several students and other devotees present in *Ajarn's* humble *kuti*, and one of them immediately brought cold water to the weary travelers from Isan. *Phra* Asoka showed the Abbot and Pompam where they would sleep, gave them clean towels, and showed them where they could bathe and refresh themselves before joining the evening's opening ceremony.

"Please relax," *Ajarn* said, "and then we will go to the main *'viharn'* together at eight o'clock." Pompam was surprised that the Indian monk spoke the Thai language so beautifully, having been in the country for such a short time.

Clean and refreshed, the Abbot and the *nene* from Buriram joined *Phra* Asoka and strolled over to the large *viharn*, or temple auditorium, which was located at the center of the *wat*. The roofline was high, and mirror-covered "*nagas*," or stylized wooden snakes, curved skyward from the eaves. Hundreds of monks were already seated on the open floor, either silently engaged in meditation, or chatting with their neighbors, waiting for the Supreme Patriarch to show up and start the convention. When the august person arrived and took his place on the dais beneath the huge golden Buddha image, the chanting began in ancient *Pali*, the liturgical language, a derivative of Sanskrit. Although he didn't understand the meaning of the "*sutra*," or hymn, they were chanting, Pompam joined in with the others and allowed himself to be absorbed by the subtle vibration and steady, pulsating rhythm, the heady scents of incense and perfumed candles almost overpowering him.

About a half hour later Pompam, tired to the bone from the long day's journey, was jolted out of his reverie by the sudden sound of bells and gongs. The Supreme Patriarch gave a brief welcome address and then, with ceremony, adjourned the Council for the evening and led the procession from the room. Afterwards, *Phra* Asoka invited *Phra* Prateep and Pompam for a tour of the great temple.

He took them into the "*mondop*," a building that housed the magnificent gilded "*chedi*," or shrine, that stood at least forty feet tall and contained the physical relic of the Lord Buddha's body. All three of them bowed three times with their foreheads to the ground, then paused to sit at the *chedi*'s base while Pompam examined the awe-inspiring room, bordered at the edge by a dozen full-size Buddha images from kingdoms of the past.

"When I first came to Thailand I was allowed to live and sleep here in the *mondop* my first year," *Phra* Asoka explained. "I was the only person permitted to live within the inner courtyard of the temple, and I had this sacred place to myself every evening," he continued. "His Holiness, the Supreme Patriarch, knew that my meditations would deepen quickly in this environment, and that I would learn how to teach the foreign students that came here for training — from listening to my heart deep in the night."

Even though *Wat* Mahathat was one of the primary temples in Bangkok under Royal patronage, it was not one that was customarily on the "city and temples" tour. But due to the fact that it was so near Sanam Luang, the Grand Palace, and other famous temples, museums, and landmarks in the area, foreign visitors would occasionally find it and explore.

Pompam and *Phra* Prateep were later to learn that *Phra* Asoka also spoke English, German and French in addition to his native Hindi, so when foreigners came to the temple the *wat deks* invariably led them to meet their resident linguist from India. In time, word was spread about him in many countries, and he would, for many years, welcome a steady stream of foreigners who wished to learn about Buddhism and study the art of meditation from a master.

"Enough for tonight, my new friends from Buriram," *Phra* Asoka exclaimed. "Now I will take you back to my room to sleep as we all have much to do tomorrow." *Ajarn* led them back to his room, settled them for the night, then went back to the sacred *mondop* to sit for several more hours in deep meditation. He was later to reveal that he only slept two hours each night, and that once in a monsoon retreat he had sat in meditation for twenty-four hours without breaks or interruptions. Pompam had never before heard of such a feat, and from that moment on the wise professor became a role model for the aspiring novice.

Unfortunately for him, that night Pompam had a dream about his Golden Buddha that was far more disturbing than any he had ever had. This time the wild, satyr-like Buddha wasn't dancing or laughing. He was sitting in the middle of a large room filled with stacks of money crying a river of tears. As the tears flowed away from the Buddha, so did the golden flesh from his body until there was nothing left but a pile of gold-stained bones. Pompam jumped straight up off of his pallet on the floor, dripping wet with sweat, his breath choking, and tried desperately to calm himself. He surely didn't want to wake up the other young *nenes* who were sleeping nearby; they would tease him mercilessly for having nightmares. He laid down and eventually went back to sleep; the bad dream dissolving into images of Bangkok, excitement dispelling the fear of night.

The next four days of the *Sangha* Council meeting passed pleasantly for *Phra* Prateep and Pompam. The Abbot *did* take Pompam to *Wat* Prakaew the day after their arrival, and treated him to savory snacks from the street vendors. Even though Pompam had seen pictures of the Grand Palace compound all his life, he didn't expect the

14

exalted, rapturous feelings he would experience when he actually visited it in person. He almost floated through the maze of brick-paved courtyards, golden *chedi*s, seemingly endless murals depicting the Ramayana, royal temples, and European-inspired palace buildings; eyes wide, he was unable to speak, proud of being Thai.

Pompam quickly made friends with several other *nene*s and young monks who were more or less in the same position as he, serving older monks in the *Sangha* Council; together they explored the historic Rattanakosin area: *Wat* Po and the Temple of the Reclining Buddha, The National Museum, Amporn Palace, the amulet market, and Khao San Road where bearded, be-sandalled Western backpackers made their headquarters in the myriad of guesthouses and cheap hotels.

Pompam couldn't believe the countless numbers of automobiles — so many of them expensive and chauffeur-driven — with well-dressed, wealthy-looking Thais sitting in the back seats, looking so confident and happy; they were not at all like the villagers back home, like his Maa and Paw, who spent all their time under the hot sun, knee-deep in muddy rice paddies. For the first time in his life Pompam wondered what it would be like to be rich.

Every evening Pompam contrived to spend some quiet time with *Phra* Asoka, whom he had already begun to love. Abbot Prateep was pleased with their budding friendship, knowing that *Phra* Asoka always spoke in such a way that no matter what he said to the boy it would be related in some way to the teachings of the Lord Buddha. Although his sense of humor was keen, the Indian never spent words frivolously or used them without good intent; every story, anecdote, and lesson in some way picked up a thread of the Buddha's "Middle Way" and his "Eightfold Path" and was neatly woven into the conversation. He took Pompam each night to the *mondop* to sit with him for a while at the base of the sacred *chedi*. He gave him personal instruction in the technique of meditation, and for the first time Pompam was able to see a glimpse into the truth and deeper reality of this practice.

When the Council meeting was over and Pompam and the Abbot had extended their thanks to *Phra* Asoka, they walked down to the pier called Tha Chang and took the *"leau hang yao,"* or long tail boat, up the river to Nonburi Province. They had been invited by the Abbot of *Wat* Chalaw, a close friend of *Phra* Prateep's for nearly twenty-five years, to spend a few days at his shady temple by the river, to relax before going back to Buriram.

As the noisy, high-powered engine propelled the narrow, low-slung boat down the wide River of Kings, each time it crossed the wake of another vessel it bounced, blew spray inside, and Pompam squealed in delight. The boat, its prow draped with colorful protective talismans and rising forty-five degrees up out of the water, soon turned into a *"khlong,"* or canal, and continued on for nearly an hour. They passed dozens of ornately-decorated temples, small villages, and lively "postcard" scenes of the age-old water lifestyle that had been the care-free way of Thai people for countless generations. The boat stopped a number of times to let off and pick up passengers before finally arriving at the pier of *Wat* Chalaw where Pompam and the Abbot disembarked.

Pompam said, "Please, *Phra* Prateep, take me on the boat every day." *"Mai pen rai*, Vichai," the Abbot replied, using one of the most-used phrases in the Thai language which means "never mind." "It is possible that in the future you might be on these boats so often that you'll get bored with them." Pompam couldn't imagine ever getting bored riding the swift, ear-splitting longtail boats — or enjoying the ever-changing view of the riverside.

They made their way to the temple's principle *viharn* where the monk knew they would find his old friend, *Phra* Voravut, the Abbot of *Wat* Chalaw.

"Welcome, *Phra* Prateep and friend," the fat, jolly Abbot called out as they entered the contrasting darkness of the small *viharn*, the pungent smell of incense heavy in the air. "Give me the news of the Council meetings and tell me about life in Buriram," he continued. After Pompam was introduced and performed his three deep *wais* touching forehead to ground, he was forgotten as the two old friends started talking and laughing, catching up on their lives since they had last met almost three years before.

A few minutes short of noon they were called out to their lunch. A group of elderly ladies from the neighborhood had prepared a delicious meal for them, a weekly merit-making activity they had engaged in for over twenty years. After the customary pre-luncheon chants the two Abbots and Pompam went down to the small *"sala,"* or open air pavilion, by the *khlong* to eat their meal in the cool breeze.

"Vichai, what did you learn at the *Sangha* Council meeting in Bangkok?" the jovial Abbot asked timid Pompam.

The youth hesitated before answering, feeling uncertain and shy, and then said, "I learned that so far I know nothing about life other than planting rice and catching frogs."

"That's not so bad," *Phra* Voravut replied as he leaned back and laughed at the boy's honest answer. "At least you know you won't starve to death, and you have learned something about the cycles of life. You would like to learn more than this?" Pompam, thinking he had given an impolite response, was too ashamed to answer, but the look in his eyes gave away his desire to learn more — much, much more — than he could ever learn in his poor, dry village in Buriram. Abbot Voravut and Abbot Prateep exchanged glances, but said nothing — returning once again to their personal musings, leaving Pompam alone.

During the three days they spent at *Wat* Chalaw Pompam became friends with another *nene* who lived there named Supachai. He was also from Isan, but had been born in Ubon Ratchathani, far to the east of Buriram near the Laotian border. Supachai was three years older than Pompam and was a student at a school for *nene*s and young Buddhist monks in Thonburi, across the river from Bangkok. His father had died when he was only two years old and his mother when he was thirteen. He had four brothers and sisters — all younger than he. Having no money, they had been divided up between various relatives in his village after his mother died, and Supachai was sent to live in the local temple, first as a *wat dek*, and later as a *nene*. He studied hard, and when he was fifteen he passed the entrance test for the Buddhist high school.

"You can speak English?" Pompam asked.

"*Nit noy,*" or just a little bit, Supachai replied. "In school they teach us vocabulary, grammar, reading and writing, but not *speaking*. I have to learn to speak it on my own, so whenever I get a chance to talk to a *farang* I practice with them. One thing I found out in Bangkok is that if you're going to be successful, it's a good idea to know English."

Pompam and Supachai quickly developed a close, natural relationship like they were *"pi-chai-nong-chai,"* or big brother-little brother. Supachai talked about his schoolwork and his dream of one day mastering English and becoming a guide for *farang* tourists.

Each night while he was there Pompam heard him weeping softly in the night, and he guessed that it was because he was missing his young siblings scattered among uncaring relatives in his old village in Ubon. The young man wanted desperately to make some money so he could take care of them and help them get educations of their own.

The last day during their stay at *Wat* Chalaw, Supachai got permission to take Pompam to school with him. They woke up before dawn to catch the long-tail boat through the ill-smelling *khlongs*, the Chao Phya River, the ferry over to Thonburi, and finally two public buses through choked-up traffic to the school. Supachai introduced Pompam to his friends as his *nong chai* from Buriram. This made Pompam feel extremely proud.

After school Pompam, Supachai, and three of his friends bought iced fresh coconut juice from a street vendor. They rested for a while in a shady spot on the riverbank, watching the endless stream of boats float by, including "trains" of rice barges, many of them so heavily-laden their gunnels barely topped the waterline.

"Why don't you come here to school, Pompam?" Kittisak, Supachai's friend asked him.

Supachai replied first, "I will speak to my Abbot, *Phra* Voravut, and see if you can stay at *Wat* Chalaw with us — that is, if you pass the entrance test."

Pompam suddenly saw a whole new world open up for him with the possibility of going to high school near Bangkok — even if it was only a high school for "junior monks." Then he remembered his family responsibilities back in his home village; and he knew his chances were slim to none that he could pass the entrance examinations — even if he was allowed to try.

"I will have to speak to *my* Abbot first. He depends on me at the temple in our village — and my family does too," Pompam replied, not betraying his self-doubt.

"Well then, we'll both speak to our abbots and I'll find out when they hold the entrance tests. I graduate after next year, so you can take my place; but before I leave we'll be able to live and go to school together for a whole year," Supachai said with enthusiasm. Pompam said nothing, not wanting to raise his hopes.

The next morning at the pier Pompam and *Phra* Prateep said good-bye to *Phra* Voravut and Supachai, and Pompam *waied* three times on the ground and thanked his host as best he could. Nothing had been said about school, but Pompam was convinced that he would never be able to overcome the obstacles that stood in his way. *Mai pen rai,* he thought; just forget it.

Chapter 3

Pompam's mother, father, brother Nuu, and the younger ones rushed over to the temple to see him when word got to them that Pompam had returned. Nuu had missed his *pi-chai* so much that he wouldn't leave his side even for a moment during the next three days; he even slept with him at the temple, refusing to go home. "Pompam, don't ever leave me here alone again," his younger brother whined, tears welling up in his eyes.

"Don't worry, *nong chai*," Pompam replied, suddenly feeling guilty about his desire for school in Bangkok. "I'll always be there to look out for you — forever." Pompam truly loved his brother, and he meant what he said.

As this was the month of October, the rice was high and dark green and nearly ready to be harvested. The rains that season had been good, and everyone in the village expected a plentiful harvest that would keep them alive another year; perhaps they would even have some left over to sell to the Chinese broker in Nong Ki who, unbeknown to them, would make a huge profit when he re-sold their produce in Bangkok. The extra cash would enable the village families to buy some extra food and much-needed clothing, things they hadn't been able to afford since the bad drought ended.

In his free time Pompam diligently pursued his studies. *Phra* Prateep had noticed the difference in Pompam's attitude towards books since their return from Bangkok. The Abbot continued to teach Pompam all he could, given his own limited knowledge; but he himself hadn't even finished high school. Pompam found a few tattered, discarded self-teach English texts in the cupboards of the one-room temple school. One was called "English in 79 Hours." It took him at least 379 hours just to get through it the first time, but he stuck with it, remembering Supachai's words about the importance of English. He, like Supachai, learned some English words, acquired an elementary feel for sentence structure, and memorized as much as he could; but he still had no idea how the words *sounded.*

He decided that he himself wanted to get really good at English and become a tourist guide — maybe work with Supachai one day. He was also excited about all the other possible opportunities that Bangkok presented, and started to become more and more obsessed with grand ideas and schemes about how he would become a wealthy and successful Thai businessman someday.

In some intuitive way he already knew that his Buddhist service and training was only a stepping stone to much greater things. The haunting Golden Buddha dreams began to fade, and Pompam began to focus intensely on his desire to live, study and work in the grand avenues of Thailand's biggest city. Pompam gradually began to believe that he really might be as clever as *Phra* Prateep had so keenly discerned on the day of his ordination, several years before.

The young man made sure he performed well all his duties at the *wat,* and he fulfilled all his obligations to *Phra* Prateep; but he began to feel twinges of guilt about the strong desires that were growing within him. "Maybe the Lord Buddha has other things in mind for me," Pompam said to himself one day as he was on his knees scrubbing the wooden floor of the monks' sleeping quarters. "Perhaps I can make merit in other ways."

The time for harvest came upon the village. Pompam, lanky and skinny like a rail, tied his yellow robes up around his loins like a diaper and spent many hours each day toiling in the steamy fields. Paw and Maa were happy to have their oldest son working beside them again, cutting and collecting the stalks of rice. Each village family helped out the other families, which numbered only about thirty-five, clearing one field at a time until all the work was done in everyone's fields. They all knew that they had to support each other with their collective labor or one day they all might starve. Maa was pregnant again and prayed earnestly to the Lord Buddha for a girl. This was not to be, however, as yet another son would come into the family. This one would be nicknamed "Black" because of the full head of hair he was born with, totally unlike his older brothers who had come out of the womb completely bald.

Around the middle of harvest time Pompam received a letter from Supachai in Bangkok. This was the first letter he had ever received in his life and his heart thumped with excitement.

After the appropriate greetings and salutations for his family and the Abbot, the letter read, "...I spoke to my Abbot, *Phra* Voravut, and he has agreed to let you come and live here at the temple because of his friendship with *Phra* Prateep. I also spoke to the monk at my school who is in charge of admissions, and he has put your name on the list to take the entrance exam this coming May. If you pass, you will start the new term next October." Pompam was shaking with excitement.

Phra Prateep awakened from his afternoon nap about this time and came out into his garden where he found Pompam and young Nuu, giggling and joking. "Vichai, what has put that smile on your face? You look like you just raided the candy vendor's cart."

"*Khatote cap*," or excuse me, Pompam replied. "I just received a letter from Supachai in Bangkok. He sends his best regards to you and..."

"Go on, Vichai, get to the point..." the old monk replied with a sly grin.

Pompam hesitated because up until then he hadn't had the courage to tell *Phra* Prateep about wanting to study at the monk's school in Thonburi; he also didn't want the kind old Abbot to know that he didn't think he could pass the exam because of the limited education he was presently getting.

One look in the monk's eyes told Pompam he had better come clean and tell the truth, so he took a deep breath and said, "Supachai says I can come to Bangkok and take the entrance exam for his school — and if I pass, *Phra* Voravut will let me live at *Wat* Chalaw."

Phra Prateep paused for a moment before responding, intentionally keeping Pompam in suspense. He had, in fact, already discussed the matter of school with *Phra* Voravut, but had said nothing to the boy. "I guess if you plan on going to school in Bangkok we had better get you prepared for the examination," *Phra* Prateep replied.

Pompam was thrilled, but then quickly remembered his obligations and put on a serious look. "How can I leave you and my family here? Do you really think I could go?"

"*Mai pen rai*, Vichai. We can do without you for a while. If you get a good education you can come back here later and help us out," the old man replied, already sad thinking about the dangers that lay ahead for the young man. Having long-since acquired a good insight into Pompam's destiny and true nature, he worried for the boy; the temptations of Bangkok might prove to be too great for him.

"The examination isn't until May so I have six or seven months to get ready," Pompam explained, his guilt and worries dissolving as his chest swelled with hope. A tear or two trickled down Nuu's sunburned face as he thought about his *pi-chai* going away again. Pompam noticed and said encouragingly, "Don't worry, Nuu, if you study hard maybe you can be ordained, take the exam the following year, and come to Bangkok, too." Nuu so far hadn't demonstrated even the slightest interest in school; he didn't even know how to speak Thai properly yet; passing a difficult entrance exam and finishing high school wasn't very likely for Nuu, and he knew it.

Later that evening Pompam went to his family house and gave the good news to Maa and Paw, who were genuinely pleased. The word about Pompam's letter eventually reached *Khun* Direk, the village headman, and he also expressed his pleasure. He had always liked Pompam, and he had noticed that his little girl, Rattana, had something like a crush on him. He decided to do what he could to help Pompam pass the entrance exam; he wanted him to become one of the first in their village to get an education and go beyond inherited poverty, backbreaking rice farming, or seasonal construction work in the capital. He brought Pompam books from Buriram — and at his own expense he even arranged for the *"khroo,"* or teacher, from the nearest local high school to give Pompam private lessons in math, Thai history, and other subjects.

The months before the examinations passed slowly with no major incident. The village harvest was a good one again, thanks to ample rains. In November the annual celebration of *Loy Kratong* arrived, and was a joyful, long-awaited time for everyone.

During *Loy Kratong* every person in Thailand either builds or buys a small floating object called a *"kratong,"* made out of a cross-section of banana tree and adorned with flowers, incense, a candle, and a small coin. In Bangkok, and wherever else there are rivers or *khlongs*, these objects are released into the water with silent, hopeful prayers: a personal ceremony letting go of all the bad luck and negativity from the year before. One night each year the many rivers and canals of all of Thailand become alight with thousands of *kratongs* being borne away by gentle, timeless currents.

Poor naked children oftentimes swim out to capture the coins that are sure to be found on each and every one. In Buriram the *kratongs* were all home-made, and were taken down to the small pond that served as the village reservoir. Afterwards there were lively parties everywhere, much drinking, singing, and dancing the *"ram wong,"* the traditional Isan dance.

Pompam kneeled down and let go of his *kratong* with the fervent prayer that his impoverished country beginnings would soon be behind him, and that next year he would float his *kratong* in the *Chao Phya* in Bangkok.

The "cool" season came, and with it the New Year; a bit later Chinese New Year arrived, usually in early February. Those who worked in Bangkok for Chinese employers received a New Year bonus — usually the equivalent of one month's wages. Bangkok streets were practically deserted during these holidays; all of the exiled workers who could afford it went back to home villages to be with the families they missed.

For several days prior and several days after the declared holidays, trains and buses were filled to over-flowing. Thousands stood up all night because the bus and train companies sold three and four times the number of tickets for actual number of seats. Every vehicle going out of Bangkok was jammed to capacity with people singing, clapping their hands to country rhythms, drinking whiskey, and smiling broadly — knowing they were going back home with New Year bonuses in their pockets. No one seemed to even notice the traffic as they slowly inched their way deeper into the countryside.

After a long absence Pompam's closest friend from childhood, Kittipong, or Kitti as he was nicknamed, returned to the village with his family for *Loy Kratong*. During the bad years of the drought Kitti's family simply decided to pack up and leave for good. His father found work as a taxi driver in Bangkok and sat behind the wheel for sixteen hours a day. His mother purchased a small push-cart and got herself a spot on the sidewalk near fashionable Silom Road, selling *"somtam,"* the spicy, pungent green papaya salad made with garlic, lime, chilies, dried shrimp and peanuts — a dish that everyone in Thailand dearly loved. Kitti's mother made her *somtam* Isan-style and added raw black crabs from the river, and some fermented, odorous fish paste. In this way both parents were able to work, and both were their own bosses which gave them a feeling of independence. Together they were able to earn barely enough *baht* to keep their small family all together in the big city.

Kitti went to intermediate school in the Bangkok neighborhood where they rented a stuffy, one-room apartment. Every day after class he would rush to his mother's stall and help her prepare the ingredients for *somtam* for the evening rush that would come. He had only one older sister, and she had a job as a chambermaid at the Ambassador Hotel on Sukhumvit Road.

Pompam and Kitti had run around naked together like two barnyard puppies when they were small, and when they were a little older they were the ones who took their families' precious buffalo back and forth to the rice fields, riding on their swaying backs like Asian cowboys. While the buffalo were grazing or cooling off in the mud, the two boys would go off hunting for small animals: frogs, snakes, lizards, water beetles — anything that could be turned into a tasty meal for the family. Kitti loved Pompam like the brother he always wanted; he looked up to him, and happily conceded the role of leader to his friend.

Kitti was surprised to hear that Pompam had become a *nene* and was living in the village temple. As soon as he *waied* his ancient grandparents he threw off his shoes, put on an old pair of shorts, and ran off to the *wat* as fast as he could.

Kitti found Pompam sitting under the big tree behind the monks' *kutis* reading a book. Kitti couldn't believe his eyes. Pompam, who had before never much cared for being a student, was actually *reading*.

"What the fuck are you doing, Pompam?" Kitti screamed. The *nene* was so startled his book dropped to the ground as he turned to see who would have the nerve to use such a bad word in the temple.

"I'm studying my English, you stupid buffalo," was Pompam's reply. Then they rushed toward each other and grabbed at one another in a playful bear hug. It had been more than five years since they had been together.

Kitti then picked up the book Pompam had been reading and said, "*You* are studying English?"

"I'm going to take the examination in May to try to get into the Buddhist school in Thonburi next year. If I am to be successful, I *have* to study English," Pompam replied. Kitti's eyes widened at the thought of having his best friend not too far away from him near Bangkok.

"I hate going to school, but Maa and Paw make me get good grades or they'll send me back here to work in the rice fields. Then I would miss out on all the fun I have on Silom Road," Kitti exclaimed. "You just have to pass this test, Pompam, so you can come to Bangkok; then I can teach you how it all works!" He did his best to one-up his friend, and impress him by how street-wise he had become.

The two old buddies spent the next five days scheming and nattering about what fun and excitement they would drum-up together in Bangkok. "*Mai pen rai*, Pompam," Kitti kept saying, "you won't always wear those *nene* robes." Kitti and Pompam cooked up endless adventures for their future together in the capital, a place full of opportunities for clever young men such as themselves; or so they believed with boyhood confidence.

The cool season ended abruptly around the end of January, and the slow but steady rise in temperature finally brought on summer. In April came *Songkran*, the Thai New Year. Foreign visitors are the only people who seem to notice the irony that *Songkran*, which is also the water festival, should be celebrated in April — not only the hottest, but the *driest* month of the year. During this four or five-day festival real life is suspended and everyone wears the spirit of childhood; squirt-guns are drawn and buckets of water are dumped on everyone with total abandon; no one gets even the slightest bit angry — even the adults carry on like five-year-olds.

The original *Songkran* ceremony involved the slow pouring of scented water over the hands of one's parents while reciting good luck wishes for the new year. This simple observance somehow expanded into wild escapades of drinking, dancing, and massive water throwing. It also is another traditional family time in Thailand, and the migratory city workers flock back to their villages to pay homage to their families

— very much like the exoduses of New Year and *Loy Kratong.*

Pompam, being a *nene*, had to content himself with the traditional parental ceremony and otherwise confine himself to the temple — in spite of his yearning to play water games with the rest of his village friends. Fantasizing about a possible future in Bangkok was the only thing that kept him from feeling sad and left-out. "One day..." he kept saying to himself.

As the exam date in mid-May approached, Pompam was excused from nearly all of his temple duties so he could concentrate on last-minute reviews. Abbot Prateep and the high school tutor seemed pleased with Pompam's progress over the past six months, and both of them felt he was ready for the examinations.

Once again *Khun* Direk, his wife, and daughter, Rattana, took Pompam in their banged-up old pick-up to the train station in Buriram; this time the young man would be making the journey alone. Just before they left the *wat* Pompam received blessings from his dear Abbot, the nine other monks, and his mother and father. These blessings were bestowed in a small, age-old ritual that involved each person winding plain white string around his wrist three times while intoning some good luck words; then they tied the string in a knot and blew on it. To foreigners this practice seems somewhat Biblical, and the phrase, "Bestowing the breath of Life" often comes to mind.

Khun Direk purchased Pompam's train ticket, his wife handed him a small basket of snacks for the journey, and *Khun* Direk presented a small white envelope containing two-hundred-fifty *baht* for expenses. *Tambon* Direk knew for certain that both Pompam's family and the old Abbot had no money to give Pompam. Although he could ill-afford it himself, *Khun* Direk felt that it was not only his responsibility as headman to help the young man, but young Rattana had emphatically insisted he give Pompam the money. *Khun* Direk and his family *waied* Pompam as he boarded the train, and waved him off with heart-felt wishes for good luck.

At Hua Lampong train station he found himself a *tuk-tuk* to take him to Sanam Luang, but the driver tried to cheat Pompam by quoting a ridiculously high fare. Pompam stanched his anger at the thought of someone trying to rob a poor Buddhist *nene;* he calmly considered how it would affect the greedy man's karma in his next life on earth. He quietly kept his temper, told the driver what he was willing to pay, and gave him a searing, knowing look. The driver reluctantly acquiesced to the price, but gave Pompam more than one life-threatening scare as he recklessly ripped his way through the heavy, late-afternoon traffic.

Since Tha Chang Pier and the boat that would take him to *Wat* Chalaw was so near to *Wat* Mahathat, Pompam went first to pay his respects to *Phra* Asoka; he wanted to receive his blessing for the exams. Pompam found the venerable monk where he knew he would find him — in the towering white-washed *mondop* with its red, green and yellow tiled roof, sitting at the base of the sacred golden *chedi*. *Phra* Asoka was talking with some English-speaking visitors: a man and a woman, both wearing sandals, army fatigues, and T-shirts from Bali. When the monk saw Pompam approaching he smiled warmly, a light came to his dark features, and he stopped his discourse.

"You have returned, Vichai. But where is your Abbot?" *Phra* Asoka queried.

"He let me come alone, *Ajarn*, to take my entrance exams for the Buddhist school in Thonburi. I don't think I can pass them, but I'm going to try anyway. *Phra* Prateep sends you his regards," Pompam replied politely.

"After you have finished your obligations here, and you're on your way home, come back to see me; I have something to send back to *Phra* Prateep." Pompam gave his promise that he would do so, bowed three times and departed, intuitively knowing he had secured *Phra* Asoka's unspoken blessing, which gave him some encouragement.

Ajarn's eyes followed Pompam as he left the *mondop*, and then he turned his attention back to his foreign guests who smiled, sensing the warmth between the Indian monk and the awkward young teenager. *Phra* Asoka was telling them that, "Buddhism is a religion about personal freedom. The caste system in India keeps the masses from being free, and it only maintains the status-quo of the old-fashioned social hierarchy. Should the masses embrace Buddhism, then they will have a chance to grow to their full individual potentials." These particular foreign visitors, who had wandered into the temple by accident, thought about *Phra* Asoka's statement more than once during their visit to India, which was their next stop after they left Thailand.

On the way to *Wat* Chalaw Pompam purchased some fresh durian at the market pier for *Phra* Voravut. He really didn't know anything about buying durian, the large spiny greenish-yellow fruit that smelled to foreigners like over-ripe cheese, but *Phra* Prateep had told him to buy some, so he did. The long-tail boat was just ready to depart as he walked down the gangway, so Pompam jumped in and took the last available seat, happy to think that he could look after himself in the big city. He thought about how he would be able to enjoy that boat ride every day should he pass the examinations — and not have to spend the rest of his life planting rice.

Phra Voravut and Supachai were delighted to see their young guest. The kindly Abbot, who reminded Pompam of a smiling Buddha, was particularly happy with the durian — and proclaimed that he would enjoy it the next morning for breakfast. After the pleasantries of greeting were over, the Abbot went off to meet some local businessmen who were waiting for him in his riverside *sala*. Pompam and Supachai were free to go off on their own to ask and answer the many questions they had stored up inside.

"Well, Pompam, will you be ready for the exams in two days? I heard that nearly four hundred *nene*s will take the tests, but there's only room for about two hundred in the school. What have you done to prepare yourself?" Supachai asked. Pompam replied, giving Supachai a verbal run-down of the books he had studied and the tutorials he had been given by the high school teacher in Buriram.

"I know about as much as possible to know, having studied only in my village. I don't think I have a very good chance," the boy concluded despondently.

They talked in Supachai's room until both of them, almost simultaneously, fell asleep where they sat, leaning against one another.

Supachai had classes the following morning and left the temple early, as usual. Pompam intended to rest and review the few texts he had brought with him. All the next day he kept to himself, tried to be positive, and do what *Phra* Prateep had always told him to do: be mindful!

It was just before daylight when Pompam awoke, immediately aware that it was the most critical day of his life. He quickly washed and put on his robe, then walked out in the cool dawning to the small *viharn* where he wanted to spend a few minutes in quiet meditation before catching the water taxi into town. He found *Phra* Voravut already seated before the tranquil image of the Buddha looming high above them, almost touching the ceiling. Pompam sat beside him and did his best to control his racing mind, not an easy feat for a boy of fifteen facing a crucial moment.

After a few minutes he heard the soothing voice of the Abbot say, "Vichai, I have prayed for the Lord Buddha's blessings for you today. Go now with good luck." Pompam *waied* to him, then to the Buddha image, and ran off with hope.

When the examinations were over the young *nene* felt totally numb and exhausted. He didn't — or rather couldn't — say much until he and Supachai were finally in the long-tail boat on their way back to *Wat* Chalaw.

"Don't worry about it, Pompam. You prepared for it, you did your best, and there's nothing you can do now but wait for the results — which you won't get for about six weeks." Pompam thought of the agony he would have to endure during the wait-time. Be mindful, be mindful, he admonished himself repeatedly, trying to resist feeling anxious, worried or depressed.

The following day regular public school was closed, so Kitti came all the way to the temple in Nonburi to meet his old friend. "Do you think you passed, Pompam?"

"I don't think I did, but I won't know for weeks," he answered glumly.

"*Mai pen rai*, Pompam. Now is now. Let's hurry to Silom Road before noon so my mother can make you some *somtam* for lunch."

Pompam had not yet been to the main financial and business district of Silom, and he felt totally out of place with his rubber slippers, shaved head and well-worn yellow robes. There were seemingly thousands of young people his own age, and it occurred to Pompam that Bangkok was truly a city of the young; all the wrinkled-up old ones were back home in the villages, planting rice and taking care of babies that belonged to sons and daughters who had gone to Bangkok for jobs and money, he assumed correctly.

The two boys walked through the Siam Square shopping area and Pompam was envious of the long lines of teenagers waiting for the cinema to open; he wanted so badly to see the latest action-hero flick the huge posters advertised. He had heard about the massive, six-story Mahboonkhrong Center which was just across the street, and was aching to go inside; he didn't dare, however, as it would be inappropriate for him to enter as a *nene*. The two boys settled for strolling along the scorching sidewalks, darting from awning to awning, stopping every now and then for something cold to drink. They occasionally saw busloads of foreign tourists pass by, inspiring them to speak enthusiastically of the time when they both would be guides, earning thousands of *baht* a month.

Pompam constantly teased Kitti about his resistance to learn English. "How do you ever expect to get ahead if you don't study, you buffalo?"

"*Mai pen rai.* I'll always have you, Pompam," he joked in return, giving his friend a healthy poke in the ribs.

When it came time for them to part, both were sad, knowing it would be many months before they could see each other again. "Write to me with your test results, Pompam. I'm counting on you to get your education so you can help me get a good job."

Pompam tried his best to be cheerful, but he felt his smile showed little heart as he waved good-bye from the departing bus.

The next morning after thanking his hosts, Pompam headed down the river to *Wat* Mahathat to see *Phra* Asoka as he had promised. He found the *Ajarn* in his normal place inside the *mondop*. Pompam was expecting to hear the familiar question of, "Did you pass?" Instead, *Phra* Asoka never said a word about the examinations. He only inquired about his health, and asked how *Phra* Voravut was getting along.

"Come Vichai, I have something in my room that I want you to take home to *Phra* Prateep."

When they got to *Phra* Asoka's *kuti* Pompam saw the familiar collection of Buddha images that the *Ajarn* liked so much to have around him. There was one very large gold-leafed one about six feet tall in the courtyard, and another five-foot-high standing Buddha in his room; it had been cast and presented to him by some of his students. The two statues would accompany *Phra* Asoka the following year to India where they would be donated to a temple near Bombay that he and his group sponsored.

Phra Asoka picked up a smaller figure and handed it to Pompam. "I brought this image of the Lord Buddha from Bodgaya, the place in India where He attained His enlightenment. Notice the peaceful smile on its face. I want you to take it to *Phra* Prateep as a gift for your village temple."

Pompam stood motionless, stunned for a moment as he stared at the little Buddha statue in his trembling hands. Suddenly its peaceful face turned into the wild Golden Buddha's face that used to come to him in his dreams! For a second Pompam was completely lost in shock until *Phra* Asoka's voice brought him sharply back to the present. "Do you think *Phra* Prateep will like it?" he asked.

Pompam looked down at the statue and saw that its face was peaceful again, back to normal. He took a deep breath and quickly recovered his composure. "I am hardly worthy to hold such a precious object in my hands, *Ajarn*," he stammered, though it pleased him to know that it was partly because of *Ajarn's* affection for him that he had chosen to make such a presentation to his Abbot.

Phra Asoka smiled, his long lashes shading sparkling eyes, and he sensed Pompam's feelings. He said, "Go now, Vichai. I will see you in October." Pompam took those words as a prophecy and his spirits lifted as high as the sacred *chedi* in the *mondop*. He *waied* reverently, then politely took leave of his kind friend and mentor.

He held the Buddha image in his arms while concentrating on his mindfulness all the way back to Isan. The bus to Hua Lampong station, the train to Buriram, and two more buses to Nong Ki finally took him to his dusty, poor village — a journey of nearly ten hours, but he arrived not feeling tired at all. Somehow he began to know in his heart that he had passed the examinations, and he could allow himself to anticipate the reality of his first big opportunity.

The weeks passed slowly for Pompam as he waited for the

examination results, even though he tried not to think too much about them. Finally the letter came, and once again he and his brother ran off to the Abbot's garden to read it in private. He scanned the letter quickly and the words reached up to him from the page.

"I passed, Nuu! I did it!" He immediately sprinted over to the *viharn* and performed his prostrations three times before *Phra* Asoka's image of the Lord Buddha. He looked up at the statue and was happy to see that it still wore its original serene, peaceful expression. He felt his heart fill up with gratitude, the determination to be good, and the desire to achieve success for his family.

Chapter 4

Pompam arrived at *Wat* Chalaw during the first week of October. He had been sent from his village with the usual blessings and his wrists were covered nearly up to the elbows in white strings. *Khun* Direk had thoughtfully taken up a collection among the village families — usually ten *baht* or twenty *baht* each — and presented it to Pompam to help pay for his books, school supplies and personal necessities.

Pompam had grown about three inches over the rainy season, almost as if the monsoons had nourished his body as well as the lush, green fields of rice. He had indeed become a handsome youth, with a well-proportioned frame, distinguished forehead, straight nose, full lips, and perfect white, even teeth that enhanced his charming, open smile. His years as a *nene* had given him grace, poise and an elegant posture — all of which would support his life-long image as a man of self-confidence and strong character. He indeed was a favorite native son of his poor village; everyone expected great things from him — and they all told him so in no uncertain terms. It made Pompam feel apprehensive to know that so many hopes were based on his success.

Supachai, true to his word, took the new boy under his wing and helped him adjust to his life away from home. Supachai's well-developed study habits rubbed off on Pompam, despite the younger boy's chronic tendency to make "*sanuk*," or fun, with his new school friends. Even with Supachai's companionship Pompam still experienced some acute moments of homesickness during those first few months; and his lonely brother Nuu, left behind in the village, missed his *pi-chai* desperately.

"You've been here only two months, Pompam, and you already have more friends than I do after three years," observed a teasing Supachai, who was shorter than Pompam, had much coarser features, and uneven teeth that were pitted and discolored from childhood malnutrition. It was true that Pompam had quickly become popular, a leader among his fellow students. His above-average height and his outspoken, *sanuk* personality seemed to set him up quite naturally for the starring role.

Foreigners often notice that the Thai people — particularly those from Isan — are an especially affectionate, "touchy" race, and Pompam and his friends were no exception. Groups of schoolboys were always piling up against one another, resting their heads on each other's shoulders or laps, arms entwining, joking and entertaining each other with teenage nonsense. Pompam was always at the center of an animated klatch of shaven-headed youngsters in yellow robes, truly enjoying and needing the sense of closeness it provided; all the boys did.

Kitti visited *Wat* Chalaw whenever he could escape from his after- school duties at his mother's *somtam* stall. It became his habit to stay overnight at the temple on Saturdays so he could stretch out his Sundays with Pompam, the highlight of his whole week. Kitti was the antithesis of his best friend in terms of physical appearance. He kept hoping that he would grow tall and handsome like Pompam, but so far in his short life he had been dramatically disappointed. He was chubby, had very dark skin, wiry, kinky hair, and a wide Isan nose with virtually no sign of a bridge. His eyes were alert and cunning, however, and he had an infectious laugh that drew others to him in spite of his looks. For a while he was jealous of Pompam's close friendship with Supachai and the dozens of other friends that were always around to claim his attention. This jealousy eventually subsided — only to be replaced by a fierce protectiveness as he continued to follow Pompam through life.

"Pompam, why do you have to always listen to the English radio station? It's not like you can really understand what they're saying; they talk too fast," Kitti commented one day.

"How else do you think I'm going to learn English if I don't hear it sometimes? There is no English TV channel, and as a *nene* there's no place I can go and talk to *farangs*; and I *have* to learn English if I'm going to be successful," he replied, full of determination.

Supachai, who was in the room at the time spoke up, "One day I'll take you to *Wat* Po and we can try to catch some *farang* tourists and speak to them. Even though the Abbot of *Wat* Po forbids this, many of us go from time to time and rarely ever get caught."

"Why would the Abbot of *Wat* Po not want us to speak to

farangs in the temple?" Pompam innocently inquired.

"Because in the past, many *nene*s have posed as official temple guides, and have given out incorrect information about the *wat's* history. There have even been some who have asked *farangs* for money," answered Supachai. Pompam found it almost impossible to believe that a *nene* could ever ask anyone, much less a *farang*, for money. He had been too well trained by his Abbot, *Phra* Prateep, to even imagine such impoliteness.

"Why *not* ask them for money? Everyone knows that all *farangs* are rich!" put in the opinionated Kittipong, buying into the common belief about the wealth of all foreigners. The feeling that they were *"only farangs"* was an attitude ingrained in the collective Thai mind ever since the European colonial powers repeatedly tried to conquer Thailand over a period of three hundred years — but were *never successful*; the Vietnam war only reinforced these sentiments: *farangs* were "fair game" for exploitation — especially by the poor.

"I would like to go to *Wat* Po sometime, Supachai, and approach *farangs* to practice my English. But I will *never* take any money from them," declared Pompam self-righteously.

The long-awaited New Year season finally rolled around and Pompam made plans to return to his village. Kitti and his family were also going, and Pompam thoughtfully invited Supachai to come along. Supachai desperately wanted to visit his younger brothers and sisters in Ubon Ratchathani, but he had no money to make the trip. Pompam had circumspectly saved some of the money his village had given him in October, and he had just enough left to be able to get Supachai and himself to Buriram.

The five day holiday was a real joy for Pompam. Although he had to stay in the temple with *Phra* Prateep, he was allowed to spend as much time with his family as he wanted. He had Supachai with him as his guest, and was proud to be able to entertain his new *pi-chai* in his home village. He also had the company of Kitti, who felt some resentment at having to share his best friend with the older boy from Ubon.

Khun Direk and his family were to be the sponsors of a large *"thamboon,"* or merit-making and fund-raising ceremony on New Years' day at the village temple. *Khun* Direk and his brood had been working on the *thamboon* for six months, following the custom of enrolling every-one in the family and all their close friends to help solicit donations for the *wat;* his two sons and daughter in Bangkok had even collected a modest sum from their acquaintances and fellow workers in the capital. *Khun* Direk canvassed the entire province of Buriram for contributions, putting himself much in debt whenever any of his subscribers would ask him for help with future *thamboon* ceremonies of their own. *Mai pen rai,* thought generous *Khun* Direk, the Lord Buddha will always provide the money I need for making merit.

Khun Direk and his group had miraculously managed to collect his goal of 30,000 *baht* for the *thamboon.* This gave him huge "face" in the province where he was already widely known as a righteous and religious man. *Khun* Direk's wife conscripted every able-bodied female in the village to help prepare food for the event, and the last two days prior to the ceremony saw a buzzing flurry of activity in at least a dozen homes where the women worked hard getting the feast organized. The "kitchens" of the villagers' modest houses consisted of one or two small charcoal braziers; they were usually set up beneath the house next to the animal pens. Thus, preparing food for over two hundred people was hardly an easy job.

There were thousands of details for *Khun* Direk and his family to attend to in addition to food preparation — the most important being gifts for the monks. Traditionally these were orange plastic buckets filled with things like laundry detergent, body soap, toothpaste, tissue, and other personal items. They usually included an umbrella, a new robe, and several cartons of processed milk and other foodstuffs that could supplement morning alms collection. At the end of the ceremony each monk was also presented with an envelope containing a small amount of money, a package of incense sticks, and three white lotus blossoms.

The whole village gathered for the *thamboon.* The monks and *nenes* (including Pompam and Supachai) seated themselves on low cushions — all twelve of them lined up in a row. They chanted for about forty-five minutes, each of the monks holding in front of him his personalized bamboo fan, its handle resting on the wooden floor. The droning sounds of the ancient chants could be heard all through the deserted village.

When the chanting stopped the monks gathered in three groups of four to be fed their lunch. They were personally served by barefoot *Khun* Direk and most of the other males — each one sincere, each one wanting to share in making the merit which would be added to their personal spiritual accounts when they died.

When the luncheon was finished, all the dishes were cleared and the monks returned to their places for more chants. *Khun* Direk, his family, and the whole host of villagers sat Thai-style facing the monks; hands that had known many seasons of planting rice were reverently raised in *wais,* and they all joined in the chanting of the *sutra* as best they knew how.

Afterwards, *Khun* Direk and his wife presented their monetary and ceremonial gifts to the monks. By custom, whenever the wife approached to make a presentation, the monk would put down a small square of saffron cloth onto which she would place the object. Only in that way could it be accepted from a female.

After the benefactions were handed out *Khun* Direk modestly, but also proudly, presented the Abbot, *Phra* Prateep, with an envelope containing the entire 30,000 *baht* he had raised. This ultimate act was followed by another short chant, then *Khun* Direk — along with every-one else — bowed three times to the ground and *waied.*

Phra Prateep, assisted by Pompam, rose to his feet and liberally sprinkled the audience with holy water; thereafter he departed, followed by the other monks and the *nenes.*

The removal of the clergy left the villagers free to feed them-selves on the leftovers, and to enjoy the big celebration that would quickly get under way. Since it was New Year, and many of the villagers still had their bonus money, there was no shortage of excellent Thai beer and local whiskey.

By two o'clock in the afternoon the party was in full swing. Music blared from a tape deck in someone's pick-up truck, and nearly everyone — especially the men — were decidedly drunk and dancing the *ram wong.* The party would go on all day and throughout the evening, until the last revelers finally crawled off to find a place to sleep, many of them not making it all the way to their homes.

Kitti and his friends managed to swipe and polish off two whole bottles of "*see-sip degee,*" a clear rice whiskey from Laos that was forty percent alcohol. He turned up in the room where Pompam, Supachai, Nuu and two of the other young monks were playing cards, trying hard not to think about all the fun they were missing at the party roaring full-swing just outside.

"Kitti, you are drunk and disgusting!" Pompam complained as he tried in vain to push Kitti off his lap where he had collapsed, reeking of the whiskey he had spilled down the front of his filthy plaid shirt.

"*Mai pen rai*, Pompam. I am happy. I will be even happier in a few years when you can drink with me. For now, I'll drink enough for both of us — for Supachai, too!"

Pompam and Supachai reluctantly went back to Bangkok when it was time for their classes to resume. *Phra* Prateep used a small amount of the 30,000 *baht* donation money to provide the two with train tickets and a little extra for supplies and expenses in Bangkok. Parting from his family was easier for Pompam this time, knowing that when he returned he would have seven weeks' holiday during summer break.

The following week Supachai made good on his promise to take his friend to *Wat* Po to "catch" foreigners for English practice.

"Do you think you're ready, Pompam?"

Although he was intensely fearful of this adventure, Pompam put on the face of confidence and replied with bravado, "What can be so difficult about talking with some *farangs*?"

On Saturday, after morning classes, Supachai, Pompam and three other *nene* friends took the ferry across the river from Thonburi and entered the vast compound of *Wat* Po. The temple covered many acres with *viharns* of varying sizes, *chedis*, statuary, monks' living quarters, and even a medical school — Thailand's first — founded two hundred years before. They arrived at the famous landmark just as two busloads of *farang* tourists were disembarking at the main gate. These groups already had their Thai guides to escort them, so they were of no use to the boys.

Supachai and friends positioned themselves opposite the famous *Wat* Po School of Traditional Thai Massage, near a group of animal sculptures and angry-looking Chinese guardian gods. One foreign couple sporting straw hats, sneakers, shorts, and expensive cameras approached the boys and asked them if they could take their picture.

The request was made in French, unfortunately, and was met with five brown shaved heads all tilted in unison to one side; five pairs of non-existent eyebrows raised in an attitude of complete puzzlement. Then the boys' initial moment of shyness quickly segued into an eruption of squeals and giggles, rapid-fire Thai slang, and numerous pokes and jabs at each other's stomachs.

The French couple looked quizzically at one another and then reverted to sign language; they held up their cameras, smiled at the boys, and motioned for them to get close together for a snapshot. The five *nenes* at once assumed serious faces and regained their composure. The tourists tried their best to get the young men to lighten up and smile, but to no avail. They finally had to content themselves with a photo of five very dignified young faces that showed absolutely no hint whatsoever of the high-spirited, fun-loving personalities that lurked within. As soon as the camera clicked, of course, the young group broke out in riotous gales of laughter, only to be suddenly silenced when an old monk passed by and gave them a scowl that said "shame on you!" The French couple moved on.

About two hours passed and no further contact had been made with any more *farangs*. Finally, Pompam, taking the leadership role, left his group and walked directly up to a sixtyish-looking couple that had tour company tags from the US hanging from their carry-ons, and wide-brimmed hats shading their pink, perspiring faces.

"*Sawasdee-khrap*," Pompam spoke the traditional Thai greeting of respect and smiled broadly.

To his surprise the foreigners responded with "*Sawasdee-khrap*" from the man, and "*Sawasdee-ca*" from the woman, using the correct gender forms.

Pompam, encouraged, bravely started with the normal list of questions Thais ask foreigners: "Where are you from?" "What is your name?" "Where do you stay?" "Do you like Thailand?" "Can you speak Thai?" He received answers in English to every question, under-standing only about forty percent of what they said, then *waied* to them politely, said "Bye bye," and went back to his watchful, admiring group.

Pompam was teased relentlessly by his friends after this encounter, causing him to make no other attempts that day to "catch" foreigners. Pompam felt quite good about his first effort, however, and knew that he had won the unspoken approval of his bashful companions.

Pompam would often repeat excursions of this kind over the next two and a half years; never alone, always in the company of friends. He would learn to avoid the *wat dek*s, security guards, and sour elderly monks as he skirted through the maze of temple buildings. A few times he barely escaped being caught when the Abbot periodically clamped down on the forbidden activities of brazen and impolite young *nene*s such as himself.

Pompam's fear of cold introductions was forgotten after his first half-dozen encounters, and he met many people from America, Australia and Europe. Tourists from other Asian countries were of little help to Pompam since his purpose was to learn English, but later on he would have occasion to wish he had taken the time to learn some Japanese.

Several of the kind *farangs* he met would exchange home addresses with him, and a few became pen pals. Most of these would enclose some money with their letters, enabling Pompam to learn early in life the equations of foreign currency exchange. He was very careful to keep his vow and never ask any of the tourists he approached for money, but he quickly learned how to use his natural charms to subliminally extract it from them. After a while Pompam would be the one to argue, "Why not take their money? They're giving it to me of their own free will. I never ask for it. Besides, they're rich and I'm poor!"

Toward the middle of his senior year he was receiving between five to ten overseas letters a month — at least ninety percent of them containing cash — and Pompam religiously kept up his correspondence with these valuable far-away friends. Some of them would periodically visit Thailand and make arrangements to meet him somewhere for a friendly visit, and they would always bring gifts from home. Pompam never disclosed to his fellow students at the Buddhist school exactly how much money he collected this way, but seeing the amount of overseas mail his friend received, Supachai, for one, knew that the sums must have been considerable.

From time to time Pompam would send money he had been given back home to his parents in the village, giving himself a great sense of pride. They were always happy to receive it, and developed the habit of never asking where it had come from; Pompam never told. They still had four young sons at home which meant six hungry mouths to feed in economic conditions that were always right there "on the edge." Any money from the outside was considered a gift from the Lord Buddha himself.

Around mid-term time of his senior year an event occurred that would change Pompam's life forever. Supachai had, by this time, already graduated and gone on to the Buddhist University at *Wat* Mahathat. Although they still kept in contact, Pompam was, by this time, quite comfortable on his own.

One day he had planned on going to *Wat* Po, but he couldn't get any of his friends to accompany him. Either they had something else to do, or they had grown tired of constantly being dragged out by Pompam to play the game of "catching" *farangs*. Pompam, happy with his progress in English, was determined to go, however, and for the first time he went alone.

After about an hour of hunting through the grounds he spotted a lone American (Pompam could, by then, tell a *farang's* nationality) sitting on a bench, writing in a notebook. Pompam calmly approached the man and greeted him with the familiar, "*Sawasdee-khrap!*" and a practiced smile.

To Pompam's astonishment the *farang* responded with, "*Sawasdee-khrap! Khun sabai dee rip row?*"

Pompam stammered out, "*Cap, khrap khun khrap, pom sabai dee.*" In all of his approaches Pompam had never encountered a *farang* tourist who could ever get past, "*Sawasdee-khrap,*" much less ask him, "How are you?" in return, and reply to him, "I am fine, thank you very much."

Pompam next came out with, "*Pom dok jai. Pom mai keuy jeu farang poot Thai dai.*"

The *farang* replied, "*Khatote, cap, pom poot Thai nit noy.*"

They had just completed the exchange, "I am shocked. I have never met a foreigner who could speak Thai," and, "Excuse me, but I speak Thai only a little bit."

This small dialogue got the two of them off to a good start. Pompam grinned and sat down on the bench next to the *farang* and was soon to learn that the visitor had exhausted almost all the Thai language he knew in just those two introductory sentences. Their conversation then moved into English; Pompam, by then, had not only grown to be proficient, but was considered the best English student in his school.

Pompam was to learn during the next few minutes that this American *farang's* name was Dr. Jim Everett, *Professor* Jim Everett, from the University of California at Berkeley. "*Ajarn* Jim" had taken a year's sabbatical from his teaching duties and was exploring the Far East in depth. His field was sociology, and he had already been to Japan, China, India, Indonesia and Malaysia; Thailand was his last stop before going back to America. The notes he was making were for a paper he would write later for publication.

Ajarn Jim had only arrived in Thailand earlier that week: hence the obligatory visit to *Wat* Po and other landmarks in the historical district. They talked for a while and then Pompam, without really thinking about it, suddenly offered to show him *Wat* Mahathat, which was nearby. He also mentioned the possibility of introducing his new friend to his *Ajarn*, *Phra* Asoka. Dr. Jim Everett, who felt he had already seen enough of *Wat* Po, was more than agreeable to escaping from the hordes of foreign tourists; he left with Pompam who negotiated a ten-*baht tuk-tuk* ride for them at the gate.

Pompam had never before dared to take a foreigner to meet *Ajarn* Asoka. He was afraid of the scolding he might get if *Ajarn* found out he was "pestering" *farangs* at *Wat* Po. This particular foreigner seemed different, though, and he somehow sensed that a meeting of the two *ajarns* might prove to be interesting for both of them.

Ajarn Jim was immediately taken by the serenity and charm of *Wat* Mahathat. As they passed through the courtyard gates they were greeted by the delicate sound of wind chimes, and Jim was pleased to notice that so far he seemed to be the only foreigner in the compound. It delighted him to see the dozens of Thai people of all ages that were napping, eating, and relaxing on mats spread out in the shade of the quadrangle and under the trees in the courtyard. He was glad that he had accidentally stumbled upon "the real thing," and he marveled at the beauty of the graceful, elaborately-adorned *viharns*.

Professor Everett already knew the rule about taking off one's footwear before entering a *wat*, but he was surprised when Pompam insisted that he not leave his shoes outside, but carry them with him indoors instead. "Sometimes there are '*kamoys*' here. This is the Thai word for 'thieves.' They usually don't mean to steal, and they're not bad people, but they are very poor and have no shoes of their own," Pompam compassionately explained, trying to save the "face" of his fellow impoverished countrymen. Dr. Jim smiled in response to this ingenuous explanation.

When they entered the high-ceilinged, glittering *mondop* where *Phra* Asoka usually could be found, Dr. Jim was momentarily over-whelmed by the grandeur of the magnificent, soaring *chedi*. *Phra* Asoka was sitting on the raised platform at the base of the *chedi* speaking with a young Thai family that had come to pay their respects. Upon seeing Pompam and his foreigner, *Ajarn* Asoka immediately motioned for them to come forward and have a seat near him. The Thai couple and their two children politely bowed three times and departed, giving the foreigner their warmest smiles and gentlest "*Sawasdee*" as they backed away.

It turned out that the two *ajarns* did indeed have much to talk about. *Ajarn* Asoka was particularly interested in *Ajarn* Jim's impressions of India, as he had only just come from there a few days before. Dr. Jim was curious to hear *Phra* Asoka's views on why the masses of India would be better off if they converted to Buddhism. After a while he pulled out his notebook and started making some notes. He told *Phra* Asoka that he would make these views known in the paper he was planning to write; hopefully it might gain some support for his cause.

"If you ever have the time, please accompany me on one of my visits to India. As you have more than just a casual interest in Asia, I believe that you would be quite intrigued by what you might encounter with me," *Phra* Asoka said very graciously. Dr. Jim only smiled, knowing that he would probably never have the chance to make such a journey again.

Dr. Jim seemed to be impressed by the learned monk, and Pompam was very proud that he had brought the two important men together. When they were about to depart, they exchanged addresses and phone numbers, and Dr. Jim promised to telephone *Phra* Asoka before he left Thailand; the monk wanted to give the professor the contact information for one of his meditation students in the Bay Area.

Pompam bowed three times to the ground in front of *Phra* Asoka, and was more than pleasantly surprised when the American professor joined him and copied his actions. This is a very unusual *farang*, Pompam thought to himself, and smiled.

Since the following day was Saturday and it was mid-term season, Dr. Jim invited Pompam to be his tour guide; he said he needed someone to show him around Bangkok. Pompam suddenly lit up; he couldn't believe his good luck. They agreed on the time and place they would meet, then parted: Pompam back to his tiny room at *Wat* Chalaw, and *Ajarn* Jim to his five-star hotel on Silom Road.

The following morning they met as arranged at the Tha Chang pier at 8:00 a.m. Dr. Jim had not yet been on the river, so Pompam suggested they charter a long-tail boat for a couple of hours. Pompam negotiated the price with the boatman and off they went down the wide, murky river, under the Taksin Bridge, and into a big *khlong* on the Thonburi side, passing houses, apartment buildings, factories, and temples; from there they wove their way through many smaller *khlongs* where the vegetation on the banks was dense with palms and unseen reptiles; Thai-style houses perched on stilts grew helter-skelter amidst banyan trees and Tarzan vines. Dr. Jim enthusiastically snapped away with his camera at people, moss-covered Buddha images, floating vendors, and picturesque riverine tableaux that one after the other arrested his attention.

"I want to take you now to a very famous temple — famous for Thai people, that is, but never visited by *farangs*," and he instructed the boatman to take them to *Wat* Paknam.

The former Abbot of *Wat* Paknam had died four or five years before, but his fame for good works and mindfulness had spread from one end of Thailand to the other; he was, by then, revered as almost a saint. Thousands upon thousands of devotees wore his picture on amulets around their necks; they swore it protected them against sickness and accidents.

They were in luck that day as there happened to be a casting ceremony in progress in the temple garden: three large seated Buddha images were being cast in bronze. The casts, filled with the molten metal, were connected by a thin piece of white string that stretched all the way into the main *viharn* of the temple. As the string wound through the *viharn* it passed through the *waiing* hands of dozens of chanting monks who were seated before the twenty-foot-high Buddha image behind the altar; the string ultimately made its way into the hands of the sitting Buddha statue itself. In this way the energy — or power — from the Lord Buddha would be directly transmitted through the monks and into the newly-cast statues. Dr. Jim found all this both poetic and fascinating.

They continued their journey through the *khlongs*, past coffin makers, coffee sellers in small rowboats, and several groups of giggling, brown-skinned, naked children frolicking in the polluted water; they competed with one another to see who could make the biggest splash on Pompam and the laughing American traveler who crouched to protect his lens.

They made another stop at *Wat* Arun, the spectacular Temple of Dawn. This landmark temple, another site reported to contain one of the Buddha's relics, was teeming with both tourists and locals alike when they disembarked from their long-tail boat. The magnificent, pointed, photogenic *chedi*s of *Wat* Arun were famous for their colorful, intricate skin of broken pieces of pottery, most of it from China. Pompam and Dr. Jim climbed up to the top of one of them for a better view.

Finally back at Tha Chang pier the two new friends stopped at a stall for "*guit dio*," or fragrant, tasty, steaming bowls of noodles with fishcake balls and slivers of pork and vegetables. Pompam knew he should eat something soon, as the noon hour was approaching and afterwards he could have nothing solid until the next day's dawn.

Pompam wished that he could take the American to some of the more secular places of commerce and entertainment, but this, of course, wasn't possible for him to do as a *nene*. While enjoying some sweet Thai iced coffee after their noodles Dr. Jim asked Pompam, "How many more days before you finish your exams?"

"Today is Saturday. I still have two more tests, but I'll be finished next Wednesday afternoon," he replied.

"What will you do during your mid-term break, Vichai?" At that point Pompam hadn't yet told him his nickname.

"Thursday morning I will be leaving on the train for Buriram to see my family and my Abbot. While I'm there I will have to help them plant the second rice crop," he answered cheerfully.

"I've been reading about Thailand for several months now, and the Isan region interests me the most, especially after having met you. Will you take me there? I mean, may I go with you to Isan on Thursday?"

Pompam couldn't believe his ears. He was actually being asked to be a tour guide again, and outside Bangkok! Even though he knew he couldn't possibly accept such an important job, he got so excited by the mere idea of touring Isan with the *farang* that he unconsciously started rattling off a lengthy refusal in idiomatic Thai, provoking a mystified look on the mustachioed, sunburned face of Dr. Jim. Pompam eventually caught hold of himself and switched back to English, saying, "I appreciate your offer, Dr. Jim, but I am not sufficiently prepared."

Dr. Jim ignored Pompam's answer and pulled out a map of Thailand and started discussing the route he wanted to take. Pompam had never been to any of the other Isan provinces in his life, so once again he politely declined the professor's invitation, pleading gross inexperience. Dr. Jim brushed aside Pompam's excuses, however, and after a few minutes the boy convinced himself that he could, in fact, do an excellent job.

"I'll pay you 1,000 *baht* per day for your time and services, Vichai, plus food and lodging." Pompam was totally overwhelmed. They had discussed a trip that would take about nine days; Dr. Jim would rent a car and drive them himself, so that would be 9,000 *baht* for him!

Dr. Jim also insisted that Pompam accept a fee of 1,000 *baht* for the present day's excursion. At first Pompam was reluctant to accept the fee, and said, "No, Dr. Jim, I cannot accept any money from you. It is my pleasure to show you Thailand."

Dr. Jim protested vigorously, and Pompam finally decided, why not? I would earn a total of 10,000 *baht* for ten days' work! How crazy these *farangs* are with their money, he thought, shaking his bald head in disbelief.

They shook hands when they parted that afternoon with the promise that Pompam would be waiting in the lobby of the Dusit Thani

Hotel at eight o'clock sharp the following Thursday morning.

Later, when he was alone, Pompam said to himself, "I have fallen upstairs." Then he closed his eyes and silently thanked Lord Buddha for his good fortune.

Chapter 5

The remainder of Pompam's mid-terms were a breeze, although it was difficult to keep his mind on his studies; he was distracted by the prospect of earning so much money, and of seeing so much of Thailand for the first time.

Prior to his departure he managed to get together with Supachai and tell him of his upcoming adventure; his friend tried not to appear jealous when he heard Pompam's astounding news. He extracted a promise that he and Dr. Jim would visit him when they reached Ubon, where Supachai would be spending his own mid-term break; he also extracted a loan of bus fare and a small amount of expense money.

"How lucky you are, Pompam," he said, trying to force a smile. "I just don't understand why."

He bade farewell to *Phra* Voravut at first light on Thursday and headed towards Dr. Jim's hotel. He received more than one surprised, if not disapproving, glance from the liveried doormen, front desk staff, and security guards as he entered the opulent five-star Dusit Thani. He had never before been in a hotel, and had never imagined that the many *farangs* who visited Thailand were ensconced in so much beauty and luxury. He couldn't believe there was actually a fountain in the lobby, and even at that early hour in the morning, sounds of violin and piano floated up toward him from the lounge on the lower level.

As Dr. Jim had instructed, he asked for the location of the house phone, called Dr. Jim's room, then seated himself in a big silk-uphol-stered chair in a corner of the huge room. He felt more than slightly uncomfortable — and even a bit ashamed. In the midst of such opulence there he was, a poor Isan *nene* wearing faded robes and worn-out rubber slippers on his dusty bare feet. He vowed that one day he would come back to the Dusit Thani looking prosperous and successful, just like the well-dressed Thai businessmen near him that were greeting their *farang* guests. I will know what it feels like to have money myself, he decided then and there.

Dr. Jim finally appeared at the elevator, disembarking with the bellboy who was toting his luggage. Pompam couldn't help but remark to himself, "So many bags for just one man. All I've got is my small cloth monk's bag with nothing in it but my toothbrush and an English-Thai dictionary."

They made their way out to the rental car that Dr. Jim had picked up on Rama IV Road the night before. Then they inched their way out into the heavy morning traffic and headed toward Don Muang area, to the North. Although the car was only a small, light blue Toyota, it was far better than the back of *Khun* Direk's pick-up. "There's even air conditioning and a cassette player! If only I had some tapes to play," he said to himself, almost feeling them in his hand.

Their destination that day was Nakorn Ratchasima, or Korat, as it was familiarly known. Seemingly endless hours of barely moving traffic passed by as they crept through highway construction, thick clouds of white dust almost reducing their visibility to zero. They made it through Rangsit, Nakorn Nayok, Saraburi, and finally arrived at Pak Chong, the "Gateway to Isan," where they stopped before noon for some lunch. Pompam had already observed that *Ajarn* Jim was picky in terms of where and what he would eat. Pompam also knew that from that point on — throughout the whole trip — there would only be Thai food, much of it of questionable quality; Dr. Jim would see no more *farang* food until he returned to Bangkok in nine or ten days. They chose a Chinese noodle shop where they each had two bowls of *guit dio* with duck.

They arrived in Korat at about 3:00 p.m., and drove through the lively, medium-size town in search of a decent place to spend the night. There were no hotels that came even remotely close to the high caliber of the Dusit Thani, so they settled on a small local inn not far from the night market. As the days passed they would get used to the blatant gawking they got from surprised front desk clerks as they checked into their lodging each evening.

The thought of staying the whole night in his own hotel room nearly scared Pompam to death, so he insisted on sharing one with Dr. Jim. After paying a small fortune for his room at the Dusit Thani, Dr. Jim chuckled to himself when Pompam translated that their first night in Korat would cost them 250 *baht*, the equivalent of US$10; the boy even apologized for the high expense. At these prices, and from the look of the rather dimly-lit, threadbare lobby, Dr. Jim didn't expect much in the way of comforts, but Pompam was delighted with their room, especially the clean bed with real sheets — and a TV! The boy had never used a western-style bathroom before, and Dr. Jim started to think Pompam might never emerge from the cloud of steam that billowed out of his first hot shower.

At dinnertime they visited the nearby night market. Dr. Jim gave Pompam some money and he purchased for him his first truly Isan meal: *"gai yang, somtam* and *khao nio,"* or marinated barbecued chicken, green papaya salad, and sticky rice. Dr. Jim, wary at first, absolutely fell in love with the delicious food, but felt sorry that Pompam couldn't join him.

"Mai pen rai, Ajarn. I am more than happy just to watch you eat while I drink my Pepsi." Pompam was to teach the professor the meaning of *"mai pen rai"* as well as numerous other words and phrases over the next few days. At that moment Dr. Jim felt happier and more content than he had felt in longer than he could remember. He was thirty-eight years old, of medium height and build, not very handsome, divorced, and well-educated; but this was the first real adventure of his life, and he had been looking forward to it for nearly seven years. Pompam could tell even during their first meeting that Dr. Jim was *"jai dee,"* or a person with a good heart.

After dinner they strolled through the night market until Pompam felt uncomfortable again with his robes and shaved head, getting disapproving looks from elders, and they returned to the hotel, collapsing on their beds from exhaustion.

The next morning they visited the statue of Thao Sunanari, the heroine of Korat who had saved the city from invading barbarians several hundred years before by organizing all of the women of the town for its defense. It is said that during the night the women went to the enemy army camp to "entertain" the men. They succeeded in getting all of the soldiers drunk, and when they passed out the women used knives to murder each and every one of them. Together, Pompam and Dr. Jim reverently lit some incense, and placed *"puangmalais,"* or flower garlands, at the statue's base.

Afterwards, they drove about thirty miles out of their way to visit Phi Mai, a vast compound of stunning Khmer ruins that had recently been restored. Dr. Jim seemed exceedingly interested in such places of antiquity, and told Pompam to make sure they visited all of them along their route.

Their next destination was Buriram province for Pompam's much-anticipated visit with his family in their impoverished dusty village. Pompam apologized to Dr. Jim in advance for how poor and primitive he would find his home. The kind professor listened to the remarks with a smile and said, "*Mai pen rai.*" But even though Pompam had painted a pretty bleak picture of the scene, it did not fully prepare him for the reality of what he would encounter.

Pompam was very proud to be returning to his birthplace in a rental car as the paid guide for an important visitor from California. He knew that the presence of *Ajarn* Jim in the village would create quite a stir; this was, after all, a village that had never had a *farang* guest in its entire history.

Ajarn Jim didn't want to arrive at Pompam's family home empty-handed, so they stopped at the market in Nong Ki to purchase supplies. Pompam told Dr. Jim that Nong Ki was famous for having the best *gai yang* in Isan, the delicious marinated barbecued chicken *Ajarn* had eaten the night before in Korat. As a result of this news, he cleaned out two entire stalls of all the *gai yang* they had, bought several orders of sticky rice and *somtam*, several different kinds of "*khanom*," or sweets, and an entire case of packaged milk for Pompam's young brothers.

Then Dr. Jim got carried away and bought shorts, shirts and new rubber slippers for Pompam's brothers — including the babies and Paw. Pompam timidly helped him select a new blouse for Maa, and some assorted gifts for *Phra* Prateep and the other monks at the temple.

"For sure there will be a party tonight, *Ajarn*. Everyone in the village will want to come and see the *farang* I brought home with me," Pompam commented with a broad smile.

"Well, in that case, we had better make sure it's a *good* party," Dr. Jim replied grinning. With that, he made off towards the nearest stall selling Thai whiskey; he purchased half a dozen bottles, a case of large beers, a case of soda and soft drinks, and at least ten bags of ice.

Pompam was startled by the excess, having never before encountered a *farang* in a party mood, but knew he would have big "face" in the village as the result of being the one who had brought such an unforeseen, happy occasion to the dirt-poor community of his birth.

"Please, *Ajarn* Jim, stop! Enough! You are making me embarrassed!" Pompam screamed, waving his arms around. Dr. Jim just looked over at the boy with an intent, exhilarated look on his face, and Pompam realized that *Ajarn* was happy. *Mai pen rai*, Pompam sighed to himself with pleasure; let him buy as much as he wants.

They followed the winding dirt road for seven miles, dust-encrusted weeds growing high on both sides. They stopped first at the temple where, out of respect, Pompam said he needed to check in with *Phra* Prateep before proceeding on to his family home.

The temple was seemingly deserted when they arrived; the heavy mid-afternoon heat had forced everyone to seek shelter indoors, and even the ubiquitous stray dogs and cats that populated the temple were nowhere to be seen. They parked the car in the shade of a banyan tree, unloaded the gifts they had brought for the Abbot and the monks, and headed toward *Phra* Prateep's *kuti*.

"Vichai! I'm over here," *Phra* Prateep called from the entrance to the *viharn*. Dr. Jim noticed that the main *viharn* of the temple was nothing more than a large wooden *sala* with a tin roof and no walls on three sides. Crude wooden stairs (more like a ladder, he thought) led up to the *viharn* entrance where the Abbot was standing barefoot, wearing only his loose-fitting under-robe. Dr. Jim could see the Buddha images, clocks, plastic flowers and ceremonial umbrellas that adorned the simple altar behind him. It suddenly occurred to Dr. Jim that he was really just about as isolated in the Thai countryside as one could get: a thought that completely thrilled and excited him.

Pompam and Dr. Jim made their way up the rickety steps into the *viharn* carrying their gifts, leaving their shoes at ground level on a small concrete platform. Abbot Prateep had quickly put on his formal outer robe and seated himself on the dais in front of the Buddha image; he silently looked in amazement at the odd pair as they bowed three times to the ground before him. *Phra* Prateep had *never* seen a *farang* perform this gesture before, and he reacted with feelings that alternated between shock and sheer pleasure. He concealed his emotions behind a solemn face, however, and merely smiled politely at the two after they completed the formality.

Then Pompam began explaining the unusual situation to the Abbot in their native dialect while Dr. Jim patiently pretended to listen, glancing around at the rustic surroundings, seated on the rough-hewn plank floor.

The lengthy explanation at last concluded and *Phra* Prateep nodded and smiled at Dr. Jim, showing him teeth in grave need of a dentist's attention. The two pilgrims then proceeded to present their gifts, and the Abbot elegantly touched each one of them with his fingertips in acceptance.

Afterwards *Phra* Prateep rattled off a few rapid sentences to Pompam who translated for Dr. Jim. "*Phra* Prateep says you are welcome here. He also says that you are to sleep in the temple tonight in my old room with me. He will make sure that mats are on the floor, a mosquito net is hung, and an electric fan is placed in the room so you will be comfortable."

"Please tell the Abbot that I am very grateful for his hospitality, but I don't want him to go to any trouble on my account."

Pompam translated this for the Abbot, who was shaking his head from side to side, and then turned to Dr. Jim and replied, "He says that it's no trouble at all to have you here as his guest. He is very honored to have an American professor from a famous American university become a friend to his temple."

Leaving the bulk of his luggage in the car, Dr. Jim and Pompam carried what they would need for the night to the small room at the back of the *wat*. They found Nuu asleep in the tiny room when they entered. The dazed young boy thought he was still dreaming and became alarmed and started to cry out when he saw Pompam enter with a *farang*. Pompam put his arm around the boy's shoulders and calmly explained everything.

"I knew you would be coming home soon, Pompam, and that you would come to the temple first. That's why I've been waiting for you here for three days," Nuu said, obviously elated to see his *pi-chai* again, whom he had sorely missed. Nuu politely *waied* to Dr. Jim, then the three of them went out to the car and drove the short distance to the family house.

They found Paw, shirtless in a *sarong*, sitting on a mat in the open space under the house, weaving one of his delicate Isan-style baskets. When she heard the car drive up Maa, wearing a faded *sarong* and a once-white sleeveless top, appeared upstairs at the front door holding the youngest baby. A mystified expression crossed her weathered face, unlike any Dr. Jim had ever seen before, as she watched her two sons get out of a brand new Toyota driven by a *farang*. She just stood there staring at them, slowly chewing on her betel nut, the mild narcotic that had permanently stained her mouth a blackish red.

By this time the other two young boys had awakened from their mid-afternoon naps, and sleepily followed their mother down the railless wooden steps to greet Pompam and his strange companion. It saddened Dr. Jim to see the children in such a state. All of them were barefoot, one of them was completely naked as was the baby. The older ones including Nuu wore filthy short pants covered with holes, and all of them looked under-nourished and had nasty sores in various places on their skin.

Dr. Jim had never encountered such a combination of fear and shyness in his entire life; it was as if the group in front of him had just come face to face with an extraterrestrial, standing there staring at him, frozen in a tableau of disbelief and rural poverty.

Pompam began his explanation speech in the same rapid-fire manner he had already used with the Abbot and Nuu; they all stood there speechless until he was done. Finally Pompam stooped over and grabbed the young naked one who appeared to be about six years old. He kissed him Thai-style on the cheek and started patting and hugging the rest of them, teasing and making them laugh.

"Please forgive them, Dr. Jim. They have never had a *farang* come to their home before. They have never even *seen* a *farang* before. Just give them a little time and they will get used to you," Pompam reassured softly, seeing the astonished look on the professor's face.

Dr. Jim went over to the car and started unloading the gifts he had purchased for the family. Pompam and Nuu helped him, and eventually the rest of the young ones joined in. Then Dr. Jim let the four boys finish the job of getting everything out of the car and onto the low Thai-style table under the house. Near the table the baby sat up in the hammock where Maa had placed him, and started to wail. Pompam went over and lifted him up, spoke to him gently, and eventually got him to stop howling. Who would blame him, Pompam thought; a *farang* has come today to play Santa Claus!

Play Santa he did, too, and nothing in his life had ever given Dr. Jim such wild pleasure. Before too long the boys that weren't already naked stripped off whatever they were wearing and put on their new outfits, fighting over who would get which size and color of rubber slippers. Paw and Maa were more discreet and put their gifts aside to open and examine later. Dr. Jim couldn't resist the urge to get out his camera and take pictures of the newly-clad, happy group.

It wasn't too long before the neighbors started trailing over one by one, unable to contain their curiosity any longer. So Dr. Jim broke out the whiskey, the beer, and the food, and the inevitable party quickly got going. One of the neighbors retrieved his ghetto blaster and cassettes from his house, and soon the strong beat of twangy Isan country music attracted even more villagers to the unexpected, late-monsoon celebration. All the more unexpected since it was hosted by the mysterious, smiling *farang* who, thanks to the many villagers who wanted to toast him, never held an empty glass in his hand.

Pompam, of course, couldn't drink alcohol, but his abstinence didn't in any way hamper his enjoyment of being together again with his family and neighborhood friends. *Ajarn* Jim was obviously enjoying himself to the maximum level, and seeing the professor dance the *ram wong* barefoot in the dirt with the open-hearted, grateful village peasants gave Pompam a new sense of respect and liking for him.

By sunset almost all of the party supplies had been exhausted, and *Ajarn* Jim insisted on driving back to Nong Ki for more, in spite of the weak, half-intended protests made by Pompam. "Don't spend any more of your money, Dr. Jim. This is enough," he proclaimed, but in reality he, too, wanted the celebration to go on longer.

"How can it be enough when we still have guests?" replied the intoxicated sociology professor from Berkeley as he started up the car, giving no thought whatever to the shoes he left behind.

"It will never be enough for these people. Can't you see that they will stay on for days as long as you keep providing the drinks?" Pompam replied, laughing.

"*Mai pen rai*, Vichai. You taught me to think like that, remember?"

Dr. Jim was by now totally caught up in the novelty of the event. Pompam smiled and made no more objections.

When they returned with more liquid supplies it became apparent that the entire village was now on hand, including *Khun* Direk and his family. Pompam proudly introduced Dr. Jim to the village headman who could only mutter a small "*Sawasdee-khrap*" as he stared at the *Ajarn's* filthy bare feet and rolled-up pants. Young Rattana clung close to her father and shyly *waied* and curtsied when she was presented to the strange visitor.

Maa then walked up to them and bestowed on Dr. Jim an Isan-style silk *sarong* and a traditional plaid "*pakomah*" that she had woven herself. She gave him a wide, black-red grin when he *waied* to her and accepted the gifts.

Pompam dragged Dr. Jim behind the outhouse, made him take off his pants, and showed him how to tie on the *sarong*. The "*pakomah*," a versatile garment, could be worn on the head for keeping off the sun as well as tied around the waist. Pompam proceeded to tie the *pakomah* on the *Ajarn's* head, creating an Isan turban for the academic sultan from America.

Pompam returned with a grinning Dr. Jim who gracefully, but ostentatiously, bowed to wild applause and drunken shrieks of approval. Pompam grabbed Dr. Jim's camera and snapped a silly picture of him in his bizarre costume. He would keep this photo on his desk at Berkeley forever.

An early-evening thunderstorm began to pelt down rain on the happy crowd, the dust and dirt turning instantly to thick, rich mud. Many of the neighbors *waied* the *Ajarn* and scurried for the cover of home; the die-hards merely crowded into the space beneath the house and kept on going. About nine o'clock the second batch of supplies was gone and everyone, including Maa and Paw, was completely drunk.

Pompam then began the slow process of dragging a reluctant Dr. Jim away from the party and back to the temple to sleep. Everyone was sad to see the fun come to an end, but with toothless or beetle-stained grins, slurred speech, and glassy eyes they took their turns bidding a fond goodnight to blissful *Ajarn* Jim. Following custom, nearly all of the men gave him affectionate hugs, and the professor was deeply moved by their warmth and sincerity.

On the floor and under the mosquito net Dr. Jim collapsed and slept like the dead. Pompam and Nuu curled up next to him, one on either side. Pompam's last thought before he himself drifted off to a sound sleep was, how is it possible that a *farang* can be this *jai dee*?

The next morning they were up at daybreak. Dr. Jim welcomed with pleasure and relief the hot cup of instant coffee Pompam brought to him. His head was pounding from all the Mekhong Whiskey he had consumed the night before, but this soon subsided after a cold sluice bath in the grungy temple outhouse, and a couple of aspirin from his shaving kit.

Dr. Jim and Pompam *waied*, bowed formally, and took their leave of *Phra* Prateep. Dr. Jim discreetly gave the Abbot an envelope with some money in it when they were about to depart, and *Phra* Prateep gave them both his blessing, tying the customary white strings around their wrists for good luck. "Please take good care of my boy, *Ajarn* Jim," admonished *Phra* Prateep. Pompam translated, adding his own emphasis to the words "good care."

They next said their good-byes at Pompam's home. A few stragglers were still sleeping it off next to the animal pens under the house, and an unshaven, scruffy-looking Paw met them with drooping red eyes, obviously the victim of a monstrous hangover. He did manage, however, to gather his wits and modestly present to Dr. Jim a small basket he had made. The young boys climbed all over Dr. Jim, their shyness of the day before long since abandoned. Maa *waied* gracefully to the kind professor from Berkeley, and then gave a sharp signal to her unruly young sons to do the same.

Paw and Maa blessed the two with the ritual of the white strings, and Dr. Jim pressed 2,000 *baht* into the palm of Paw's hand while the poor rice farmer looked bashfully off to the side. "Vichai, tell them to take the boys to the doctor for a check-up, and to keep them healthy," Dr. Jim instructed. Pompam dutifully communicated this to his parents, knowing full-well that they would never spend the much-needed money on preventive medicine.

The first few miles down the highway were spent in silence as Dr. Jim reflected on the amazing human experience he had just had.

Hopefully he would be able to come here again; but he knew that if he did, it would never be the same without Pompam, and there was no telling how or where the young boy would end up in the future.

"Turn right at the next crossing and I will show you Phanom Rung," Pompam politely commanded. Unquestionably the greatest landmark in Buriram is Phanom Rung, an eleventh-century Khmer ruin that is perhaps the second most spectacular of its kind — after Anghor Wat in Cambodia.

They had been to Phi Mai in Korat only two days before, and Dr. Jim had been both pleased and impressed with the elegant symmetry of line, and the grand scale of the massive temple complex created by the ancient Khmer builders. When he first gazed upon the magnificent Phanom Rung, however, perched on top of its solitary hill in the midst of miles and miles of flat Isan plains, Phi Mai paled in comparison.

They spent about two hours exploring the site, taking dozens of photographs and admiring the view that stretched out over nearby Cambodia. Dr. Jim was stunned by the timeless beauty of Phanom Rung, and tried his best to imagine the highly cultivated human beings who had built it. He sadly reflected on the fact that the descendants of the builders were the very ones who had massacred over one million of their own kind in the "killing fields" of their recent civil war.

His favorite photograph of Pompam taken during the entire trip was one of him sitting astride an ancient stone lion on the wall at the western end of the temple, his yellow robes shining brightly in the morning sun. The exultant expression on Pompam's grinning face was a sight he would never forget, and that photo would also remain on the professor's desk at Berkeley for as long as he did.

From Phanom Rung they continued on to the main town of Buriram. They had lunch, but since there wasn't much to see, they drove on through the back roads to Surin Province. Unfortunately, they were a few weeks too early for the Surin Elephant Round-up, an annual event that attracted locals as well as visitors from all over the world. The tourist brochure says, "Where else can you see elephants play a game of football?"

Pompam and Dr. Jim managed to find one elephant, and for a not-so-small price, got his *mahout* to take them on a short ride through the town, attracting more than one curious gaze from passersby below.

It was the first time either of them had ever ridden on one of those amazing creatures, and it was difficult to tell which of the two was the most excited; both of them were absolutely equal in their child-like rapture.

They checked into the best hotel in town and Pompam immediately attached himself to the television set, a major treat for him since *Phra* Voravut refused to allow one at *Wat* Chalaw. In the early evening they browsed through some shops and Dr. Jim purchased a few lovely pieces of colorful, locally-woven silk to take back to America as gifts.

Early the next morning they made their way towards Ubon Ratchathani, the eastern-most province in southern Isan. On the way, they passed through the normally dry fields of Si Sa Khet Province, perhaps the poorest in all of Thailand. That day the rice fields were the most brilliant color of emerald green that Dr. Jim had ever seen. It looked to him like the people who lived there would have a good crop that year and survive yet another season; this thought made both Pompam and Dr. Jim feel good.

They once again checked into the nicest hotel they could find, left their bags in their room, and went off in search of Supachai. The village was about ten miles away, and they were able to find it without too much difficulty. After making three or four inquiries they finally found the right house, and Pompam could understand at once why the resident family could only afford to take care of one of Supachai's younger siblings. Dr. Jim thought that by comparison this house makes Pompam's house look almost orderly and prosperous. It was depressing for him to even look at, ramshackle to the point of collapse, the stench of the primitive toilet out back nearly overwhelming him.

They found Supachai sitting outside the one-room, wooden dwelling reading a book. He was alone except for his younger brother who was taking a nap on a rush mat rolled out on the dirt floor. Supachai and Pompam greeted each other warmly, and with great excitement Pompam told Supachai all about their journey so far, with emphasis on the part about the big party at his family's house two nights before.

"You should have seen *Ajarn* Jim all dressed up in *sarong* and *pakomah*, with no shoes, drunk on Mekhong, dancing the *ram wong* with Pi Noi from next door!" This remark was made by Pompam in English so Dr. Jim could feel the full benefit of his playful teasing. Dr. Jim looked not in the least bit embarrassed. He merely smiled at the two boys and started waving his arms around like he was once again doing the *ram wong*. They doubled over in hysterics at his clumsy, exaggerated version of their native dance.

"Why don't you and your brother come back to town with Vichai and me, Supachai. We'll have the hotel bring in a roll-away bed and we can have a slumber party," Dr. Jim offered, knowing how much it would please Pompam to spend the night with his good friend.

Supachai looked warily at Pompam as if to say, "Are you sure it's all right?" Pompam said, "Yes, come with us; we'll make our own party in the hotel," knowing that the enticing part about "the hotel" would clinch his coming with them.

Even though he knew they didn't really care, Supachai wrote a note to his relatives letting them know where he and his brother had gone, and that they would return some time the following day.

"Why don't you be our tour guide here in Ubon, Supachai. What can we see while we're here?" Dr. Jim asked and smiled at the serious young man.

"There are some old temples and a few shops to see in Ubon town that we can go to this afternoon. Then tomorrow morning, if you have time, we can go to Moon River," Supachai replied eagerly. From that moment on Dr. Jim found it difficult to free his mind from the tune of Andy Williams' signature song, "Moon River." The melody and even a few long-forgotten lyrics came back into his head and wouldn't go away. So there really is such a place, he mused, smiling.

The four of them bonded quickly and had a great time sightseeing in Ubon that afternoon. Then Supachai and Pompam drank cokes and watched while Dr. Jim and Supachai's ten-year-old brother, Nut, consumed a delicious-looking meal of Isan food bought from a street vendor. The three local boys were amused to see the *farang* eat their peasant fare with such enjoyment. Even though it made him turn bright red and sweat like hell, Dr. Jim ate the chili-infested food like a native, his fear of food germs long-since tossed aside.

Back at the hotel Dr. Jim ordered up the extra bed and some more towels. Pompam claimed the roll-away for himself and let the two brothers sleep in what would have been his own double bed.

Everyone had long hot showers and Pompam enjoyed playing host, showing off his new, albeit temporary, lifestyle. Sleep for all of them came early, the newcomers experiencing the cool luxury of air conditioning for the first time.

Moon River the next day was indeed as beautiful as its namesake song, Dr. Jim reflected. Gentle cascades of water rushing over large smooth rocks in the wide stream made it a river unlike any he had ever seen. They all took off their rubber slippers (Dr. Jim had by now purchased a pair for himself) and waded out into the shallow clear water, the two *nene*s hoisting their robes up around their thighs. They were in the middle of an immense national park which had been mercifully set aside by the government some years before, so far preventing it from being seriously spoiled by loggers and other shameless polluters.

Later, Dr. Jim and Pompam dropped off Supachai and Nut at their relatives' house in the small village, the two *nene*s agreeing to meet up in Bangkok when the school term began. Dr. Jim off-handedly gave Supachai a thousand *baht* when they parted; he told him it was for being their tour guide in Ubon. Supachai *waied* him in thanks as he fought back grateful tears. He had desperately needed money in order to get back to Bangkok, and had no idea how he would get it. The money he had taken from Pompam was already spent on food and necessities for his younger brothers and sisters who were scattered among relatives throughout the district.

"Next stop Mukdahan Province, Dr. Jim," Pompam exclaimed as he gave the directions. That night they stayed in a quaint, rustic guest house on the high bank of the mighty Mekhong River, and spent the evening fighting off killer mosquitoes and gazing out over the wide expanse of water at the lights of a Laotian village on the far side. Dr. Jim enjoyed a cold beer while Pompam sipped on a Pepsi.

The professor experienced a warm feeling of peace and contentment being there in that strange and exotic corner of the world. He realized that having Pompam with him for company, and the countless meaningful insights that the good-hearted teenager had unselfishly shared, was the best thing that could have happened to him on his first — and perhaps last — big adventure. He had never before been around anyone like Pompam, an original, truly beautiful person with a clean, pure mind, and bright, loving spirit. He made a decision at that moment to help the young man try to secure a decent future for himself.

The next night they stopped in Roi Et Province where they saw the tallest standing Buddha statue in the world, and some small (very, very small) Khmer ruins; they were not impressed, remembering the grandeur of Phanom Rung.

The following day they made it to Khon Kaen, a large Isan town that produced the reputably best hand-woven silk in the region. They visited some shops and Dr. Jim once again made some purchases to take back to friends in Berkeley.

The last night on their journey through Isan was spent back in the same hotel in Korat where, only a few days before, they had spent their first. An oppressive sadness hung about them since they realized they would be parting company the following morning, maybe to never see one another again. Pompam would be taking the bus to Buriram where he would spend the remainder of his mid-term holidays helping plant rice. Dr. Jim would drive back to Bangkok alone, spend one more night at the Dusit Thani (a night of "re-entry into the real world" as he thought of it), and then catch a flight early the following morning that would take him back to California. He would not forget to make his promised phone call to *Phra* Asoka.

While walking in the park near the statue of Thao Sunanari, the heroine of Korat, Dr. Jim asked Pompam, "What do you plan on doing in a few months when you graduate from your Buddhist high school, Vichai?"

"If I can, I will go to the Buddhist University at *Wat* Mahathat with Supachai, although I would rather disrobe and take further study as a layman," Pompam replied with honesty.

"What if I were to pay for your tuition and some small expenses at Ramkampheng University? I've read in my guidebook that it's on the 'open' system so you can study and work at the same time. You would only have to go to classes when you wanted to, and when it fit your work schedule. You could also take as much time as you needed to graduate. I would love to send you to Chulalongkorn or Thammasat, but since you would need to devote full time to your studies there, and not work to help with living expenses, I just don't think I could afford it."

Knowing he had to refuse, Pompam's heart pounded as he thought of an appropriate response.

"I could never accept such a gift, *Ajarn* Jim, but I am grateful to you for offering," his voice was shaking.

"Well, why not, Vichai?" the professor asked, surprised.

"Do you know the word *'graing jai,' Ajarn*?" Pompam knew that he hadn't taught that word to Dr. Jim himself, but the smart man may have read about it in one of his Thailand books.

"No, Vichai, I don't know that word. Teach me about *'graing jai,'*"he responded, still trying to understand why the boy had refused his offer.

"There is really no direct translation for the phrase in English, so I will try to explain it as best I can." Pompam thought hard about how to interpret the uniquely-Thai expression that all Thai people use from time to time when at a loss for words, or the need to politely say "no."

"It's like, just now you offered me a great gift, a wonderful opportunity, and I feel *'graing jai'* to you. It means, 'I am not worthy of such a gift,' or 'How could I possibly accept such a gift?' Or, 'You are on such a higher level than me' or maybe, 'I owe you so much already that I could never take more.' Do you understand now, Dr. Jim?"

"I think I understand a little bit. I know the second word *'jai'* means 'heart.' I suspect that the concept of *'graing-jai'* is something very near the heart of your Thai culture. So many of your words end in *'jai'* and all of them seem to refer to one emotion or another."

Dr. Jim continued with, "I cannot stop you from feeling *'graing jai'* with me; but I can tell you that because of the feeling in my *'jai,'* I want to do this for you very much. Don't forget, Vichai, that I *work* in a university, and I feel that you *deserve* to have this chance. Please say yes."

Pompam, speechless, brought his hands together in a *wai* near the top of his forehead and bowed low in the most respectful manner possible, usually a gesture reserved for the highest monk — or the King.

He looked up at Dr. Jim and with tears streaming down his face said, "Thank you very much, *Ajarn*. I will accept." He said this in the politest form of the Thai language, and he knew that Dr. Jim would understand.

PART II
FOR LOVE OR MONEY

Chapter 6

The remaining term of Pompam's high school career was pleasant, and passed for him with feelings of optimism and expectation. He no longer had to worry about how to further his education; Dr. Jim had generously taken care of that. He kept his mind on his studies and maintained good grades; no one in his class knew English better than Pompam, and this alone earned him no small amount of respect among his fellow students.

Pompam diligently kept up his pen pal correspondence, and he occasionally went to practice English with *farang* tourists at *Wat* Po. These days he always went alone, however, as he had had some close calls with the fearsome Abbot's temple security; he didn't want any of his colleagues to get caught if he himself should ever have that misfortune.

Dr. Jim wrote to him from California at least once a month, and since there was always money enclosed in each letter Pompam had ample funds, given his small needs. The final month before his graduation Dr. Jim sent Pompam his university entrance fees so he could enroll before he went back to Isan for his last summer vacation.

Kitti would be graduating from high school at the same time as Pompam and his parents had given him the nod to enter Ramkampheng with his friend. The two boys decided they would rent a room near campus and hopefully find jobs at the same place so they could work, live, and study together; neither could bear the thought of being alone.

During the last month of school both Kitti and Pompam were busy preparing for final exams and saying good-bye to friends, so they agreed to meet up in their village in Buriram after it was all over. Kitti had miraculously obtained permission from his reluctant parents to spend his holiday with his grandparents, giving the lame excuse that, "It's the last time I will still be only a boy in my village."

It had been the custom since the beginning of time for monks and *nenes* to shave their heads and eyebrows during the full moon of every month. However, that last month before graduation Pompam and other students who would be disrobing were told that they did not have to shave. This would give their hair and eyebrows a head start in the growing-out process, which would be awkward and embarrassing for a while as they resumed their lives as laymen. Pompam decided that he would not disrobe until he had returned to his village and received ceremonial permission from his dear Abbot, *Phra* Prateep.

As all graduations were, Pompam's was bitter-sweet. Afterward, the boys said their good-byes, shed a few tears, and made the customary promises to keep in touch, not knowing they probably never would.

The following morning Pompam made his prostrations to *Phra* Voravut at *Wat* Chalaw before heading off to the train station with his tiny cloth bag that contained all of his possessions. He owed so much to the dear old monk, and he promised himself that he would help this temple whenever he could.

"May the Lord Buddha bless you always, Vichai," *Phra* Voravut said softly and affectionately, and then Pompam bid farewell to the shady temple by the *khlong* that had been his home for a little over three years.

From the pier at Tha Chang he made his way to pay his respects to *Phra* Asoka at *Wat* Mahathat, and to inform him of his future plans.

"Welcome, Vichai," *Ajarn* spoke warmly to Pompam as the *nene* bowed three times before him.

"I have graduated from high school, *Ajarn*, and I'm on my way back to Buriram for the summer. When I return in May I will enter Ramkampheng University."

"I thought I might be seeing you here at Buddhist University, studying alongside your friend Supachai," *Phra* Asoka replied in a concerned voice.

"I want to study as a layman, *Ajarn*, and Dr. Jim from California has generously given me a scholarship." Dr. Jim had, in fact, already given the Indian monk this news in a letter.

"You must always follow the direction of your heart, Vichai. Fate seems to have given you good fortune, and the Lord Buddha has given you many gifts as well. Never forget that you alone have the greatest control over the wheel of your karma. So make sure you are mindful — and avoid doing things that will make you suffer later on."

Pompam remained silent for quite some time, reflecting on what the holy man had told him. He felt that *Phra* Asoka had somehow looked right through him to the center of his being; and he sensed that the monk had seen into the future, and knew more about his life than he was telling him.

"Remember also to always show compassion for others, Vichai, just as the Lord Buddha has always shown you."

A thoughtful — almost alarmed — Pompam bowed before his teacher, thanked him for his blessings, and then departed on his journey to Isan, determined to make sure he always obeyed the Indian monk's wise words.

The first thing Pompam did when he arrived at his village was head straight for the *wat*, seek out *Phra* Prateep, and ask him for permission to disrobe; he was more than just a bit eager to begin his new life.

Phra Prateep looked Pompam directly in the eye and said, "You know that you have already given yourself permission, Vichai, and I cannot stop you. But you have been like my son for many years, and as your second father I cannot help but be concerned about you."

"Why *Phra* Prateep? You don't have to worry about me. My life is in the hands of the Lord Buddha, and I will be fine," the boy replied, sincerely believing in the protection of his faith.

"Just make sure you *stay* in the hands of Buddha, Vichai," the old monk admonished him, frowning with concern.

Relieved of his obligations as well as his status as a *nene*, Pompam went to his old room and changed into layman's clothes, then returned to the *viharn*, kneeled, and *waied* his dear Abbot. Afterward, he prostrated himself three times before the Buddha statue that *Phra* Asoka had years before presented the temple as a gift. Ever since Pompam hand-carried it from *Wat* Mahathat it had occupied a prominent place on both the altar and in his heart.

When he rose up after the third bow he did a double-take on the familiar Buddha image: he thought for sure he had seen it cast a glaring, wide-eyed grin at him — with big, shiny, golden teeth.

He felt a shock of electricity shoot up his spine and he turned quickly towards *Phra* Prateep, who merely sat there calmly watching him, a curious expression on his face.

Pompam immediately glanced back at the Buddha statue again and it was grinning even wider than before — and this time it was biting down hard on a large gold coin! Pompam felt another flash of heat that momentarily left him dizzy and disoriented; he closed his eyes and covered his face with his hands.

Phra Prateep approached him slowly, put his hand tentatively on the boy's shoulder and said, "Are you all right, Vichai? What did you see?"

Pompam exhaled his breath slowly as he had been taught, opened his eyes, and looked up for the third time at the Buddha statue; it appeared to be serene and peacefully normal.

The young man turned and met the steady, hard gaze of the old monk and many things unsaid passed intuitively between them. Without another word Pompam stood up and left the temple. He was clear that he had received both a blessing — and a warning — from the kindly man who was his second father and, perhaps, from the lord Buddha himself.

The following day Kitti arrived from Bangkok to begin his last summer in his native village as a "boy," and his immature attitude soon reflected it. Pompam and Kitti had a little over six weeks of idle time in which to indulge themselves, and Pompam felt he had a great deal of making-up to do; this was the first time he hadn't worn the yellow robes of a monk in nearly eight years. As a matter of fact, it took him several days just to get used to the confinement of having to wear underpants and trousers again.

"Let's have a party tonight to celebrate our freedom, Pompam," Kitti exclaimed. "We can start the party tonight, and end it when we go back to Bangkok to start classes," he laughed.

So that was exactly what they proceeded to do, and the pile of whiskey and beer bottles behind Pompam's family outhouse grew higher with each night's chapter in the two boys' on-going celebration.

Much to Maa's consternation, Paw became a willing participant in the nightly drinking bouts, and he went to bed smelling of whiskey every evening; he usually stumbled on the way to bed and woke up the new baby that Maa had recently delivered. Pompam's younger brother Nuu was also eager to join in the party, even though he was only thirteen years old. Pompam, who had never tasted alcohol in his life, quickly developed a keen taste for it, and several of Pompam's and Kitti's indigent boyhood friends who had never left the village promptly took up the habit of dropping by Pompam's house every afternoon when the drinking would begin.

Pompam was shy about his hair growing out and never took off the old baseball cap he wore to hide the coarse black spikes that protruded unevenly from his skull. He couldn't wait for it to grow to the point where a barber could shape it into something decent so he wouldn't feel uncomfortable about leaving the village.

"When are we going into town for a *real* party, Pompam?" a jaded Kitti asked after about two weeks of hanging out in the backyard. This meant a trip to the main town in Buriram for a sample of its cafes and gaudy music halls.

After consulting the mirror Pompam decided that he would be ready for a haircut in about another week, and that they could go then. There had been much talk among the boys about Pompam's virginity and his need to get rid of it so he could finally be a real man. Many alternating plans had been discussed to this end, and Pompam decided he would remedy the situation during his first trip to town.

That Sunday Pompam paid a visit at *Khun* Direk's house to pay his respects to the kind village headman who had always been one of his strongest supporters; Pompam hadn't seen him since the big temple *thamboon* ceremony the previous year. He told *Khun* Direk all about his scholarship to Ramkampheng, and the opportunity Dr. Jim had given him to get a proper university education.

"I am pleased for you, Vichai. I know that in the future you will bring great honor to our village," *Khun* Direk solemnly predicted.

Young Rattana shyly emerged from the house and gave Pompam a brief, courteous *wai*. Pompam noticed that she still had that same gaze in her dark eyes whenever she looked at him. She was only fourteen years old, but the young man could see that one day she might become a beautiful girl.

"Rattana has become quite a good student herself, Vichai; she has the best grades of anyone in her class. Perhaps she will also go to a university one day." *Khun* Direk spoke proudly of the person he loved above all others in the world, and Rattana blushed and looked away.

The day finally came when Pompam was satisfied that he could get a haircut so he and the boys could go to town and have their "real" party, as Kitti had called it.

He returned from the barber still wearing the green baseball cap, fuming with rage. "Look what that idiot did to me!" he exclaimed to Kitti as he dramatically yanked off the hat.

Kitti stifled both his giggles and a cutting remark when he saw how the barber's electric clippers had practically shaved Pompam over the ears and up the neck, leaving the gelled top sticking straight up like a bundle of harvested rice.

"It's fine, Pompam," his friend tried to soothe him, choking back a laugh. "What does it matter how it looks here in Buriram. By the time we get to Bangkok it will be totally grown out and you can have it properly cut at Mahboonkhrong Center. *Mai pen rai.*"

Pompam eventually calmed down and the two boys, along with Nuu and two others, made ready for their departure on the local bus for their big night out in the provincial capital. Maa had forbidden Nuu to go with the other boys, stating emphatically that he was simply too young. When she was busy tending the new baby, however, he sneaked out the back of the house and was gone before she knew it.

The five young men — all wearing their best rubber slippers — walked into a coffee shop in Buriram looking exactly like what they were: sons of poor, uneducated rice farmers from the backwaters of Isan. From the very beginning it was tacitly understood that Pompam was the host for the outing; none of the others carried even a single *baht* between them.

Pompam ordered beers for everyone, along with some spicy plates of food that might be called *hors d'oeuvres* in more civilized places; in Isan it was barbecued pigs innards with a chili paste dip.

"So what's the plan, Pompam?" Nuu inquired, imitating some gangster movie he had seen on television while waiting for Pompam in the barber shop.

"Let's just drink for a while here; later we'll go to the cafe where we can listen to music and see some girls," Pompam replied, pretending to know what he was doing.

By the time they got to the much-talked-about cafe, all of them were well on their way to becoming very drunk. When they had finished their beers at the coffee shop they sat outside on the sidewalk and polished off a whole bottle of Thai whiskey. Once inside the dimly-lit cafe they began teasing each other boisterously, dancing the *ram wong* with each other, and drawing frowns of disapproval from the more "sophisticated" clientele. They innocently displayed their rice-field roots with more abandon and enthusiasm than they had intended.

About an hour later the "*nak-rong*" began to appear on stage. These were the singers — most were female, but a few were male — who made at least a part of their living by performing in establishments of this sort; a daytime job or illicit after-hours liaisons with customers made up the balance of their careers.

Most *nak-rongs* had absolutely no talent whatsoever, and just stood on stage like dressed-up dolls, reciting lyrics off-key without the slightest trace of feeling or musicality. The girls wore the gaudiest evening clothes imaginable, with skirts so short they could barely sit down without embarrassing themselves, beads and sequins galore; and they wore enough make-up on their pert young faces to scare a water buffalo in broad daylight. The group of intoxicated boys, Pompam included, thought they were not only ladies of extreme beauty and sex appeal, but were immensely gifted singers as well.

If someone in the audience admired a particular *nak-rong*, they would purchase a *"puangmalai,"* or traditional flower garland, with *baht* notes tied onto it, and present it to the singer mid-act. After the set, she or he would give the *puangmalai* to the captain who kept track of how much would be owed at closing time. The singer would then proceed to the table of the customer who had presented the floral/monetary tribute, *wai* deeply, smile, and then sit down to chat and drink for a while. If the chemistry was there, they might negotiate an arrangement for an amorous meeting later on.

This particular cafe in Buriram had about thirty *nak-rongs* that would rotate performances until the bar closed. Some of the larger establishments in the suburbs of Bangkok may have as many as 70 to 100 outrageously attired "singers" who performed for *puangmalai*, and for whatever else might be offered after closing time.

Pompam was particularly interested in one young lady wearing a tight little skirt that barely covered her shapely bottom. Silver sequins and multicolored "pearls" were sewn into a pattern that swirled aimlessly all over her tiny green creation. She wore too-high heels that required all her concentration while trying not to trip over the tangle of microphone wires that covered the floor.

Pompam went up to the captain and purchased a *puangmalai* for 100 *baht*, then swaggered over to the foot of the stage and held it up to the girl mid-way through a song, amazed at his own audacity. He was encouraged by loud catcalls and whistles from his disorderly table, but he never once looked back. The cute, diminutive girl carefully bent over in a *wai* to receive it from Pompam, and nearly fell over head-first while struggling to keep her balance and her knees together at the same time.

The boys from the farm wandered back onto the dance floor, trying to look "cool" as they danced with each other. They swayed back and forth with their arms up over their heads and did their best to adapt the Isan *ram wong* to modern Thai pop music from Bangkok.

Pompam ordered several dishes of food, including an entire fresh-water fish in a fragrant sauce made of chilies and bitter vegetables, steaming and bubbling over a can of sterno. Dancing had made the boys hungry, and they dug into the rare delicacy with noise and relish while the young waiters and waitresses continually re-filled their glasses with Thai whiskey and "*so-co,*" soda and cola mixed together.

When her set was finished Pompam's young *nak-rong* came over to their table, *waied*, and sat down with the unruly boys. She was quite shy, and said she had only been working there for six weeks.

Pompam bravely excused himself to go talk to the captain about the girl, find out whether or not she could be "offed" to have sex with him, and how much it would cost. He was informed that it was "up to the girl," but if she did he would have to pay the cafe a bar fine of 150 *baht*, and then give the girl at least 500 *baht* as a "tip" after they had done their deed. Pompam frowned, realizing there was no way he could afford the gorgeous, sexy girl in the shimmering green dress.

"We have other girls in a room behind the stage that you can 'off' for a 50 *baht* fine," the captain informed Pompam when he saw the disappointed look on the poor boy's face. "You can take her to the short-time motel next door and get a room for 50 *baht*, then give her a tip of about 100 *baht*. When you're ready just let me know and I'll take you back there so you can choose one." Pompam felt relieved that the evening might not be wasted after all.

In about twenty minutes the *nak-rong* finally left their table when she figured out there would be no further transactions with the farm boys. Pompam then took leave of his rowdy friends and sought out the captain to lead him to the back room where he would select his girl.

The boys lewdly cheered him as he went off. Kitti screamed out, "Pompam, take me with you; I'll show you how to do it!" Kitti, of course, was also still a virgin, but *mai pen rai*. Pompam was embarrassed to the teeth when he caught the winks from three or four lecherous-looking older men at neighboring tables; he held his head down as he followed the captain through the smoky, crowded nightclub.

The captain took Pompam to an alcove where he could peer through a glass partition into a shabby, fluorescent-lit room that contained between fifteen or twenty females of varying ages, seated on folding chairs, idly watching television to pass the time. None of them were as pretty as the *nak-rong* Pompam really wanted; some even seemed almost old enough to be his mother. All looked disinterested and bored, and even Pompam could figure out that this was just a part-time night job for the girls, to help them keep rice on the table for families at home.

One reasonably attractive girl looked up at Pompam; she appeared to him to be about 22 or 23 years old. She smiled, winked, then seductively re-crossed her bare knees, a gesture she had obviously picked up from an American movie. At least she seems to have *some* interest in me, Pompam thought.

He pointed to her and told the captain, "I'll take that one over there, the one in the blue dress." The captain signaled to the girl with a small penlight. Pompam then paid him the 50-*baht* bar fine, and the captain led the pair to a side exit and pointed the way to the motel next door, a purple neon sign said in Thai, "Playboy Hotel".

Pompam felt so uncomfortable that he didn't think he could go through with it. The girl didn't say one word. She merely grabbed

Pompam's sweaty hand and led him over to the "curtain" motel. Normally a customer would drive up in his car, the attendant on duty would motion to an open curtain with a flashlight — like one of those signalmen on an airport tarmac — then close the curtain after the car was discreetly parked in the stall. In Pompam's case there was no car, of course, so the boy signaled them to a curtain and they *walked* into the stall; then he closed the curtain behind them and ushered them into the bedroom beyond.

The room-boy switched on the electric fan and Pompam paid him 50-*baht*, the rate for three hours' use of the room; the girl already had her shoes off when Pompam closed the door. He looked around at the tacky, over-used motel room which featured a double bed made up with only a fitted bottom sheet and two smallish pillows. There were mirrors behind the bed and on both side walls; Pompam looked up at the pale pink ceiling and was shocked to see a wavy, discolored mirror up there too.

"What's your name?" Pompam said softly, trying to break the ice.

"Num," replied the girl with no emotion. She didn't bother to ask Pompam his name, but motioned toward the bathroom where it appeared she wanted him to shower.

Pompam began by removing his T-shirt and hanging it up on the rack near the door, which he locked. Then he wrapped a threadbare bath towel around his waist and modestly removed his jeans and underpants beneath it.

He went into the tiny, poorly-ventilated bathroom and kept the door ajar so he could keep an eye on the girl. He had heard plenty of stories about girls like this stealing the customer's valuables, and then running off before doing their work — especially if the customer was drunk, and Pompam knew he was.

He stepped under the lukewarm water and started soaping up when the door suddenly opened and Num, now completely naked, stepped in to join him. He had never seen a totally nude woman before except in some trashy magazines Kitti had bought at a stall on Silom Road. Pompam thought the girl was quite lovely, though not very tall. He would have preferred that she had worn less make-up: her eyelids were painted orange, and her lips bright red. She had surprisingly full breasts with brownish-pink nipples which pleased him; Pompam had no way of knowing she was nursing a baby she had delivered just three months before. She pinned up her long black hair to keep it from getting wet, and stepped in next to him.

She took the tiny bar of soap from Pompam's quivering hand and began by lathering his back. "You have the strong healthy body of a young man," she commented almost admiringly, her first spoken words. "So many of my customers are old and ugly."

She soaped Pompam's body from his shoulders to his feet, leaving his private area for the last. When she began soaping there, Pompam, who had been erect since she first walked into the bathroom, giggled and said "*Jakutee,*" or, "I'm ticklish," and quickly made her stop when he thought he might come and spoil his first time.

Num completed her shower as Pompam was toweling off — not able to stop himself from staring openly at her small but well-proportioned body. She led him into the room, took his towel, hung it on the back of one of the two side chairs, and guided him onto the bed. She made him lie on his stomach while she straddled him on his back and began to massage his broad, youthful shoulders.

Pompam closed his eyes and enjoyed the undulating sensation of Num massaging him with her entire body. Then she laid down beside him and pulled him onto his side; he tentatively began to lightly touch and caress her. Pompam took a deep breath and inhaled for the first time the female scent, exhaling slowly.

Pompam climbed on top of Num and she wrapped her slim legs around his waist; with her left hand she swiftly and expertly guided him inside her. Pompam closed his eyes and shivered once or twice. With a gasp, unable to control himself, he came quickly as she grabbed hold of his firm buttocks and pulled him toward her as he pushed and pushed, trying to make it last.

They relaxed for a few minutes, lying on the bed side by side. Num made the motion to get up and shower, but Pompam begged her to wait until he was ready to do it again. The next time he would be slower, he promised.

"If you want to do it again you have to pay me double," the girl said bluntly, making it sound very business-like.

"*Mai pen rai,*" was Pompam's quick answer, "I'll pay you twice if you'll wait for me."

Pompam was more pleased with his second attempt, and he managed to hold off his coming while she tacitly taught him how to give her pleasure as well as prolong his own.

A little later Pompam paid Num the 200 *baht* he owed her for "double" and she left him in the room alone, to shower and dress before returning to his friends. When Num got back to the nightclub she repaired her make-up and went immediately to the room behind the stage where she waited patiently for the next man to "off" her. She never gave Pompam another thought. This was her work, and her humble means for providing rice for two fatherless children, one just an infant. If she was lucky, she might have two or three more customers before closing time that night.

Pompam felt relaxed and pleased with himself. He was eighteen years old and still a virgin until that night; by Thai standards he was way behind schedule. He was glad to be a man at last.

The music was still blaring at full volume when he stepped back into the smoke-filled music hall. As he approached his table he was appalled to see the mess his drunken friends had made. Kitti and one of the other boys were on the dance floor, clearly oblivious to the fact that they were the only two people out there. They were embracing each other for support, stumbling dramatically out of step to a slow number being crooned by a tuxedoed male *nak-rong* on stage. Pompam couldn't help but laugh when he saw how silly they looked.

At the table his brother Nuu was slumped across two chairs sleeping soundly. His slippers were on the floor and his stained and crumpled shirt was completely unbuttoned. The other two boys were sitting up but dangerously listing to one side, unaware of the fish bones strewn about, and other debris that littered the table in front of them. They both started shouting at Pompam when they saw him moving toward them, making vulgar, obscene remarks about the sexual act they knew Pompam had just performed. Kitti and his dancing friend joined in on the teasing when they heard the catcalls of the other boys.

Pompam sat down, the waiter immediately made him a fresh drink, and the questions began. "What was she like, Pompam?" "Which one did you do it with, Pompam?" "How many times did you come, Pompam?" And on and on...

Pompam tried without success to calm them all down. The captain passed by and coldly gave them a straighten-up-or-you're-going-to-get-thrown-out-on-your-ass look. Pompam smiled at him helplessly, smiled, and shrugged his shoulders.

After a few more drinks Pompam was drunk all over again. Kitti and the rest of the boys were out of control, falling off their chairs. Finally the captain *did* come over and firmly asked them to pay their bill and leave. The *nak-rong* were all complaining that the boys were making such a disturbance they couldn't concentrate on their singing.

Pompam paid the tab, shocked that he had allowed himself to spend so much money on one evening. With some help from two or three of the waiters, he got all of the boys out of the cafe and into the street. Now where do we go? Pompam wondered to himself; it's far too late to catch a bus home; Maa will be furious.

Pompam decided they would sleep on the platform at the train station, less than two blocks away. They all held onto one another and staggered down the main street of Buriram in a shabby, drunken chorus line. A security guard at the depot looked at them threateningly when they walked through the gate, but kindly left them alone once he saw them all collapse unconscious in a big heap. At least they were far enough away from the tracks that they were in no danger of getting run over when trains came through in the middle of the night, he thought.

At one point during the wee hours, thirteen-year-old Nuu crawled away from the huddle to throw up, and somehow managed to make it back and fall asleep again. All piled up on top of one another as they were, out cold, they looked like an abandoned litter of mangy kittens, put out to be adopted by some kind-hearted passerby.

Two trains passed through the station sometime during the early hours of the morning. One of them even stopped and passengers got off, but the boys didn't stir. It wasn't until daybreak when Pompam was awakened by a horrible smell and he opened his eyes to the sight of a fur-less stray dog licking his face. Pompam poked and prodded, and slowly got the other boys up on their feet; they sleepily stumbled into the public washroom where they did whatever they needed to do. In the case of Kitti and one of the others, this was to endure a violent case of prolonged dry heaves.

When they were more or less restored, Pompam treated them

all to hot coffee and *"khao tum gai,"* a nourishing, revitalizing hot rice soup with roasted garlic and bits of chicken. After their stomachs were settled, Kitti bravely suggested they have a round of beer. Pompam, against his better judgment, ordered two bottles and let the party begin again.

They finally arrived back in their village around noontime, Pompam relieved of both his virginity and about 2,500 *baht*. Each of the boys went off to their respective homes to sleep through the heat of the day. They were ready to get together again about sunset time for some more Mekhong and *so-co*, but without the company of disobedient Nuu, whom Maa punished severely by making him clean the outhouse and weed the vegetable garden until well past dark.

After about another week of the party routine it began to dawn on generous Pompam that he was the only one in the group who had any money to pay for their drinking binges, and he was spending far more than he could afford.

Pompam realized that he and Kitti would be going back to Bangkok in about three weeks' time, and there would be clothes to buy, things for their room to purchase, and expense money needed for survival until they could both find work. Besides, it was rice-planting time, and that was certainly no fun with a big hangover every day.

Thus, the last couple of weeks of boyhood freedom were spent quietly, with only the bare minimum of drinking and an occasional party. Pompam's parents, especially Maa, were happy to see him settle down again into their simple way of life, perhaps for the last time all together as a family.

When the time came, good-byes were said at home, the temple, and throughout the village, as the two old friends made their exit from Buriram and moved on to Bangkok, the University, and hopefully a better life. Although *Khun* Direk once again offered to drive the boys to the train station in his old pick-up, Pompam insisted they take the local bus. The young girl, Rattana, stood by her father, as always, and waved good-bye, silently hoping that Pompam would return for *Loy Kratong*.

Chapter 7

It only took Kitti and Pompam a few hours to find a room to rent near the university, just three small streets away from Ramkampheng Road itself. Even though classes were still two weeks away, the area seemed filled to brimming with young people. The first two of the half-dozen major shopping centers on Ramkampheng were already built, and for the first time Pompam could enter such places as a normal layman and not be concerned about his yellow robes and shaved head. He bought himself several outfits of new clothes, mostly from the stalls of street vendors, however, and not from the air conditioned shops in the malls. He got his hair cut at the gigantic Mahboonkhrong Center as he had long-ago promised himself, and generally felt quite pleased with his new image.

The room the two boys rented was about ten feet by twelve feet in a five-story, rabbit-warren walk-up. It only cost them 1,000 *baht* each month, but they did have their own bathroom with cold water, and a window to the outside with a view of laundry hanging out of the mildew-covered tenement next door. They considered themselves very lucky to have a window facing anywhere at all, as many of the rooms in their building were *inside* rooms with nothing more than slats for ventilation near the ceiling.

Their first purchases for the room were bedding and straw mats to cover the green linoleum tile floors, an electric fan, a plastic zip-up wardrobe for their clothes, and a small ice chest. They bought cleaning supplies and scrubbed the room down thoroughly, unpacked, then sat back to relax and plan their next move.

"We'll find jobs tomorrow, Kitti," Pompam said. "I think we should try that big seafood restaurant down toward Klongtan; you know, the one with the big crab on the roof. If we're lucky we could start out as waiters and not have to work our way up from busboy."

Kitti didn't much like the idea of working in a restaurant; he had been helping his mother with her *somtam* stall for the past nine years. But Pompam stressed the importance of getting night jobs so they could attend classes and study during the day. It was also important to find work not too far from their rooms so they could avoid long bus trips through the intense heat and traffic of Bangkok. Kitti saw the merit in Pompam's logic, and agreed to go with him the following day in search of a restaurant job.

Once again their luck was good, and both got jobs at the big restaurant in Klongtan with the crab on the roof. Unfortunately, they *would* have to start out as busboys. Also, unfortunately, their meager starting salaries would only be 1,500 *baht* per month each, plus dinner every night.

Later, Kitti looked downcast when they talked the situation over in their room, but Pompam said with optimism, "*Mai pen rai.* Our two monthly salaries together will cover our rent, utilities, and part of our food. I still have some money coming every month from Dr. Jim. We'll make it okay until we can find something better." Kitti just groaned.

They gradually began meeting their neighbors. It was hard *not* to meet them as living quarters were so close. When tenants were home, doors were always kept open to catch the occasional breeze; there was virtually no such thing as privacy, and it was noisy as hell, all the time.

One day they introduced themselves to Ott, the boy next door, who was from Sukhothai Province. He had been in Bangkok for about five years, studied part-time at the university, and had dreams of becoming a professional photographer. They had seen him going out every evening on his motorbike wearing very fashionable clothes. Sometimes he returned about two or three o'clock in the morning; sometimes he didn't return until the following day. He seemed to rarely attend class or lectures, and it didn't appear that he had a job either. Pompam and Kitti wondered where he got the money to pay his bills and buy his nice clothes and camera equipment.

"The first thing you guys had better do is buy a padlock for your door," Ott warned the two new boys, noticing they didn't already have one. "Never trust the people in this building — or in any building for that matter. There are *kamoy*s everywhere."

Pompam and Kitti were smart enough to believe the likelihood of thievery in such a place, and they purchased a sturdy lock the next day.

It took them only three nights to absolutely hate working at the restaurant. The owners were Chinese, of course, and they treated the help like slaves, especially the lowly busboys who, to them, were barely even human. Within a week, however, their luck improved when two other boys quit and they were both promoted to waiter, each with a 300 *baht* per month wage increase. In spite of the tough working conditions and the degree to which they detested the place, they agreed with one another to stay there for one month. "At least we don't have to worry about what to eat for dinner every night; it will always be left-over something — with fish bones to watch out for," Pompam remarked sarcastically.

They registered for classes, making sure they took an identical schedule. In the beginning they never missed a class or a lecture. About two months into the term, however, they were lucky to make it to twenty percent of them, either because they were too tired from working the night before, too lazy, or too bored.

Ramkampheng was an "open" university, designed for students who had full-time jobs and couldn't attend class on a regular basis. All a student basically had to do was pass the exams and sooner or later he would get his diploma. Degrees from Ramkampheng were obviously less impressive than degrees from "normal" universities where class attendance was imperative and standards were much higher. Degrees from Chulalongkorn and Thammasat, ranked number one and two in Thailand, were the most highly prized. Admission to those fine institutions, however, was open only to those who achieved the highest examination scores, or had powerful connections who could pull strings.

About six weeks after the boys had begun their new lives at Ramkampheng, they came home from work a little after midnight one night, tired to the bone, and were greeted by Ott, their neighbor, who was sitting on the floor in his room with the door open. "Come in and drink with me. I have some Black." he called.

Pompam and Kitti had been good about not drinking since they started their school term, but since the next day was a rare holiday from both school and work the two boys cheerfully accepted Ott's invitation for some "Black," whatever that was. Since it was a hot night the fan was on "high," and Ott was wearing only a pair of shorts; Kitti and Pompam changed into the same before going next door.

"Black" turned out to be Johnny Walker Black Label Scotch. Neither Pompam or Kitti had ever tasted *farang* whiskey before, so they were curious about the new treat. As they toasted each other with their first glass Pompam asked, *"Pang, mai?"* "Is this expensive?"

"Pang mak," he answered, or "It's very expensive." "It runs about 700 *baht* a bottle, but it was a gift from a foreigner friend," Ott continued.

The three boys talked way into the night, drinking and laughing, exchanging stories of their families and hometowns. Pompam and Kitti had never been to the ancient royal capital of Sukhothai, located mid-way between Bangkok and Chiang Mai in the north. Ott, on the other hand, had never been anywhere near Isan where Kitti and Pompam were from. They compared notes, however, and discovered that all three of them were equally destitute, and that each had come from similar farming backgrounds. They all dreamed of a better life through education, and they were impatient for some of the rewards they saw around them every day in the booming material world of cosmopolitan Bangkok.

Ott was about twenty or twenty-one years old. He was two inches shorter than Pompam, had a slight build, dark skin, and one of those good-looking Thai faces that shows almost no hint of the Asian mix; it gave him a blended "international" look which made his ethnicity difficult to pin down for a non-Thai. He had a girlfriend that he was rarely able to see, even though she too lived in the capital. She was from a well-off Chinese family who owned a shipping company on Rama IV Road; Ott was a pure-blooded Thai and the offspring of impoverished rice farmers in Sukhothai; this, according to Ott, was not a relationship destined to go very far. His only hope was to complete his studies and make enough money to earn her family's respect — hopefully through developing his love of photography into a successful career.

"I've made some contacts in the advertising and media fields, and one day I'll have enough material to put together a portfolio and show it to them; I think I'm good," Ott announced with confidence.

"How can you afford to live in your room alone, have all your nice clothes, a motorbike, camera equipment, and not have a job?" asked Pompam who, like most Thai people, thought nothing at all about asking the most direct personal questions.

Ott's face turned slightly red and he replied, "I have sort of a job, in a small nightclub down off Silom. Here, have another drink," and filled their glasses. They were already tipsy by this time, and the bottle was nearly empty.

"I'll tell you about my work if you like, but you must promise never to repeat to anyone what I say. I'm not really ashamed of it because I do what I do to survive — not because I like it. But I never want my girlfriend, Kim, to find out; I really love her," Ott began in a whisper, suddenly needing to confide in someone. He had kept his feelings to himself for a long time.

Pompam and Kitti couldn't imagine what kind of work Ott did that he wanted to keep so secret. They both had openly shared with Ott that they were waiters in a goddamned Chinese seafood restaurant. What could be worse than that? they wondered.

"What I do every night when you see me leave here is go to work in a bar where I sell my body." Ott bluntly said these words then paused and poured himself some more whiskey.

Pompam and Kitti weren't sure they had heard him right; they didn't even begin to understand what he meant.

"What do you mean you 'sell your body'?" Pompam asked in all innocence, looking questioningly back and forth between Ott and Kitti.

"I mean I work in a bar where men who like men come to rent out boys for sex," Ott replied softly, looking down at the floor.

"Then you are gay, that's all," Kitti blurted out. The two boys from Isan had heard about being 'gay,' but thought little of it as their own culture understood and allowed intimacy between men, although such a practice was rarely, if ever, spoken about in public. They were an extremely affectionate people and it was simply no big deal, certainly not regarded as unnatural in any way.

"No, I am *not* gay. As I told you, I have a girlfriend and I want to marry her one day. It's just that I have learned to *act* gay in a sexual way with men who will pay me for it," Ott tried to explain. "When I first came to Bangkok I, too, worked in a restaurant and struggled to pay my rent and put food in my stomach. After a while it just wore me out. Then I discovered I could make more money working in a bar than any other way, and I've been doing it for about two years now. I don't like it, and I'm certainly not proud of it, but I can at least afford to have the things I need, keep up with my classes, and still have a little left over every month to send to my family in Sukhothai."

Pompam and Kitti, of course, knew that girls often sold their bodies this way. Pompam had bought one for himself in Buriram only a few weeks before. Then he visualized Num for a second, her silken skin, and the way he had felt inside her; it began to arouse him just thinking about it. He also thought that even if he was starving to death he wouldn't — *couldn't* — sell his body to another man. It made him squirm to even think about what two men might do together in bed.

"Now that you know what I do for a living, please keep your word and don't tell anyone," Ott spoke gently. "I hope that since we have drunk whiskey together we can be friends and understand one another. We're all the same, guys. We're just poor Thai farmer boys who want more out of life than planting rice and herding buffaloes."

"*Mai pen rai*, Ott, we'll be your friends, and we'll keep your secret," Pompam spoke sincerely, putting his hand on the older boy's shoulder. "Now it's time to go to bed. I'm drunk and tired."

The next day Pompam couldn't stop thinking about Ott's startling revelation about how he earned his livelihood. He seemed like a nice, perfectly normal young man, and yet he could do things with a man that should only be done between a man and a woman. How very horrible and strange. *Mai pen rai...*

During the next few weeks they made friends with other neighbors, and they got together with Ott from time to time — usually very late at night. They discovered that there were other boys — and girls — in their building who also sold their bodies. There were two pretty young girls who lived on the same floor who worked at one of the huge massage palaces down on Petchburi Road; everyone in Thailand knew that the services of a masseuse in a massage parlor only *began* with the massage. There were also two boys down on the third floor who were really more like girls, and everyone called them "lady-boys." Those two allegedly worked in a cabaret show down on Sukhumvit Road, dressed up like women. Kitti and Pompam also found out that a big, strong-looking boy from the second floor worked out with weights every afternoon at the Ramkampheng sports field, and then sold his body to men who were turned on by muscles at a bar that specialized in that commodity, down on Suriwongse Road near Patpong, the main red light district.

After a while Pompam and Kitti got used to the idea that it takes all kinds in this world, and they ceased to be concerned about the different sorts of people and lifestyles that made up their youthful neighborhood. "Who cares?" Pompam would say to Kitti. "We're all in the same boat here in Ramkampheng. None of us come from 'good' families with money or social background. We all come from the dirt."

Pompam eventually got promoted from waiter to captain, and then from captain to head captain. He also had a chance to spend some time tending bar, which he enjoyed for a while until he got bored, preferring contact with the customers. After about two years he was promoted to assistant manager, having won the confidence of the fat, arrogant Chinese owner who Pompam thoroughly despised. However, he was able to learn the inner workings of a large eating and drinking establishment, and he considered it part of his education.

Kitti, who turned out to be good with figures, gradually gained the trust of the Chinese owner as well, and was promoted from waiter to cashier. He always balanced his register to a *baht* at the end of each night, and there was never a shortage or a discrepancy when he turned in the money to the Chinese. After a little more than a year he was put in charge of the restaurant's bookkeeping because the owner realized he could save money by having Kitti do the work, rather than pay a professional accountant. The Chinese, being the masters of money in many parts of Asia, were able to teach Kitti many tricks in terms of handling it and making it multiply. Kitti paid close attention and learned a great deal about creative accounting, investing, and finance.

The attitudes of the Chinese owners were oftentimes difficult for the Isan boys to endure. Because they, themselves, were not ethnic

Chinese and members of the boss's family, they were always treated like outsiders of a lower rank. Even though they did their jobs well and worked hard, with each promotion their salaries were only increased by a token amount. Pompam and Kitti resented the miserliness of their bosses, but realized they probably had the best jobs they could get given their circumstances.

During the first three years of their university studies they only managed to get back to Buriram twice for New Year and once for *Loy Kratong*. Even though it was so seldom, they still had to threaten to quit their jobs in order for their bosses to let them have their holidays.

Both boys had a student deferment from the obligatory two-year military service demanded of all twenty-year-old Thai males. Normally, all non-students that age were required by law to report to the military office in their home province for the annual lottery. If they picked a white ball out of the hopper they were inducted on the spot; if they picked a red ball they were let off the hook. Boys who came from families with money routinely bought themselves out of the lottery with a bribe. The amount would be anywhere from 7,000 to 20,000 *baht* depending on the province — and the avarice of the local commanding officer.

Pompam was twenty years old when his mother gave birth to her seventh son. It surprised Pompam that his mother was still having babies at her age; but it literally *shocked* him when she had another one the following year when he was twenty one. It was also a boy.

"No more babies for me, Pompam. I'm too old, and I can't seem to be able to make any daughters," she told her eldest when he came home for his annual visit.

Pompam and Kitti made few close friends during this period in their lives, and had virtually no social life other than drinking whiskey with Ott every now and then after work. The two boys obviously had very little time and money for girlfriends; their sex lives had been limited to a few small affairs with lonely waitresses who were more than happy to bed them with no expectations. It was simply a way to escape the hardships of life for a few moments and make their bodies feel good. Neither the waitresses nor the poor students from Buriram had many other pleasures, or much to which they could look forward.

All of Pompam's brothers adored him. Nuu dropped out of school when he was fourteen to help Paw with the rice fields. The next one, named Att, was more inclined towards academics and remained in the local school, helping out on the farm in his spare time. All the rest were either children or babies and Pompam regretted that he wasn't home enough to really get to know them. As time passed he also became increasingly more frustrated at his inability to send more than 300 or 400 baht a month home to help support his family; this will all change in a few years, he continually promised himself.

Each year he saw Rattana during his home visits, and marveled at how much she had grown and matured during his absence. She was indeed a beautiful young woman now, and still the true love of *Khun* Direk's life. He never saw Rattana except in the company of her father, but each time he encountered her he noticed that she still gazed at him the same way she had that day in the back of the pick-up years before — on the way to the train station in Buriram. It still made him slightly uncomfortable.

"I'm going to send Rattana to Khon Kaen University to get her Associate of Arts degree when she finishes high school," he told Pompam. "A Bachelor's Degree won't be necessary for her, but I at least want her to have two years."

Unbeknown to anyone, Rattana was already deeply smitten with Pompam. There was something special and mysterious about the young man that she had never been able to understand — even though she had known him her whole life. To her, he always had a sort of golden glow, and his scent would simply overwhelm her every time she had a chance to stand near his strong, healthy body. In a way, Rattana also feared Pompam's powerful charisma and charm, but she had long ago given her heart and soul to him and she could think of no one else. So many nights she had laid in bed fantasizing about their future life together while she massaged her centers of ecstasy. Rattana couldn't help it that Pompam excited and aroused her, and she prayed to the Lord Buddha that one day he would love her and make her secret romantic world become real.

Whenever Pompam was in the village he would spend time with *Phra* Prateep at the temple, mostly talking over old times. He would also visit *Phra* Asoka once every six months or so in Bangkok,

more out of respect and to keep the connection going than to listen to
his advice. Both monks would ask Pompam when he was going to do
his time as a monk since he was of the age to do so. Pompam's reply
would be, "I'll become a monk when I have money to take care of my
family." Secretly, however, Pompam knew that he had left the
monastery forever, and it would be unlikely if he ever returned.

Supachai finished his degree at the Buddhist University and,
much to Pompam's surprise, decided not to disrobe and be a tour
guide, but to remain a monk and become a teacher of other monks at
the Buddhist school in Chonburi, south of Bangkok. From that point
Pompam and his old friend would gradually lose touch with each other
over time.

Dr. Jim remained true to his word and religiously sent
Pompam's expense money every month. Pompam dutifully kept up his
correspondence with Dr. Jim, not only because he wanted to make sure
his important monthly stipend didn't stop, but because it made him feel
good about himself to have such a fine, high-level person in his life.
Pompam also still wrote to a few of his old pen pals from *Wat* Po days,
and occasionally received much-appreciated money from them as well.

During their third New Years season at the restaurant Pompam
and Kitti were dealt a severe blow, along with all of their other fellow
employees. One night at a staff meeting after closing time the Chinese
owner announced that since they hadn't made enough profit the previous year there would be no bonuses. When he said this he looked
directly at Kitti and gave him a threatening frown; he knew that Kitti
was aware the restaurant had actually made a tremendous amount of
profit.

Kitti was disgusted by such a blatant lie, and he cursed the
Chinese silently under his breath. Later, he couldn't help but tell
Pompam about the lie, and Pompam became enraged; he had counted
on the bonus money, and had worked hard for it all year; he had already
promised Maa and Paw a portion of it for the family, and he knew they
were depending on it. "Surely there is a better way to make money
than working for the fucking Chinese," he said to himself. That night
when he laid down to sleep he thought about his poor family and rolled
over and faced the wall and wept, feeling totally helpless.

The week following the no-bonus announcement, Kitti and Pompam passed Ott's open door after work one night and Ott invited them in for a drink. Both boys were exhausted to the bone. Kitti went off to sleep, but Pompam agreed to join Ott for just a short time, sensing his friend needed to talk.

Ott was approaching his twenty-fourth birthday, and even though he had already graduated from University, he couldn't make the switch to a "real" job; he had gotten too used to the good money he could still make by selling his body. He knew, however, that after five years of it he would soon be past his prime, and have no choice but to stop. He had never known any boy in the business who had survived more than seven years; at that point they would either be too old, or too burned out physically and emotionally to be able to handle it any longer.

"How was your night tonight, Ott?" Pompam asked when settled in with a full glass. Pompam noticed that Ott was looking tired and drained lately, and it worried him.

"Not so bad, Pompam. A *farang* bought me out early and took me to a curtain motel for about an hour, then paid me 700 *baht*," he replied in a dull monotone, dark circles under his eyes.

Pompam couldn't help but think that 700 *baht* for one night was more than one quarter of what he made at the restaurant in an entire month. "What did you have to do with him for 700 *baht*?" Pompam asked, curious, never before having discussed the subject before.

"You know, the usual. I've had enough practice by now that I can let them do it to me without it hurting too much. If the customer is nice to me, and not too old, it can even be almost enjoyable. This guy tonight books me out two or three times a month and occasionally takes me to a restaurants or to the disco; it's almost like we're friends," Ott explained cynically.

"Do you have to go with everyone they tell you to, even if you don't like them?" Pompam asked.

"That's the worst part of the work. If the captain tells me to go with someone then I have to go; otherwise he would fire me on the spot. The captain would also pass the word around to the other bars in town that I was no good with customers — and get me blackballed from working someplace else. So I go with them all. It's only something to put up with for an hour or two," he replied with resignation.

Pompam was yawning and about ready to fall asleep when Ott said, "Pompam, tomorrow night is the third-year anniversary of the opening of my bar and there's a party. We're going to be very busy and short-handed for waiters. Why don't you come with me and help serve the food and drinks. You won't have to be a 'boy' and go with any customers; besides, my captain will pay you 250 *baht*."

Pompam was shocked that Ott would even *think* of asking him to go with him to the bar — even though the 250 *baht* was tempting, and he was curious about where Ott worked and how the system operated. He said, "I can't go, Ott. I have to work tomorrow night. Besides, you know how I feel about the kind of work you do; no offense."

For a moment Ott felt hurt by Pompam's remark, but he replied with good humor, "*Mai pen rai*. It's probably just as well. The customers would all want you — and when they found out they couldn't have you they'd leave and go someplace else; then none of us would get any work."

The next afternoon when Pompam was getting ready to go to the restaurant he suddenly felt a flash of anger, and his resentment at the Chinese owner surfaced again. "Fuck him!" Pompam said out loud. "Fuck the restaurant."

Pompam knocked on Ott's door. "I've changed my mind, Ott; I'll come with you tonight and earn the extra 250 *baht*," Pompam said on impulse. "I'll get Kitti to tell the restaurant I'm sick and can't work. Just remember, I am *not* a bar boy, and I *won't* go off with some customer," he said adamantly.

Kitti took the news about Pompam going to the bar with Ott rather poorly. He expressed worry and concern for his friend, but inwardly he was also jealous that he hadn't been asked to go too; but Kitti knew he wasn't good-looking enough to work in such a place — even if it was only to serve the food.

"Okay, Pompam. I'll cover for you at the restaurant. Just don't do anything you'll be ashamed of later," he admonished firmly.

Pompam climbed on the back of Ott's motorbike and they zigzagged through the snarled traffic to Silom Road. Pompam was glad to see that the tiredness in Ott's eyes from the night before had disappeared.

Pompam, dressed in his best shirt and slacks, looked like he had just stepped off the page of a fashion magazine. By this time there was no evidence whatsoever in the young man's appearance that he had ever lived as a *nene* in a Buddhist temple for a little more than eight years. "We'll have to keep you hidden in the back, Pompam, or you'll be too much competition for me and the other boys," Ott teased, but half meant it.

Ott introduced Pompam to *Khun* Somkid, the owner of the bar, who smiled and looked him over with more than just a hint of interest in his eyes. Pompam immediately felt ill-at-ease and regretted his decision to come.

"If you change your mind, Pompam, and you want to go with a customer, just let me know," *Khun* Somkid said jokingly.

"Relax, Pompam; you'll be okay," Ott said reassuringly when he realized Pompam was about to bolt.

Pompam took a deep breath and said, "Just this once, Ott, but never again." He cursed himself silently for being so stupid to have gone along with Ott's foolish scheme.

The bar was in an old, wooden, two-story Thai-style house located in one of the small lanes between Suriwongse and Silom. The boys removed their shoes, and Pompam noticed the place looked more like a comfortable old home than any kind of bar he had imagined. It was furnished much like a home, too, with groupings of chairs and sofas in what were previously the drawing room, dining room and study. There were some tables and chairs set up on the verandah at the front of the house as well, and Pompam caught a whiff of acrid-smelling mosquito coils that were being burned at each corner of the railing.

There was live music in one end of the drawing room, and some of the boys were dancing. Several customers had arrived, many of them Thai, but a good percentage of them were *farangs*. *Khun* Somkid greeted the customers at the front door as though they were old friends; since it was an anniversary party, all of his regular patrons had been invited.

Before too long each of the guests had at least one or two boys by his side, smiling, flirting, massaging necks and knees, doing their best to secure their wages for the evening. Pompam helped himself to several glasses of whiskey and *so-co* in the kitchen, and before too long noticed that he was beginning to enjoying himself; he didn't feel nearly as threatened as before.

Around ten o'clock a well-dressed group of four men entered the bar. *Khun* Somkid *waied* profusely when he greeted them, particularly to the older Thai gentleman in the party. He treated them like guests of honor and seated them in a reserved grouping of easy chairs near the entertainment area. The *farang* who was with them handed Somkid a large bottle of Chivas Regal and asked for ice and mixers. All four of them were speaking English, but the only one in the group that seemed interested in the boys was the *farang*; he kept craning his neck from side to side, looking around, hunting for something special.

Three or four boys were presented to the *farang* for his approval, but after a few minutes with each one the foreigner would say something, and then the older Thai gentleman would discreetly signal to the boy that it was time to leave. After a while the *farang* got up and excused himself to go to the washroom, obviously using the excursion as an excuse to do a survey to see for himself what else was available. When he passed the door to the kitchen he stopped and looked in. About a half-dozen boys — Pompam included — were standing around drinking and joking. When they saw the *farang* they all turned towards him, smiled, *waied*, and became silent, shy.

When the *farang* spotted Pompam he smiled broadly, *waied* back, and returned to his table. The other boys pounced on Pompam and mercilessly teased him about his *farang* admirer; Pompam blushed dark red from embarrassment, and tried to divert their attention with some macho remark about how much he needed a woman to fuck that night.

About ten minutes later *Khun* Somkid came into the kitchen and politely summoned Pompam. "There's a *farang* out there who wants to meet you, Pompam. I know you don't work here as a boy, but since the Thais the *farang* is with are important friends of mine, please just go to the table and sit with them for a while."

Pompam was revolted by the idea of playing such a ridiculous charade, but *Khun* Somkid had asked in such a polite way that he felt he couldn't refuse. "What harm can there be just sitting with them for a while?" he asked himself.

Khun Somkid made the introductions and Pompam sat on the sofa beside the *farang*. He *waied* to everyone politely and did his best to use the good manners he had learned in his temple up-bringing.

After a while the elegant older gentleman summarily explained to Pompam the situation at hand, using the Thai language. "*Khun* Somchai here is the general manager of the Thailand Pavilion hotel over on Silom Road. Ek is his boyfriend, and I am the hotel's public relations manager. The *farang* is *Khun* Hans from Holland. He is the owner of a very large tour company in Amsterdam that brings our hotel hundreds of guests every year, which makes him a very big customer.

"*Khun* Hans thinks you are the most handsome boy here, and he wants to take you out with him. *Khun* Somkid explained that you don't work here as a boy, but if you will change your mind and spend the night with *Khun* Hans, then we will give you 1,000 *baht* over and above what *Khun* Hans gives you — but you must *not* tell *Khun* Hans of this arrangement. Please think it over and let me know your answer within ten minutes. *Khun* Hans, by the way, is a very generous tipper." Pompam, shocked and slightly outraged, tried hard not to show any emotion on his face, which had suddenly reddened at the ears.

After another drink, Pompam politely excused himself to go to the men's room; he immediately headed back to the kitchen where he had seen Ott disappear.

"Ott, now look what you've gotten me into!" Pompam hissed angrily. "That *farang* over there wants to 'off' me and the old Thai man had the nerve to tell me that he'll pay me 1,000 *baht* on top of what the rich *farang* gives me! What shall I do?"

"I told you you'd be competition, Pompam," Ott said with a teasing scold. "Do it if you feel like it — or don't do it; it's really up to you. By the way, the old Thai gentleman is a distant relative of the royal family, and a very close friend of *Khun* Somkid. Make sure that you treat him properly even if you refuse — only out of politeness," Ott told him seriously, understanding the required cultural protocol.

Pompam had never been near anyone even remotely related to the royal family. As all Thais, he held the monarchy in such high esteem that he almost felt he couldn't deny a request made by someone of such superior rank. The lure of the money he would make also tempted him, remembering the bonus he wouldn't be getting, and his disappointed family back in the village. After all, he thought, how bad could it be for one night? Many thoughts raced through his mind as he tried desperately to make a decision. He knew in his heart that he was a good person; he ultimately came to the conclusion that nothing he did with his body could ever change that.

He went back to the *farang's* table and very politely told the older Thai gentleman that he would be honored to go out with their friend from Holland. He winked at Pompam, smiled, and said to the *farang* in English, "Pompam would be more than happy to accept your invitation to join our party tonight." *Khun* Hans, the *farang*, was obviously delighted by this news, and he turned to Pompam with near-brimming eyes and said, "I am so happy." Pompam only smiled and tried his best to hide his nervousness.

Khun Somchai settled the tab and they prepared to leave the bar. Every boy in the room, as well as many of the Thai customers, got up from their seats, approached, and deeply *waied* the noble gentleman as he departed. *Khun* Somkid had charged *Khun* Somchai the bar fine of 100 *baht* for "offing" Pompam, even though the young man didn't officially work there; and he surreptitiously slipped the promised 250 *baht* for his night's work into Pompam's shirt pocket when he went out the door. Their eyes met briefly and Pompam quickly turned away, embarrassed.

They all got into *Khun* Somchai's large, silver Mercedes Benz and headed off to another night-time place where the older Thai man and Somchai's boyfriend, Ek, said they liked to sing. By the time they got there Pompam had mentally made himself feel half-way comfortable with the situation, and didn't mind too much that the *farang* had his arm around his shoulder and was cuddling up to him as if they were off on their honeymoon.

A new bottle of "Black" was opened at Chez Studio, and they were served many more rounds of drinks — along with chilied peanuts, deep-fried squid, and several other plates of delectable Thai snacks. Pompam found himself having a really good time, something he had rarely had during the past three years of slaving away at his menial restaurant job. *Mai pen rai* that everyone in the club can see that I am the *farang's* boy, thought Pompam, the alcohol having its magical effect; I could care less...

The older Thai gentleman, whose name was *Khun* Arun, got up and sang a few old Cole Porter songs. His voice wasn't too bad for his age, and Ek leaned over and told Pompam that *Khun* Arun had sung professionally about twenty years before, and had even appeared in a couple of classic Thai movies. Pompam was not only impressed, but by that time he genuinely felt some affection for the happy, child-like, titled gentleman, who wore an ascot and a navy blazer like he had just stepped off a yacht at Monte Carlo.

Ek was the next one who got up to sing. He chose "Desperado," a *farang* song that Pompam had never heard before, but seemed to be a big favorite at Chez Studio, which at the moment was filled to capacity. Everyone kept teasing Pompam to take his turn on stage, and he surprised even himself when he finally went up and sang a Thai pop song that had been a big hit the year before. His voice cracked and went off key, but the crowd and the band gave him big cheers for his bravery and good nature. When he got back to the table the inebriated, uninhibited *farang* appeared to have become hopelessly smitten with him.

They finally arrived at the hotel on Silom about 2:30 a.m. and went up to *Khun* Somchai's suite for a nightcap. The security guards would normally not allow Thai boys — or Thai *girls* for that matter — onto the guest floors, but they were with the hotel manager so the uniformed staff *waied* deeply as the noisy, laughing group got on the lift.

Pompam and *Khun* Hans were on the verge of collapsing from drink and exhaustion when they finally got to the *farang's* suite about an hour later. Pompam had only stayed at fourth-rate hotels in Isan with Dr. Jim, so the magnificence of Hans's suite nearly bowled him over. He was glad he had studied English so thoroughly; he and the *farang* were able to communicate quite well in spite of the large quantities of alcohol they had both consumed, and the fact that the *farang* was Dutch.

Hans showed Pompam into the giant marble bathroom and handed him a thick white towel, indicating it was time to shower. Pompam thanked him, closed the door, and undressed, hanging his clothes on a hook next to the sink. He was enjoying the rare luxury of hot water sluicing down over him when suddenly he heard the bathroom door open. Before he knew it the pale-skinned *farang* had stepped naked into the shower and was lathering him with scented soap.

Pompam couldn't help but remember his first girl, Num, doing exactly the same thing a few years before when he had bought her off at the cafe in Buriram. When Hans began soaping up Pompam's private parts he was surprised to notice that he easily got an erection and, as with Num, had to stop the kind man before he finished too soon. Pompam then took the soap and bathed the *farang*, returning the same favors.

When they got into bed the *farang* was gentle and loving with Pompam, knowing it was his first time. Pompam's fear had largely dissipated by then, and he began to almost enjoy what was happening to him. Pompam finally relaxed to a certain extent, and the two of them made love: the rich European and the buffalo boy from Isan.

In his initiation, Pompam quickly learned the various roles he was being taught and persuaded to play, and when the ultimate act began, Pompam was able to gradually ease himself from pain into comfort with very little difficulty at all. He was totally surprised at himself that not only had he allowed it to happen, but that he had not minded it as much as he thought he would. And in some strange way it pleased Pompam to see how much *Khun* Hans enjoyed the experience of having him.

They eventually dozed off, satisfied and exhausted. They awoke surprisingly early in the morning, given the time they had finally gone to sleep. Pompam smiled at *Khun* Hans and didn't feel the least bit uncomfortable when the *farang* reached over and took him in his arms and said, "I think you are the one." Pompam merely smiled and said nothing, not having any idea how to respond.

When they were showered and dressed they went downstairs to the coffee shop to meet *Khun* Arun, *Khun* Somchai and Ek for breakfast. After they sat down *Khun* Arun teasingly asked the *farang*, "Are we in love yet?" *Khun* Hans blushed demurely, and his glowing face told the whole story.

Khun Somchai said, "Everything is arranged for Pattaya. I suggest we pack up and leave right after breakfast."

The *farang* turned to Pompam and said, "We're all going down to Pattaya for two nights' holiday and I would love for you to join us." *Khun* Arun had known from past experience what a glutton this *farang* was for young Thai boys. He was surprised that Pompam had made such an impression on Hans that he would want to take him to Pattaya and forego the additional young male treats that were so plentiful at the seaside resort.

Pompam had never seen the ocean before, and he was very tempted to go. But then he thought about Kitti back in their room alone, and the dreaded job he hated that he had to go to that evening. He was torn between going with the group to Pattaya, and doing what he knew in his heart was the right thing.

"Okay. I'll go," was Pompam's impulsive response, "but I'll need to go back to my apartment to get some more clothes and let my roommate know what's going on."

Pompam then told *Khun* Somchai where he lived, and it was agreed that they would stop by his building on their way out of town so he could collect his things.

Kitti was sorely shocked at Pompam's story when he flew into their room to pack just before ten in the morning. "I was so worried about you, Pompam. I woke up Ott around eight o'clock and he told me that you had gone off with a *farang*. Now you are telling me that you're going to Pattaya with him for another two days!"

"Calm down, Kitti. I'm earning us some money that we really need right now. Don't forget we're not getting bonuses this year; and I promised some for my parents. And please don't complain about having to tell the boss tonight how sick I still am. I'll see you in two days. Be good."

"How can you say to me, 'be good,' when you are being so bad! How much more bad could you be?" Kitti practically screamed.

Pompam quickly gathered what he needed for the seaside outing in a small carry-all and left the room, not responding to Kitti's outburst. Three or four of his neighbors knowingly raised their eyebrows when Pompam got into Somchai's Mercedes and they drove off. News of this will spread through the building like a slum fire, he thought to himself, momentarily alarmed. *Mai pen rai...*

Pattaya, about two hours to the southeast of Bangkok, was a place Pompam had been dreaming of visiting for years, but had never had the time and money to go. He never imagined that his first time would be with a *farang* from Europe, an important Bangkok hotel man, the GM's Thai boyfriend, and a distant relative of the royal family.

A hotel-manager friend of *Khun* Somchai's had arranged for two large adjoining suites for the party at his lovely beach-side property. The Pattaya hotel was also heavily used by the Dutch tour operator, so Hans was treated like a king, which was standard for him.

After getting settled in their rooms they changed into their beach outfits and went down for a huge buffet lunch by the pool. Pompam thought he must have died and attained nirvana; he had never seen such a fancy spread. After lunch they chartered a speedboat down at the beach and had the boatman take them over to Koh Larn Island where they swam, snorkeled, and tried out the new jet-skis that had just then made their appearance at this Gulf of Thailand "paradise."

None of them could have predicted that within a few short years Pattaya would become over-developed, sleazy, and polluted, and would turn into a place where no self-respecting tourist would even think of going; eventually it would become populated by pedophiles and sex addicts of every persuasion who didn't seem to mind the raw sewage that was routinely dumped just a short distance from the famous beach.

While the *farang* basked in the stern, soaking up sun, the four Thais sat under the boat's canopy trying to avoid it. "Why are you sitting up there? You'll never get a tan that way," the *farang* shouted to them.

"We don't want to get dark and look like rice farmers," shouted Pompam who jokingly spoke for the Thai faction aboard. The *farang* just smiled, admiring the way Pompam looked in his brief black swimsuit.

In the late afternoon they went back to the hotel, showered, and took a siesta before gathering later for drinks, dinner and the evening's entertainment. *Khun* Hans and Pompam made love again before drifting off to sleep; this time the young man knew what was expected of him, and how to both give and receive enjoyment.

Pompam looked over at the napping foreigner beside him and determined that he was about the same age as Dr. Jim — and wasn't too bad looking as *farangs* go. His white skin was now a medium pink, and his blondish-red hair seemed to have gotten lighter during the day. Pompam also noticed that Hans's muscle tone was still good, and his body was firm to the touch.

A sharp feeling of shame passed through him when he thought

about Dr. Jim, and what his kind benefactor would think about what he was doing at that very moment. He scolded himself silently and said, "Dr. Jim is sending me money every month to go to school, and here I am in Pattaya skipping classes for two days — not to mention the fact that I'm having sex with a man for money." But as he drifted off to sleep an inner voice soothingly told him that he was still the same good person he had always been; nothing was really changed; he was only helping his parents and young brothers back home.

The manager of their hotel, a rather lady-like German named Dieter who sported a Van Dyke goatee, hosted the group to a multi-course dinner in their European dining room that evening. Pompam didn't know how to cope with the artfully-prepared *farang* food and the many utensils that were used. He kept his eye on his experienced companions, however, and meticulously copied them, managing to survive the ordeal with hardly any embarrassment.

Towards desert *Khun* Arun spoke up, "I think I would like a little company this evening, Dieter. Where do you think I should go shopping?" Dieter, in a thick German accent, told him the name of a new place that had a huge tank of water at one end of the bar where naked boys gave erotic performances in front of large lighted windows.

"That's a novel approach to fishing," *Khun* Arun said amusingly. They all laughed and agreed to go there for a drink when they finished their coffee. Afterwards they might do something absolutely crazy like go bowling, an activity they would never dream of doing in Bangkok.

They all enjoyed the unusual new bar, and the revue of lithe male sea nymphs who cavorted nude and naughtily under the water. One of them seemed particularly good at holding his breath, and *Khun* Arun chose him for his night's amusement. He decided to take the boy and go back to the hotel early and forego the bowling expedition. "I have better things to do with my own balls and pin," he announced to the giggling and, by now, intoxicated group.

The rest of them continued on to the bowling establishment where they attempted to aim their bowling balls in the right direction while consuming another whole bottle of "Black." Pompam got a special kick out of the way *Khun* Dieter wiggled his rear end each time he bent down to release his light-weight ladies' ball, and then watch in squealing frustration as it rolled each time into the gutter.

Everyone thoroughly enjoyed the Pattaya holiday, but after another day at the beach and another night on the town, it was time to return to the real world of Bangkok.

"I come back here every six months for business, Pompam, so I will see you again before too long. I'll write to you often and send you pocket money so you will stay out of trouble." This was an obvious hint to Pompam to discourage him from taking up the bar game, and getting "offed" by more *farangs* while he was away.

"I'll send you off at the airport tonight and then it's back to work at the restaurant for me tomorrow." Pompam wondered if he would still have a job, especially since he wouldn't be showing up again that evening. He would have to depend on Kitti to cover for him for the fourth night in a row, and he started feeling even more guilty about putting his best friend in such an unpleasant, awkward position; the Chinese owners could be nasty as hell when it came to lame excuses.

Before they left the hotel they had sex for the last time, and Pompam did his best to make it a good finale. Afterwards, *Khun* Hans gave Pompam 4,000 *baht* along with a big hug. Pompam was stunned to think that this one chance encounter had landed him a windfall of 4,000 *baht* from the *farang* — plus the additional 1,000 *baht* that he had already received from *Khun* Arun. And it was only for four days of "work." Pompam's guilt about Kitti seeped away as he thought to himself that perhaps this wasn't such a bad way of life after all. Maybe I could do this work for a short time; the money would mean so much to my family. Pompam pondered the possibility all the way to and from Don Muang Airport.

Chapter 8

Pompam got back to his room that night after seeing *Khun* Hans off at the airport only to find an enraged Kitti waiting up for him, ready to kill.

"I hope you're proud of yourself, you fucker!" Kitti raged. "Tonight you got yourself fired from your job. They almost fired me, too, because they knew I was lying for you!" Pompam had never seen Kitti so angry in all the years he had known him.

"It's okay, Kitti, I don't want to work there any more anyway," was Pompam's cool reply. He had brought home a big bottle of Mekhong whiskey and some ice, and fixed them both a drink before he sat down to tell his story.

"I suppose you're going to be a bar boy now and sell your body to weird, sex-crazed men night after night," Kitti almost spat out.

"Be quiet, Kitti, or everyone in the building will hear you." He then took out his wallet and handed Kitti the 5,250 *baht* that he had earned in four days. "Why should I work for those ungrateful Chinese bastards when I can earn this?" he asked.

"Where did you get the *250 baht*, Pompam? What did you have to do for that?" Kitti made an obscene gesture as he delivered the insult.

"I got 4,000 from the *farang*, 1,000 from *Khun* Somchai for agreeing to go with the *farang*, and the 250 *baht* from *Khun* Somkid, the owner of the bar, for helping serve drinks and food at the party," Pompam replied, keeping calm.

Kitti stared in disbelief at the money. It was almost the same amount both of them made together in one whole month at the restaurant. "You might as well tell me about it, Pompam, from the beginning," he said after a while, stunned by the idea of earning so much money in only four days.

Pompam told the whole story, from *Khun* Somkid's bar all the way to his farewell performance at the airport. Kitti asked one or two questions about Pattaya, but other than that he kept quiet and concentrated on his whiskey, re-filling his glass three times during the telling.

He finally asked in a huffy voice, "Well, Pompam, are you going to go back to the bar again and see if your good luck will repeat itself?"

"Yes, Kitti, I am. Tonight." Pompam was surprised; he had already, unconsciously, made this decision.

Kitti tried to resign himself to having to work alone at the restaurant, and come home to an empty room. He also tried hard to accept the fact that Pompam was actually going to go off and sell his body to anyone who could pay the bar fine. Kitti, of course, wouldn't dare tell anyone, because any shame on Pompam would certainly reflect on him, Pompam's best friend and roommate. It would take him months, however, to get used to the images that frequently flashed across his mind whenever he thought about the actual sex acts Pompam was paid to perform. He knew that he, himself, couldn't do what Pompam did, even if he were good-looking enough to try.

The next morning Pompam went next door to tell Ott both the news of his adventure with the *farang*, and his decision that he would be going to work with him at the bar on Silom that night. Ott was pleased on the one hand, and not so pleased on the other, considering the competition for customers handsome Pompam would become. He kept thinking about how old and tired he, himself, was beginning to feel, and feared the day when he could no longer attract clients at the bar. What will I do then? he wondered grimly; work the street?

"You had some beginners luck, Pompam. You can't expect to meet customers like your first one every single night. Sometimes I sit at the bar until closing time three or four nights in a row and never get bought out by anyone," Ott replied.

The idea of wasting his time several nights in a row without making a single *baht* didn't appeal to Pompam at all; he realized he still had much to learn about this new game.

"How long have you been working at the bar on Silom, Ott?"

"At this one about two years. Before that I worked at a go-go bar in Patpong for a few months, but I hated taking my clothes off in front of people. The first places I worked at were in Saphan Kwai — horrible little bars that only had Thai customers, never a *farang*. Then I learned some English and moved to better places that had *farangs*," he replied. "But it's been a pretty sad story for the past five years, and I still have nothing to show for it." He just sat there on the floor looking defeated.

"If I'm going to do this kind of work, Ott, I want to make sure I work out of a bar where I can make some good money; I don't see any point in it otherwise. I know nothing about any of the other bars in town, and you've been out of circulation for two years. Let's make a plan to stay at *Khun* Somkid's for another week, and if we don't get bought out six nights out of seven, then we'll start looking around." Pompam found it hard to believe that Ott had become so down and lazy for two years; he hadn't even bothered to look for a place where he could earn better money.

"How can we look around when we have to work every night?" Ott asked, sounding weary.

"We'll make up some story for *Khun* Somkid and buy ourselves out for two or three nights. Then we can go on your motorbike to every bar in Bangkok, if necessary, and decide for ourselves which one is best."

That sounded like a reasonable plan to Ott, so the two boys agreed.

Later on that day Kitti went off to the restaurant alone, nowhere near happy, but nearly resolved to the fact that Pompam was striking out his own. "Just take care of yourself, Pompam. Don't forget that if anything should happen to you, I would be the one to do the explaining back home."

"Don't worry, Kitti. I can take care of myself. We'll soon have lots of money in the bank that we'll save for setting ourselves up later on. In the meantime we'll be able to afford everything we need, and I can still help support my parents and brothers," was Pompam's confident reply.

At the bar that night both Ott and Pompam were bought out. Ott's customer was one of his regulars, a Thai/Chinese banker in his late thirties with a wife and two children at home. Pompam's was another *farang*, this time a man from Germany out in Bangkok on business. He took Pompam to a short-time motel, and Pompam got so disgusted he almost couldn't do his work; the *farang* was ugly, had bad body odor, and was nearly sixty years old. He had second thoughts for a few moments about his new calling, but he closed his eyes, made himself numb, and did his best not to hate himself.

Both boys were back in Ott's room before midnight to compare notes. Ott had made 400 *baht* while Pompam had been paid 500. Ott was jealous that Pompam had once again bested him in the money department, but he tried not to show it. Pompam mostly stayed quiet, trying not to think about what he had done for the money.

The following night Ott was "offed" by a *farang* and Pompam was left sitting in the bar the entire evening. Ott stayed out all night with his customer so Pompam wasn't able to connect with him until the following day. Ott felt somewhat better knowing he had done better than Pompam for a change.

That night Pompam got bought out by a Thai customer, his first. He found it very strange to go to bed with another Thai man. It almost felt like he was having sex with a male relative. It was also his first time the customer was the one who wanted to be on the receiving end in sex. Pompam hadn't even considered this possibility, but he managed easily enough to switch roles and thoroughly please his client.

The next three nights were dead for both boys, and by the end of the week they had made the decision to search for a new venue in which to peddle their good looks and youth.

They paid their own bar fines for two nights, telling *Khun* Somkid that Pompam's previous *farang* customer had a friend come into town and needed two boys for a trip to Pattaya. *Khun* Somkid took their money and asked no questions, naively believing they were telling the truth.

For the next two nights Pompam and Ott investigated the entire spectrum of the Bangkok bar boy scene. After looking into two or three small bars in Saphan Kwai they ruled that area out because there still weren't any *farang* customers. Why work there when they had put so much energy into learning English? they thought. They also went to a number of bars in Patpong, Silom and Suriwongse that were strictly go-go format. Ott had already gone through that routine, and Pompam really couldn't imagine exposing his body on some tiny stage, cranking up and down against a cold steel pole to last year's music.

Ott took Pompam to the two bars on Suriwongse that were

notorious for their complete nudity and live sex shows. Pompam watched in horror as the boys — at least half of them underage — paraded down the narrow catwalks wearing absolutely nothing, smiling, and showing off their self-manipulated erections in the "Mr. Big" part of the show.

He couldn't imagine how the poor young boy in the candle dance could bear the pain of the hot wax that dripped onto his completely naked body from the fistful of lighted altar candles he held aloft. The act was performed to the tune of "It's a Wonderful World" by Louis Armstrong, a rather sad irony, Pompam thought.

The most embarrassing act for Pompam to watch — embarrassing because he was watching Thai boys just like himself — was the three naked boy-boy couples who performed real, non-simulated acts of penetration not two feet away from him on the stage. They did their best to make a good show of it using violent, exaggerated theatrics, painful-looking contortionist maneuvers, and exaggerated facial expressions. Pompam felt sorry for those rather average-looking farm boys — most of them obviously from Isan — who had sunk to that level to survive.

They were shocked to see several female *farangs* in the audience who were staring in fascination at the fifteen-year-old Thai boys copulating in front of them. Apparently these women and their male companions had become bored by the run-of-the-mill man/woman live sex shows down on Patpong. For them it must have been no longer stimulating merely to watch a naked Thai man and woman fornicating for real on the back of a black and chrome Harley-Davidson suspended from the ceiling; they needed more, and they weren't afraid to explore the deepest depths of what Bangkok had to offer late at night. Everyone knew that whatever the action, all of it was under the watchful eyes of paid police protectors who raked in fortunes every month. Pompam and Ott definitely ruled out these two places.

Even though Ott and Pompam were considered good-looking by any standards, they also eliminated the muscle bars on Suriwongse. The boys employed there worked out with iron several hours every day; they needed to look appealing to the Thais and *farangs* who came to rent-out macho-looking sex objects that could satisfy their particular brand of fantasy.

There were several bars scattered around the small *"sois,"* or lanes, and sub-*sois* of the Sukhumvit area, and they managed to inspect a half dozen of those during the second night of their search. That district seemed to be more to their liking, but in each place something was wrong. There were either not enough customers, not enough *farangs*, too many lady-boys in one place, all fair-skinned northern boys in another. They all seemed to specialize in some particular customer taste or look; Ott and Pompam felt they didn't fit in any of them.

Pompam finally decided to contact *Khun* Arun at the Thailand Pavilion Hotel and seek his counsel on where to find the best work of this kind; he had a strong feeling that the elderly Thai gentleman would know.

He rang up *Khun* Arun at the hotel and was glad that the older gentleman seemed happy to hear from him. "Can I come to see you, *Khun* Arun? I need your advice on something that concerns a matter of employment," he asked.

Khun Arun chuckled to himself, immediately sensing what kind of employment guidance Pompam was seeking. "Of course, dear boy. Why don't you come to the hotel around four o'clock this afternoon and have coffee with me. Call me from the house phone in the lobby; I'll be in *Khun* Somchai's suite," he replied.

Pompam showed up promptly at four o'clock with Ott. He made the call upstairs and *Khun* Arun cleared him with the security guards at the elevator.

"I brought my friend with me, *Khun* Arun; his name is Ott. I think you met him before at *Khun* Somkid's bar." Ott *waied* low to the distinguished gentleman who showed them in and seated them in the living room of *Khun* Somchai's luxurious suite.

"Thank you again for your kindness regarding *Khun* Hans, *Khun* Arun. It was a good experience for me, and I really enjoyed the trip to Pattaya," Pompam politely began the conversation. "It changed my life in a way, *Khun* Arun, and I've decided to work as a bar boy for a while. I might as well use the gifts the Lord Buddha has given me while I still can, and save up enough money to help my family and set myself up when I graduate from University," he said with sincerity.

Khun Arun smiled and said, "Perhaps you have made a wise

decision, Pompam. There is no shame in what you are doing, and if you are clever you can easily cover your tracks later on if you need to."

"I worked with Ott for a week at *Khun* Somkid's bar, but since I only had three customers in seven days I don't think it's the right place for me — or for Ott. As long as I'm going to do this kind of work I want to do it every day and waste no time," Pompam explained. "Ott and I have been to practically every bar in town and we still haven't found the best one for us."

Khun Arun thought for a moment before answering. "I know one place where I could send you with an introduction from me. It's called 'Number Ten' and it's near the Nana Entertainment Plaza on Sukhumvit *Soi* 4. I am acquainted with the owner, a Thai-Chinese who dresses and behaves as half-man/half-lady. He/she — whatever you want to call it — collects expensive jewelry and gambles too much, but she is well-connected and runs the most exclusive boy bar in Bangkok. Many of her customers are models, movie stars, politicians, police officers, and big businessmen. She does a lot of her business by phone, and many of the customers are never even seen in the bar. She can do this successfully because she is known for her discretion and for having the best-looking, best-behaved boys in the business." Pompam was surprised that Ott had never heard of Number Ten.

"How much can a boy make in one month working at Number Ten," asked Pompam.

"She, by the way her name is Anuwat, runs an average of about forty boys and is usually sold out every night by eleven o'clock. Each boy should make between 500 and 1,000 *baht* per night, so he should make between 12,000 and 24,000 *baht* per month. I know for a fact that several of them make much more than that — up to 50,000 *baht* a month — depending on how many customers they service per day, how many of them are regulars, and how rich they are. It also depends on how good-looking the boy is and how well he can take care of his customers," he replied with a wink.

Pompam and Ott looked at each other with total surprise. "Number Ten sounds perfect for us, *Khun* Arun," Ott said after a moment, while Pompam silently contemplated the potential earnings.

"Then I'll call *Khun* Anuwat now and make an appointment for you to see her."

Khun Arun made the call and informed the two boys that *Khun* Anuwat would see them at six o'clock that evening. "The bar is on a small *soi* off Sukhumvit 4 to the right. You will see a small sign saying, 'Number Ten,' on the main *soi* at the end of a row of townhouses. Hers is the last townhouse on the left at the end. You will find it strange to see a boy bar in a neighborhood where there are mostly expensive residences, but she has powerful friends, and no matter how much any of the neighbors complain, there is nothing anyone can do about it."

Pompam and Ott said good-bye to *Khun* Arun who told them to keep him informed, and to come around to see him again when they had the time. He also said that he would refer to them any guests at the hotel who might want their special services and companionship. The two boys politely *waied* the older man, and expressed their thanks.

Pompam and Ott arrived at *Khun* Anuwat's townhouse at precisely six p.m. They left their shoes at the front door and waited for him on the ground level, which was where the boys were put on display in the evenings in sort of a "pen" near the cash register. They would later learn that the second story was also part of the bar. It had a small go-go stage in one corner and pillows and small tables scattered around where the customers could relax, chat, and drink with the boys. *Khun* Anuwat lived on the third and fourth levels with his muscle-man lover.

When he sailed into the room Pompam and Ott were completely taken aback by *Khun* Anuwat's appearance and demeanor. They had never before seen a man wearing satin lounging pants, a floral kimono, an armful of golden bangles, and huge diamond rings on three painted fingers. His hair was cut in a long/short shaggy design that had been dyed at least four different shades of red. Anuwat hadn't yet applied his make-up for the day, and his pock-marked face looked pasty-white. Not a pretty sight, they both thought with a shiver.

When Anuwat came to a stop in front of them he greeted them with, "So, you are friends of *Khun* Arun? He thinks you might be suitable as employees here." He looked both boys over critically and had them walk back and forth across the room.

"Take your clothes off," he ordered in a hard, bitchy tone. "I need to see if your bodies have any marks that might displease my customers."

The boys then took off everything but their underwear and stood uncomfortably, somewhat dazed, before the strange and possibly cruel, androgynous creature. "Turn around," he said coldly. The boys turned around as *Khun* Anuwat inspected their strong, youthful physiques.

"Okay, now take off your underpants and make them big. We are known for perfection here at Number Ten, and we can't have any little tiny ones running around."

The two boys silently obeyed, more embarrassed to do this in front of each other than in front of the mamasan of the house, who just sat there and stared at them. Never in his life had Pompam felt more cheap.

He went over and felt the quality of their skin, then availed himself of a free grope down below. "You can put your clothes back on now. You both at least pass the equipment test. Not too bad..."

He then proceeded to ask them about their background, what kind of experience they had working in this field, what they did in the daytime, and other questions he thought were pertinent to the interview. He never asked them how old they were, however, being totally unconcerned about hiring underage boys, as he very often did.

He finally asked, "Can you do everything in bed?" Both boys shyly nodded their heads up and down. "Sometimes we have women come in here to buy the boys for sex. Can you do it with women?" Once again the two boys nodded in the affirmative, this time a little more vigorously than for the last question. He could tell by the response that the boys weren't gay; they obviously preferred women, but could do the work with men in whatever way the customer preferred. He had seen literally thousands of young, handsome boys just like them.

"Go and make me copies of your Thailand ID card and your house registration form and you can start tonight," *Khun* Anuwat informed them; he needed these documents if there should ever be a problem involving the police. "Be back here no later than eight o'clock and meet with Joe, the captain; he will explain our rules." He turned around and left them without another word.

Pompam and Ott now had jobs in the most exclusive house of its kind in Bangkok. They smiled at one another thinking about all the money they would make; the feelings of shame and embarrassment during their interview with Anuwat were already fading.

"Pompam, can you imagine? We'll even get bought out by women. I would do women for free, but at Number Ten they'll actually be *paying* us for it!" Ott exclaimed with no small amount of excitement at this unexpected and ironic bonus.

Luckily Ott had his motorbike so they were able to get their documents copied, have showers, change clothes and get back to Number Ten by eight o'clock. They didn't bother to call *Khun* Somkid and tell him they had quit working for him. Pompam felt fortunate that Kitti had already left for work; he was excited, and in no mood to hear another one of Kitti's lectures about the perils of selling his body.

When they checked in at Number Ten there must have been at least twenty-five handsome boys sitting in the "pen," ready and waiting to begin work. Pompam and Ott introduced themselves to a few of them, and each one carefully sized up the new boys in terms of competition for customers. *Khun* Anuwat was behind the counter on the telephone taking out-call orders for the evening, and making assignments, matching caller requirements with the talents and virtues of his boys.

The captain, Joe, arrived and took Pompam and Ott off to one side to explain the house rules. "First of all, if you want to work here you have to show up every night at seven o'clock. If you're late, it's an 80 *baht* fine. If you want time off, it's 150 *baht* per night, the same as the customer pays to 'off' you. When the customer 'offs' you, you don't get anything back from the 150 *baht* fee. *Khun* Anuwat keeps that. If you are sitting with a customer and he buys you a drink, you get a twenty percent commission. If he buys a whole bottle, you get ten percent.

"You can't refuse any customers assigned to you for any reason. If you do, then you're automatically fired. You must never discuss any of the customers, whether they're yours or another boy's, with anyone outside the bar. If you do, then you'll not only lose your job, but be blackballed from ever working in a bar again in Bangkok or Pattaya. *Khun* Anuwat has his way of making sure this happens. That's it for the rules. Any questions?" Joe, a former bar boy himself, asked the two newcomers, who just sat there trying to absorb it all.

"I understand," they both answered in unison.

"Come in early tomorrow," Joe continued, "someone will be

here to take your pictures for our photo album. The photographer is a professional so the pictures will make you look good. Wear something nice. He'll take your pictures naked as well, so the customer can see in advance what he's paying for. No need to be embarrassed, all the boys have to do it," he continued matter of factly.

The idea of nude photographs shocked the two boys. To have to strip and be groped and examined by *Khun* Anuwat was one thing, but to have nude photographs in a book for anyone to look at was another. What if they somehow got out?

Joe, as if reading their minds, said, "The photographer gives all negatives to *Khun* Anuwat and there will be only one print in the book. It *never* leaves the bar, so don't worry."

The two new boys joined the rest of the young men and waited for customers to show up. It wasn't long before they started arriving, and Pompam was one of the first to be called over by Joe to be introduced to one of their regulars, an older man who couldn't resist a new face, and had an insatiable appetite for them.

The customer was a *farang*, a wealthy Englishman, who came to Number Ten practically every night. When he didn't come for one reason or another, he would usually telephone Anuwat to have a boy sent over to his house. According to one of the boys whose name was Pop, this *farang* had "offed" all but about five boys in the entire stable. He only liked masculine, straight boys; if he thought they were gay, or were in the least bit effeminate, he didn't want them. He got his thrills from making the straightest ones he could find perform the most debasing, non-straight acts for him.

Many of the boys became his regulars, and they would sometimes phone him to make afternoon appointments; that way they could make extra money before they had to report for work at the bar.

The Englishman was a heavy drinker and always kept one or two bottles of his favorite brands open in the bar. He would occasionally come in late in the evening and entertain those boys who hadn't been "offed," and sometimes take them all out with him to an after-hours disco such as NASA Spacedrome. From there he would take one or two of them home to bed. He was very popular at Number Ten only for the reason that he never tipped the boys less than 1,000 *baht* each time. He, in his conceited state of ignorance, thought all the boys adored him and were his friends.

"Pompam," said Joe, "this is *Khun* James, one of our very favorite guests. *Khun* James, this is Pompam, our newest boy." At first sight Pompam disliked the man, but he quickly disguised the feeling with a big smile.

Khun James was instantly attracted to the "new face" called Pompam, and suggested they go upstairs to the more comfortable part of the bar and have a drink or two. On the way up he waved to Anuwat who demurely winked back at him. He was on the telephone again making an arrangement for one of the boys to meet the number two man in the police department at a "curtain" motel later on.

Upstairs, almost every boy in the room greeted *Khun* James with a *wai* and a fake smile; nearly all of them had been to bed with him, and had earned his 1,000 *baht* at least once; it was almost like a "house" initiation. James and Pompam sat down and polished off nearly half a bottle of Chivas before they said their good-byes and strolled out to the big Benz parked out front. He took Pompam home with him, but was so eager to get started that he forced the young man to lean over him and begin his sexual performance in the car while driving down Sukhumvit Road.

This meeting would be the first of one and a half years'-worth of commercial encounters Pompam would have with the wealthy, happy Englishman, who had retired to live in Bangkok because he found it entertaining — and so full of pretty, inexpensive little amusements in a never-ending supply.

Pompam's career at Number Ten took off like a rocket from the very beginning. He became a "star of the bar," and was booked in advance nearly every night, sometimes three or four days ahead. It was very rare for him to have to sit in the "pen" with the other boys and compete to catch the eye of a "shopping" customer.

During his first month at Number Ten Pompam cleared a little over 30,000 *baht*. At the end of the second month his combined income from the bar, Dr. Jim, and his old pen pals from *Wat* Po came to nearly 50,000 *baht*. Pompam decided that for convenience sake it was time to put a down payment on his own motorcycle and pay it off over the next six months. He bought lots of clothes, a television, stereo and hundreds of cassette tapes. He also began sending 2,000 *baht* each month to his family in Isan, and he bought Kitti anything he wanted to keep him from complaining. He kept up to date with his schoolwork, and had only one term to go before graduation, an event he and Kitti eagerly looked forward to.

In a very short time, Pompam learned how easy it was for bar boys to spend everything they made on birthday parties, discos, drinking, and going out every night after work. They wound up living from hand to mouth — even though they earned far more than "normal" workers in their age bracket. Pompam felt he was smarter than they, and was determined to save his money and not fall into this trap. In a year or two he figured he could accumulate enough to open some kind of business of his own.

"Pompam, do you think we could go back to our village for *Loy Kratong*? It's only two weeks away, and it would be our first visit in nearly a year," Kitti asked plaintively, still miserable and stuck behind the cash register every night at the restaurant.

"I don't see why not, Kitti. This time we can go back with presents for everyone, and give a party the village will never forget," he replied enthusiastically, looking forward to doing what Dr. Jim had done four years earlier.

Both of them truly needed a break from their arduous routines. Pompam knew he desperately had to feel normal again — even if only for a short time — if he were to retain his health and sanity; selling one's body day after day took it's toll, he had begun to realize.

Kitti had to threaten to quit his job before the Chinese owner finally gave him the six days off he requested. Pompam reluctantly paid Anuwat a six-day bar fine which amounted to 900 *baht*. "That's a lot of money to have to pay just for a few days off, *Khun* Anuwat. Can't you give me a break?" Pompam pleaded.

"No breaks, Pompam. This is business and you know the rules," he replied curtly.

Pompam hated those rules, especially the ones that cost him hard-earned money. He developed a strong hatred for Anuwat, seeing every day how he treated the poor young men who worked for him. He had often seen Anuwat's cruel nature come out when he viciously banished one of the boys for some slight infraction of a silly rule. One day I'll get even with that filthy bitch, he thought to himself.

The arrival of Pompam and Kitti created quite a stir in their village. The two of them were so well-dressed and prosperous-looking that their old friends and neighbors were almost afraid to approach and say hello.

"You are looking very well indeed, Vichai," *Phra* Prateep remarked almost caustically, when fashionable-looking Pompam came to the temple to pay his respects.

"The Lord Buddha takes good care of me, *Ajarn*," Pompam replied with composure. "I have my good health, my studies at the university are going well, and I have a job that provides me with all I need, over and above my scholarship. By the way, I recently received a letter from Dr. Jim in California and he sends you his best regards."

Phra Prateep thought fondly of that strange *farang* professor bowing before him alongside Pompam. "You are very lucky to have his support, Vichai; make sure you live up to his expectations of you."

Pompam handed the kind Abbot an envelope containing 2,000 *baht* which was his gift to the temple for *Loy Kratong*. "How can you spare so much money, Vichai? This, and what you send your parents every month — surely your job at the restaurant doesn't pay *that* well?" Pompam realized there were no secrets in the village as far as finances were concerned.

"*Mai pen rai, Ajarn*. I work hard, save my money, and I am provided for. I need to have the chance to make merit, too, don't I?" Pompam answered with his most charming smile, ducking any further questions about his money and its source.

The actual day for celebrating *Loy Kratong* was two days away, and Kitti and Pompam were busy organizing their big party. "Maa, here's some money for food. Get the neighbors to help prepare everything," he instructed her.

He sent Paw and his brothers to buy supplies to stock the bar, and they borrowed the neighbor's boom box for sound, since Pompam had brought with him all the latest cassettes from Bangkok. Nuu was thrilled to have his *pi-chai* back home again, and he followed him around like a shadow.

The whole village turned out for the party, and Pompam and

Kitti gained much "face" for being able to provide such lavish entertainment for *Loy Kratong*. Everyone got thoroughly drunk, danced the
ram wong, and ate their fill of Maa's good cooking.

Mid-way through the evening many of the revelers made their
way down to the retention pond and floated their *kratongs* in the age-old
ceremony of getting rid of negativity and bad luck. As he was about to
set his own *kratong* on the water he heard someone behind him calling,
"Pompam, let me float my *kratong* along with yours."

"Rattana," exclaimed Pompam, "it's you! How you've grown
— and so pretty you are now, too!" He thought to himself that since he
was twenty-one, she would have to be seventeen years old. What a
change can come about in only a year, he marveled; before she was
only a child.

"I'm living in Khon Kaen most of the time now, Pompam," she
began. "I'm doing a two-year program at the University. My father
calls it 'finishing school.'"

"I'm very glad you're able to continue your education,"
Pompam replied, "you always were the top student in your class. Are
you learning English?"

"Yes, from a *farang* professor so I can learn how to speak it, too. I
hope to be as good at it as you are one day," she said with a laugh.

"Learn everything about the *farang* world you can, Rattana. It
will come in handy one day," he replied, thinking about how he used
his own abilities.

Pompam noticed that Rattana still looked at him the way she
always had, and realized for the first time that it was actually a very
loving, wanting look. The girl had perhaps always loved him, Pompam
thought back. What a good feeling to have someone love me simply for
myself, he thought; a pleasant contrast to the shallowness of all the
customers who paid him for his "love." Rattana's presence was comforting, and a warm glow began to swell up in Pompam's heart.

"Let's light the candles and incense on our *kratongs* and tie
them together with this piece of string," Pompam said softly.

They released the small objects into the pond and remained
crouched next to the water, watching as the little flickers of light floated
off towards the center. Pompam looked over at the lovely young girl
and shyly reached for her hand; he held it as they recited their silent

prayers of acceptance for all the good things that would come; the past was already out there on the water, being carried away on moonlit ripples.

They stayed like that quietly for a while, a feeling of peace settling on both of them. After a while, Rattana's father called her and said it was time to go home; she stood up and reluctantly said good-night — even though she wanted nothing more than to stay there with Pompam forever. They smiled at one another, Pompam squeezed her hand, and she walked away, leaving him alone in the darkness.

Pompam, no longer in the mood to drink himself into a stupor with Kitti, sat down next to the pond and fell into deep reflection.

After a few minutes he noticed that the warmth of the moonlit evening had turned into a cold and biting breeze. Suddenly, in his peripheral vision, he caught a glimpse of the menacing Golden Buddha that had haunted him so often in years past; he thought it had long since left him for good, but there it was — just under the surface of the pond. He wanted to turn his eyes away from the hideous visage, but instead he crouched closer to the ground with his face peering over the edge. He was compelled by some mysterious force to concentrate and look deeper into the black waters.

The Golden Buddha appeared to be dancing the *ram wong* to the beat of the music back at the party. He still wore the same devious, toothy grin on his dissolute face, and little children scurried around its feet, polishing and shining its golden skin. Then Pompam watched in horror as the Buddha gathered up the children, crying and screaming, and locked them in a tiny cage. Just at that moment a small, wind-driven wave splashed against Pompam's face and he almost fell head first into the water; he recovered his balance and strained to see the fading images at the bottom of the shallow pond. He felt sick to his stomach and vomited, trying desperately to make some sense out of what he had seen, thinking he might be going crazy.

After about an hour he pulled himself together, got up, and walked back towards the party which was still going strong. He wished that he could simply make the soiled reality of his existence float out of sight like his small *kratong*, and disappear forever into the hidden realm of the night.

The return to Bangkok at the end of *Loy Kratong* and the harsh realities of the life he had chosen for himself, came only too quickly for Pompam. From the train station, he and Kitti barely had enough time to go back to their rooms to prepare themselves for their night's work. Kitti trudged off to the restaurant with a long, sad face, and Pompam went off to Number Ten feeling anguish and dread. I want to feel love, he thought to himself, not pain, day after day.

"I hope you had a good rest, Pompam," *Khun* Anuwat said when the young man walked in. "*Khun* James called and wants you at his house right now for dinner. Tomorrow night you're booked to see *Khun* Yod who is coming down from Chiang Mai. Then the following evening you'll be going to a party at *Khun* Pan's penthouse. He has a *farang* guest from New York he wants you to entertain." Again, Pompam felt sick to his stomach.

"Pompam, my dear, please come in and meet my friends," *Khun* James ebulliently exclaimed, greeting Pompam with a kiss, and whirling him into the drawing room to meet a klatch of half a dozen queens from London. Pompam forced himself to be pleasant, and did his best to endure being put on display as *Khun* James' "trinket" of the evening. He drank far more than he should have, but it helped him get through the dinner, the pawing and groping of *Khun* James' silly friends, and the inevitable, demeaning sex acts that later concluded the evening.

"Ott," Pompam complained the next morning, grieving for his innocence, "I've been living this kind of life now for six months. I will do it for one more year until I turn twenty-three, just to save up some money. After that I'm going to start my own business." But he wondered at the same time if he could actually survive it one more year.

As their graduation date approached, Kitti and Pompam kept up their study program as well as their work schedules, and got through their final exams. A couple of weeks later they received word that they had passed them all, and could sign up for the graduation exercises in May. Pompam and Kitti discussed whether or not they would even bother, but their decision was clinched one day when Pompam received a letter from Berkeley.

"I have managed to clear a few days in my schedule so I can attend your graduation, Vichai. I wouldn't miss that event for anything in the world. I am so proud of you," so read the letter from Dr. Jim that both shocked and pleased Pompam at the same time. So many mixed feelings came to the surface, and he needed to sit quietly for a while as he contemplated his response.

"Dear Dr. Jim," began Pompam's return letter. "I will be so happy and honored to have you here for my graduation. It doesn't seem possible that a little over four years have already passed since we first met at *Wat* Po. I can never thank you enough for all that you have done for me, and I would not be graduating at all if it weren't for you. I will meet you at the airport."

As Dr. Jim came through the doors from Customs into the Arrival Hall Pompam waved his arms and called out, "*Ajarn*, over here, it's me!" to get his attention.

"Vichai, you've grown up! I hardly recognized you with hair and civilian clothes. How different, and how handsome you look!" Dr. Jim enthused, embracing him warmly.

"You look great too, *Ajarn*. Four years doesn't seem to have changed you at all," Pompam replied, but in fact the American did look older and grayer, he thought sadly.

As Pompam rode in the taxi with Dr. Jim to the hotel (not the Dusit Thani, but a less-expensive place on Sukhumvit) the two of them spoke rapidly back and forth, filling each other in where their letters had left off, trying to cover the four years that had elapsed since they last met.

Dr. Jim told Pompam he was engaged to be married, and showed Pompam a picture of his fiancee; Pompam was surprised to see that she looked Chinese. "She teaches Oriental literature," explained the professor.

Dr. Jim was interested in Pompam's job with the "entertainment company" and wanted to know exactly what he did for them. Pompam blushed slightly, feeling ashamed, and answered that he was the assistant manager of a small nightclub on Pattanakarn Road. He said it really wasn't such a great place, but it had paid him enough so that he could supplement the money he received from Dr. Jim, and comfortably survive. "I only work part time, *Ajarn*, but after graduation I'll be able to get a better, full-time job and work days." Pompam hated himself for having to lie to this kind and devoted friend.

He left Dr. Jim at the hotel so he could get some sleep; the flight from San Francisco via Tokyo had been exhausting. Dr. Jim told him he would only be in Thailand for five days, and they agreed to meet the following day for lunch. "It's my treat," insisted Pompam.

The next morning, before he met Dr. Jim, Pompam stopped by Number Ten and grudgingly paid off *Khun* Anuwat — buying himself time he truly owed the man who had come half way around the world to see him graduate.

"I told you before, Pompam, no breaks!" Anuwat said with an arrogant sneer to the angry young man.

The day before the graduation exercises Pompam took Dr. Jim to see *Phra* Asoka. Pompam had to tell the revered monk the same stories he had told Dr. Jim when he was asked about his work. He felt even worse about lying to the Buddhist *Ajarn* than he had to Dr. Jim. The monk told Dr. Jim about his missionary activities in India, and Dr. Jim gave *Phra* Asoka a copy of an article he had written about Buddhism in India and had quoted him, which greatly pleased the Indian *Ajarn*.

"Congratulations on your university graduation, Vichai. You have much to be grateful for in your young life. You owe a great debt to *Ajarn* Jim for giving you your scholarship. How you repay that debt, either to him or to another, is up to you. But you must never forget."

The graduation exercises, unfortunately, fell on one of the hottest days of the year, and the outdoor event was miserable for everyone. It became an absolute mob scene which made the heat even worse. Traffic had been blocked up for miles in every direction near the university, and there would be more of it to look forward to on the way home.

Kitti's and Pompam's parents sat in the sports stadium with Dr. Jim, along with two of Pompam's younger brothers, Nuu and Att, and Kitti's sister. Pompam had sent extra money back home to pay for the train tickets, and had arranged for his parents and brothers to stay in a vacant room next to his and Kitti's for two nights. This was the first trip to Bangkok for all four of them; Maa's younger sister was baby-sitting the youngest brothers back home.

Dr. Jim, coming from the cool Bay Area in California, thought he would die of the heat before the interminable ceremony was over; there were moments when he had wished that he had never come and just sent a card instead. When the great moment finally arrived, he watched with pride and snapped several photographs as Pompam marched across the stage, *waied* before the royal presenter, and was handed his diploma. Dr. Jim reflected that he had sent Pompam approximately 100,000 *baht* over the previous four years; seeing the results that day of what he had paid for convinced him that even though it had been money hard-earned, it had truly been well-spent.

Afterwards Pompam took the whole group to a large, open-air Thai restaurant that consisted of a series of *salas* surrounded by fish ponds — all connected by bridges; the place was famous for being so huge its waiters had to use roller skates to deliver the food. There were lots of toasts to the two grads, a great deal of spicy food, which added to Dr. Jim's heat discomfort, and endless conversation in the Thai and Isan languages that Dr. Jim couldn't understand. He felt awkward and out of place, even though Pompam did his best to look after him and include him as one of the family.

The professor from California was indeed grateful for the cool comforts of his hotel when Pompam brought him back at the end of the long day. In the lobby as they were saying goodnight, Dr. Jim handed Pompam an envelope and said, "I couldn't think of anything to give you for a graduation present, so I thought a few *baht* would help you get started in your new life."

Pompam vigorously protested accepting the gift, and said that he couldn't take anything more from Dr. Jim, especially more money.

"*Mai pen rai*, Pompam. You heard what *Phra* Asoka said about repaying your debt — to me or to another. It doesn't matter. I am happy to see you off to a good start in your career, and that is enough for me. I'm sure you will find someone else to help along the way," the kind man replied.

Pompam silently began to weep; he just stood there, his body shaking, his head on Dr. Jim's shoulder. Dr. Jim perceived them as tears of happiness and gratitude, but in actuality, Pompam was crying painfully bitter tears of guilt and shame. "I promise you, Dr. Jim, that one day when I can, I will give a university scholarship to someone who deserves it."

When Dr. Jim was ready to return to America he was both satisfied and pleased. He felt content, knowing that his protégé in Thailand had a direction in life, and some worthy goals that he would surely achieve.

At the airport they both shed some tears, albeit for different reasons. "You must promise me that you will visit me one day in California, Vichai, when you are rich and successful," he said as he was about to pass through Immigration.

"I promise you that, *Ajarn* Jim," Pompam replied, and made the same promise to himself. They both recognized that they had created a strong bond between them that would last throughout their lifetimes. Dr. Jim went away feeling quite good, and with a few more choice photographs to add to the collection on his desk in Berkeley.

A couple of weeks after his graduation Pompam and Ott were having a bowl of noodles together in a *soi* near their apartment, and once again discussed the future. Pompam was more determined than ever to go into business for himself when his "Year of Torture," as he had come to call it, was over.

"What kind of business will you make, Pompam?" asked Ott.

"I'm not quite sure, but whatever it is I want you to join me. I'll bust my ass, literally, for the remainder of my Year. I'll simply make myself numb, do my work, and get every last *baht* I can out of my stupid rich customers. And from today you will never hear me complain about any of this again," Pompam said defiantly as he fought back burning tears.

It is true that he never complained again. He endured the humiliation, the degradation, the indecencies, and the revolting sexual practices of selfish, fat old men like *Khun* James without any comment whatsoever.

Kitti, however, sensed that Pompam was becoming damaged. What else could be expected when a person let others drain off his vital energy day after day? He was nothing more than a self-winding toy for bored and foolish men with money, and Kitti knew that when Pompam's beauty faded, they wouldn't hesitate to quickly throw him away.

Kitti and Pompam could both see the toll that five and a half years of this lifestyle had taken on poor Ott. His love for Kim, his Chinese girlfriend, and his hope of one day being a professional photographer, were all he had to keep himself from going around the twist. Kitti hoped and prayed that Pompam could hold himself together until his self-proclaimed Year of Torture finally ended.

Khun Hans came back from Amsterdam twice during that year. He demanded all of Pompam's time, even though he would sneak off every two or three days for a "quickie" with some fourteen-year-old street urchin he picked up in front of Robinson's Department Store on Silom — or go prowling in one of the bars near Patpong that opened early in the afternoon. He felt no loyalty whatsoever to Pompam, and Pompam didn't in the least expect it given the fact that he had no loyalty to Hans — or to anyone for that matter other than Kitti, Ott and his family back home. Business for *Khun* Hans in Amsterdam had been good that year, so he was perhaps *too* generous with his monetary gifts to Pompam, which the young man pocketed with a coy smile.

He took care of his regular customers (*Khun* James was only one of many), and whoever else bought him out of the bar; he no longer cared who it was or what he had to do. He worked hard every day of his life, constantly spending his essence, and he was getting tired.

His twenty-third birthday was approaching, and he began to mark the days off the calendar. His frugal lifestyle had paid off, and he had saved a remarkable sum of 300,000 *baht*. His motorcycle was his own, he owed no debts, and he could seriously begin to plan for his emancipation.

He would finally have his freedom.

Chapter 9

When it dawned on Pompam what his next move should be when he turned twenty-three, he broke out laughing at himself because the answer was so obvious and had strangely been there all the time: Pompam would open his *own* boy bar.

He had the money saved (almost all of it anyway), and he had Kitti and Ott to work with him, the only people he trusted in Bangkok. He felt that his year and a half in the business had taught him every conceivable aspect of running such an establishment, and he was confident that he could do it far better than *Khun* Anuwat. This was how he would get even with that bitch, Pompam thought, in addition to stealing all her best boys. When he analyzed the situation he realized he would have to begin with a compromise or two, but he knew that somehow he would prevail in the end.

He called up *Khun* James and asked him if he could come over: there was something very important he needed to talk to him about. *Khun* James thought, oh my, this could only be one thing: money. James was continually being asked for money by the boys he had "befriended" in the bar. Even though he paid them well for their hard-earned favors, his familiarity with them left the door wide open for all sorts of emergency requests, which he occasionally accommodated. He felt that over time he had heard every possible sad story in the book; Pompam, however, had never asked *Khun* James for anything, and he was curious to hear what his tale would be.

"Come in, my dear; give mummy a kiss." *Khun* James greeted Pompam in his dressing gown, looking like he had just gotten out of bed. Pompam politely *waied* and teased *Khun* James about the extra weight he had put on, as was his custom with this chubby, long-time customer and "friend."

"*Khun* James, in three weeks I will celebrate my twenty-third birthday. On that day I will be retiring from my career as a bar boy once and for all, and I want to start my own business." Pompam had rehearsed his speech for several days.

"Well, what do you have in mind, darling?" James asked, surprised by Pompam's announcement, wondering how much he would ask for.

"I want to open my own boy bar, *Khun* James. I've already found the perfect location, off Sukhumvit *Soi* 11, and I've saved almost enough to open it on my own, but I'm afraid of running short. I want you to loan me 200,000 *baht*, and I will pay it back within two years, if not sooner. As collateral for the money I'll sign over twenty-five percent of the shares, which you can return to me when the 200,000 is paid off — or you can continue to be my partner; it would be your choice. You also have the experience of being a top designer in London, and you could make the bar truly beautiful," he explained, throwing in a little flattery to help the sell.

James was momentarily taken aback by the proposition, the amount requested being enormously greater than any he had ever been asked for before. However, as Pompam explained his ideas and went over the numbers he began to see that the clever boy was on to something with real potential. James didn't like the idea of raiding Anuwat's boys at Number Ten for workers, but in the end, who really cared? He would never again need to go back to Number Ten; owning twenty-five percent of his *own* bar would enable him to enjoy his *own* boys for entertainment; the social possibilities were endless, and they titillated his imagination. The idea began to sound better and better the more they discussed it.

"Let's go upstairs to my room and talk about this a little bit more, Pompam." James had a suspicious grin on his face, but Pompam dismissed it as just another prelude to one of the revolting bedroom games the man liked to play. He reasoned that James wanted to humiliate him one last time, just to show him who was in control of the money.

Mai pen rai, Pompam thought as he steeled himself; I can certainly do it one more time for the 200,000 *baht* I need. So he accepted his fate, went upstairs to the bathroom, took a shower, and entered *Khun* James' familiar master bedroom, the black-out curtains drawn tight against the morning sun.

When his eyes adjusted to the semi-darkness, Pompam was shocked to see *Khun* James sitting up naked in his bed with two very young boys, one on either side of him. The boys were skinny, dark-skinned, also naked, and couldn't have been more than twelve or thirteen years old, maybe younger; they looked terrified, thought Pompam, nearly tripping over a pile of clothes on the floor.

"Come join us Pompam. I need you to teach these two children how to do it like a real professional," James commanded with a lurid smile on his dissipated, sagging face.

Pompam took a deep breath, dropped his towel, crawled onto the bed, and reluctantly tried to get the four-way into gear, in spite of his aversion to doing anything with youngsters like those two.

After a few minutes of playing around, and no one was yet really turned on, James, getting bored, had a sudden inspiration and ordered Pompam to do something that completely repulsed and revolted him. An inner rage welled up inside that nearly boiled over, but Pompam thought about the money he wanted, and somehow kept himself under control, determined to get what he had come for.

Pompam closed his eyes and obeyed *Khun* James: he laid on his back and submitted to both boys, one after the other, allowing them to enter and use him until they climaxed. James, no longer bored, watched the spectacle with gleeful amusement, cheering the young ones on with lewd comments about what a good fuck Pompam was. When both boys were through, James then climbed on top of Pompam and cruelly added his own poison to the young man's already defiled body.

Pompam was devastated, but became more resolved than ever to get what he wanted out of this evil, depraved *farang*, and then punish him. An idea had already begun to form during those last few moments of the most outrageous abuse he had ever endured.

Later, while *Khun* James was in the shower, Pompam spoke to the two boys like he was their *pi-chai*, and made them promise to meet him at the noodle shop at the end of the *soi*. He gave each of them a hundred *baht* so they could get something to eat. Pompam learned that James had picked up the two kids about four o'clock that morning on Silom Road where he had gone trolling in his big Benz. The boys had just arrived in Bangkok the previous day from the countryside, had no place to go, and were practically starving. Pompam looked at them with pity, knowing that there were hundreds more just like them out on the streets that very moment, willing to do anything for a few *baht* just to keep themselves alive.

After a bit of joking and small talk downstairs in the elegant, tastefully-decorated drawing room, *Khun* James perfunctorily paid off the two boys and sent them away, not giving them a second thought. He and Pompam then resumed their business conversation as if nothing at all had just happened upstairs. Pompam realized that James was completely oblivious to anyone's feelings or circumstances other than his own. The *farang* had become used to using people less fortunate than he, and then throwing them away; it had become as natural to him as eating or breathing.

"How long will it take you to have the business documents drawn up, Pompam?" *Khun* James inquired. Pompam had already engaged the services of an attorney to get the paperwork started. "I will contact *Khun* Prawin, my lawyer, and tell him to have everything ready to sign by the day after tomorrow. We can go and see him together and you can bring the money with you then."

It was also agreed that *Khun* James would meet Pompam at the future bar site the next morning so they could begin planning the renovations. Pompam had found a four-story shophouse with a good lease on a small *soi* just off Sukhumvit Road. The neighbors on the *soi* consisted of two or three restaurants, two small hotels, three or four Indian tailor shops, and a camera store on the corner.

The shophouse had formerly been a beauty salon/barber shop, but when the lease expired the salon owners decided to retire rather than renew it. Like hundreds of similar businesses all over Bangkok, the former barber shop had had private cubicles for its male customers, so that after their haircuts and manicures they could be treated to "a little something extra" by the pretty young female operators.

"Pompam, this location is *wonderful*. You'll get all the business from the Ambassador Hotel next door, and from all the other small hotels in this part of Sukhumvit," *Khun* James exclaimed cheerfully when they met to inspect the premises.

Pompam soon realized that *Khun* James truly was the interior design expert he had claimed to be; he began rattling off all the changes that would be needed, materials that should be used, how the decoration should be handled, seating arrangements, and hundreds of other details. Pompam carried around a notebook and pen and wrote down all of *Khun* James' ideas; he also made rough sketches of room layouts and other alterations that James said needed to be made. The ground floor of the townhouse would be the main bar area. The second and third floors would be showers, massage rooms and VIP rooms where the customers could take the boys short-time for sex. The fourth floor would be living quarters for Pompam, Kitti and Ott.

The next afternoon Pompam and *Khun* James met with the attorney and signed the documents for the 200,000 *baht* loan, the twenty-five percent interest in the bar, profit sharing, and other pertinent items. Afterwards, when *Khun* James gave Pompam the 200,000 *baht* in cash, it was hard for the young man not to show his excitement.

"Partners!" exclaimed *Khun* James as he held out his hand. Pompam looked the man directly in the eye, grasped his hand firmly, and answered him, "Partners!"

That evening Pompam went to Number Ten and told *Khun* Anuwat he was quitting. "You'll be sorry, you shitty little slut!" Anuwat proclaimed, scowling imperiously at Pompam. "You've gotten used to easy money, and you'll never be the same. But if you change your mind, don't bother coming back to me."

Pompam was seething inside but he kept his mouth shut. He just glared at the androgynous bitch, knowing it was the last time he would ever see him. Ott came in about the same time Pompam was leaving, the two boys winked at each other in passing, then Ott gave his own resignation to an angry, screaming *Khun* Anuwat.

"Get out of here you ungrateful whores. I'll make sure you never get work again," bellowed Anuwat in the wake of their departure.

At about that same time Kitti was also giving *his* notice at the Chinese restaurant. Kitti, however, couldn't contain his pent-up feelings as well as the other two boys. When he walked out the door he yelled back at the Chinese owners, who stood there with their jaws hanging open; he screamed out the worst possible thing a Thai could say, which translated as "Go fuck your mother!"

He had been a slave in that restaurant for five long years and had saved the Chinese a fortune by doing their accounting for a fraction of what it would have cost them to hire a professional. Kitti had never gotten over the lie they told that New Year to get out of paying the poor employees their much-deserved bonuses. He felt that in his own way he had suffered as much as Pompam, and he felt a great sense of relief as he walked home.

That evening at a "freedom" dinner Pompam hosted, he laid out his plan. "Ott, you'll be captain of the bar and in charge of the boys — doing the job Joe does at Number Ten. You'll get a salary of 5,000 *baht* per month plus ten percent of our monthly net profits. I know it's a lot less than what you've been clearing from Number Ten, but it will get bigger, I promise you."

Ott, who had never made anywhere near the kind of money Pompam made, and never was able to save much said, "*Mai pen rai,* Pompam. I'm with you all the way."

"Kitti, you'll keep all the accounting records and take care of paying the bills; you can order supplies, play bartender, and oversee the room boys who'll keep the place clean. I'll also pay you a salary of 5,000 *baht* a month plus ten percent of the profits."

Both boys were more than happy with Pompam's generous wage program, and the three of them smiled and clinked glasses.

"Ott, you hire away the best boys at Number Ten; tell them they can work six nights a week and have one night off without having to pay a bar fine. We'll take good care of our people." Pompam hated *Khun* Anuwat for all the times he had had to pay bar fines whenever he needed time off. I'll fix Anuwat, Pompam thought; all the boys will want to work with me now.

"*Khun* Prawin, the attorney, has fixed an agreement with the townhouse owner so we can move in this week and start getting the place ready for business. *Khun* James gave me all the ideas for renovations, and they're very good. It's going to be the best bar in Thailand," Pompam said, beaming.

"Opening night will be my birthday. Have all the boys who come with us from Number Ten invite their regular customers. For the next week we'll go to the most popular bars in Bangkok and steal the best boys in each place," he told Ott. "I want at least forty experienced boys to start out with, and I want all of them to be 'stars.'

"Ott, you start taking their photographs as soon as they're hired. Instead of a photo book I want to have a slide show. We'll get one of those carousel slide machines and have a continuous showing on the wall opposite the bar. We'll have pictures of each boy with *and* without clothes; that should get the customers motivated, don't you think?" he asked with a big grin.

Ott and Kitti couldn't imagine where Pompam got all his ideas, but they instinctively knew they had hitched their fortunes to a big winner. Pompam was suddenly moving very fast with his career plans. Though he appeared to Ott and Kitti as supremely confident and sure of himself, Pompam was feeling the effects of a mysterious power coming from somewhere deep within his soul. At times, the sensation terrified him. Other times, it thrilled and filled him with intense passion. He wasn't sure, but he felt that he might be losing control of part of himself; but he had no idea which part it might be.

The following morning at eight o'clock sharp the two street boys *Khun* James picked up on Silom Road showed up at Lumpini Police Station and made a formal complaint against *Khun* James. They were far below the legal age of eighteen, and the police knew how much the press loved to get hold of juicy stories like this one; it made the law enforcers look like they were doing their jobs, protecting young girls and boys from the legions of pedophile foreigners who flocked to fertile Thailand in search of prey. In reality, however, no one was fooled; everyone knew pay-off money got most offenders off the hook.

In their police report the two boys made no mention of Pompam or his part in the event that took place in *Khun* James' bedroom. Pompam had paid each boy 3,000 *baht* to press charges against the *farang*, and made them promise that they would leave Bangkok and go back to their families in the Northeast as soon as the whole episode was over.

The two boys led the police in a squad car directly to *Khun* James' walled compound in one of Sukhumvit's most fashionable neighborhoods. The frightened maid opened up the gate and let them into the house, then ran upstairs to wake her dissipated boss who, lucky for him, had slept alone for a change. *Khun* James came downstairs in his pajamas and robe — absolutely enraged that he had been disturbed.

When he saw the two boys, however, standing in his drawing room with uniformed policemen, he was suddenly struck still in terror.

The boys pointed their fingers at the *farang* and spoke to the police officers in rapid Thai, identifying *Khun* James as the one who had solicited them on the street and used them for sex. At the police station they had already described in detail the sex acts *Khun* James had made them perform with him. Apparently James had really worked the young boys over and, as they were virgins, had caused them both severe physical pain before Pompam ever arrived on the scene.

As they placed *Khun* James in handcuffs and dragged him out of his house, still dressed in his pajamas and robe, he screamed in protest, "I am a British subject. You can't do this to me. I will sue you!" The two police officers didn't say a word. They merely shoved him roughly into the back of the police car and he continued to shriek at them, tears streaming down his horrified, unshaven face.

It was quite a scene at the police station when the police officers entered with the two underage boys and the handcuffed *farang* in his royal-blue, paisley silk dressing gown. They made *Khun* James sit at a desk behind a placard with his name printed on it, and told the two boys to hold out their arms and point at him with their backs to the cameras. The police photographers, as well as photographers from both the Thai and English-language newspapers, snapped away. Big front-page articles complete with unflattering photos would appear the next day for the whole country to see.

By this time *Khun* James no longer thought of Thailand as being a paradise for great sex and easy retirement. He was experiencing first-hand the wrath of the Thai police bureaucracy in one of their moods to be self-righteous and to publicly punish a *farang*. They didn't even give him the opportunity to buy himself out of his unattractive, unfortunate predicament until the damage against him was already done.

Khun James spent that entire day and night in the police jail, not allowed to make a phone call to his embassy or to his attorney until the following morning. The night he spent in jail the police watched through the bars with amusement as *Khun* James was beaten and repeatedly sexually assaulted by the twenty or so other inmates — all of them Thai — who shared his filthy cell.

By the time his lawyer and the British Embassy got James released, he was battered, bruised and nude except for what little was left of his royal-blue dressing gown. He remained completely mute, and stared off into space like a zombie. His mind had been severely shaken during the ordeal, and his conservative, unsympathetic Thai attorney suspected he might be permanently scarred.

Khun James and the lawyer negotiated to pay the huge fines and compensation money the police demanded for the two boys (who never received one *baht*), and James was allowed to board a plane for London under armed escort that night at midnight. Immigration had quickly issued deportation orders, and blacklisted him from ever being able to enter the country again. Later, when his mind was lucid enough to remember, *Khun* James would feel lucky to have been spared a long prison sentence. If the torment he had suffered during his one night in jail was any indication, he knew he wouldn't have survived too long.

The police pocketed almost all of the money *Khun* James had paid, the two boys went back to their village in Isan with the 6,000 *baht* Pompam had given them, and Pompam was rid of *Khun* James forever.

The next morning he instructed *Khun* Prawin to strike *Khun* James' name from the shareholders list for the new business. The agreement between Pompam and *Khun* James was destroyed, leaving no trace whatsoever that Pompam had ever received the 200,000 *baht* loan. Pompam was now the sole proprietor of his new bar which he named, ironically, "The Jamestown Pub."

Pompam felt not a little satisfaction when he reflected on the sad fate that had befallen his former customer and business partner. "It serves him right, the stupid *farang* prick," Pompam muttered to himself, feeling totally justified to have done what he did. It would take some time for his mind to heal from that last sordid scene in *Khun* James' bedroom; however, Pompam thought, I *did* get the 200,000 *baht*, which must be the most expensive tip a prostitute in Thailand *ever* received.

That night, in the shophouse that would soon be transformed into the Jamestown Pub, Pompam regaled Ott and Kitti with the details of the finale to *Khun* James' story in Thailand. They all roared with laughter at the thought of the elegant British gentleman's awesome reversal of fortune. Pompam even proposed a toast, "To *Khun* James; may he never forget 'The Land of Smiles.'" Then they proceeded to get drunk on a new bottle of "Black," and finalize their plans for Pompam's birthday party and their grand opening the following week.

After that night, they never once gave *Khun* James another

thought.

Ott persuaded seventeen of the boys from Number Ten to come over and work for their side. He and Pompam together hand-picked another nineteen from other bars around town as well. Approximately ninety-odd customers showed up for their big party; most of them were regulars that had been invited by the boys, but a few of them were walk-ins, attracted by the colorful signs and bouquets of balloons outside on the *soi*.

In addition to the countless drinks and bottles of beer that were consumed, they sold nearly forty bottles of whiskey to be kept for the purchasers' next visits — a very good sign of repeat business. All thirty-six boys were "offed" that night (many of them more than once) and the action in the VIP rooms upstairs kept the room attendants busy changing sheets and towels until nearly dawn.

"I guess we've done it, Pompam," shouted Kitti over the loud music. In spite of the fact that he was *"mau maak,"* or very drunk, he had been an admirable bartender, and had kept track of everyone's bar chits with no mistakes.

"I absolutely *love* your slide show, Pompam," cooed one very effeminate Thai patron. "How much will you charge me to make a complete copy of it?"

"The slides are not for sale, I'm afraid," Pompam responded in a friendly tone. "You'll just have to buy out all the boys and take your own pictures."

The lady-like patron giggled with delight at the thought of such a project. He couldn't wait to tell his old friend, *Khun* Anuwat at Number Ten, all the stories about the celebratory evening, knowing he would turn absolutely purple with rage, finding out he had been bested by his former star rent-a-boy. As a matter of fact, Anuwat lost big-time at the gambling tables the next evening as a result of losing his cool over Pompam's success.

After the opening Ott and Pompam had between ten and fifteen boys per day come by to apply for work. They would, perhaps, select one or two, oftentimes none, but before too long they had a stable of nearly eighty extremely good-looking boys. All of them had been brought up in similar sad life situations that had caused them to sell their bodies in the first place; but at least the working conditions were better, and the management more sympathetic at Jamestown than at any of the other places they could have worked doing the same thing.

By the end of their first month the profits were already substantial; good, in fact, by any standard for a business in its first month. Ott and Kitti were both pleased with their salary plus ten percent; Kitti's take was nearly the equivalent of *eight* months of his salary at the Chinese restaurant; and Pompam was able to recoup nearly one quarter of his initial investment.

"Ott, since there's not much for you to do during the day here, why don't you work on getting your portfolio together so you can start being a professional photographer," Pompam suggested one night.

"I'll need to find a place for a studio and darkroom when I really start," he replied, immediately liking the idea.

"You should check right here on the *soi* and see if any of these shop-houses have upper floors for rent. At the beginning you won't need a street-front location," Kitti wisely suggested.

Ott began looking around and soon found just such a situation. It would be perfect for his modest professional needs, and he could move out of Jamestown and live there as well; it would also be a place where he could entertain his Chinese girlfriend, Kim. With a sense of optimism he was able to put down a deposit using his first month's income, and he began at once to plan his new business and expand his portfolio. So far he had mostly pictures of young boys, with and without clothes, but he was determined to soon change that.

Pompam started to send a minimum of 5,000 *baht* home to his parents each month. His younger brothers were growing fast, and the family had acquired more needs in the process. Maa and Paw still never asked any questions about where the money came from — and they never would. Pompam was satisfied that he had finally reached one of his goals.

At the end of the third month when Kitti finished tallying up their accounts, he said, "Pompam, you've done it; you've completely recovered your initial investment. How does it feel?"

"I couldn't have done it without you and Ott, Kitti; but our job isn't over yet. By the time my birthday rolls around again next year I want us to have saved enough money to open *another* business;

Jamestown Pub is only the beginning."

One night a tour guide from one of the big travel companies came into the pub and brought two Japanese clients with him. The Japanese customers selected and bought off boys, then took them upstairs to VIP rooms for sex. While the guide was waiting for them downstairs at the bar, Pompam went over and *waied* to him and said, "*Sawasdee-khrap*. Thank you so much for the customers. My name is Pompam, the owner here."

"I am Chai, professional tour guide," the pleasant Thai-Chinese in his early thirties replied in a friendly manner.

Pompam bought Chai a drink and they started up a conversation. Pompam instantly liked the man; he had a quick wit about him, and Pompam sensed an innate cleverness that lived behind his beguiling round face.

"Do you only work with the Japanese?"

"No, Pompam; our company deals with tourists from Taiwan, Hong Kong, Singapore, and nearly every country in Europe — as well as America. I work as the *Thai* guide and give my narration in English; most of the tours have their own escorts who translate what I say into whatever language the tourists speak."

"Do many of them want to 'off' boys, like those two Japanese upstairs?" Pompam was curious.

"Not so many; they're usually too embarrassed to ask, but when they do, we usually just tell them to go down to Patpong and look around. The boy bars don't pay us a commission, so there's really no reason for us to push it," Chai replied, suddenly turning on a light in Pompam's head; he knew tour guides raked in huge commissions from the dozens of big, female massage palaces.

"What if I raised the 'off' fine when customers were brought in by tour guides, and I paid commissions? Would I get some business that way?" asked Pompam.

"I think you might get a lot of business, Pompam. Our salaries are small, and nearly all of our income comes from commissions on jewelry, shopping and massage parlors. If we could offer boys, too, it would give us another chance to make money off the *farangs*."

"Would you help me get the word out? I could pay you an

override on everything I pay to all tour guides," Pompam was thinking fast now.

In the end, Chai agreed to give it a try, and the two of them mapped out a program for developing the tourist market for Jamestown Pub. Before too long, the two satisfied Japanese tourists came back downstairs, and were smiling and snapping photographs of their cute young "conquests" to take home as souvenirs.

"You get the referral cards and fliers printed tomorrow Chai and keep track of your expenses. I think we can get the twenty-four-hour escort call service started within two days." Pompam felt excited about the new challenge.

Chai jumped into the exploitation of call boys and bar boys with great enthusiasm, seeing the potential in it for himself. Guides were soon bringing in tourists on a regular basis, making Pompam more per head from them than he made from regular Thai and *farang* walk-ins. Ambitious Mr. Chai did a good job, and before too long he and Pompam were good friends.

About six months later Pompam got the money together and opened another bar to meet the increased demand, this time in the Pratunam area near the garment market. Tourists were brought in by guides, and drawn in through the extensive advertising program Pompam launched in several visitor magazines.

Each year, thousands of travelers to Thailand were shocked to find ads for female massage parlors and escort services in the tourist publications they picked up in their hotel lobbies. They were even more shocked when they turned the page and saw Pompam's ads featuring a group picture, and a caption that read, "Eighty handsome young boys — come visit us, or hotel in-call available."

"Pompam, we're making money hand over fist. The investment in the Pratunam bar is already recovered, and you've got nearly a million *baht* in the bank. What are you going to do with all of it?" Kitti asked a few months later when they all got together for drinks.

"My twenty-fourth birthday is coming up soon, and I told you last year that by then we would open up a new business. I don't want to sell the two boy bars right now; they're making too much money for us. I want to branch out into a completely new field. Any ideas?" he asked.

Ott, whose photography studio had been steadily growing said, "Why don't we do something with *girls* for a change. I'm tired of taking pictures of naked boys." They all laughed.

Pompam was already been thinking along the same lines. He and Chai met the following week and discussed the possibility of Pompam opening a massage parlor with young female masseuses. "Do you think the guides would support us if we start a girl business?" he asked.

"You've been totally honest with all the tour guides, Pompam, and you've taken good care of them. I can guarantee they will send you more massage business than you could handle," replied a very confident Chai.

"Then let's start looking for the right place and the best deal; we're on a roll right now, Chai, so let's keep it going."

In the back of his mind, however, Pompam was concerned that he only had one million *baht* to invest; he was quite sure it wouldn't be enough, figuring start-up costs for a good massage parlor would be astronomical. He hoped that Chai would come up with a good solution.

Never once, after the success of the first boy-bar, did an ethical or moral question arise in Pompam's mind regarding the lucrative business of selling sex. It was already too much of an ingrained feature of the modern day Thai landscape to have concerned him — or most people in the country, for that matter. By now, he was only concerned about making money, just like everyone else.

Chapter 10

Pompam was already familiar with Paradise City, a medium-size massage parlor on Petchburi Road, not far from Atami and Verandah, two giant massage parlors, each the size of small office blocks.

"The owner, Khun Jeo, has let his business slide during the past year, and he's run up some huge gambling debts; the interest charges are eating him alive. He hasn't been able to keep up his police protection payments, and his only choice right now is to sell the business and pay off his usurious creditors — or wind up floating face down in the Chao Phya River," Chai explained rapidly, excitement in his voice, still catching his breath after racing over to Jamestown to give Pompam the news.

Pompam's first thought was that it was far above his reach financially. "What does the owner want for it?" expecting to hear a ridiculously high price.

"He doesn't own the land or the building, just a ten year lease; but he put in all the equipment and decoration at his own expense. To answer your question, Pompam, he wants three million *baht*. That's for the lease, the business, and the licenses," he replied.

"You know I don't have three million *baht*, Chai," Pompam responded with a frown.

"I know that, but I think he'll take your one million now, and some post-dated checks for the remaining two million over the next six months. He *needs* a million *baht* right now or he'll be dead within a week; he's desperate, and has no other offers."

Pompam knew immediately that three million *baht* with these terms was a steal. Getting the licenses alone could cost at least that in under-the-table payments to officials at the liquor commission and the police.

"When can we see this man?" Pompam asked seriously.

"Pipop, a colleague from my tour company, just told me about this only today. He is a good friend of the owner, *Khun* Jeo, and he knows you and I are meeting now. I told him that if you were interested I would call him and he would set up a meeting for tonight," Chai replied.

"There's the telephone," Pompam pointed, feeling that his knack for sudden luck and opportunity had struck again.

Chai set up the appointment with Pipop and they met the owner, worked out an agreement within an hour, signed a contract. Pompam handed over one million *baht* in cash, and post-dated checks for the balance. Jeo turned over the lease, license and door keys in return. Everyone noticed the visible look of relief on *Khun* Jeo's sweating face; the poor man was a nervous wreck, smoking one cigarette after another.

Petchburi Road was a major entertainment district in Bangkok, and was usually choked to a standstill with four lanes of traffic moving each direction, a smoggy haze over the whole area. Most of the bars and massage parlors had originally been built during the Vietnam war era for American GI's on R & R, and the huge, garish neon signs that fronted the buildings had a dated, late-sixties look to them. Many gigantic, new massage operations had started up in more recent years. The local economic boom had caused an increase in demand, as had the ever-growing popularity of Thailand as a sex-tourism destination; one place, at the Makasan intersection, was twenty stories tall and employed over 250 girls.

Pompam knew he desperately needed help running the new business, since he, Ott and Kitti couldn't possibly handle everything themselves. "Chai, will you give up your position as tour guide and manage Paradise City for me? I'll pay you 20,000 *baht* a month and ten percent of the profits to start," asked Pompam, feeling confident that Chai would be good at it.

Even though Pompam was younger than Chai, and it was against the custom, he *waied* low to Pompam, silently thanking his new boss for giving him the opportunity.

Pompam then brought in his brother Nuu from Buriram, who had just turned eighteen. He needed to have people work with him that he trusted, and he thought it was about time Nuu got out of the rice fields and into a decent job.

Chai and Pompam weeded through the Paradise City's existing employees and kept most of the girls, nearly all of the maids, and most of the waiters and waitresses in the coffee shop. They summarily fired all of the cashiers, captains, and mamasans; these positions would have to be re-filled using their own new people.

The place itself needed a major re-vamping. It had become seedy and run-down over the years; *Khun* Jeo had done nothing to keep it up to date. They decided to close for two months for renovations, and then re-open with a big blast on Pompam's twenty-fourth birthday. Kitti found a way to pay for the renovation out of cash flow and operating profits from the two boy bars.

Kitti brought in his mother to manage the coffee shop; she was more than willing to leave her *somtam* stall on Silom in exchange for a good salary with security. Kitti's father also came on board and started organizing Bangkok's public and private taxi drivers on a sliding-scale commission program. For captains they hired five of the boys from Jamestown Pub; they had been with them since it opened and were more than ready for retirement.

"Pompam, how can you do it? You've fucked thirty girls in two weeks. Aren't you getting tired?" Chai teased him.

"I don't think I'll *ever* get tired. I believe this is called 'reaping my rewards,'" he replied with a laugh. He had been trying out the girls who now worked for him, as well as exploring other massage parlors, gathering tips on the business, and hiring away beauties who pleased him.

With no restraint, Pompam allowed himself to express his healthy appetite for beautiful girls; he reasoned that his tenure in a boy bar had repressed his natural instincts. Even though he knew it was expected of him to get married and raise children some day, he felt that it would never stop him from whoring around as much as he pleased. In this respect, his attitudes about sex were normal, not at all unlike the prevailing sentiments of the entire Thai male population.

By the time Paradise City was ready to re-open, everyone on Pompam's team agreed that even though it wasn't one of the biggest, it was certainly one of the most attractive massage parlors in all of Bangkok. It's early-Las Vegas look, including red flocked wallpaper, gold-streaked mirror tiles, massive "Louie" lobby furniture, faux-crystal chandeliers, and marble floors, greatly pleased Pompam and the boys; they knew their customers would be impressed, and enjoy being surrounded by such luxury.

The night of Pompam's twenty-fourth birthday party, combined with Paradise City's re-opening, finally arrived. Chai and Kitti's father had rounded up the tour operators, tour guides, hotel taxi drivers, bell-boys, and other service workers who could refer customers to them in exchange for commissions. Many members of the police had been invited; several even came in their uniforms. *"Phuyais,"* or big-shots in the business community, had been asked to attend in great numbers, and the parking lot was stuffed to capacity with Mercedes Benzes and all the other luxury cars that had become the primary statement of one's worth and rank in modern Thailand.

They put up a big search light out front, and traffic on Petchburi Road slowed to a crawl as passing motorists stopped to get a good look. In Bangkok there are consumer magazines that specialize in "massage parlor industry" news. Reporters for those rags were invited, as well as representatives from all of the Thai dailies.

The coffee shop had a stage at one end that provided a non-stop revue of sexy female singers and live bands playing Thai pop music and country songs. It reminded Pompam of the night he lost his virginity to the prostitute, Num, because he couldn't afford 500 *baht* for the *nak-rong* in the green dress he really wanted. Now he could afford hundreds of such girls, one right after the other, he mused.

Complimentary Black Label and Chivas flowed abundantly, and the sixty-five girls who provided the massage services were also available free of charge that night. The "girl room" had been re-carpeted, re-painted, and re-designed; it had three rising tiers of daises where the girls sat smiling, waiting to be chosen. Pompam had new uniforms made up for all the staff, but he had paid particular attention to the shocking pink, "shorty" chiffon negligees the massage girls wore. He had the idea of employing three full-time beauticians to do the girls' hair and make-up before work every day; this extra "perk" not only made the girls happy, it also made them look more sexy and appealing, which was good for business.

Pompam, as host, stood in front of the glass wall that separated the pink-lit "girl room" from the lobby, and welcomed the guests as they arrived. He was so handsome and well-dressed; the girls on the other side of the glass looked at him dreamy-eyed, wishing all their customers could be like him. This, of course, would rarely be the case, since most of their patrons would be middle-aged locals, *farangs*, or Asian tourists brought in by Chai's friends — literally in busloads.

The girls, just like the boys in the boy bars, had no say. Their job was to entertain whoever chose them, make sounds like they enjoyed it, and endure the disgust and humiliation so they could collect their tips at the end. The majority of Pompam's girls were over the legal age of eighteen, but about thirty-five percent of them were from fourteen to seventeen years old; management felt it had no choice but to employ the younger ones, since so many customers demanded them.

"*Sawasdee-khrap!*" Pompam said, *waiing* low to his most important guest that evening, the Chief of Police for all of Bangkok. He had been invited, of course, but Pompam really hadn't expected him to show up. Pompam guessed correctly that his former customer, now good friend, *Khun* Surapong, the number two officer in the Department, had persuaded him to make an appearance.

"My name is Vichai and I am the owner here. I am honored that you have come to our opening, Sir, and I hope that you will be our guest here whenever you have the time." Pompam overdid his welcome a bit, but the Police General seemed satisfied and perfunctorily returned his *wai*.

"*Khun* Surapong has been telling me what a clever young man you are, and I wanted to stop by and wish you good luck," the portly, middle-aged General responded politely to his host.

The General was ushered into the coffee shop where he was greeted with a profusion of *wais* from all directions. He settled at a table with a group of his "own," and proceeded to finish off nearly a whole bottle of complimentary Chivas by himself. Later Pompam found out that he had taken two girls upstairs for a "special" bubble bath body massage, and had passed out naked on an air mattress.

Even though the official closing time, by law, was 1:00 a.m., the party didn't end until about four-thirty. Pompam and his crew had nothing to worry about since nearly all the top brass in the police force stayed until the end, drinking their whiskey, and having sex with their underage girls.

After the last guests finally departed, Pompam, who was by then totally exhausted, decided to do a bit of relaxing himself. He picked out three of the best-looking, best-trained girls who were still awake and able to walk, and headed upstairs for a massage. He chose the biggest and most opulent VIP room and stripped off all his clothes.

The three girls got naked quickly, filled up the huge bathtub, eased Pompam into the fragrant, bubbly hot water, then climbed in with him. Each girl concentrated on a different part of his smooth, firm body and massaged it gently; all his tensions from the long night began to melt away in the bubbles. Then with one girl behind him, one astride him, and one sitting facing him so he straddled her, they gave him the "ultimate" body massage, an item that was *not* on the regular menu.

His strong, good-sized manhood was hard and pulsing, and he thought for sure that he would come right there in the bath water the next time one of the girls rubbed up against it. He controlled himself, though, until they were out of the tub and piled onto a large soapy air mattress on the floor. For a while the four of them writhed around in one slippery mass of flesh until his seeking member found entrance in one of several available orifices — not caring in the least which one it was. He quickly came, totally engulfed by the complex sensations of his flesh bonded together on all sides by the slick, undulating bodies of the three beautiful young girls.

"I think I like being the owner of a place like this," Pompam said to himself as the girls rinsed him off in the shower.

"I want to go back to our village for *Loy Kratong*," Pompam whined to Kitti one night late in the rainy season. "By the time it gets here I will have been away from Isan for a year and a half. I miss my family."

"My mother and father are here in Bangkok, Pompam, so I don't need to go back to the village. I think that you should go, though; by now I'm sure all sorts of stories about Paradise City have gotten back to everyone back home, and you might need to go and do some explaining," replied Kitti.

Pompam had recently increased his family's allowance to 10,000 *baht* each month and they had instantly become the most affluent residents of their small community. Kitti was right and word *had,* in fact, gotten back to Buriram about Pompam's massage parlor; but as it turned out, no one thought it was wrong or even cared. *"Mai pen rai,"* was everyone's general attitude. Despite the sordid nature of the business, everyone was envious of Maa's and Paw's oldest son's success in the capital city; after all, the only thing that really mattered was the money.

"I think I'll send Nuu back to the village with money to build my family a new house," declared Pompam, getting a sudden inspiration. "I want it to be ready when I go there for *Loy Kratong.*"

Pompam summoned Nuu and drew a design of the house he wanted; then he sketched a rough site map of their property and showed Nuu exactly where he wanted it to be built. He made a list of the building materials he wanted to be used, and where; then he phoned a contractor he knew in Buriram and told him to meet Nuu at the village in two days' time.

Nuu was absolutely bowled over with both pride and surprise, having been entrusted with such a major responsibility. The next day Pompam gave him a half-million *baht* in cash and sent him off to Buriram.

"Don't forget, Nuu, I'll be there for *Loy Kratong* in exactly two months and I want to sleep in my own new house!" Pompam called after him.

"I'll do my best *pi-chai;* don't worry," answered Nuu.

Thinking about building a new house for his parents reminded Pompam that he and Kitti still lived secretly on the fourth floor of Jamestown Pub. Over time they had made their little apartment as comfortable as possible and had equipped it with electronic equipment, nice rugs, and other furnishings to make it livable, even though it was really only a place to sleep. The idea began to enter his mind that he would like to have a nice home, a bachelor pad where he and Kitti could entertain friends and family, and enjoy themselves for a few years before they eventually settled down and got married.

"Kitti, when I come back from *Loy Kratong* I want us to start making plans to move out of the bar. They need the space there anyway for more VIP rooms. Where do you think we should go?" Pompam asked his friend a few days later.

"*Soi* Tonglor, Sukhumvit 55, might be a good place to buy

property, Pompam. It's becoming very fashionable right now, and land values are sure to keep going up; it might be a good place to invest some money."

"You mean, *build* our own house in Bangkok?" Pompam asked in surprise. He had only been thinking about leasing a nice condo somewhere, but he could see some sense in what Kitti was saying about buying land.

"Why not?" Kitti answered. "You've certainly got the money now."

Why not, indeed, Pompam thought, and decided he would follow Kitti, for once; he knew that Kitti had been keeping up with Bangkok's booming business trends better than he himself had.

The massage parlor operation on Petchburi Road was proving to be more of a success than Pompam and his boys had ever dreamed. They gradually up-graded the quality of entertainment at Paradise City, and soon drew a crowd in their coffee shop that was completely separate from their massage parlor business; they even began to treat it as a separate outlet. Pompam had always loved music, and the entertainment aspect of Paradise City was something he truly enjoyed. They no longer felt they needed the gaudily-attired *nak-rongs* who sang for *puangmalai*, and instead began booking groups of local pop performers who attracted a younger, mixed clientele. Ott had a good feel for the entertainment business, so he was put in charge of talent.

Pompam's favorite music, which he loved dearly, was the country music from Isan. He missed the old-style music from the temple fairs in Buriram, and regretted that there was nowhere to go in Bangkok where he could get up and do the *ram wong* if he felt like it, eat Isan food, and drink Lao whiskey. Pompam thought there might be a business opportunity in such an idea; I'll think about it in during *Loy Kratong*, he decided.

"I'm going off to Buriram next week, Kitti. Do you think I've earned enough money to buy myself a car?" Pompam, from training and habit, practiced frugality when it came to spending money on himself, and he still drove his first motorcycle. Lately, however, he hadn't enjoyed taking his life in his own hands every time he went out on the road, and he had had a couple of close calls that had nearly cost him his life.

"I think you owe it to yourself to buy a nice car, Pompam, and drive it home to Nong Ki. Everyone in the village knows you have money now; don't be so embarrassed about it," Kitti advised.

"Okay, Kitti, I'll buy a car. But what should I get? I don't want anything too expensive or too flashy. I just want transportation."

"Then buy something Japanese — maybe a Toyota or a Honda. They're both good cars and either one will reflect your modesty," Kitti teased.

That night Pompam went out and looked at Japanese automobiles. He decided on a Honda because his old motorcycle was a Honda, and it had kept him alive through five years of dangerous Bangkok traffic.

The next morning Pompam asked, "What should I buy for Rattana, Kitti?" Pompam had already brought presents for his family, and he suddenly had a notion to get something special for the girl back home.

Kitti was surprised by the question, and sensed that there might be more news about Rattana in the future. "Why don't you get her a small gold chain and a Buddha amulet," was his reply after a few moments of thought.

"What a great idea, Kitti! I'll get *Phra* Asoka to go with me and help select it." Pompam had been meaning to visit the monk for quite some time, feeling guilty about neglecting him.

"You are all grown up now, Vichai," welcomed *Phra* Asoka, smiling. Pompam *waied* and bowed three times, and when he rose up he could still see the warmth and love for him in *Ajarn's* sparkling dark eyes; there was no sign of any scolding for staying away so long, and Pompam was relieved.

"In some ways I *have* grown up, *Ajarn*, and yet in many other ways I'm still the same barefoot buffalo boy who showed up here with his Abbot nearly seven years ago."

"You look well, Vichai, but I can see in your face that you come to me today with a great many more experiences than you did the first time we met — not all of them good, if I'm not mistaken." The monk shifted his posture, looking concerned.

Pompam almost flinched, and feared for a second that *Phra* Asoka knew by intuition the complete book of his life — including the body-selling chapter. "Yes, *Ajarn*, that is very true. Some of the experiences I am proud of, and some I'm not. I suppose I'm not much different than most others."

"Are you still in touch with Dr. Jim in California?" the monk asked, mercifully changing the subject.

"Yes, *Ajarn*. He still writes me every now and then, and when he does he always asks about you. Do you ever hear from him?"

"He used to write to me regularly, but I haven't heard from him for a while now. He has been a big help with my foundation in India. He has sent several people to talk to me about Buddhism, and he has made donations to the temple we support in Bombay." Pompam winced as he picked up the hint, and made a mental note to give *Phra* Asoka a big donation for his foundation very soon.

"I want to buy an amulet for a girl in my village; I'm going home for *Loy Kratong*. Will you walk over to the market with me?" he asked.

"Is this girl you want the amulet for someone special in your life, Vichai?"

"I suppose so. She's the youngest daughter of our village headman, and she has always been around me. I'd just like to get her something nice," he replied honestly.

The well-known market that specialized in amulets and Buddha statues was located across the street from the temple next to the river; there were rows upon rows of stalls in a maze of open-air corridors. *Phra* Asoka, somewhat of an expert regarding these objects, helped Pompam choose an antique Buddha image encased in lovely gold filigree. *Ajarn* said it had a nice feeling about it.

"I don't see much value in buying an amulet for good luck that contains the image of a holy monk, long since dead," he added. "I'm not superstitious, Vichai. Luck is something you have to cultivate from inside your heart, and then you realize it's not really luck at all, but the creative intention of the mind — and karma, of course."

Pompam realized he would have to think about that statement for a while, before he could fully digest its meaning.

"*Ajarn*, would you help choose one for me, too?" he asked,

suddenly wanting one for himself.

They looked through several stalls and finally found one that pleased *Phra* Asoka's eye: another handsome Buddha image encased in gold.

The second one, which was quite large, also appealed to Pompam, so he told the dealer he would take it. When the seller told Pompam it was 6,000 *baht*, *Phra* Asoka was more than a little surprised to see the young man peel off the twelve 500-*baht* notes and pay for it without even trying to bargain.

"So, Vichai, you not only have your good health, but you have money now, too. I am happy that you are doing so well."

"I'm not very superstitious either, *Ajarn*. I must have cultivated some small amount of luck in my own heart over the years," Pompam modestly replied, smiling.

Pompam's next stop that day was in Chinatown at the gold sellers' shops on Sampheng Road. He wanted to wear the Buddha image that *Ajarn* had selected for him, and he wanted to buy a chain for Rattana's as well.

When Pompam walked in the office, Kitti noticed the heavy gold chain around Pompam's neck right away. "Oh my Buddha! Yesterday a new car and today a gold chain! What will it be next, Pompam?"

When he drove up to his parents' house he first saw the familiar old, dilapidated, wooden structure where he had been born and raised. Then behind it he saw the new white, concrete block, two-story modern house that he had commissioned his brother to build only two months before. The contrast between the two dwellings was indeed quite startling — on many levels.

He could see immediately that the new house wasn't yet entirely completed, but he hadn't realistically expected it to be. He knew, however, that if he hadn't given Nuu an almost unrealistic deadline it still wouldn't even have a roof on it. Even though he could see that in every respect the house looked totally out of place, he felt proud of it, and knew that his parents were proud of him for building it.

"*Sawasdee-khrap* Maa, Paw!" Pompam *waied* to his mother and father when he got out of the car. They hardly even acknowledged

Pompam's presence, though, because they couldn't take their eyes off of the new Honda.

Maa offered a wide, beetle-stained grin and said, "Pompam, you are supposed to be a struggling young businessman. Where are you getting all of your money? Have you become a thief?" she asked, teasing, never knowing how he got his money, never really caring. But now, she and everyone else knew all about Paradise City.

"No, Maa," Pompam replied, "I've had some good luck lately with a new business opportunity. Aren't you going to invite me in and show me the new house I built for you?" he asked with a big smile.

They all removed their shoes before they entered the new home. Pompam could see that the quality of construction and finishing was inferior by Bangkok standards, and he made a grimace when he saw how his younger brothers had already blackened the newly-painted walls with hand prints everywhere. Maa had mistakenly set up her kitchen in the living room where she had spread out some reed mats and put a charcoal brazier on the new parquet. Pompam winced as he went from room to room and realized that he would have to teach his parents how to use and take care of the house properly. He knew he couldn't blame them for not knowing how to live in the *farang*-style house; after all, they had lived in an ancient wooden shack on top of a buffalo pen their entire lives.

"This is your room, Pompam. No one has been in here since the house was finished. When you are here, this is where you will stay," Maa told her oldest son as she opened the door.

"No, Maa. This is the master bedroom. This room is for you and Paw. I don't need to have my own room here; I only come once or twice a year. You need all the rooms you have for you and Paw and the six boys," he replied with irritation in his voice.

"Thank you, Pompam, but *no*, this is *your* room," Maa said adamantly.

Pompam realized it would take a little time to change her mind about the use of the big bedroom, so he stopped arguing.

After he had changed into some shorts, T-shirt and rubber slippers, he took Maa and Paw and the youngest three boys with him in the car and drove down to the market. It was the first time any of them had ever experienced auto air conditioning. The young brothers giggled and screamed in the back seat with Maa, who just sat there quietly looking out the window, not able to fully comprehend the incredible miracle that her boy, Pompam, had driven his own brand new car all the way out to Buriram to see them. And wearing a thick gold chain, too. Not much escaped her close examination.

"Maa, we'll buy everything we need for our meal tonight, and maybe some whiskey so we can invite our neighbors and friends. The *farangs* call it a 'housewarming,'" Pompam announced.

They proceeded to load up the car with mountains of food and supplies. Maa protested that he was buying too much, but he told her she could keep most of it in the refrigerator and it wouldn't spoil. Maa still knew nothing about the magic of modern refrigeration; Pompam had peeked in the fridge before they left home and saw that she was storing the raw, uncooked rice in there, while some fresh meat was sitting out on the floor wrapped up in old newspapers.

Back at the house Pompam had a few moments alone with his brother who had just returned from an errand and told him, "Nuu, you've done an excellent job on the new house. Now I know for sure that I can trust you to do everything for me. Do you think Att is ready to come back to Bangkok and work with us?" Att was the next younger brother after Nuu and he was now seventeen.

Nuu was pleased and grateful for the way Pompam acknowledged him about the house; he still worshipped his older brother as he had since he was a child. "Att is a good boy, Pompam. He's finished with his studies here at the local school and has already told me several times that he would like to live in Bangkok with us. Do you think there might be a job for him at Paradise City?" he asked.

"If not Paradise City then undoubtedly somewhere else. I have enough ideas for new businesses to keep *all* my brothers busy; I just wish they were all grown up!" Pompam laughed, thinking it would be a long time before the youngest could be put to work; he was only four and a half years old.

That evening they drove to a temple fair in a neighboring village so Pompam could listen to the Isan country music he had been missing. Somehow they managed to squeeze the entire family into the small Honda: Maa and Paw and their eight sons, including Pompam. On the way they laughed about being stuffed in the car like pigs in a market pen, and thoroughly enjoyed the warmth of being all together again.

Pompam had put on a *sarong* and his old *pakomah* before they left home. He was the lightest-skinned member of the family; his night-time work in Bangkok kept him out of the sun most of the time. His parents and brothers, however, worked in the rice fields and were always out of doors; their skin was the color of teak.

Like Pompam, there were a great many Isan-born workers in the villages who had just returned from Bangkok for the holiday. He enjoyed seeing the variety of happy expressions on the faces of those who had just stepped back into their birth culture for a while, away from the social and financial alienations of Bangkok, and its many prejudices against them. The twangy music, the *ram wong* dance, the Lao whiskey, camaraderie, and the cool night air were all lovely to Pompam, and he wished that he could somehow capture the same feeling in the capital. Perhaps he would open a place himself where Isan people could come together and re-experience who they were. He would discuss this idea with Kitti and Chai when he returned after *Loy Kratong*.

That night Maa sat on a rush mat one of the boys spread out on the ground, her two youngest ones fast asleep at her side. She watched as the rest of her men were lifted up in an almost spiritual ecstasy, so rich was the soul of their unique Northeastern culture. They danced the *ram wong* together, barefoot in the dirt; huge loudspeakers amplified the potent music, centuries-old instruments of their native country still alive. Dozens of other men and women were moving along with them, laughing and waving their arms to the pulsing, ancient Isan rhythms. Even though Pompam had built the family a new house and had come back home in a new car, Maa could see that he was still just a regular buffalo boy like the rest of her brood. She, herself, hadn't been as happy for many years as she was at that very moment.

The next morning Pompam woke up before dawn to help his mother prepare the food offerings for the monks. He had never done this before, and it made him feel good inside to *wai* and put food in the alms bowls when the monks passed their house. He remembered the eight years of his own life when he had been on the receiving end of such merit-making.

"You look like you have returned to us even more prosperous

than last time," the canny old Abbot told Pompam when he called on him at the temple. "I am sure that with the good Buddhist training you've had, you are mindful about how you make your money," he continued, raising his non-existent eyebrows.

"My training as a *nene* taught me many things, *Ajarn*," Pompam replied. "I've done my best to be able to provide for my family." He tactfully side-stepped the remark about "mindfully" making money. Pompam was sure, however, that the Abbot, who knew everything that happened in his village, must have heard about Paradise City; but it was the ever-practical Thai way to accept only the reality of having the money in present-time, and not to pry into its origins.

That evening was the actual night of *Loy Kratong*, the last full moon of the harvest season. In the afternoon Pompam went to the house of *Khun* Direk, the village headman, to pay his respects, and to make sure that he could meet Rattana later at the village reservoir so they could float their *kratongs* together and he could give her his gift.

Khun Direk was genuinely happy to see Pompam again, but was somewhat reticent about letting this handsome "city boy" escort his precious daughter to celebrate *Loy Kratong* alone. *Khun* Direk had also learned of Pompam's latest business venture, but was polite enough not to mention it directly.

"Pompam," *Khun* Direk announced, "we will *all* meet you this evening to send off our *kratongs*." Rattana stood close by and smiled at Pompam, but it was impossible to maneuver herself any closer to begin a conversation. That would have to wait until later that evening, she thought to herself.

Pompam couldn't help but notice how truly beautiful Rattana had become. He had, over the last year or so, seen and been with a great many young girls, given the nature of his new business, and his complete freedom to express his strong sexual urges as he pleased. But he could tell right away that Rattana was indeed very special. She was taller than most Thai girls, had shining black hair that fell to her shoulders, perfect white teeth that gleamed through her radiant smile, big round eyes, and a small nose with a real bridge, unlike most Northeastern girls he had known. He could sense by her poise that the two-year Associate of Arts program at Khon Kaen University had helped her to develop and mature; she somehow seemed much more worldly, more confident, and wiser than most girls her age.

Khun Direk noticed Pompam's close observation of his young daughter, and even though his instinct was to be overly-protective, he could see that there was a possibility of a strong attraction between the two that he could not prevent.

That evening under the full moon Pompam and his family went down to the reservoir to "play" *Loy Kratong*. Rattana and her parents arrived early, and she had insisted that they wait for Pompam before sailing their small, colorful, hand-made vessels.

The two families greeted each other politely, and then each person lit a candle and incense, and performed his or her own brief, personal ceremony at the water's edge — including Pompam's young brothers who seemed to enjoy it the most. Pompam and Rattana once again released their *kratongs* tied together as one, just as they had done on the same occasion two years before.

"*Khun* Direk, why don't you and your family join us for some refreshments," suggested Pompam when the *kratongs* had reached the middle of the pond, a cluster of small, flickering lights on the still water. As they had not yet been inside the house that Pompam built, Rattana and her parents were more than happy to pay a curious first call.

"You certainly are a good son to provide such a lovely new home for your family," Rattana's mother, duly impressed, commented after the house tour, thoughts already in her mind about what a nice son-in-law Pompam would make. They all admired the new house, the men had some drinks, and then *Khun* Direk announced that it was time for him and his family to go home.

Rattana looked expectantly at Pompam who said, "Would it be all right with you, *Khun* Direk, if I took Rattana out for a drive in my new car? I promise I won't get her home too late."

Khun Direk, who had never let his daughter go out alone with a young man before, said solemnly, "I'll let her go, Pompam, but only because it's with you," his message clear to everyone.

Once in the car Pompam suggested, "I've always wanted to see Phanom Rung in the full moon, but never had a car to take me. Would you like to go there?" Rattana smiled, and her wide, dark eyes gave him her answer.

When they arrived at the ancient Khmer ruin, the entire hill upon which it stood was illuminated in radiant silver moonlight. The massive stone structures of the temples looked as if they were heated by some fire within their walls. The two young people carried with them the rush mat Pompam had brought along, and walked quietly through thousand-year-old portals that seemed to them to have been crafted by sorcerers from some forgotten, mythical age. They knew they were probably the only people there that night, but each of them felt they could sense other presences who had long ago looked up at the same moon.

In the walled-in courtyard on the east side of the hilltop, Pompam spread out the mat so they could sit down and enjoy the enchanted nightscape.

"I've never seen anything so beautiful in my life, Pompam. Thank you so much for this moment," the young girl said softly.

"I brought you something from Bangkok to remember me by, Rattana. I want you to wear it always and think about our being at Phanom Rung together under this *Loy Kratong* moon."

He handed her the small, red, satin-covered, drawstring pouch which she opened carefully and slowly removed the fine gold chain with the Buddha amulet hanging from it.

"*Phra* Asoka, the Indian *Ajarn* at *Wat* Mahathat, helped me choose it for you, Rattana."

The young girl couldn't believe her eyes. Never had she received such a beautiful and important gift. She reached over and put her arms around Pompam and gave him a Thai-style "kiss" on his cheek.

When the *farangs* first came to Thailand several hundred years before, the Thai women couldn't understand why the *farangs* tried so hard to join their lips with their own. They thought the whole idea of the *farang* kiss was disgusting. They preferred to nuzzle their noses next to the man's cheek and neck, and sniff, absorbing the clean, fresh scent of their consorts.

Pompam put his arms around Rattana and returned the Thai "kiss" while remarking to himself how absolutely pure and gentle (as well as sensual) it was to breathe in the essence of the unspoiled young girl. In all of his sexual encounters, with both men and women, he had never had such a uniquely-arousing experience.

They remained quietly in each other's arms for a few minutes, simply enjoying the pleasure of being with one another, feeling close. They watched the moon slowly make its way across the sky, letting their minds drift like clouds; a spell cast by the ancient masters of Phanom Rung enveloping them.

"I had better be getting you back home, Rattana. Your father will be worried about you, and upset with me for keeping you out late," Pompam said almost lovingly.

They silently got up, rolled up the mat, and walked back down to the car below. They spoke very little on the drive back to the village. They listened to the soft, romantic Isan music that Pompam had put in the tape deck, and occasionally looked over at one another and smiled. They both knew at the same moment that they would soon be lovers.

When they reached her home they could see *Khun* Direk waiting, sitting on the top step, smoking a hand-rolled cigarette.

"Will you come and drive with me tomorrow evening, Rattana?" he asked.

"Of course, Pompam. I will tell my father." She waved back to him from the front porch, then kissed Khun Direk on the forehead and went inside.

The next morning Pompam woke up early, bathed, dressed, and called out to his mother, "Maa, I'm going to take all the boys to the big market in Buriram today. Get them ready; I want to leave right after I've had my coffee."

When the boys heard this announcement the three youngest ones stripped naked on the spot; since they hadn't yet been allowed to use the shower in the new house, they sprinted off to the old outhouse like little foxes. Nuu had already used the shower, but Att and the next younger two had also not yet bathed, so they crowded into the tiny privy with the others. Pompam laughed out loud at the sounds of crying and shrieking coming from the small building out back. All six brown-skinned boys, ages four, five, seven, eleven, fifteen and seventeen, fought each other for space in the tiny room that measured only four feet square.

They finally started off, all eight brothers in the small car, singing along to the country music Pompam played full blast. When they got to the main town in Buriram, Pompam and Nuu made a joke about the last time the two of them were there together, spending the night on the railway platform, hung-over to their very fingernails.

The open market was busier than usual that day. Many Bangkok returnees and their families were stocking up on all sorts of supplies. Pompam led his crew to the clothing stalls and began fitting each of them out in new duds. They kept at least six stall-owners busy for the better part of an hour while trying things on, arguing over who would get what, the smallest ones clinging to Pompam for fear of getting trampled in the crush. Pompam was a good bargainer that day, and thought he had done rather well with the final totals. Each boy followed him back to the car with an armload of clothes and their first new shoes.

"We can't forget Maa and Paw, can we?" Pompam joked.

"No, Pompam! No, Pompam!" they shouted back in unison.

They went back to the market a second time and bought clothes for Maa and Paw, laundry soap, bath soap, cleaning supplies for the new house, sheets, towels, dishes, and numerous other odds and ends. Pompam stopped at a furniture stall and ordered a dining set, sofa, chairs, some beds and other locally-made furnishings. He drew a map of the house's location, and the shop owner promised to deliver it all later that afternoon. Pompam found himself having the absolute time of his life opening up his wallet for his big Isan family.

Back at the car he had each of the boys change into one of their new outfits and told them he was taking them out for lunch, an announcement that produced great screams of delight.

They walked over to a Chinese shophouse that had a red and gold-lettered sign over the door; on the sidewalk in front were glass-fronted, stainless-steel cabinets filled with ducks hanging by their necks, chunks of roasted pork, and trays of fresh *dim sum*; it all looked very appetizing to the boys, and Pompam ordered them a feast. "Pompam, why don't you stay here with us in Buriram and take us out to lunch more often?" one of the middle ones inquired of his rich *pi-chai* from Bangkok.

"I can't take you out to lunch like this if I don't work; and I can't work if I don't live in Bangkok!" Pompam proclaimed. He did make a firm mental decision to come back home more often. He had never imagined that being in Buriram could be so much fun, and then soon figured out that it was having money that made the difference; Buriram was still the same.

A visit to the ice cream shop was their last stop, and by the end of that treat Pompam wished that the boys had kept on their old clothes. *Mai pen rai*, he thought, Maa can clean everything in her new washing machine; I'll teach her how to use it.

Within an hour after getting home and showing off all their loot to Maa and Paw, who stared at Pompam in total amazement, the truck arrived to deliver all the furniture and household items Pompam had bought. They worked the rest of the day putting everything in place, making up the beds with unfamiliar things called "sheets," and sorting out the new dishes in the kitchen cabinets.

"Well, Maa, now you have a real *farang* house, just like down on Sukhumvit Road," Pompam joked with his mother. He could tell by the sparkle in her eye how pleased she was with everything he had bought. Pompam suddenly had a morbid thought and wondered how pleased she would be if she knew that all of those things had been purchased with money he had made by using young people who sold their bodies for sex — himself included. *"Mai pen rai,"* thought Pompam, "just look at all the things I have provided for my family!"

Just after sunset he showed up at the Direk family home to call for Rattana. She appeared at the door looking even more enchanting than the night before. Pompam suspected for the first time that he might be falling in love with her. He had never before had a serious girlfriend, and this was the first time he had experienced feelings of this kind.

"Don't be back too late," *Khun* Direk admonished as the young people waved good-bye. "Don't worry, Paw," Rattana assured him, "we're only going down to Nong Ki for a bowl of noodles."

Pompam wondered where she thought up the idea of going for noodles, but they did in fact have some, and then drove on a few more miles to a lovely wooded park near a small stream.

They spread out the rush mat on the ground and seated themselves. There didn't seem to be much to say to one another, and it wasn't too long before they were laying down, holding each other tightly, and kissing each other in both the Thai and *farang* styles. Pompam knew for certain that Rattana had never even come close to being intimate with another man. He thought that even though he himself had been sexually involved countless times with hundreds of people, he also had never actually been *intimate* — at least with his heart.

As time passed, one article of clothing after another was removed from the two young bodies, very slowly with no rush. When they were nude, illuminated by full-moonlight shining through a lattice-work of trees, they searched each others' bodies with their hands and their lips, and with quickening breaths inhaled each others' secret scents. Pompam's smooth, silken, Isan skin against Rattana's own, sent shock waves through their inflamed and entwined bodies .

He waited until she was moist and ready, and then entered her slowly, with more gentleness than he thought he was capable given the surge of his rising passion. He could tell that it was hurting her and she wanted to cry out, but she buried her face in the crook of Pompam's neck instead and stifled small sounds of pain and joy. She had long dreamed of this moment and wanted so much to share the pleasure she knew Pompam was feeling and, to some extent, she did; but she knew that for her it would take more time to truly appreciate and savor all the riches of the body. When Pompam finished, fulfilled, they lay there side by side, and Pompam watched the subtle movements of moonlight on the delicate gold chain that encircled the isthmus between her throat and breast.

"*Pom rak khun*, Rattana." "I love you, Rattana," Pompam spoke the words as he sniffed her ear. He knew for certain that he would go with many other women in his lifetime, but he would love only one of them: this beautiful girl from his native Buriram.

They were together almost every minute that remained of Pompam's holiday in the village, and they tried to be discreet when they went off to make love; but it was impossible to hide from their families and friends what they had become to each other.

Their parting was sad, but not *too* sad, as they both had confidence in what they had experienced. Pompam would return to work in Bangkok, and Rattana would go back to Khon Kaen to finish her last term. They agreed to meet again at New Years.

Later, after the ritual of the white string, Maa and Paw lit incense at the temple and thanked the Lord Buddha for the many blessings that had been bestowed upon them through the eldest of their three sons who had just driven away.

Chapter 11

He didn't much like the idea, but Pompam moved Att in with Nuu in a staff apartment at Paradise City; about twenty-five of the service personnel lived in a dormitory on a corridor near the laundry room. It wasn't a very good environment for an impressionable seventeen-year-old fresh out of the countryside, but for the moment it would have to do.

His brother Nuu had no interest whatsoever in furthering his formal education. He had stopped going to high school when he was about fourteen and told his parents that he simply could endure no more. Att, on the other hand, had shown pronounced skills in academics, and Pompam decided he should continue his schooling. On the way back from Buriram Att agreed to follow in his older brother's footsteps and enter Ramkampheng University next term. Pompam would have liked him to enter one of the more prestigious institutions, but the truth was, he needed him to work in the business, and the "open" system at Ramkampheng would give him the time to do so. Besides, Ramkampheng wasn't that far geographically from Petchburi Road and Paradise City.

Pompam thought the next brother, Chatree, nicknamed Toy, a quiet, sensitive youngster, would go to Chulalongkorn University if he was so inclined.

"While I was home in the village I had an idea about opening up a place here in Bangkok where people from Isan can go to hear our country music, dance the *ram wong*, eat Isan food, and drink Lao whiskey. What do you think, Kitti?"

"Do you really think Isan people in Bangkok have any money to spend on entertainment?" the money-minded finance man asked during their meeting the next morning.

"Yes, Kitti, I do. Besides, the place I have in mind won't be expensive. I want it to be affordable for the thousands of construction workers, taxi drivers, hotel service workers, and all the other Isan people who come to Bangkok to make money to send home to their families in the villages; I know there will always be a little left over for a modest night out on the town."

Pompam then proceeded to explain how he would go about creating such a place. "I want you to help me develop this project, Kitti, and when it's finished we can train Nuu to be the manager; and I want Att to learn how to take over if one day we have to move Nuu somewhere else."

The young entrepreneur continued, "I think right here on Petchburi Road is the perfect area for such a place. With all the construction going on in the Sukhumvit, Rama IX, Ramkampheng and Silom areas, Petchburi would be the most central location. Besides, I think we can lease some land cheap and put up our own building."

Kitti reflected for a while on all this, remaining silent.

"Start looking for the land tomorrow, Kitti. The facility should be big enough to accommodate four to five-hundred patrons, and there need to be kitchens, service areas, and decent living quarters for the staff — better than here at Paradise City. The building shouldn't be that complicated to build, so I think we can get the whole thing together within about four months."

"Four months!" Kitti screamed. "How am I supposed to get a whole operation like that together, including building a building, in only four months?"

"Don't worry, Kitti, I'm sure it can be done — and I'll help you," Pompam answered calmly. Kitti sat there deep in thought, pondering his latest mission.

"Now, Kitti, I want to talk about your idea of buying some land and building a house up on *Soi* Tonglor," abruptly changing the subject.

"Before we start on that, Pompam, I want to say that for this new Isan entertainment project you should use some of your contacts to find a good banker who will loan us the money. It's time you got your feet wet in the financial community."

Pompam had never thought about borrowing from banks; he had always assumed they would never listen to a buffalo boy from Isan. "That's an excellent idea, Kitti. We don't owe anyone anything right now, and all three of our businesses turn good profits. I don't see why the banks won't cooperate; our money's as good as anybody else's."

"Just one more thing, Pompam. I think for any further projects after the Isan entertainment one, we should start a policy of buying the land, not leasing it. Property values are going up very quickly right now and I really want us to buy some land before it gets too high. This is what brings me to *Soi* Tonglor," Kitti began.

Pompam thought about this and once again saw the good sense in Kitti's feelings about buying land.

"This land thing has been on my mind for quite some time, Pompam. Just look at who is rich right now in this town: mostly the Chinese and a few of the old Thai families. They're the ones that have been buying and holding on to land over the last thirty years. They own blocks and blocks of it right here in the city. We need to start putting some money into real estate ourselves," he said with authority.

Pompam felt that this was probably true, and admired Kitti for thinking ahead.

"*Soi* Tonglor is beginning to develop, Pompam. Lots of rich people are building big homes on that side of Sukhumvit from *Soi* 23 up to Ekamai. Several high-class shops are opening up on Tonglor, and there are plans in the works to start building houses and high-rise condos around there — mainly for *farangs*. While you were in Buriram I made several trips to investigate Tonglor, and I found a few interesting pieces that I want to show you. The land is expensive *now*, but I have no doubt that it will be dearer than gold in just a few years."

"If we're going to have a new house, then we might as well do it right and build in a good neighborhood," responded Pompam, who had just come from his native village where every place was the same: dirt poor.

They located a parcel of land on the east side of Petchburi Road, between Asoke and *Soi* 39, for their Isan-style nightclub, and leased it for fifteen years from the Chinese owner.

Kitti immediately went to work lining up the architect, contractors and various consultants they would need. He also found an artist to paint the murals of scenes from Isan country life that Pompam dreamed up to cover the interior walls. Pompam said, "I want a *total* Isan experience."

In the meantime, Pompam asked his friend, *Khun* Surapong

from the police department, to make an introduction for him to the right banker. When the loan was arranged, Pompam had to secretly pay a large sum of money not only to the banker for getting it approved, but to *Khun* Surapong as well, for making the connection. He learned that extra "commissions" like these were standard procedure in Thailand, but "*Mai pen rai*"; it got the job done.

After much careful looking, Kitti and Pompam also selected a five-*rai* parcel, about two acres, on *Soi* Tonglor that they thought would be perfect for a new house; they bought it on credit for three million *baht*. This was incredibly expensive for them at that time, but Kitti was adamant that land prices would soon skyrocket in the area. "Pompam, it's an investment!" he droned until Pompam, still unconvinced, relented.

The land was on the corner of one of the *sois* that was mid-way between Sukhumvit Road and *Khlong* Saen Sap, a filthy, polluted canal that once flowed with clear water. It had 150 feet of frontage on *Soi* Tonglor itself and continued along the side *soi* to make up the rectangular-shaped five-*rai* parcel. They decided to build the house on two *rai* of the property at the back, down the small *soi*, and let the front three *rai* sit vacant for a while; they would wait for the property values to go up and sell it off when they could make a big profit.

Pompam immediately began his search for an architect who could design the house of his dreams. He finally selected one by driving around Bangkok and observing some of the opulent, Greco-Roman, nouveau riche palaces that were just then coming into vogue, and then found out who had designed the one he liked best.

About six weeks after he returned from Buriram Pompam received a rather nasty letter from an irate *Khun* Direk informing him bluntly that Rattana was pregnant. *Khun* Direk was steaming, and Pompam was stunned. His plans at that point in his life did *not* include a wife and child, and Rattana hadn't even completed her Associate of Arts degree. Pompam knew, however, that he was totally stuck, and the only solution was to go to Isan and marry the girl. If he did otherwise, he would never again be able to show himself in his home village, and his parents would be mortally hurt and lose tremendous "face."

"Oh my Buddha!" Pompam moaned out loud, sitting alone in his apartment over Jamestown; alone for the first evening in months.

He wrote two letters back to Buriram. The first was a very formal one to *Khun* Direk, apologizing for having created the touchy situation, also saying that he would be highly honored if he would grant him permission to marry Rattana. The second letter was to Rattana herself, professing his love and his desire to marry her. He told her to select a date for the wedding as soon as possible, and to let him know how much money he should send her to help pay for it.

"Kitti, what am I going to do now?" Pompam lamented. "I'm not quite twenty-five years old and I have no place to live with a wife and baby. Besides, I just don't want to be married yet; I'm simply not ready!"

"*Mai pen rai*, Pompam," Kitti replied. "You go to the village and do your duty and get married. Send Rattana a monthly allowance, have her continue to go to the university in Khon Kaen, and then after graduation go back and live with her parents for a while. The baby can be born in Isan; no problem. When the house on Tonglor is finally finished, in about a year, Rattana can move to Bangkok and live with you. This will give you more time as a free man, and more time to prepare yourself for married life."

Pompam felt better after listening to Kitti's sensible solution. He reasoned that even after Rattana moved to Bangkok he would still be able to have his own personal life. She would be the "*mia luang*," the major wife, and he would give her all the respect to which that title traditionally entitled her. He would love her, give her money, buy her presents, and make her as happy as he could. But he still deserved to have his "*mia nois*," or minor wives, on the side, and do anything he damn well pleased.

"No wife is ever going to stand in the way of *my* enjoyment," he said defiantly to himself. "I am, after all, a Thai man!"

Two weeks later Pompam, Kitti, Ott, Nuu and Att drove to Buriram in Pompam's Honda for the hastily-arranged wedding; Chai reluctantly stayed back in Bangkok to watch the "store." Pompam had sent Rattana 50,000 *baht* to cover all the expenses, even though he thought *Khun* Direk should have been the one to pay. Given that amount of money, it should be the grandest event the poor village has ever witnessed, Pompam reflected moodily.

They all resented having to take time away from their busy work schedules, so they agreed to drive to Buriram one day, have the wedding the next, and drive back to Bangkok the following day. Rattana wouldn't get a honeymoon, but Pompam would make up for it by inviting her to Bangkok later on. He promised her they would stay at the world-famous Oriental Hotel down on the river for a few days.

That evening upon arrival, Pompam had a meeting with Rattana and a somewhat dour *Khun* Direk to go over plans for the ceremonies and reception the next day. He swore his eternal love to his bride-to-be, and nodded his head up and down to everything she and his future father-in-law told him to do. He couldn't wait to get out of there.

Afterwards, Kitti, Ott, and Pompam's brothers got all of the available boyhood friends together and gave the groom an Isan-style bachelor party. They had the shindig in Pompam's old wooden house so they wouldn't wreck the new one, and the guys got so drunk it looked like a war zone at the end. Everyone was barefoot wearing *sarong* and *pakomah,* loud Isan music blared out, toasts and raucous cheers split the night every minute or two, until Maa finally pulled the plug about 3:00 a.m.

The boys had only been asleep for three hours when they were rudely shaken awake by Maa yelling it was time to get ready. The ceremonies were would begin at seven o'clock when the monks came to the bride's house to start chanting. "Hurry up, you drunken buffaloes!" she screamed.

"Oh, my Buddha!" Pompam groaned, his head throbbing with pain. "I'll never get through this day!"

Kitti, Ott, and Paw seemed to be in even worse shape than Pompam, but they somehow managed to get themselves pulled together and accompanied Pompam to the home of *Khun* Direk. The rest of the brothers and Maa soon followed them; everyone was dressed in their finest clothes — including shoes — and Maa looked almost pretty in a new pink lace blouse, Pompam noticed, in spite of her permanently-stained mouth.

Three tents had been set up in the front yard of the bride's house: One was to shade the nine monks who were seated on a raised dais, the biggest was set up with tables to seat the entire village for the meal, and the third was to hold the bar and the live band. The thought of having to drink more alcohol again that day was enough to make Pompam start to heave.

Pompam's spirits rose, however, when he got his first glimpse of his bride, dressed in a beautiful Western-style wedding gown complete with train. "I really do love this young girl," he said to himself, "so this torture has to be worth it in the end."

She smiled at Pompam when they joined hands in front of the monks, and her wide black eyes clearly showed everyone how much she loved her handsome, but terminally hung-over groom.

The chanting began and the guests seated themselves on mats that had been spread over the ground in the space in front of the monks. They all held their hands in the *wai* position as was the custom, and at least pretended to listen; Pompam thought he would keel over and pass out long before it was all over.

Ott was the official wedding photographer, and he darted from one place to the next snapping photos. Pompam wondered how the poor guy could even manage to look through the lens, knowing that Ott's poor head was in the same condition as his own.

When the chanting mercifully stopped, the bride and groom knelt at a special wedding rail with their hands in the *wai* position over a huge bowl of purple orchids. White string joined the couple together at their heads, and trailed around behind the monks to a Buddha image.

The monks were the first to file by and pour jasmine-scented lustral water over the *waiing* betrothed hands; they were followed by every family member and guest, each person whispering a special good luck wish to the couple as they tipped water from the ceremonial vessel, which was shaped like a nautilus shell. Pompam and Rattana kept their heads bowed and softly thanked each person as they passed. Then more chanting...

Finally, it was time to feed the monks their lunch. The bride and groom had to place the first dishes ceremoniously in front of the holy group, and then members of both families helped serve the rest of the food. When they finished their meal, a new session of chanting began and Pompam was in such agony he thought he would surely die.

The monks were eventually escorted back to the temple after

accepting money, flowers, and orange buckets of necessities from the bride and groom. The last thing *Phra* Prateep did before departing was to sprinkle holy water on the heads of the bridal couple and their guests with a straw broom-like implement. A spray of water hit Pompam directly in the face and he felt momentarily revived.

With the monks out of the way the eagerly-awaited party could at last begin. It wasn't long before Pompam was handed a "pick-me-up" drink, then he and Rattana proceeded to visit each table to formally welcome their guests, and to respond to everyone's merry toasts. Rattana, never a drinker, faked taking small sips with every "*chai-oh!*" or cheers! Pompam, on the other hand, as the macho groom, had to completely drain his glass each time, as did the toasting guest. By the fifth table Pompam realized his hangover was gone and he was already building up to another one; but as he looked down the line at the next fifteen tables he wondered if he would make it to the end. I really should have eaten the rice Maa held under my nose this morning, Pompam thought too late.

Afterwards, Rattana and Pompam finally got to sit down and have a bite to eat, but by this time Pompam had lost his appetite; all he could do was sit there in a stupor and let Rattana feed him like a baby from her plate. The mothers of the bride and groom, Rattana's sisters, and other female guests went over to Pompam's new house and made up the marriage bed in the master bedroom. This was the custom the women enjoyed the most since it gave them a chance to get away from the men and gossip freely. Even though Pompam had finally persuaded his parents to move into the master bedroom, he couldn't begrudge his Mother's wish for her oldest son and his bride to sleep there on their wedding night.

"Please, I beg of you, I've got to lay down!" Pompam looked up and pleaded to the sky, dragging Rattana from the party. Everyone just laughed at his pitiful cry for mercy, and headed for the bar to fill up their glasses.

The inebriated groom followed his bride upstairs to the bridal suite and collapsed on the bed unconscious, fully clothed. Rattana undressed, bathed, put on her new lace nightgown, and laid down next to her whiskey-smelling, snoring new husband.

I am so very happy, she thought to herself; I have the only man

I've ever wanted. Pompam had become the young, handsome prince of their poor Isan village, and on this special night she felt like she had at last become his princess. She felt very blessed by the Lord Buddha, who had obviously also blessed Pompam with exceptional good luck. She believed that Pompam had passed his luck on to her that night at Phanom Rung when he gave her the gold chain and gold-encased Buddha image. She had never once removed that precious amulet, thinking that if she did, it would break the spell that was cast over them that magic evening in the moonlight. She finally closed her eyes and re-lived the wedding in her mind until she drifted off into sleep.

Pompam woke up after a couple of hours, feeling slightly disoriented. He quietly slipped out of bed, took a bath, then laid down in the nude next to his beautiful young wife. He looked at himself and was surprised to see that in spite of all the alcohol he was fully erect. He gently began stroking Rattana's shoulder and she soon awoke, removed her gown, and began to respond to her husband's caresses.

The gentleness that had characterized their love-making during *Loy Kratong* was quickly replaced by an almost athletic physical passion, and Rattana became the aggressor instead of the passive schoolgirl. Pompam was amazed at this change in her behavior, but it pleased him that she took the initiative to try her best to satisfy him in ways he thought she would never even consider.

Pompam was, in time, able to bring Rattana to her first climax, and once she learned how to relax and let herself fully enjoy the experience, she peaked again several more times. At the end, Pompam was exhausted and spent; Rattana, still tingling, was pleased with herself and excited about the thought of many rapturous nights with her special "prince."

"I love you, my husband," she whispered.

"And I love you my Isan Sweetheart," he said soothingly, liking the way those words sounded: Isan Sweetheart. "Don't be angry with me for going back to Bangkok tomorrow. I have much to do right now, and I must build you a house so we can live together forever."

"*Mai pen rai*, Pompam. You will find me to be a very patient wife." Pompam was very glad to hear these words.

Rattana, however, was already thinking about how she could be with her husband sooner. Even though she truly loved Pompam, she felt a nagging fear about him that had troubled her many times before. She worried about the problems he might step into without her — as a result of his boyish and charming over-confidence. She also didn't want to be alone without her husband during the whole term of her pregnancy — and she was curious about all the rumors surrounding Paradise City. If she could just be by his side, she thought, she could look after him and everything would be just fine.

Rattana was also ready to leave her present life behind. While away at school in Khon Kaen she had developed tastes and interests of her own; and though she loved her father dearly, she had grown tired of his over-protectiveness and was eager to move on.

Of all these thoughts, however, Rattana decided to keep quiet — at least for the moment — and be a dutiful, obedient wife.

The following evening back in their office at Paradise City, Pompam, Kitti, Chai and Ott gathered for a "board meeting." Kitti said, "Good news: construction is on schedule, so we can have the grand opening of Isan Sweetheart on your twenty-fifth birthday, Pompam." That their first two openings, and the coming one, fell on Pompam's birthday were lucky omens, they all agreed. They also approved of the name Pompam had just come up with for their new venue.

"I think you should put Pop in charge of Jamestown Pub and the Pratunam bar, Pompam," Ott stated. "I'm getting too busy with my photography business, and I can see that my PR and entertainment-booking duties around here are just about to double."

"Good idea, Ott; I think Pop is the perfect choice. How many boys do we currently have working at the bars now?" Pompam inquired.

"We have seventy-four at Jamestown Pub and another eighty-three at Pratunam," Ott answered. "More and more boys come into the bars every day who want to sell their sex — younger and younger ones. A few years ago I thought boy bars would die out before too long, with our national economy growing like it is. But it seems that just the opposite is true. We even have young boys coming in who come from good families right here in Bangkok! We used to work as bar boys because we were poor and had no other choice."

Pompam shook his head, then turned to Chai and asked, "How

many girls do we have working the massage rooms here at Paradise?"

"Right now, Pompam, we have about sixty, but we could use about fifteen or twenty more good ones, and they're hard to find. Most of the girls that come looking for work these days have already been around too long or have kids back in the village; they all look like they'd whine all night and cause problems. We really need some fresh young ones," he exclaimed, "or we'll soon see business start to fall."

"Well, I think it's ironic that boys are easier to find than girls, but what can I say? *Mai pen rai.* Since we need more girls right now for Paradise City, and we're going to need a whole group of new ones for taxi dancing at Isan Sweetheart, I think we'd better start going out into the provinces and find them ourselves. Right?" They all nodded their heads in agreement. "Besides, I have the notion that our construction-worker customers at Isan Sweetheart will need to get laid from time to time. They can't afford our prices at Paradise City, so where do they go?" Pompam was thoughtfully considering this new concern.

"There are hundreds of low-class brothels scattered all over Bangkok, Pompam," Kitti replied. "That's where our poor Isan brothers have to go when they feel the urge. Those kinds of places charge only fifty to one hundred-fifty *baht* a pop, and they make the girls work twelve to fifteen hours a day and service twenty to thirty customers — like slaves. It's not very glamorous, but it's the only thing the men can afford."

Pompam thought for a moment, considering what Kitti had said. He, himself, didn't much like the idea of virtual slavery, but he knew the character of the average Thai male very well, and he knew that commercial sex was a customary part of their lives. If he didn't capitalize on it others would — and are — and nothing could be done to change the fact, he reasoned.

He finally said, "Kitti, I think we should open our own low-class brothel business, particularly if we're going to start hunting down girls for our other operations. See if you can find a place near Isan Sweetheart that we could pick up for a business like that. Once we've got the right market coming in, we might as well capitalize on it and sell them some sex." The four of them paused to think about this.

"Chai," Pompam continued, "why don't you find out where the best places are to find young girls, and learn how the system works.

I've heard the easiest places to get them are up North."

"I have a friend in Chiang Mai who owns a bar near the Night Bazaar. He's got connections in all the Northern provinces and I'm sure he could help us out," Chai replied.

"Good. Why don't you go see him. If he can do it for us, come back to Bangkok and I'll make a trip back up there with you. Before we spend any money buying young girls I think we should learn everything there is to know about it," said Pompam.

He spoke next to Ott, "I want really top-notch entertainment for Isan Sweetheart's grand opening on my birthday. Get all the top performers you can — including dwarfs and comedians — and see if you can get some of your movie star connections to show up too. Since you're in charge of PR and the guest list be sure to invite all of the Members of Parliament from each of the provinces in Isan; and I know you won't forget our good friends at the police department, our bankers, and the media people. Get a list of Chai's top customers from Paradise City and invite them, and any big customers from the boy bars, too."

"By the way, Pompam, what did you mean about 'taxi dancing' at Isan Sweetheart," Chai asked, bringing up a subject Pompam had just introduced for the first time.

"Most of our customers will be men: men without wives or girlfriends in Bangkok. The guys are going to drink, of course, and when have you ever seen an Isan man drink whiskey and listen to Northeastern music and not get up to dance? We can't have a great big dance floor full of men! Everyone will think we're running a gay bar!" They all laughed out loud at Pompam's irony.

"I want to have about thirty or forty young girls wearing white blouses, skirts and socks — like schoolgirl uniforms — standing by the dance floor, available to be asked for a dance. But in order to dance with the girls, the lonely men have to buy coupons. The coupons can sell for ten *baht* each, and when the girls turn them in at the end of the night they can get three *baht* out of each ten. If they get friendly with a customer and want to go off and sell their bodies they'll have to wait until closing time. We don't want to run out of taxi dancers while we still have customers who want to buy coupons," he explained with a laugh.

Kitti, Ott and Chai shook their heads in amazement at Pompam's novel idea; all of them had been working for a while in the flesh trade, though, and could easily see its potential.

"Okay, boys. I'm tired as hell and I'm going home to bed. Did I say *home*? I look forward to having a *real* home one day so I won't have to climb four flights of stairs and walk past a row of cubicles where I can hear young boys getting poked," Pompam said, amusing the others.

"We can go over the blueprints for the new house tomorrow, Pompam," Kitti grinned.

"I think the plans look great, Kitti, but how much is it going to cost?" Pompam asked admiringly as he viewed the section drawings the next morning.

"Four and a half million, Pompam. The guy wants 500,000 to get started, mainly to buy materials. The rest can be paid out in install-ments until it's paid off."

"Tell the guy I'll pay 500,000 *baht* now to get it started, another two million when the roof is on, and the final two million when it's finished right down to the last nail. That'll make him get the damned thing built faster," Pompam proclaimed.

"Okay, Pompam. I'll pass that along," Kitti replied with a smile. "Where are you going to get the money?"

"From the bank. Where else?" was his reply.

"I'm leaving tomorrow for Chiang Mai, Pompam. I talked to my friend, Nopadon, the one who owns the bar up there. He's got a field trip organized for me to teach me how to buy girls," Chai announced a few days later.

"Bring me home a sixteen-year-old virgin for my birthday, okay?" Pompam called out in jest as Chai was leaving the room.

Ott showed Pompam the list of entertainers that would be performing for the grand opening, as well as the list of those that would be scheduled at Isan Sweetheart for the next three months. "You're really well-organized, Ott; it looks good. By the way, how's Kim these days?"

"She's just fine, Pompam. I'm moving into my new apartment next week and there's a good chance I can get her to join me. Her dear, Chinese parents still won't give us their consent to marry, so she thinks the only way to get them to give it is for us to live in sin for a while," he replied in his humorous way.

"Kim sounds like a smart girl, Ott. Just don't get her pregnant," Pompam warned him with a smirk.

Pompam was so busy he delayed having Rattana come to Bangkok for their honeymoon until the opening of Isan Sweetheart; that was when he really wanted her to be there. The delay really wasn't a big problem for Rattana since she was back in Khon Kaen completing her last term at the university, something that allowed her some freedom of her own and also meant a great deal to her father. The Associate of Arts program had really helped her to grow up, Pompam reflected. He was happy that she had worked to improve and make herself better prepared for her life with him — especially since he suspected they might often be in the public eye. Perhaps he would open a business for her; or maybe she would like to spend her time doing charity things for the community; either one would be good for his image, which mattered a great deal to him.

They greeted each other warmly at Hua Lampong train station, but were restrained by Thai custom from hugging and kissing each other in public; that would have to wait until they were behind closed doors in their hotel room.

Although it was unusual for Thai people to stay at the Oriental Hotel, the staff greeted Pompam and Rattana warmly. He had reserved one of the big corner suites in the new tower, directly over the Chao Phya River, and Rattana took one look at the view and became ecstatic. "Oh, Pompam, I can't believe we're together again — especially *here* in this hotel."

"Don't forget, Rattana, this is our honeymoon and we want it to be something we will always remember," he replied lovingly.

"How could we ever forget it, Pompam. It's not only our honeymoon, but it's your birthday — and a big opening night for you. I'm so excited I can hardly stand it," she giggled as she ran through the suite inspecting every detail.

"Pompam, did you see this? Quick, come and look!"

This was also Pompam's first time in the "number one hotel in the world," as it is often ranked by several sources, and both of them stood in the doorway and stared into the huge bathroom, gray marble covering practically every surface. There was a shower, a giant bathtub, toilet, bidet, double sink, bathrobes, shampoos, all sorts of little bottles all over the counter — and even a telephone. Pompam, with all of his grand ideas, had never thought of having a telephone in the bathroom.

"Our bathroom in the new house will be even more wonderful than this one," Pompam exclaimed, and made a mental note to speak to his contractor.

"Come on Rattana, we're going shopping. We have to get you a new dress to wear tonight," he announced.

"You must be reading my mind, Pompam. I brought with me the best dress I have, but I was afraid it wouldn't be good enough," she said modestly.

"One of the best ladies' shops in Bangkok is in the Plaza right next door to the hotel. Let's go." It pleased Pompam to see the look of pleasure in his beautiful, pregnant wife's face.

Later on, they walked out of the store with a pale blue silk number that concealed Rattana's pregnancy beautifully; Pompam couldn't believe he had just spent 15,000 *baht* on one garment — and another 12,000 on a pair of shoes and a handbag!

They ordered room service, the first time for both of them, and dined on their balcony over-looking the magnificent River of Kings. Pompam thought about the countless times he had commuted back and forth on the noisy long-tail boats between *Wat* Chalaw and the Buddhist school over in Thonburi. This was the first time he had seen the Chao Phya from a high-rise perspective, and it made him feel very happy and pleased with himself.

After their meal they bathed, spent some time making love, then bathed again before getting ready for the party. Pompam put on a suit that had been made for him by a well-known tailor down at River City Complex. He looked in the mirror, straightened his silver and blue silk necktie, and knew he looked great. When Rattana emerged from the dressing room wearing her new designer outfit Pompam's heart nearly stopped; she was his very own beautiful wife, and she looked radiant.

She came toward him smiling and gave him a Thai-style kiss and a big hug. "Thank you for everything, my dear husband. I hope I look good enough to stand by your side this evening."

"You look good enough, Rattana, but actually, not *quite* good enough." The poor girl's joyful expression nearly drooped to the floor when she heard those words.

"I don't think you should wear your gold chain and Buddha amulet tonight, darling. I think you should wear this instead," and produced a black velvet box from his pocket and presented it to her.

Rattana took the box in her trembling hands. When she opened it and saw the large diamond pendant suspended from the white gold chain she thought she would surely die. Pompam reached up and unfastened the simple Buddha amulet and Rattana almost started to protest, remembering the good luck she felt it brought her; she had sworn to herself that she would never remove it. Then she thought, *Mai pen rai*, a diamond has to be even better good luck — it's so much more expensive. Pompam put the diamond on and affixed the clasp at the back of her neck. She turned to him and smiled, then ran to the nearest mirror to have a look at herself, beaming.

"Now do I look good enough, Pompam?" she asked expectantly.

He paused for a moment and then spoke, "It's still not quite right, Rattana. I think you should take off your little gold earrings. They don't match the necklace."

Rattana agreed at once and went to he bathroom to remove them. When she returned for Pompam's inspection, he said, "And now, I think you should replace them with these," and handed to her, one in each hand, a set of diamond studs that weighed a little over one carat each.

"Now I know I must be dead, Pompam. There isn't a girl alive where I come from that has jewelry like this!" she cried.

"Now there is just *one* girl, my dear."

When Pompam and Rattana arrived at Isan Sweetheart there were already a few guests that had gotten there early. The staff was assembled, of course, including Kitti, Ott, Chai, Nuu and Att.

Everyone took a deep breath when the stunning young honeymoon couple walked into the room. Ott rushed up with his camera and said, "This one's for the society page," as he snapped their photo. Chai hurried over at once and congratulated the couple. Kitti, Nuu and Att, who had known Pompam and Rattana all their lives, could only stand there mute and stare at them.

"What's the matter, you guys? Can't you wish me a happy birthday?" Pompam joked.

They began to stammer some greetings. The two younger brothers did a better job of it than Kitti, who couldn't take his eyes off the diamonds, thinking about what Pompam must have paid for them. "Happy Birthday, Pompam; Happy Honeymoon, Rattana," he finally managed to get out with a crackly voice.

The evening turned out to be sensational, and the reception of Pompam's new entertainment concept was better than anyone had dared anticipate. Pompam and Rattana were like magnets to all of the guests; everyone wanted to meet these heretofore unknown newlyweds, and the photographers from the media outlets Ott invited had a field day.

Pompam was proud of his new wife at this, their first public appearance together, and he had her stand beside him when he went up on the stage to welcome his guests and proclaim the opening of the new establishment.

"I would like you all to meet my new bride," he said to the crowd, "*Khun* Rattana!" Everyone cheered and applauded until Pompam signaled for the music to start. He and Rattana descended to the dance floor and Pompam extended his arms to her in the traditional invitation to the *ram wong*. The two of them, smiling, danced the *ram wong* together under the roving spotlight to wildly enthusiastic cheers. No one in the room could take their eyes off of them.

Spontaneously, Pompam motioned to Rattana to follow him and they moved toward the Police General and his wife, their highest-ranking guests. In the style of the Isan custom Pompam invited the general's wife to dance with him, and Rattana invited the General, himself; the older couple were both surprised and delighted. Pompam motioned for everyone else to follow their lead, and soon the dance floor was crowded to capacity. Seeing so many people uninhibitedly dancing the *ram wong* to the sounds of traditional Isan instruments (amplified over what must have been the best P.A. system in town) made Pompam know for sure he had a hit.

For a short moment in time, for that one evening at least, Pompam had turned being born in Isan into something to be proud of, not ashamed. One look at Pompam and Rattana convinced everyone in the room that all people from the Northeast were *not* just dirt-poor rice farmers with dark brown skin, uneducated, possessing no skills or backgrounds. The politicians that had been invited from that region were proud to see Pompam drawing attention in such a positive way to the culture of their native land. They all wanted to meet and congratulate the attractive young man, and a few of them hoped they could draw him into their various causes when he had accumulated a few more years.

The room was filled with fragrant bouquets of flowers and other gifts that people had brought for the opening and for Pompam's birthday. Dozens of bottles of imported whiskey and mountains of Isan food were consumed by the celebrants. Everyone was enthusiastic about Pompam's novel idea of the taxi dancers. No coupons were sold that night, of course, but all of the young girls were kept busy throughout the evening, and they enjoyed themselves, for that one night only, as if they, too, were invited guests.

The evening drew to a close with the unanimous opinion that Pompam and the boys had a major success on their hands. Nuu, having been introduced as the manager, suddenly had great "face." Pompam was pleased to find out that his faith in both Nuu and Att had not been unfounded. "You worked your asses off tonight, and I love you for it!" Pompam complimented them as he and Rattana said their good-byes.

"I was so very proud of you, Rattana. You were such a natural at being my hostess. I just don't know where you get that from," Pompam said sincerely when they were unwinding back at their Oriental suite.

"It's easy to be your hostess, Pompam. All I have to do is stand by your side and follow your lead. I also paid attention while I was at the University; it really paid off, I think," she added confidently.

They were both exhausted from the long day. Rattana had

started out early in the morning from Buriram on the train — and she was pregnant. Pompam had worked hard since just after dawn.

They slept until nearly noon the next morning, neither of them wanting to leave the soft warmth of the other. Rattana stroked and teased Pompam's body until he became aroused, and they indulged themselves in a long session of love-making. "This is what honeymoons are for, Pompam. Are you having a good time?"

Pompam made a few phone calls to "the boys" that afternoon, but was determined to stay uninvolved with business until after Rattana had gone back to Buriram. During those phone calls he was given glowing reviews of the party, and a short briefing on some projects that he said could wait until their next meeting, which would be in four days.

Rattana and Pompam never took the car out of the garage the entire time. They took massages in the health club across the river, dined in their room or in the restaurants, and took walks through the lovely, romantic gardens behind the old colonial-style wing of the hotel.

One evening at sunset they got the boatman at the pier to hire a long-tail boat for a private cruise down the river and *khlongs*. Rattana enthusiastically shared Pompam's excitement about the *Chao Phya*, and they had a marvelous time observing the same timeless scenes of Thai history and riverside life that Pompam had learned to love so much during his student days.

Rattana begged to see the building site of the new house on *Soi Tonglor*, but Pompam persuaded her to wait until it was finished, saying he wanted to surprise her. After the diamond pendant surprise she had no problem whatsoever waiting for any others that Pompam had to offer. They generally relaxed, enjoyed their time together, and made love often like any normal honeymoon couple.

Pompam felt sad when he said good-bye to Rattana on the train. He had gotten used to her company, to her sleeping beside him, and he was reluctant to let her go. Rattana wanted very much to stay as well, and she tried very hard to be a good sport and conceal her impatience; but she also knew the time wasn't yet right for her to move — even though she couldn't stop worrying about leaving her husband alone in Bangkok.

"*Mai pen rai*, Pompam. The baby will be born in a few months and the house will be ready before too long. It's better if we wait until then," she said to him with a forced smile. Pompam realized how lucky he was to have such a loving, sympathetic mate.

"Greetings, friends," beamed Pompam as he walked into his office at Paradise City where they were all gathered to await his arrival.

"Funny, but you don't look any different, Pompam, after five nights at the Oriental," Kitti teased. "I thought you would have at least grown a bigger nose after all that *farang* food."

"I only ate *farang* food two nights, Kitti, and I couldn't stand it. Rattana enjoyed it, though, so I guess it was okay," he replied, laughing.

"So, how has business been at Isan Sweetheart since the opening?" Pompam inquired, getting down to business.

"The word seems to have gotten around very quickly about our 'Little bit of Isan right here in Bangkok' and we've been packed every night. Just as you predicted we're getting the construction workers, tuk-tuk and taxi drivers, hotel service workers — mostly single men. Believe it or not, we've also gotten several groups of Isan people with big money. There seems to be quite a few of those, surprisingly, and they're all coming out of the woodwork. We've had rich men bringing in their *mia nois*, businessmen bringing in their office staff. We've had lots of policemen, and they've even paid their own bills; your friend, *Khun* Surapong must have passed the word around the force. We sold nearly 1,000 bottles of whiskey in four nights, can you believe it?" Kitti answered.

"How do they like the taxi dancers?" Pompam asked, curious.

"The poor little girls are completely worn out by the end of each night; most of them are only fifteen or sixteen years old, you know. They have nothing to complain about, though, as each girl has collected at least one hundred 10-*baht* coupons each night which nets her 300 *baht* in commissions."

"Maybe we're giving them too much," Pompam remarked.

"Let them make some money, Pompam. Otherwise they'll start selling their bodies to customers after hours even more than they already are," said the finance man with a big grin.

"What about a location for our low-class brothel, Kitti, have you found anything?" Pompam asked.

"Just down the side *soi* behind Isan Sweetheart, near that smelly *khlong*, is an old run-down curtain motel. It needs quite a bit of work, but I met with the owner yesterday and we can rent the whole thing for only 25,000 *baht* a month. It has forty rooms, a small lobby, and an old coffee shop that hasn't been used in years."

"Go ahead and take it, Kitti. It sounds like a good deal if we don't have to spend too much money on renovations; the location is perfect," Pompam replied. "But we can only make money if we have the girls to work there. Chai, what did you find out up north?" Pompam asked.

"Sometime in the next few days when you have time, I want to take you up to Chiang Mai for a meeting with *Khun* Nopadon, my friend I told you about. He can get us fifteen top-quality girls who can work in Paradise City right away. We'll have to pay him a commission of 5,000 *baht* each, plus the expenses for moving them to Bangkok; but they're already working in first-class places in Chiang Mai, so they're experienced and won't cause us any trouble."

"Sounds good so far, Chai; what else?" asked Pompam.

"Nopadon tells me we can get an unlimited supply of second-string young girls from the hilltribes and northern provinces. He can also get us some from Burma and Southern China — illegals smuggled over the border. These girls will cost us 10,000 *baht* each — which will go to their families who'll sell them to us outright. But the girls will have to work off the 10,000 *baht* as a debt to us before we pay them anything at all for their work. I figure that if we credit them ten *baht* per customer, then they'll have to take care of 1,000 customers before they start getting paid. These girls are either underage and/or illegal, most of them, so our payments to the police each month will be high.

"If we get that motel with forty rooms, then I suggest we get forty girls to start with; that way they'll each have their own room to live and work in. That comes out to 400,000 *baht* in girl costs to start up, but when you figure that each one will owe us 1,000 services before we have to start paying her, that's 100,000 *baht* at 100 *baht* per "service" — times forty girls — that equals *four million baht*," Chai concluded, almost out of breath; the enormity of the figures astounding Pompam, Ott, and Kitti, who sat there trying to comprehend.

Pompam hesitated a moment as he considered what might be

called the "morality" of the proposition. Thoughts came to his mind about things *Phra* Prateep and *Phra* Asoka had said to him long ago about compassion. What will this do to my karma? he asked himself. After a few seconds he justified his decision to move forward with the project by telling himself that the young girls would eventually be better off, and that they were performing a service for their families. He, himself, had made sacrifices for the folks back home; these girls would be no different.

"Okay, Chai and Kitti, let's get all this rolling as soon as possible. Every night Isan Sweetheart is open and there are no young girls to sell next door, we're losing money," Pompam said as he gave his approval. "Realistically, when can the motel be ready and the girls be in Bangkok ready to work?"

"If we started right away on the motel and you go with me to Chiang Mai, Pompam, I don't see why we can't get started in one month," Chai summed up. "One other thing, Pompam," he continued, "you asked me to bring you a sixteen-year-old virgin for your birthday. Did you forget?"

Pompam's eyes brightened up with surprise, "Yes, Chai, I did forget. Did you think I was serious?"

"She's waiting in Chiang Mai for your inspection, Pompam. She's truly an exquisite specimen of the northern Thai beauty: pale white skin, dark eyes, small slim body, and she only just turned sixteen. I picked her out myself, Pompam, and I've already paid half the money to the family so they won't sell her to anyone else before we get up there. Believe me, Pompam, this one is *very* special; I think you'll probably want to get her a small room somewhere in Bangkok and keep her," Chai continued, a mischievous grin turning up the corners of his mouth.

"How can you talk to Pompam about buying a sixteen-year-old virgin in Chiang Mai when he's just returned not two hours ago from his honeymoon?" Ott asked Chai with more than just a hint of disapproval in his voice.

"I'm only following the boss's orders," Chai answered demurely.

"What's wrong with me having a *mia noi* now that I'm officially married?" was Pompam's reply, showing no hint of being disturbed by questions of morality. "And if I'm going to have one why shouldn't it be a different *type* from the one I just married? Let's go to Chiang Mai day after tomorrow, Chai. Kitti, you get a bunch of cash ready for Nopadon and we'll take it with us." Kitti gave him a funny look, but said nothing.

"How is Pop working out as the new manager of the boy bars, Ott?" Pompam asked, on to a different subject.

"He's taken on the responsibilities really well, Pompam. We have nothing to worry about there, except that he has some promotional ideas I'm not too thrilled about. He wants to enter five of his best boys in the 'Man of the Year' contest in Pattaya, and wants us to be their sponsors. By 'us' I mean Isan Sweetheart and Paradise City. I'm worried that it just might connect us to the boy bar business a little bit too closely," Ott replied.

Pompam paused to think about the idea for a moment. "I don't think it's anything to worry about, Ott. The only people who would find out the boys have worked in bars will be the wealthy gay customers who'll want to buy them and put them on yearly contracts. I think it's good advertising when you think of how popular those contests are," Pompam responded. Ott was surprised by Pompam's reaction, even though it was true that teenagers and adults of both sexes — even parents and grandparents — flocked to these competitions by the thousands, and the winners became instant national celebrities.

"Are we ready to get started on the house on *Soi* Tonglor?" Pompam turned and asked Kitti.

"The contractor has reluctantly agreed to your terms and can start as soon as you pay him the first 500,000 *baht*," he replied

"Give him the money right away, Kitti, so he can get going. Rattana and our baby won't be able to move to Bangkok until it's finished, and I miss my new wife already," he said sentimentally.

"Maybe you won't miss her so much if you buy yourself a *mia noi* in Chiang Mai," Kitti joked in return.

PART III
BODY AND SOUL

Chapter 12

Pompam had never been up to Chiang Mai and he looked forward to seeing the former northern capital which produced, reputedly, the most beautiful girls in Thailand.

Khun Nopadon met Chai and Pompam at the airport and drove them to the Suriwongse Hotel, just opposite the Night Bazaar. On the way, Pompam admired the ancient walled-in city, surrounded by a moat, and was fascinated by the golden spires of temples that seemed to tower over everything. He couldn't possibly have foreseen that just a few years later insensitive developers would completely desecrate Chiang Mai, building high-rises that put the temples in their shadows and alter the character of the mystical old city forever.

When they met for drinks in the lobby after they checked in, Pompam had mixed feelings about *Khun* Nopadon, the man who was to be their primary supply source for young girls. Nopadon, who was in his late thirties, was pleasant enough, and had a bright, eager smile; but Pompam couldn't help but sense a certain hardness, perhaps even cruelty, in his dark eyes. He decided he would ask Chai more about his background later.

"*Khun* Chai tells me that you have approved an initial order of fifteen experienced girls for your massage parlor, and another forty village girls for your secondary operation, *Khun* Vichai. I've arranged for ten of the fifteen massage girls to meet you at my bar in about an hour. If they meet with your approval, then perhaps you'll trust me regarding the other five — sight unseen. I can assure you these are only best-quality girls who are working now in first class places in Chiang Mai. Tomorrow we will go to some villages up north near the Burmese border where you can inspect some of the young ones more suitable for your motel. The countryside in Chiang Mai is lovely, and I am sure you will not be bored," Nopadon explained.

"What about the girl I picked out for *Khun* Vichai, Nop? When can he see her?" Chai asked.

"I am having her brought down to Chiang Mai from her village in Chom Thong district tomorrow evening. If *Khun* Vichai accepts her, fine; if he doesn't, I know someone else who will want her. You saw her yourself, Chai, and you know she's exceptional," Nopadon answered, all business. Pompam felt uncomfortable hearing the girl talked about like this — even though he hadn't even seen her yet.

"Last time I paid you a non-refundable half price of 20,000 *baht*. Have you already paid off the rest to her family?" Chai asked.

"Everything's been settled with the family. As I said, if *Khun* Vichai turns her down after he 'initiates' her I already have another buyer," Nopadon replied.

"Do you mean to tell me that this girl will cost me 40,000 *baht*? We're getting all fifteen massage girls for 45,000 *baht*!" Pompam couldn't believe such a high figure for only one girl.

"The price is high, *Khun* Vichai, but then so is the perfect ruby that comes from across the border in Burma," Nopadon responded. "Just wait and see her for yourself; I don't think you will be disappointed — or find the price too high."

They finished their drinks and walked over to Nopadon's bar where they were to meet ten future employees for Paradise City.

Their eyes slowly adjusted to the dim light as they entered the wooden, *Lanna*-style building, removing their shoes at the door. "*Lanna*" was the name of the ancient royal kingdom of Chiang Mai, and its distinctive, delicate style of architecture and decoration can be seen nearly everywhere in the city. Nopadon seated them on the floor at a low, carved table in a secluded corner — on piles of cushions covered in blue and white homespun cotton called "*ikat*." Nopadon ordered drinks and excused himself.

"What makes me think there's something really bad in Nopadon's past, Chai? Something that damaged him and caused him to be *jai dum*?" Pompam asked. The phrase "*jai dum*," or black heart, is used to describe someone who is very mean or cruel.

"I'm surprised you sensed that, Pompam," Chai responded. "Nopadon conceals his heart quite well from most people. His grandfather was the last King of the Shan State, that region of Burma just over the border from here. When Nopadon was very young he hid and watched as his entire family was destroyed by the Burmese nationals who sacked their compound. Later on the area was re-captured by the Shan warlords who trade in opium. I think Nopadon still helps these politically-motivated drug traders — who are very dangerous — by smuggling supplies up to them. He has seen much killing in his life and yes, his heart is hard."

Pompam reflected on this information, and in a few minutes Nopadon returned to them with four very beautiful young girls, all very heavily made up for night time. They smiled and *waied* to Pompam and Chai and then seated themselves next to them and began massaging their shoulders. Pompam smiled and signaled his approval to *Khun* Nopadon. Four more girls arrived, and the first four *waied* and departed. The second four were even more stunning than the first group. Pompam sat there imagining the happy, satisfied customers they would have at Paradise City, and all the money they would make from the practiced services of these lovely girls.

Two more girls showed up and Nopadon excused himself, telling the other four girls to follow him. These last two were even more exceptional than the first eight, and they were dressed in kimonos made out of the finest patterned silk Pompam had ever seen: one in shocking pink, the other in celladon. The girl in pink sat next to Pompam, the other crouched beside Chai. Suddenly, in unison, both of them unfastened their robes and exposed nakedness underneath, the two men gaping in surprise. Each one put a hand on one of the men's crotches, smiling, stroking. The low table between them hid the boys' regions below the waist as the girls unzipped their trousers and gave freedom to their instant erections. The two demoiselles disappeared under the table, and the young men looked across at each other with embarrassed, bulging eyes, trying not to laugh or breathe too hard, the girls performing special acts of magic until the boys reached their natural conclusion.

After these last two *waied* and departed Nopadon returned with a waiter carrying another round of drinks. "Do you trust me to select the last five without your final approval?" he asked with a wide grin.

"I'm not sure, *Khun* Nopadon," Pompam replied. "If they're any better than the last two then I think I absolutely *must* see them." They all laughed.

"Can I take you two gentlemen out to dinner tonight? I know

a wonderful place the tourists don't know about that's on a small, private lake on the road to Lamphun Province. We can take a few ladies with us if you like," Nopadon offered.

"I'll say 'yes' to dinner, *Khun* Nopadon, but 'no' to bringing girls along. It might not be a good idea if we talk business, and besides, after the visit by the last two, I don't think we'll need female company tonight. Thank you very much just the same." Chai readily agreed with Pompam as they grinned at one another.

The restaurant that evening was indeed lovely — lit only by torches and candles — and the two young men from Bangkok thoroughly enjoyed the Northern Thai food. They especially loved the aromatic *"khao soi,"* a northern curried noodle dish with chicken and pickled vegetables, and the *"nam prik num,"* a red-hot chili paste made with a combination of specially roasted chilies and shallots. The service was provided by barefoot waiters and waitresses dressed in ethnic northern costumes made from local textiles. Musicians were seated on a stage floating on the lake, performing country songs from the region, accompanied by folk dancing.

"Don't expect the merchandise you inspect tomorrow to be like what you saw today, *Khun* Vichai. We are going to some of the poorest villages in the north, and the hilltribe people who live there still wear their native clothing and speak only their own dialects. The families have too many children to feed, and their daughters are useless now that growing poppies is illegal, and they are no longer needed for the harvest," Nopadon explained.

"Do you want us to pay for the girls tomorrow in full, or just make a deposit?" Pompam inquired.

"It's better to pay for them outright and take them with us as we go. Otherwise, the families will just keep the deposit money, move away so we can't find them, and re-sell the girls. I've hired two vans; one will be used to keep them in as we buy them along the way. I'll store them in a secure place I have in Chiang Mai until you're ready, and then I'll ship them down to Bangkok all at one time on a chartered bus," answered Nopadon.

The following morning Nopadon picked up Chai and Pompam at seven o'clock. They drove northwards toward the Burmese border through some of the most scenic mountain countryside in all of Thailand. They passed through areas where a few giant teak trees still grew, miraculously escaping the vicious ax of Thai logging companies that had nearly devastated the region ten years before. Nopadon said that new laws made it illegal to harvest hardwoods any more, but there was a constant conflict between the under-staffed, easily-bribed forestry officials, and poachers who seemed determined not to leave one tree standing.

"The first village is about ten miles down this dirt road," Nopadon informed them after driving for about an hour and a half. "There are three girls there that I have already negotiated for."

When they arrived at the small compound Pompam reflected that his community in Isan seemed wealthy compared to what he saw before him. There was no electric power, and the only water supply appeared to be from a tiny brown stream. The women mostly wore brightly-colored, embroidered costumes of red, blue and black cotton, and elaborate head-dresses, necklaces and bracelets made of silver coins. According to Nopadon, the amount of silver they wore indicated their status in the tribe, and represented their entire wealth.

The family was already out front waiting for them when they drove up to the first house. They got out of the car and Nopadon spoke to them in their native dialect. He turned to Pompam and said, "There's the girl — over there," and he pointed.

Pompam looked in the direction Nopadon indicated and saw a small dirty child sitting on the stoop of the tiny shack. "That one?" Pompam exclaimed in disbelief. "She doesn't look old enough to be out of primary school, much less work where she's going. How old is she? Eleven?"

"According to her parents she's fifteen, but who can say for sure? As you can see, *Khun* Vichai, the people are small in stature here, maybe it's their diet, I don't know. Here, take a good look at her." Nopadon led Pompam over.

Nopadon lifted up her chin so Pompam could see the face. He moved the lips aside so they could examine her straight, white teeth, not yet stained by beetle-nut as was her mother's. "Stand up," he spoke roughly to the girl who silently obeyed. By Pompam's estimation she stood about five feet tall, and was rail thin. "Does she know what's going on here?" Pompam asked Nopadon.

"She knows she has to go to Bangkok to do her duty for her family. She's the oldest of five, which is just too many for the parents to care for. She's been told she'll be a waitress in a coffee shop. Once the money is exchanged she'll know there is no turning back until she's paid off the debt," Nopadon explained. "This has all become quite common here."

Pompam remained silent for a few moments and just kept looking at the child until Nopadon said almost impatiently, "*Khun* Vichai, do you want her or not? If so, please pay the father. He's the one standing over there in the blue and red *pakomah*."

Pompam didn't much like the way he felt as he handed over the 10,000 *baht* to the girl's eager father. The man couldn't have been more than forty years old, but to Pompam he looked at least sixty-five.

Nopadon read his mind and said, "It's the opium, *Khun* Vichai. He's probably been smoking it since his teens. It's very bad for the health and they don't eat right, even if they could afford to," Nopadon continued. "They can't grow poppies on this side of the border any more, so these people go back and forth through the forests to get their opium. Trust me, *Khun* Vichai, this father knows exactly what's going to happen to his daughter, but he would rather have the 10,000 *baht*."

Nopadon spoke to the girl and told her to get her things and go wait in the van. She obediently did as she was ordered and barely even looked up to say good-bye to her parents and younger siblings. It seemed that her heart was already hardened towards the world, but Pompam knew that it would have to get even harder if she were to survive her new life in Bangkok. For a moment he asked himself if he should really be doing this ugly business; once again he thought that if it wasn't he, it would be someone else; the girls' parents would see to that.

Nopadon led them to another house a few hundred feet away. The parents of the next girl, who looked fourteen, but whose father assured the men she was sixteen, were almost duplicates of the first set. Pompam began to wonder if the heads of all these families were fatally addicted to opium.

He knew from reading the newspapers that the government had been trying to persuade the hilltribe people to grow vegetables and other cash crops for years. In some districts the programs had succeeded, but in others the poor people merely took the money the government gave them and didn't grow anything at all. Young mothers with tiny, filthy babies would sometimes wind up on the sidewalks and pedestrian overpasses of Bangkok as beggars. Many of the male members of the families — and sometimes the female as well — would fall into the opium habit which would disable them for life, eventually destroying them.

Pompam paid off the parents of the second girl and watched as she reluctantly marched off towards the waiting van. It almost made him physically sick to think of her future, but he pushed the thought aside. Then he gave the bag of money to Chai and told him to pay off the parents from then on. He simply didn't want to do it again.

They collected the third girl from that village under similar circumstances as the first two, and then moved on deeper into the forest to another small hamlet, about ten miles past the first one.

Nopadon explained that the people there were of a different tribe. They were migratory primitives, basically hunters and gatherers; they didn't stop and put down roots long enough to grow anything. They built their houses out of logs and branches they cut down in the forests, and covered them with leaves for sun and rain protection. It was said that when the leaves on the roofs of the houses turned yellow the people would pack up their meager belongings and move on to another spot. This is why they were given the name, "The Children of the Yellow Leaves." The problem for these unfortunate people lied in the fact that they were running out of room, running out of land upon which to move. Civilization was hemming them in on all sides and their way of life was quickly dying out forever.

Nopadon didn't speak the dialect of these people, and apparently no one else did either except for the people themselves. Their numbers had simply become too small for anyone to bother to learn their language. The village headman spoke the dialect of the Akha hilltribe, which Nopadon understood, so they conducted their business in that tongue.

"There is only one girl here that's coming with us," Nopadon said to Pompam. "She ran off and hid when she heard us coming, so they have to go and get her from the forest; she might be a difficult one to tame in Bangkok."

Pompam shuddered at the thought of having to "tame" girls in order to get them to work. Was he going to wind up running a prison? he wondered.

The village headman finally showed up with the girl, her father tightly holding her arm on one side, and he on the other. Pompam looked at her face and saw the hatred streaming from her eyes as she glared directly up at him. The father turned the young girl towards him and slapped her hard in the jaw. Then he spoke rapidly and angrily to her in their unintelligible dialect. The girl, who looked to be about seventeen, hung her head, then meekly followed her father to the waiting van and got aboard without a single glance backwards. She apparently had no possessions whatsoever, and brought nothing with her other than the ragged, filthy clothes she wore.

Chai paid the money and they moved on. On their way to the next village Nopadon said, "Of the forty girls we'll get, you can expect about ten of them to either run away or get sick within the first thirty days. Not sick so much their bodies, but in their minds. They get sort of 'distracted.' *Mai pen rai.* You'll see what I mean."

"So does this mean you'll have to send us a new batch of girls every thirty days?" Pompam inquired.

"Sometimes yes, sometimes no; it all depends. Just keep in touch with me and call when you need some fresh ones," Nopadon replied with no emotion.

They visited three more villages that day and collected a total of fifteen girls. Nopadon explained that it would take them two more days to gather up the other twenty five. The next day they would illegally cross into Burma where they would get about a dozen more. Those would be both Burmese and Chinese girls that had either been captured or sold to soldiers who worked for the drug warlords. "Tomorrow night we'll stay in Chiang Rai so we won't have to back-track to Chiang Mai; it will make our work easier the following day," Nopadon informed them.

"Are any of the girls over eighteen?" Pompam inquired.

"Of the total forty, about a third *claim* they are over eighteen, but none are supposed to be over twenty," answered Nopadon.

Pompam was thinking that they may have miscalculated the

amount of money they would have to pay the police each month, having so many girls under the legal age. *Mai pen rai*, he thought; paying the police is like paying rent and a little tax; it can't be avoided.

When they got back to the hotel that evening Pompam and Chai were totally exhausted. "So how did you like your first day out in the field, *Khun* Vichai?" Nopadon asked.

"Sightseeing was lovely, *Khun* Nopadon, but it makes me sad to find out there are people in Thailand who are even poorer than in Isan," he replied.

"I've been to parts of Isan that are just about the same. Up in Loei Province, in the mountains, you'll find Isan villages that are just as poor as the ones we saw today. They don't hesitate to sell their daughters up there, either. If you want some of those, just let me know."

"I would just as soon stick to northerners for the time being," Pompam responded, not wishing to think about buying girls in this manner from his native region. Plenty of the girls at Paradise City and boys at his boy bars were originally from Isan, but none of them had been bought, he reasoned; they all did what they did of their own free will, just as he, himself, once had.

"I'll pick you up again at seven o'clock; we'll need an early start to cover all the ground we need to tomorrow. Be prepared for a unique experience up in Burma," Nopadon said, giving them an ironic smile.

Pompam took a long, hot shower and reflected on the day. He almost felt sorry for the young girls they had bought that were now locked up somewhere in Chiang Mai. On the other hand, their parents obviously need money in order to survive, and those girls were their only assets. Everyone has to make sacrifices in this life in order to provide for the family — which comes first. He, himself, had sold his own body for a year and a half, and provided sex to anyone who wanted him. He had endured the indignities of being violated by wealthy, drunken customers who fucked him one night, and then some other young boy the next.

"*Mai pen rai*," he said to himself, "I am one of the lucky ones — perhaps the luckiest in the history of the trade — to come out of it unharmed and rich. The Lord Buddha taught me to provide for my family first and I did; these young girls are only doing the same thing."

Pompam turned down the covers and lay naked on his bed,

relaxing, drifting from one thought to the next, when there was a sharp knock on his door. He wrapped a bath towel around his waist and opened it. Chai was standing there with the most incredible-looking young girl he had ever seen in his life. It was as if all the girls they had collected that day weren't even a part of the same species as the porcelain-skinned creature in front of him.

"Pompam, this is Joy, your sixteen-year-old virgin. She speaks the Chiang Mai dialect, but if you speak Thai slowly to her I think she'll be able to understand you," Chai explained, smiling as he saw Pompam's delighted expression.

"This is *Khun* Vichai, Joy, but I think he'll want you to call him 'Pompam,'" Chai said as he introduced them.

The young girl, who wore no trace of make-up, bowed her head, *waied* very politely, and timidly gave Pompam a half-smile. She stood about five-foot six, quite tall for a northern girl, and had thick, long black hair that reached nearly to her waist. There were tiny gold earrings in her delicate pierced ears, and she had on a modest white blouse, and a skirt of dark blue silk with a hem-line border of light blue and burgundy. On her small feet she wore shoes made of thick, black homespun Thai cotton. A small ceramic Buddha image hung from a dark cord around her neck. Pompam thought she was the most exquisite thing he had ever seen.

"Why don't you get to know Joy for a while, Pompam, then call me later in my room and we can go out for dinner. I'll be waiting," Chai said as he eased his way out of the room and winked at his friend.

When the door closed Pompam suddenly realized he was standing there wearing only a towel. He momentarily felt embarrassed in front of the innocent-looking young girl, but then he remembered that she knew exactly why she was there.

From her point of view she saw Pompam as an extremely handsome young man with gentle eyes. Since her fate was inevitable and she had absolutely no choice in the matter, she would rather have someone like Pompam buy her than an old, smelly village headman who would only want her for breeding sons. She decided to do her best to try to please the dark-eyed, muscular man standing in front of her so he would want to keep her for himself. If she were good to him, he might be good to her in return, and perhaps even give her money so she could help provide schooling for her two younger brothers at home.

In broken Thai she told Pompam that he looked tired and in need of a massage. She gave him a tentative, but warm smile, and asked him to lay down and relax. She would have a bath and join him in a few minutes.

Pompam laid on the bed and closed his eyes. Here he was, he thought to himself, a newly-married man with a baby on the way, yet undeniably attracted to this beautiful young flower from "The Rose of the North," as Chiang Mai was called in the tourist magazines.

Just as he was about to drift off to sleep he felt smooth, cool hands on his shoulders, gently massaging him. She obviously had no experience or training in this art, and he had been guaranteed that she had never been intimate with another man. But he sensed promise in her youthful hands, and he knew that she could be instructed by the mamasan at Paradise City to expertly and with strength, relax his body and give him pleasure.

She removed the towel that was still around Pompam's middle and straddled him as he lay on his stomach. Pompam remembered that it had been the same with Num, the prostitute in Buriram, when he had lost his own virginity. Joy modestly still wore the white blouse, but Pompam could feel the nakedness of her loins as she sat gently on his bare buttocks. He could feel her long silky hair as it fell loose on his back, sending shivers up and down his spine as she moved back and forth, rubbing against his bare skin with her own. He quickly became rock-hard, as if he hadn't had sex in a year.

She moved down to his legs and kneaded the muscles in his calves and thighs, gently and instinctively brushing up against his inflamed private parts with her fingertips as she did so.

When Pompam could stand no more, he turned over on his back and gazed up at her innocent, beautiful face. He unbuttoned and removed the white blouse and admired worshipfully the small, perfect breasts, tiny waist, and completely hairless body.

He drew her down to him and they kissed. He stroked and explored her with his free hand while he held her fast to him with the other. She seemed so small and fragile, like a child's doll, he thought, but then remembered that she *was* only a child. He could tell that she was doing her best to keep calm and be graceful at the same time, as she let herself submit to his body and his passion.

"Don't be afraid, Joy; I won't hurt you. I will always keep you close to me and protect you," he said to her, already knowing that he would, in fact, pay the balance and keep her.

She smiled at him and nodded, telling him with her eyes that he now had her trust. He felt her center and knew at once that she truly was a virgin; he began kneading, preparing her. He would go gently, just as he had done with Rattana, as he took from her the maidenhood that her father and mother were so willingly selling him. He thought to himself how happy he was to pay for this precious purity, even twice or three times the price if it was asked of him.

She cried out once, but softly, as he finally penetrated her flesh. Then they moved in unison as Pompam took his pleasure, slowly at first, and then faster. He held her close to him and spoke soothingly, breathlessly, as he reached his climax, shaking. Then he held her, still inside, while he waited for his heartbeat to return to normal. She smiled at him and one small tear ran down her cheek. Pompam didn't know if the tear was from pain or from sorrow, knowing that she had abandoned forever the little girl that had only an hour before walked into the room.

They showered and dressed, and Pompam called Chai to tell him they were ready for dinner. He smiled at Joy and thought about how appropriate her name was. She would surely bring him joy, and he decided he would take care of her, buy her presents, and pay over and over again the price of her virtue for the pleasure she would bring him. Pompam couldn't help but feel a pang or two of guilt when he remembered the sad fates of the poor girls they had bought that day, and the good luck that by comparison had befallen Joy. Yes, he thought, she was truly lucky to have him be the one to buy her; he was a good man, and he felt he truly deserved to own this treasure.

They went down and met Chai in the lobby and decided to have their dinner at the Thai restaurant in the hotel. Chai was happy to see Pompam beaming as the maitre d' escorted them to their table; he noticed that Joy was relaxed and seemed to be in a good mood as well. She was quiet during most of the meal and let the two men talk, but she smiled often, and fed Pompam bits of choice morsels from her plate with her own hand. Pompam was too preoccupied to notice, but Chai clearly saw the looks of jealousy and contempt on the faces of the waiters as they served them. They were obviously thinking, how dare these rich Thais from Bangkok come up to Chiang Mai and take from the poor Chiang Mai men the most beautiful girls!

"Chai, please make sure the girl's parents get the balance of the money as soon as possible if Nopadon hasn't already paid them. Clear it with the hotel management that Joy will be staying in my room until we return, and to let her sign for food and anything else she wants," Pompam instructed.

After dinner the three of them went shopping in the Night Bazaar and Pompam bought the young girl several articles of clothing and a small gold chain from which to hang her Buddha amulet. He couldn't help but remember the fine gold chain and Buddha image he had bought for Rattana, and the way it had gleamed in the *Loy Kratong* moon. Joy was thrilled with the presents and the attention she was getting from the kind young man who was to own her, and who was saving her from poverty and a sad life with some nasty old man who would surely abuse her.

Back at the hotel room Pompam phoned up Kitti at Paradise City and asked him to find a suitable apartment for he and Joy to live in when they returned to Bangkok. Kitti wasn't too happy at the thought of living above Jamestown Pub alone until the new house on Tonglor was completed. But he was careful to keep the disappointment out of his voice and convey only the deep happiness he felt for Pompam — or at least *said* he felt. "Why is Pompam always getting all the good things and I, his best friend, get nothing to make me happy?" Kitti said to himself after he hung up the phone. He did his best not to feel bitter. After all, he was getting rich by riding on the coattails of Pompam's successes. But not as rich as Pompam, he brooded.

The happy couple showered and went to bed. Pompam couldn't resist using Joy's body again before they slept. She responded far better this time, and Pompam felt sure that with a little more practice Joy would become an expert lover.

Pompam explained to the girl that he would be leaving early in the morning and would stay overnight in Chiang Rai. She was gen-uinely sad at the thought of Pompam going away, if only for one night; but then she thought of the 3,000 *baht* Pompam had given her for shopping while he was gone, and she didn't feel *too* sad.

When the sun came up Pompam hated to get out of bed and leave behind the soft, cuddly pet that he had only just acquired the night before; but business came first, and he knew he had to go.

She woke up as he was getting dressed, and sleepily smiled up at him. "You had better be good while I am gone — or else!" Pompam admonished her with a mock threat. She *waied* to him furtively and professed obedience to his every wish. He kissed her good-bye and then quietly left the room.

For a while Joy lay awake, silently thanking the Lord Buddha for her good fortune. She liked Pompam, and even thought she could learn to enjoy having sex with him, as she was sure he would want it every day. Last night it had been so painful to let him enter her the second time, but she hadn't let on. She allowed herself to fall asleep again, and dreamed about what her life would be like in Bangkok.

Promptly at seven o'clock Chai and Pompam joined Nopadon in the lobby and began their drive up to Chiang Rai; they would stop there for breakfast before proceeding up towards Mae Sai and the Golden Triangle. Pompam and Chai wore boots and jeans; Nopadon had told them they would be crossing the Burmese border on foot, and then walking several miles into Shan territory up in the mountains.

"We'll be meeting an old friend of mine named *Khun* Ahm, who works for the 'Big Man,'" as Nopadon referred to the drug warlord in control of the whole region. "He's supposed to have ten or twelve girls waiting for us at his camp," Nopadon continued.

They ate a large meal at Nopadon's urging, being advised that they wouldn't get to eat again until they were safely back over the Thai border late that afternoon. Pompam was *not* enthusiastic about making what could be a dangerous journey into some lawless section of wilderness where the weeping poppies grew.

Before reaching Mae Sai the driver turned left onto a rutted gravel road and continued until they got to a small settlement consisting of four or five crude huts. They got out of the van, which would stay there with the driver, put on their backpacks, and headed off through the jungle. Nopadon carried a rifle, which added to Pompam's uneasy feelings.

Luckily it was late in the "cool" season so the heat and humidity wasn't as oppressive as it would be in three or four weeks' time. Pompam and Chai, accustomed to the soft life in Bangkok, weren't used to trekking up hill through uneven jungle terrain. Pompam reminded himself that it had been *his* idea to come on this trip and learn all he could about the business of buying young girls, so he could only blame himself for any discomfort he felt. He could just as easily have sent Chai alone, he reflected too late.

After about an hour of hiking through the dense forest they crossed a small river on a crude, narrow log bridge. "We're in Burma now, my friends," Nopadon announced, "or rather, we're on land controlled by the Shan druglords."

About half an hour later three men armed with assault rifles suddenly appeared from out of nowhere on the path in front of them. The leader spoke in rapid dialect with Nopadon who, from time to time, gestured back at Pompam and Chai. The soldiers finally seemed satisfied with Nopadon's explanation, and two of them led the way up the trail; the third one followed last, behind the two men from Bangkok. There was no more talking from this point, and Pompam and Chai were more than just a little nervous about their unprotected situation.

They walked approximately another two miles until they reached an encampment surrounded by more heavily-armed guards. They were near the crest of a hill, and Pompam looked out into the distance and saw nothing but field after field of poppies in bloom. It was indeed a beautiful sight, he thought, but it brought immediately to his mind the reality of exactly where they were, and the fact that they had no legal rights up there whatsoever.

A man about Chai's age, with a week-old beard, emerged from a small hut wearing dirty battle fatigues and a khaki canvas hat. He smiled when he saw Nopadon and immediately went over and embraced him. "This is *Khun* Ahm. He is the highest-ranking lieutenant of the Shan State in this area. He does not speak Thai, so I will do the talking and any translating that is necessary. He and I are like brothers, but I must warn you to stay close to me as I do not know the other men."

The two "brothers" sat down under the shade of a rough lean-to by the hut, and Nopadon motioned Pompam and Chai to join them.

Nopadon and Ahm began speaking rapidly in their Burmese dialect.

"*Khun* Ahm asks if you want to buy opium as well as girls," Nopadon translated at one point.

Pompam, who had never in his life experimented with drugs, not even "*ganja*," or marijuana, politely said, "No thank you; we don't know anything about opium."

"*Khun* Ahm wants you to try some with him, just to be polite. Then he will show you the girls," said Nopadon in a firm tone that told Pompam he couldn't refuse.

"Tell *Khun* Ahm that we would be happy to join him, but only for a little, as we have never done this before." Pompam replied cautiously, wishing that he were anywhere else at that moment but where he was.

Khun Ahm called for an aged female servant to bring over the pipes and other implements that were used in the preparation and smoking of the narcotic. It took a few minutes for the woman to get things organized. Meanwhile, Ahm and Nopadon continued their conversation, which was totally unintelligible to Pompam and Chai; they just sat there and looked back and forth at each other in worried silence.

Ahm motioned for Pompam, his honored guest, to be the first with the pipe. Pompam took three lengthy drags until the small round ball of opium turned to ash. He had a nasty coughing fit, and then it was Chai's turn. Afterwards, Nopadon and Ahm smoked the pipe, congenially passing it back and forth.

After a few moments Pompam began to feel the effects of the powerful drug. He couldn't possibly have known that what he had just taken into his lungs was one-hundred percent pure, having come straight from the source itself, right there in the Golden Triangle. His arms and legs felt like they weighed a ton, and he had considerable trouble making them obey. He also had the strange sensation of being awake and asleep at the same time.

The effects of the opium were not in the least like those of alcohol, which Pompam had learned to enjoy and handle like a pro. With the opium, however, he didn't feel totally in control of himself, which he didn't like at all. "If this ever wears off," Pompam said to himself, "I vow to the Lord Buddha that I will never do it again — even to be polite!" At that moment he felt a sudden spasm of nausea, and he leaned over on his side and vomited violently. He glanced over at Chai, who looked pale as a ghost, and noticed that he had just wretched his guts out, too.

Pompam wasn't quite sure just how long he laid there in a daze before Nopadon said, "*Khun* Ahm wants to show you the girls now. Come."

Pompam gradually rose to his feet, feeling like he was floating over the surface of the earth in a balloon. He tried to clear his head, shaking it, and wondered how he would ever be able to walk all the way back to the van.

He and Chai were ushered over to a crude, small hut, then peered inside where they saw a bunch of young females huddled over to one side, cringing in fear. Pompam could see that they were filthy and in rags; they probably hadn't bathed in weeks, the inside of the dwelling reeking of human smells. When his eyes finally adjusted to the gloom he counted ten bodies. At first glance, the youngest looked to be about thirteen, and the oldest eighteen. They looked a poor sight to him, but then what did he know? He had only left the soft perfect arms of Joy a few hours before.

"It's up to you, Chai. You take a closer look. You're carrying the money; please do what you think is best. I'm going back over to the other hut and sit down; I still don't feel so good," Pompam said. He really didn't feel well at all, and before he could get back to the other hut he vomited again in the bushes. Never again, he promised himself...

Chai wound up buying all ten of the girls and handed over the money to Ahm. "Nopadon, can you ask *Khun* Ahm where these girls came from?" Chai asked his friend.

"He already told me," Nopadon replied. "Three of them are Burmese — Karen, in fact — and were taken as prisoners of war after a border fight. The other seven are from Yunan in China; their families traded them for opium."

"Do you think we'll be able to control them in Bangkok? We don't speak their languages," Chai asked.

"Don't worry about them too much. The three Burmese will stick together, as will the Chinese. Just feed them, make them work, and keep them locked up so they don't run away. Since they don't have a debt to pay off like the girls from the Thailand side, I suggest you pay them a little something after each customer to keep them quiet. Don't forget, you have *bought* these girls, and they *know* it," Nopadon replied icily.

A little while later *Khun* Ahm ordered two of his men to get the girls out of the hut and tie them together in a line for their march through the jungle. As they stood in the sunlight Pompam and Chai thought they really didn't look so bad. At least they didn't appear to have been beaten or mistreated too badly — apart from not being allowed to bathe.

After splashing some cool water on their faces the two men from Bangkok felt like they could, after all, make the trek back through the jungle to the van. Nopadon and Ahm spoke some more in Burmese and then Nopadon turned and spoke to Pompam, "*Khun* Ahm says he is happy to do business with you. He will continue to catch young girls and keep them for me. I'll keep in touch with Chai and let him know when shipments can be made. He also wants you to find buyers for the opium for him."

They said their good-byes and then began their long hike back down to the border. The leader of the guards went in front, as before, then Pompam, Nopadon and Chai. The girls followed along, roped together in their line, with the other two soldiers.

Before they got to the narrow bridge at the border the guards saluted them and silently vanished into the jungle. Nopadon untied the girls, who had nowhere to run anyway, and they willingly walked on until they reached the small village on the Thai side. A few suspicious pairs of eyes glanced in their direction, but nothing was said. Apparently those villagers were used to seeing everything imaginable go back and forth between the two countries — including young girls being sold into a life of forced prostitution.

The girls were ordered to get into the spare van which had been brought along just for that purpose. Nopadon gave the driver instructions and it departed without delay.

"Where did they go?" Chai asked Nopadon.

"He'll drive the girls back to Chiang Mai and put them in the house where I'm storing the others. A new driver will bring the van back up to Chiang Rai late tonight so it can meet us early tomorrow morning," Nopadon replied.

They got out to the main highway and turned left towards Mae Sai, the border town that thrived on mostly illegal trade with the Burmese across the river. Pompam, Chai, and Nopadon were near-starving at this point and couldn't wait to find a restaurant. It had been nearly seven strenuous hours since their last meal that morning in Chaing Rai, and Pompam and Chai had lost theirs in the bushes.

They gorged on Thai food at a restaurant Nopadon suggested that overlooked the river. Afterwards they took a stroll through the market that led down to the bridge where both Thai and foreign tourists had their pictures taken under the big "Welcome to Myanmar" banner. Even though Thai nationals could cross the bridge without a visa and buy cheap cigarettes and other items, Pompam and Chai had no interest in re-visiting Burma.

There were numerous stalls that offered Burmese and northern Thai jewelry for sale, as well as many that sold trays of loose colored stones. Chances were the rubies and sapphires weren't real, but if they were, they would be of inferior quality. Pompam bought a ruby ring for Joy. Nopadon examined it and said it was not a great stone, but it was real and acceptable. Pompam also bought some other gifts to take back to Bangkok for Kitti, Ott, his brothers, and a few of their staff — as well as an ornate, hand-made, silver hilltribe belt for Rattana.

When they arrived at the hotel in Chiang Rai they were so exhausted all they could think about was a bath and sleep, so they had a few quiet drinks in the bar and turned in before nine o'clock.

Early the next morning they set out again for the third and final day of their girl-buying safari. Pompam couldn't wait for it to end so he could get back to Joy in Chiang Mai.

They went first to visit Chiang Saen up at the Golden Triangle. The ancient rubble of brick ruins near the small town looked interesting as they passed, and Pompam thought of both Dr. Jim and Rattana who liked exploring such places. They drove up to where they were building a new hotel, right at the very tip of the Golden Triangle itself. Lucky future guests would be able to look from their balconies and see Burma off to the left, across the River Ruek — and to the right see Laos on the opposite side of the mighty Mekhong: a unique view of two countries from a third.

Just outside Chiang Saen they stopped at a small, ramshackle village where Nopadon had made arrangements to buy two young girls. By this time Pompam hardly even looked at them, so inured had he become to the poverty, the tears — sometimes screams — upon parting from their families, and the utter hopelessness of their pitiful situation. He tried not to feel sorry for them, knowing that if he allowed himself to care, he would become depressed. Nopadon was explaining that the two girls standing in front of them were not under age, as one was nineteen and had an identity card to prove it, and the other one, who would be the oldest in the whole group, was supposedly twenty. They were barefoot, had coarse facial features, and looked so shabby that Pompam had to turn away, fearful of meeting them eye to eye.

They drove over the small mountains to Chiang Khong, a lovely little town on the banks of the Mekhong River. One could see a thriving Laotian village on the opposite bank, long-tail boats crossing back and forth, unimpeded by non-existent border police. They bought four girls there and continued on.

On their way back to Chiang Mai they passed through Phayao Province where Nopadon explained there was a well-organized girl-buying outfit that had been in operation for several years. They met the ring-leader of the enterprise at a large, pretentiously-decorated concrete house on the shore of a big lake. To Pompam this flesh trade operator looked like an evil cartoon character: bald head, grossly obese, droopy purplish eye-bags peppered with blackheads, and a thin line of mustache that looked like a worm crawling on his lip. He wore massive jade, diamond and ruby rings on four of his stubby fingers; and there were heavy gold chains around his almost non-existent neck. Pompam was revolted by the ill-mannered creature, and for the first time, he began to feel dirty about the business they were doing. He looked up at a mirror on the opposite wall, and almost expected to see a likeness much akin to the black-hearted human who sat opposite him; he was relieved, however, to see his own familiar face instead.

The girls that were produced, and made to parade around nude in front of them, were first-quality. However, instead of 10,000 *baht* per girl as had been agreed, the fat trader loudly demanded 12,000 *baht*.

Nopadon, more than anyone else, was angry about the sudden change in price because it was his "face" that was on the line.

Pompam said *"Mai pen rai,"* to ease the tension between the two and Chai paid the extra money. The ten girls they bought in Phayao brought their total up to forty-one.

"We'll let you know when we're set up to receive the girls, *Khun* Nopadon. Please keep in touch with Chai and let him know your supply situation; we just can't seem to avoid expanding our entertainment businesses, so I think we'll be able to use all the females you can provide before too long," Pompam said when they were back at the hotel.

"Chai, please give *Khun* Nopadon his commission, and add another 10,000 *baht* as a bonus. Why don't you also give him an additional 10,000 *baht* for taking good care of the girls here in Chiang Mai until we're ready for them in Bangkok," Pompam instructed.

Nopadon smiled a broad smile as Chai peeled off the thick stack of purple notes and handed them to him. Pompam could see in the man's dark eyes that he loved money above all else. "I appreciate doing business with such an honorable and generous man such as yourself, *Khun* Vichai. I hope that I may be of much use to you in the future." Nopadon *waied* to Pompam, and Pompam returned it politely.

"Chai, since I'm going to be with Joy tonight, why don't you rent yourself to a nice northern girl at the massage parlor around the corner," Pompam suggested.

"I think I'll do that, Pompam." Chai replied, smiling.

"I owe you so much, Chai. I thank the Lord Buddha for the night you first came into my bar. Your ideas and connections have brought so much to us, and I am very grateful," Pompam said sincerely.

"Without you, Pompam, none of my ideas would have earned me one *baht*. Because of you, I am becoming a rich man. *I* am the one who is grateful," he replied with lowered eyes.

Pompam was completely worn out from the unfamiliar physical work-out of the past three days. He was also happy to see his little Joy again, who beamed and threw her arms around him when he walked in the room. Pompam was content just to sit and cuddle with her that evening, watch television, and eat a simple room-service meal of fried rice and beer.

Before he went up to his room he had questioned the front desk manager and found out that Joy had taken nearly all her meals in the room, and had neither made nor received any telephone calls. Pompam gave the man a 1,500 *baht* tip and smiled, glad to know that she had behaved herself.

Pompam had a long hot shower which was followed by Joy's inexperienced, but nonetheless delicious massage, and a lively session of love-making. She was absolutely delighted with the ruby ring he gave her; the idea that Pompam had actually thought about her while he was away on business pleased her immensely. Pompam, who was having trouble keeping his eyes open, finally fell soundly asleep.

Joy, on the other hand, couldn't sleep; her mind was racing. She laid quietly in Pompam's arms and kept thinking about her first plane ride the next morning, her ruby ring, and her good fortune, being the property of such a kind and good-looking man. She didn't know if he was already married or not, but she decided that it did not matter as she had already grown very fond of him. She finally drifted off to sleep after nuzzling up as close as she could to Pompam's smooth, naked body.

Chapter 13

Kitti met Pompam, Joy, and Chai at Bangkok airport the following morning, and in spite of the jealousy and disappointment he had felt two days earlier, he was delighted to see Pompam again. He had to stand back and catch his breath for a moment as he was introduced to Joy; she was even more beautiful than he had imagined.

On the way into town Pompam asked, "Kitti, have you found a place for Joy and me to live? I hope you don't mind my moving out on you for a while; it will only be until the new house is finished."

Kitti tried not to sound upset, but Pompam detected displeasure in his voice when he answered, "Yes, Pompam. I've found somewhere for you to live with your new friend. I've rented a serviced apartment on Sukhumvit *Soi* 11, so you and I won't be *too* far away from each other."

"You are really my savior, Kitti," Pompam said, trying to placate his boyhood buddy. "I don't think I could survive in this world without you."

"*Mai pen rai*, Pompam. I'd still be working at that damned Chinese restaurant right now if it weren't for you," was Kitti's reply.

"I want to drop off Joy and our things at the new apartment and then go to the office with you," said Pompam.

"Last night I moved all your clothes and personal things over to your new flat. When I saw how comfortable it looked I almost rented one for myself," Kitti continued.

"Why not, Kitti? You can afford it. And by the way, thank you so much for doing all of this," replied a grateful Pompam.

"I can wait until the new house is finished, Pompam; it will only be six or eight more months. Besides, I don't have as good a reason as you do to make a move right now," he said as he looked in the rear-view mirror at Pompam's beautiful, young lover.

Joy had been listening to the conversation, catching bits and pieces about a new house; even with her broken Thai she could understand that part. She began to wonder if one day she would be living in a brand new house with her new "husband." Maybe he would even marry her — who knows? she fantasized.

The serviced apartment was in a new building that catered mostly to short-term *farang* tenants in Bangkok for business reasons. The apartment was on the fifth floor of the six-floor building, and it had one bedroom, a living-dining room, small kitchenette, large bath, and a balcony overlooking the gardens of an old house in back; the colors were all grays, light blue, and rose. Joy was so excited, it looked to her like she was moving into a palace.

"Joy, you unpack and make yourself at home. If you get hungry there's a coffee shop on the ground floor. I've been away for four days and I have some business to see to," Pompam explained.

She wanted to throw her arms around his neck and thank him for taking such good care of her, but was restrained by the presence of Kitti and Chai; she only raised her hands in an obedient *wai* and smiled, saying nothing.

Kitti noticed the ruby ring on her finger, quite certain that Pompam had probably bought it for her. Between the diamonds for Rattana and the ruby for Joy, Kitti could see the beginnings of an expensive habit developing for his friend.

At the office there was a letter waiting from Rattana, informing him that so far everything was normal with her pregnancy and that she couldn't wait to be with him in Bangkok. Lately, she had started to plead with Pompam to let her come before the baby was born and rent an apartment until the house was finished; short of that, when could she come for a visit? For a split second Pompam experienced a slight pang of guilt about Joy.

He called Kitti in to start going over their various projects. "Before we get into this work stuff, Kitti, I've got to ask you to please help me keep any news about Joy from reaching our staff. You, Chai, and Ott will be the only ones that can know about her; if my brothers find out — or your parents — I'll be hip-deep in buffalo shit with Rattana."

"Don't worry, Pompam. Your brothers still don't even know about the boy bars and we've actually been living *there*. I don't see why they would ever find out about your new arrangement if we remember to watch our tongues." Yes, Pompam thought, just be mindful...

Later, when they went to inspect the new house, they saw that the foundations had just been completed; the size of the big hole in the ground already made it look impressive. Pompam wanted the house to be large enough not only for himself, Rattana, and their new baby, but for Kitti, Nuu, and Att, as well. There also had to be room for more babies and more brothers that were sure to eventually come along.

"Do you still think it will be big enough?" Pompam asked Kitti.

"Pompam, the main house will be five thousand square feet and the guest house out in the back will be two thousand. The house you grew up in Buriram was about five *hundred* square feet and ten people lived in it. Yes, I think it will be big enough," Kitti answered almost sarcastically.

"How long before it's finished?"

"The contractor says six to eight months. Are you in a hurry?" Kitti teased.

"No way am I in a hurry! I'm in no rush to pay out all that money," but he was actually thinking about one day having to leave Joy on her own.

Later, they visited the old motel site behind Isan Sweetheart, and Pompam was glad to see the busy construction and decoration crews. They walked the property and decided that it would, in fact, be ready for business in two more weeks. Kitti had done a remarkable job mobilizing forces in such a short time and Pompam said so, noticing his still-ruffled feathers.

"You haven't told me yet about your adventures in the north, Pompam. I can't wait to hear about the great Isan girl-hunter combing the jungles in search of fresh meat." Kitti loved to joke with Pompam as he always had, but this time Pompam flinched at his choice of words.

Pompam shared with Kitti his stories of girl-buying in the northern provinces, embellishing details just to amuse his old friend. He told him all about the excursion over the border into Shan-controlled territory, and the gut-wrenching experience of smoking opium; that part made Kitti frown. Pompam also told him about the Golden Triangle and the new hotel that was being built up there; he promised Kitti that he would take him there one day.

He told the story of the fat, evil flesh trader in Phayao, and the bottom line on how many girls they had bought and the costs. He described Chai's friend Nopadon, and lastly told him about the sexy massage girls they had "interviewed" at Nopadon's bar. When he told the under-the-table anecdote Kitti screamed, "Why am I never around when the good stuff happens? You *must* take me on your next trip or I quit!"

Pompam dropped Kitti off at the office and went immediately back to his new apartment. This time Joy didn't hesitate to throw her arms around Pompam and kiss him deeply. She slipped her hand inside his trousers and managed quickly to get him aroused; he was tempted to shower and take the girl immediately to bed since she seemed so eager. "Come on, Joy, there's plenty of time for this later. Right now I'm taking you shopping."

An hour later Joy's eyes completely glazed over when she entered the giant six-floor Central Department Store on *Soi* Chitlom; she had never seen anything like it in Chiang Mai.

Pompam treated the girl to practically a whole new wardrobe, and they bought a variety of domestic items a young couple just setting up housekeeping would need. Joy was thrilled, acting like a little girl at the circus for the first time, and Pompam remembered that she *was* only sixteen.

They went to dinner at a small Thai restaurant on *Soi* Lang Suan, just opposite Central. He was nervous about being seen with Joy in public, so he chose a place where he felt there was no danger of being spotted together.

"Pompam, this morning in the car coming back from the airport I heard you and *Khun* Kittipong talking about a new house. I don't mean to be impolite and ask personal things, but I have only known you for a few days, and you are a very kind man..." Joy began carefully, hesitating.

Pompam was startled by her remark about the new house and decided that he might as well tell her the truth, knowing the young girl would find out about Rattana and the baby soon enough.

"The main thing that you need to know, my little mouse, is that I care for you very much, and will always take care of you as best I can," Pompam said, meaning it sincerely. "Another thing you need to know, and I guess I should tell you now, is that I am already married. My wife is living in the countryside with her parents until our first child is born, and then she will move to Bangkok when I complete the house I'm building. Please do not be upset by this." Pompam felt sad that he was breaking the news to her on her first night in Bangkok, but he realized that Rattana was still number one in his life and he owned his loyalty to her before any others.

Joy did her best to fight back tears, finally learning the truth that Pompam was married and that she was, by default, to be his *mia noi*. "I suspected you might have a wife, Pompam, but I didn't know for sure. Now that I know what my position is, you will never hear me complain or ask any more questions." Even though she was still so young, she was smart enough to realize that this was the best course to take given the circumstances; she, after all, had no power to protest, and knew that she was completely at Pompam's mercy now that he owned her body and soul.

"We will live together, Joy, until the new house is completed and my wife moves to Bangkok; this will be about another six to eight months. Afterwards, I will spend as much time as possible with you — at least two or three nights each week. I am sorry, Joy, but this is all I can offer you."

"*Mai pen rai*, Pompam. You have promised to take care of me and share yourself with me as much as you can; I cannot hope for more than this," Joy responded bravely.

"I will do more than that for you, Joy. I will make sure you complete any level of education you wish. After that, I will help set you up in a business of your choosing, since I don't want you to be bored and spend all of your time just waiting for me." Pompam felt quite good about himself for making these two offers.

Joy hadn't expected Pompam to be so generous with her. She thought he might want to keep her locked up every day, allow her to see no one, and have no friends of her own. She knew that many *mia nois* were treated this way by their "husbands," and Joy expected the same from Pompam. She was, after all, only to be the minor wife, and primarily existed for Pompam's sexual amusement. She understood all of this very well as it was a custom that had prevailed in Thailand for centuries, common even in the royal family. Joy had learned in grade school that in the last century King Rama IV had had numerous "wives" who were the mothers of his eighty-two children; but the fact remained that only one was the queen.

"Thank you, Pompam. I will do my best to make you proud of me," she said gently. "Perhaps in the future there will be ways I can help you."

"That is very possible, Joy." Pompam was genuinely touched by her sweet, accepting attitude.

Throughout the evening Joy showed Pompam no sign of being hurt or disappointed by his news. She wanted their first night together in their new home — even if it was only a temporary home — to be special, and she made love to him with all the strength and ardor she could command. Pompam was glad that he had told Joy the truth, and believed that he could find a good balance between this lovely young girl — and the other lovely young girl that he had just married a few weeks before.

The next morning at the office Pompam wrote a loving letter to Rattana, annoyed for the thousandth time that there was no telephone service in the village. He told her about the progress on the new house, and he promised to visit her in Buriram as soon as he could. Once again, he told her it would be impossible for her to move to Bangkok before the house was ready. In his mind he had already eliminated any residue guilt about Joy; she was now an established part of his life and he deserved to have her. Nonetheless, he missed his wife.

After he finished the letter he called up his old friend, *Khun* Surapong, at the police department. The high-ranking official was always happy to hear from Pompam; it usually meant that there would be some money to be made, just as there had been from introducing Pompam to his banker friend. "How nice to hear from you, Pompam. What can I do for you today?" he asked.

"One of my younger brothers in Buriram, Chatree — his nickname is Toy — seems to have a talent for studies, and I want to bring him to Bangkok to finish high school and then go on to Chulalongkorn University," Pompam explained. "Do you have any connections at the International School over on Sukhumvit *Soi* 15? I'd like to enroll him there next term."

"I just happen to have an old classmate who now runs the place. I don't think that getting your brother in there will be any problem at all. As for 'Chula,' if your brother can get decent scores on the entrance examination, and if you are prepared to make a 'donation' to a certain person I know, then he's as good as in," he replied confidently.

"Just tell me what to do, *Khun* Surapong; I really appreciate the favor. When you have the time I'd like to see you regarding a new business I'm about to open, and I want to make a 'donation' to help make sure it's successful." Pompam knew that he needed to increase his monthly police pay-offs to include protection for their new brothel that was ready to come on line, featuring mostly underage northern girls.

"If it's convenient for you, Pompam, I'll stop by Isan Sweetheart early tomorrow evening and we can talk about it then," *Khun* Surapong replied. What he really meant was, "I'll be by tomorrow evening and you can pay me the money — for whatever it is you want."

In an hour or so Ott and Pop knocked on his door.

"How's the new living arrangement, Ott?" Pompam asked, not having spent much time with his old Ramkamphaeng friend lately.

"It's working out great, Pompam, and Kim's family has finally given us their consent to marry. Kim was right about our problem: to the Chinese, *marrying* a Thai is better than living in sin with one," he responded with humor.

"How is everything going at the bars, Pop? Ott tells me you have some good promotional ideas," Pompam asked.

"Everything's going really well, Pompam. We still have the best stable of boys in town, and our base of regular customers keeps coming back for more. I wanted you to know that *Khun* Anuwat from Number Ten had the nerve to come to Jamestown the other night. She sashayed in with a small entourage of queens, all of them half-pissed. She made a scene after she tried to 'off' three of our boys for herself and her friends and I lied and told her they were already booked. She made some very nasty remarks about you, Pompam; I can't even repeat the ugly things she said. When I threw her out on her ass she screamed about how one day she would get even with you for stealing her best boys and opening your own bar. But from what I hear, business lately has been going downhill at Number Ten."

"She deserves to have her business fail, the way she treats her boys. Do you think it's so bad that she may be forced to close?" Pompam, angry, asked with interest.

"She hardly wore any jewelry the other night if that's any indication. I hear she still gambles her money away every night, so who knows?" Pop answered.

"Why don't you pull another employee raid on Number Ten; I'd like to see Anuwat finished for good," Pompam suggested.

He turned to Ott and said, "I got these two letters while I was up in Chiang Mai. It seems there are some media types who would like to know more about me. Do you know who they are?"

Ott read the two letters and said, "This one, *Khun* Apisit from 'Dichan Magazine,' is an acquaintance of mine. He came to the Isan Sweetheart opening. 'Dichan' is a first-class magazine, and it's read by all of the '*hi-so*' people of Bangkok. I think an interview with him might not be such a bad idea. If you like, I'll contact him and set it up; I'll even volunteer to take the pictures for free to make sure you look good. Forget about the other letter, it's not important."

"Okay, Ott, let me know when you've got it scheduled and I'll get a haircut that day," Pompam said to make them laugh, thinking that he would like to become a part of Bangkok's *hi-so*, or high society, one day.

During the interview, in the coffee shop at Paradise City, *Khun* Apisit asked Pompam several questions about his past, which was to be expected. Pompam kept nothing back about his impoverished up-bringing in Isan, being a *nene* for so many years, going to the Buddhist school, and his degree from lowly Ramkampheng University. His answers began to get vague, however, when questions were asked about Paradise City and Isan Sweetheart, particularly where Pompam had gotten the money to start them. Pompam simply answered, "I have several investors in both operations who prefer to remain private," putting an end to further questioning along that vein.

Nothing ever came up about Pompam's life as a hustler, or the two boy bars he still owned. So far it looked like his tracks had been covered pretty well, and he breathed a sigh of relief. Ott took some terrific pictures of Pompam in his office which would appear with the article; he reassured Pompam later that *Khun* Apisit had been quite impressed, and that the article would portray him in a very favorable light.

Pompam's parents came to Bangkok for a brief visit; they had heard about Isan Sweetheart from Nuu and Att and wanted to see it for themselves. The three brothers were delighted to have them in town, and they did their best to show them a good time.

Busy Pompam spent even fewer waking hours with Joy when Maa and Paw were around, and she became increasingly cranky and moody, feeling ignored and taken for granted. Pompam tried to please her with gifts, but their placating effect would only be momentary. He knew she was getting bored, and hoped that she would soon find an interest to occupy her time.

He had an even more difficult time with Rattana, who begged him relentlessly to let her come to Bangkok with his parents so she could see him. Pompam denied her repeated requests by saying that the trip back and forth on the train wouldn't be good for a woman in her seventh month of pregnancy. Rattana insisted she was fine, and expressed her anger at his refusal in a series of nasty letters and telegrams. Pompam had never known her to behave this way before. Now both of his women were unhappy with him at the same time, and he felt frustrated and annoyed.

Pompam decided to drive his parents back to Buriram himself, rather than send them by train as they had come. He wanted to give them some extra attention and care for them personally, for one thing; he was also bone tired from working so hard, and in dire need of a good rest; he decided his home village was the best place to do that, and besides, he could see Rattana.

"Maa, when I return to Bangkok I'm planning to take another one of your boys back with me. A few weeks ago I wrote a letter to Toy and invited him, but he wrote back and said 'no thank you,' for some strange reason. I've enrolled him anyway at the International School; and when he graduates from there I've found a way to get him into Chulalongkorn; he'll just have to accept it," Pompam announced during their drive to Isan, still a bit annoyed by Toy's ingratitude.

"What will I do with four of my sons in Bangkok and only the little ones at home?" lamented Maa, not surprised by Toy's obstinance.

"I'll gradually take the little ones off your hands, too, as they grow older. Then you and Paw can relax and watch the rice grow," he answered, trying to humor her.

Maa and Paw weren't too excited about losing yet another son to Bangkok, but ever since Pompam had assumed the role of bread-winner in the family they never complained about any of his decisions — even those that directly involved them *or* their other sons.

Paw hadn't been feeling well the past few months and Pompam was worried about him. He refused to let Pompam take him to the doctor in Bangkok, denying that there was anything wrong. But all the way back to Buriram he slept soundly in the back seat of the car, and Pompam knew something wasn't right.

Rattana acted cool towards her husband when they drove up, even though she was elated to see him again. "Pompam, you were a real buffalo to not let me come to Bangkok. I haven't seen you in nearly four months and I really wanted to come with Maa and Paw."

"I know you wanted to come, my dear, but you are just too pregnant to travel right now and I didn't want to take any risks. I explained all this to you in many letters so please stop complaining and cheer up," Pompam said almost curtly, even more exhausted from six hours behind the wheel.

Rattana took her cue, backed off, and stopped whining. Pompam took a good look at her and couldn't believe how much weight she had gained. "Can we keep these big breasts after the baby comes?" he teased, trying to put them both in a better mood.

"How is the house coming, Pompam?" Rattana asked, still on edge.

"Here, I've brought some photographs to show you. Kitti took these just one week ago."

Rattana stared at the pictures in amazement. Even though the roof wasn't on yet, the walls were up to the top and she said, "Pompam, this can't be our house; it looks like a palace! Why is it so big?"

"It's big because we're all going to live together: you, me, the baby, our future babies, my brothers, and Kitti — plus two or three maids," Pompam answered.

Rattana frowned and shook her head. "Pompam, I won't know how to live in a place like that. This is a house for some *hi-so* lady; I'm just a poor Isan country girl."

"Remember what you told me after the opening of Isan Sweetheart? You said that all you had to do was stand beside me and follow my lead, right? Well, that's all you need to do, Rattana," Pompam said sweetly, wondering what was wrong with her; she had never seemed insecure before.

Maa and Paw cleared out of the master bedroom again so Rattana and Pompam could stay there; Pompam was too tired to protest this time, and almost immediately after an early dinner the two of them turned in for the night. Pompam had never felt so worn out in his life; the drive from Bangkok on top of everything else had really done him in, and he looked forward to a long, sound sleep.

Rattana snuggled up to the strong, warm body she had missed so much since their honeymoon at the Oriental. Even though she knew she was too pregnant to get involved in "serious" love-making, she played with him and tried to get him aroused, wanting to satisfy her husband in some way. Pompam only complained of being tired and turned over on his other side.

Rattana, feeling almost panicky, started imagining Pompam had either lost interest in her because she was fat and he no longer found her attractive — or he had found another woman in Bangkok. Both thoughts were equally frightful and they kept her up worrying most of the night. What if her body never went back to normal again? And what if Pompam had a *mia noi* in Bangkok? How would she deal with these things? She had no idea.

Pompam spent two more days in the village, hardly ever leaving the house. He visited the temple and his old Abbot, of course, but he mainly wanted — and truly *needed* — to rest and be left at peace for a while. He didn't want to drink with his old friends, and he didn't want to go on any marketing excursions; he didn't think he was sick, but he felt desperately tired, and realized that he had strung himself out far too long without a decent break.

Rattana had an increasingly difficult time trying to understand Pompam's behavior. He was kind and tender towards her, but all he wanted to do was sleep. Her imaginings began to take control of her, and she started to believe that she was causing it or doing something wrong.

Poor Pompam grew weary of her constant pestering and whining and need for reassurance. Finally, when he could take it no more, he yelled at her, "Just leave me alone! I've told you I'm so tired I'm almost ill and I need a rest! Why won't you listen to me? Is this the way you're going to be in Bangkok? Go away until you behave yourself!"

Rattana began to cry, offering endless whimpering apologies. Pompam, who only wanted to take a nap sat up and screamed, "Can't you hear me, woman? I said leave me alone! Now, get out of here!"

Devastated, Rattana walked over to her parents' house, locked herself in her old room, and sat there feeding her fears and insecurities with endless mind chatter and worry. Something had changed with her husband and she intuitively knew it.

Pompam continued to ignore her, and he refused to even go near her until he was in the car, ready to drive back to Bangkok. By this time Rattana was almost beside herself with anxiety.

"Maa, why doesn't Rattana understand me? You know how tired I was when I got here and how long it's been since I've had a rest. I only wanted to relax in my mother's house for a few days."

"*Mai pen rai*, Pompam. Rattana is pregnant. Sometimes pregnant women get funny in their minds. I should know; I was pregnant nine times. Don't be so hard on the poor girl; she's missed you," Maa answered wisely.

Pompam and Toy said their good-byes and then drove over to *Khun* Direk's house where Rattana was still in exile; he knew he couldn't be so cruel as to leave without saying something to her.

Rattana came out to the car when she heard the horn honking. She just stood there looking sullen, downcast and hugely pregnant. There were dark circles under her swollen, red eyes.

Pompam went up to her and put his arms around her. "We both have to do a better job of understanding one another, Rattana. I need to always try to see your point of view and you have to try to see mine. Let's both think about this while I'm gone. Okay?"

"All right, Pompam. You'll come back when the baby is born, yes? I promise not to be so insecure."

They were a few miles down the road before either one of them spoke. Finally Pompam said, "I've tried for years now to make life better for my family — and now for my wife. Why don't I feel any better about it than I do?" he asked his younger brother, Toy, riding in the seat next to him.

"You needed a rest when you came home, Pompam, and your wife took it personally and imagined you were trying to avoid her. You've been working so hard in Bangkok trying to make money to support us, but it seems you've done nothing to really make yourself happy; and the more people you try to please only makes more people who want something from you," the precocious young boy said to his *pi-chai*.

"Since when did you get to be such a wise old man?" Pompam couldn't believe the insight this sixteen-year-old boy was already starting to demonstrate. He realized he hardly knew the good-looking, serious kid sitting next to him. When Pompam left home to go to school in Bangkok Toy was only seven years old. He had always been the quietest one of the brood, and Pompam had barely even noticed him over the years. He looked over at him as if for the first time.

"I guess I picked the right brother to give the best education in Thailand to," Pompam said, grinning.

Without smiling Toy answered, "Like I said in my letter when I told you 'no thank you,' I truly appreciate what you want to do for me, *pi-chai;* but I don't want you to do it because you feel it's something you have to do. You didn't have anyone to help you out except for Dr. Jim; and I think even if you didn't have him you still would have survived and become successful. I believe I can do the same for myself — even if I only have the Lord Buddha to help me. And I would *do it* on my own if you hadn't insisted so hard the other night in front of Maa and Paw — making me feel ungrateful."

Pompam was touched by the boy's confidence and his admirable sentiments. In a way, he hated to think he was forcing Toy under his protection against his will, but he hated even worse the thought of the boy having to claw his way up in the world as he, himself had done. He shuddered, thinking that someone as innocent as Toy might have to sell his body to get ahead.

"I believe that having you around me in Bangkok will be the best thing that's happened to me in a long time, Toy. I have no doubt that you have the ability to make a success of your life with or without my help; but I have a selfish reason for wanting to see you through Chulalongkorn: I think I'm going to need you closely by my side one day, and I want you to be prepared."

Toy sat there quietly for a while, thinking about what Pompam had said. Then he answered, "Thank you, *pi-chai*. I will do my best."

"You're welcome, *nong-chai*. I am sure you will."

Pompam didn't like the idea of billeting Toy in the staff quarters of Isan Sweetheart with Nuu and Att, who had moved over there when it opened; but it would just have to do until the new house was finished. Pompam suddenly felt uncomfortable — almost embarrassed — about Toy seeing first-hand how his older brother made his money.

Recognizing for the first time how pure and unspoiled Toy was made Pompam want to shield and protect him from anything having to do with the "dark side" of life. Having him know about Isan Sweetheart and Paradise City was one thing, but God forbid he should find out about the rest, thought Pompam, as he touched the Buddha amulet around his neck.

Chapter 14

"Now that our brothel by Isan Sweetheart is ringing the cash register, what's the next step, Pompam?" asked Chai a few days later, always looking for another opportunity to make money.

"You're sure there's no problem maintaining a continual supply of girls from Nopadon up north?" asked Pompam.

"I talked to him yesterday and he has another small shipment ready that he can send us any time," said Chai. "Supply is *not* a problem."

"Then if you have any contacts with similar businesses here in Bangkok, why don't you let them know you can get girls for them. We'll buy them from Nopadon for 10,000 *baht* and sell them locally for 20,000. Why not? If we only broker thirty girls a month that's a profit of 300,000 *baht* for doing practically nothing!" Pompam exclaimed.

"You should also think about making a trip to Songkla Province and see if there's any market down in the south for light-skinned northern girls. I'm sure there must be at least ten or fifteen provinces who could use a good, reliable source of fresh young females. Why don't you just do an exploratory trip around the country and find out?" asked Pompam, by this time thinking of the girls they used only as a commodity.

"I actually think it's well worth our while, Pompam. Nopadon says he can supply us with at least one hundred-fifty a month if we can find good 'homes' for them," Chai laughed at his own bad taste.

Pompam ignored the joke and said, "Rather than increase our overhead by opening more brothels ourselves, I think being the middleman might be the best way to expand."

The following week the issue of "Dichan Magazine" came out with Pompam's interview, and the phone immediately started ringing off the hook: for donations, for jobs, for business opportunities, for public appearances, for invitations to dinner, lunch, drinks — for everything. Pompam was shocked by the amount of interest the article had generated.

"You seem to be the Bangkok star of the moment, Pompam," Ott said to him smiling. "See what a good photographer can do for you!"

Coincidentally, that same week two of Pop's bar boys came in first and second place in the "Man of the Year" contest in Pattaya. They were sponsored, of course, by Paradise City and Isan Sweetheart, but a few nosy queens soon discovered where the winning numbers were from, and business at the two boy bars nearly went through the roof.

The winners both got modeling jobs, product endorsements, public appearance contracts, immediately enabling them to retire from their previous line of work. Pompam felt glad for them, and told Ott to arrange to have them come to his office for publicity photos; he thought it would be good for business at Isan Sweetheart and Paradise City.

The photograph Ott chose to send off to the press showed Pompam standing in the middle, dressed in an immaculately tailored business suit and tie. The two handsome boys flanked him on each side wearing nothing but very brief swim suits. One daily Thai newspaper printed the photo and a caption that read, "We want to see what the man in the middle looks like in his briefs, too!" A literal flood of offers for Pompam to do commercial modeling came in; one fashion house even offered him a million *baht* to do a magazine ad. He was overwhelmed and amused by the whole thing, and still couldn't fathom why he had become the focus of so much hype. "I'm still just a buffalo boy from Isan," he said modestly to himself.

Pompam refused all commercial offers, but listening to Ott's advice, he agreed to do one modeling job, *free*: for the Tourism Authority of Thailand. He did, in fact, pose in a brief swimsuit, on a beautiful beach in Phuket Island with a sexy girl. The pictures appeared in TAT's world-wide advertising campaign, and on a series of posters that were displayed in travel agencies and tour companies from Toronto to Tasmania. Pompam had suddenly and unwittingly become such a celebrity that it even rubbed off on his brothers: Nuu and Att got paid for posing for a few pictures, but Toy, characteristically, refused to listen to any proposals.

Joy was thrilled about her "husband's" new public image, but it only made Pompam even more secretive about appearing anywhere they might be seen together. The whole thing made Rattana, who was still pregnant in Buriram, intensely jealous, furious, and even more insecure about her relationship with Pompam than ever; she became desperately worried about their marriage, and him being in Bangkok without her.

The media frenzy brought in all kinds of new business for Paradise City and Isan Sweetheart, and the massage girls and taxi dancers were busier than ever. Everything was going great until a shocking item appeared in the largest Thai-language newspaper one day: the now-famous picture of Pompam and the two beauty contest winners, and an article that claimed that all three young men had once worked as prostitutes in gay bars. This landed like a bombshell on Pompam and his group, and created a potential disaster for their businesses.

Outwardly they all remained cool and simply denied the story. Pompam laughed and joked with a swarm of reporters, and swore that the allegations were "ridiculous": the work of "envious competitors."

No one inside his immediate group, however, would ever forget how much the incident completely enraged Pompam. His temper went totally out of control and he picked up a heavy crystal ash tray and hurled it against the mirrored wall of his office, smashing both to pieces.

"Who did this to me?" Pompam demanded, his face black with fury. "Ott, I want you to find out who planted this story immediately! I want to know who did it and I want to punish him!" Pompam screamed.

Later that evening Toy, wearing a worried, sad face, came up and asked him timidly, "That story in the newspaper — it can't be true, can it?"

Pompam was mortified to the quick, being confronted that way by his innocent little brother; he felt like he had been stabbed in the chest. He said, "Of course it's not true, Toy; I would never do anything like that. In business sometimes jealous people say terrible things just to hurt others."

The next morning Pompam met with Kitti and said, "I want you to make up a good price and see if Pop wants to buy the two boy bars; I don't want them any more — it's too risky. I know you, Ott and

Chai still get percentages of the profits, but it's small-time now compared to your other income."

"*Mai pen rai*, Pompam; I understand. It'll be much safer for all of us without the boy bars. If you go down in shame, we all go down; don't you think we realize that?" replied Kitti, who was badly shaken by the scandal.

"Thanks, Kitti; and if Pop doesn't have the money, give him good terms over time — or just give him the fucking business for free — I don't care about the goddamned bars!"

It didn't take Ott long to find out that the source of the article was old *Khun* Anuwat himself, the vengeful owner of Number Ten. One night he had drunkenly blabbed about Pompam to a newspaper reporter who was an occasional customer at his bar. That reporter told another reporter who eventually wrote and published the slanderous article.

Alone in his office Pompam phoned *Khun* Surapong at the police department. "Have you seen what they printed about me?" Pompam asked through clenched teeth. Of course *Khun* Surapong had already seen it, and also felt outraged — especially when he realized that he himself could be exposed as an old *customer* of Pompam's.

Pompam said, "I will make a very large donation to the charity that can prevent that bitch from ever doing me any harm again."

Khun Surapong told Pompam to "consider it done," and he wondered exactly how large the "large donation" would be...

That night just after closing time four policemen, *not* in uniform, entered the front door of Number Ten. Each of them carried heavy billy clubs. Anuwat, who was standing behind the bar counting his nightly receipts, screamed out loud and started to run upstairs when he saw them. Four or five bar boys, preparing to leave for the night, ran from the townhouse and continued on down to Sukhumvit Road, completely forgetting about their shoes on Number Ten's threshold.

The four thugs raced after Anuwat and captured him in the second-floor lounge which was now empty. They tore off all of his frilly clothes, tied him up with the ripped pieces, and began threatening and taunting him as he unashamedly begged not to be hurt. One of them roughly stuffed Anuwat's panties in his mouth to prevent his screams from being heard by the neighbors, while another one rifled the cash box downstairs; a third one plundered through Anuwat's jewelry on the top floor to make the invasion look like a sadistic robbery. He also located the cartons Anuwat kept stashed away that contained the nude photographs of every boy that had ever worked at Number Ten. He had orders from his boss to burn every one of those photographs immediately after leaving the premises, which he did. Pompam had given *Khun* Surapong this last instruction when he remembered the compromising photos that no doubt still existed of Ott and him.

Then they began to beat Anuwat senseless, first with their belts, and then with the billy clubs. The "wise guy" in the group decided at the last minute to shove his billy club as far up Anuwat's rectum as it would go, and leave it there as a painful souvenir. They all poured themselves a drink and enjoyed a good laugh before they left the sordid scene, leaving the naked Anuwat bleeding and unconscious on the floor — the large black stick protruding from his pimply ass, pointing towards the ceiling.

Khun Surapong was thorough, if nothing else. After Pompam had called him that afternoon he phoned up an old friend who happened to be a judge, the very same judge who had been paid by Anuwat to prevent any of the numerous neighborhood complaints against Number Ten from ever getting through the judicial system. The judge, too, was outraged at what Anuwat had tried to do to the dear boy, Pompam; after all, he, himself, had once been one of Pompam's occasional customers.

The next day in the midst of the police "investigation" regarding Anuwat's assault, a team from the judiciary arrived to officially close the establishment for violation of neighborhood zoning ordinances. The well-to-do residents in the neighboring townhouses were ecstatic that Number Ten had at last been shut down.

Other phone calls were made to make sure that nothing about the assault or the bar's closing would ever appear in the press. The matter was closed for good.

Anuwat eventually recovered in the hospital, a devastatingly ruined man. Suffering from severe depression, he committed suicide three days after being discharged by cutting his wrists with a razor, sitting on the floor in his cashier's booth at Number Ten.

Pompam never said a word about the incident — ever. He completely closed his mind to it. A very happy *Khun* Surapong soon got his "large donation" from Pompam: an amount at least triple what he had thought it would be.

Only a few seconds passed from the time Pompam received the telegram and the moment he rushed out of his office yelling, "I have a boy! I have a baby son!" He took the time to phone Joy to give her the news and tell her he was leaving at once for Buriram and would return in a few days. Joy was not in the least bit happy about Pompam's fatherhood, but she held her tongue and said nothing but, "Congratulations, Daddy!"

Pompam summoned his brother, Toy, who had a few more days to go before school started, and the two of them drove non-stop to Isan. Pompam's well-used Honda wouldn't go as fast as he wanted it to, and he cursed it all the way, deciding to buy a faster car when he returned to Bangkok.

They arrived at the hospital in the main town of Buriram where he had insisted Rattana be taken when her time came, tossing aside the centuries-old custom of having the village midwife do the honors at home.

Khun Direk and his wife were standing next to the bed looking down at daughter and grandson, smiling adoringly. Rattana looked up and saw her famous husband, arriving breathless at her door, and beamed at him.

Pompam bent down and kissed her, then carefully picked up his son. "I can't believe it, Rattana; we're a real family now!" he said with proud enthusiasm. Nothing he could have said would have pleased her more.

He looked down at the baby and declared, "I shall name you Prakart Jim Polcharoen."

Toy smiled at the thought of how happy Paw would be that Pompam had named his first-born "Prakart" after him.

Pompam gave the baby the middle name "Jim" in honor of Dr. Jim from Berkeley. Pompam and Toy had discussed the baby's name all the way to Buriram and decided that "Prakart Jim" was the best choice.

"Are you happy now, Rattana? It will only be two more months before the house is completed and you and Prakart can move to Bangkok," Pompam said.

"I am happy now, Pompam, but I will be even happier when we're all together under the same roof," she replied as she stretched out her arms for the baby.

That night Pompam, Paw, *Khun* Direk, and Toy celebrated the baby's birth with a long and noisy drinking session. Toy, who refused to touch alcohol, stuck to his cola while the other three polished off a whole liter of Black Label. Maa and Rattana's mother huddled inside the house talking about the new baby, laughing at the commotion their men were making out on the front porch. They even had a few drinks of their own.

He stayed on in the village the next day and night so he could drive Rattana and Little Jim, as they had decided to nick-name him, home from the hospital. Rattana and the baby stayed in her room in her parents' house while Pompam slept in his parents' master bedroom again. Rattana didn't care much for that arrangement, but she had learned her lesson about complaining the last time Pompam was home, and she didn't want to do or say anything that might upset him. She knew that an end to her frustration was in sight, and she decided that she could be patient for two more months.

Bright and early the next morning Pompam and Toy began their journey back to the capital. The two of them had become good friends since the last time they had driven together to Bangkok, and Pompam realized that he was becoming closer to Toy than he was to any of his other brothers, even though Nuu had practically been his very own shadow when they were growing up.

"How come you didn't want to do a modeling job like Att and Nuu when you were offered the chance?" Pompam asked him. "You're just as good-looking as they are, maybe more so." Toy had the sharpest, most refined features of anyone in the family; the bone structure of his face was actually more Western-looking than Asian. It was only his crescent-shaped dark eyes and thick, jet-black hair that gave away his true origins.

"Don't you think there's got to be one of us in the family who isn't recognized in public? You might need me one day, Pompam, to be your invisible man," the boy teased, but Pompam knew his modesty really had its roots in his religion.

Since Toy had come to Bangkok, Pompam discovered that he was, in fact, a very devout Buddhist — more so than he, himself, or any of his other brothers — even Maa. Toy didn't just perform the outward rituals of his religion, but he tried his absolute best to be mindful at all times, and put into practice the Buddhist precepts he had been taught at the temple school by *Phra* Prateep. Pompam found out that Toy even managed to meditate every morning and evening in the noisy staff quarters of Isan Sweetheart.

"I see you spent some time with *Phra* Prateep yesterday. How's he doing?" Pompam asked.

"He's getting old, but otherwise he's fine. I miss him in Bangkok."

"You'll have to get to know *Phra* Asoka at *Wat* Mahathat; I'll take you to meet him soon," Pompam volunteered, thinking that Toy would enjoy having a relationship with his Indian *Ajarn*. "Is everything okay with your temporary living arrangements?" Big brother was concerned, knowing it wasn't a good environment for a boy as sensitive as Toy.

"To be honest with you, Pompam, I'll be glad to move out of there; I'm not like Nuu and Att and the rest of your staff, and I need more quiet. I also don't like the sex business," he replied, looking directly at his *pi-chai*.

"It won't be too much longer, Toy," Pompam replied, feeling ashamed.

Pompam kept his word to Joy about providing for her education and giving her something to occupy her time. After discussing all their options he enrolled her in a leading fashion design school, as she had professed a keen interest in that field. Pompam thought that if she could learn to design clothes as well as she had learned to shop for them, then she might have some kind of a future of her own after all. Joy seemed to enjoy the new focus in her life, but the main benefit for Pompam was that she whined less, and didn't demand as much from him as before.

Pompam also kept his promise to himself and bought a new BMW, in metallic racing green; he wouldn't have to worry about driving a slow car any more. He also bought new cars for Nuu and Att while he was in the mood, and gave Toy his old Honda.

During Chai's survey trip down to Songkla, other provinces in the south, and along the Eastern Seaboard, he met a number of businessmen who owned brothels and "entertainment" establishments; most of them eagerly placed orders with him for girls from the north.

"Pompam, there is such a huge demand everywhere for young girls in this country that you can't even imagine it," reported Chai, excited. "I have firm orders right now for about five hundred to start with, and once my contacts gain confidence in our ability to deliver the goods, we'll have standing monthly orders that can go on forever."

"You had better go up to Chiang Mai and get a reliable system going with Nopadon, Chai. You'll be in charge, of course, and I'll pay you everything you're presently earning plus ten percent profit sharing on this new venture," Pompam declared. Chai, who liked money as much as his relatives down in Chinatown, smiled at Pompam and nodded his head.

Pompam continued, "The main thing we'll have to be careful of is the goddamned media. I have a very high profile right now and we can't afford any more problems like the last time. We also have to keep news of this brokerage business from my brothers — especially Toy."

"I totally understand, Pompam. It'll take me about a month to get the operation organized and deliver the first batch of girls to our new customers. After that's all set up I'd like to take the next step and explore the possibilities of exporting them overseas — to Japan and Taiwan," Chai volunteered, surprising even Pompam by his ambition.

Pompam knew it would be time soon to devise some kind of a long-term plan for investing all the money they were making. He would talk to Kitti about buying some more land, he decided.

A few weeks later the house on *Soi* Tonglor was finally completed. It had been decorated and completely fitted out by a firm Pompam hired on Sukhumvit *Soi* 23; the Thai/Chinese principals had been trained in America, and Pompam, like most Thais, genuinely liked all things American. He, Kitti, Nuu, Att, and Toy piled into the new

BMW and drove up for a final inspection before they moved in.

At the entrance Pompam honked his horn and a maid ran out to open the big iron gates, the only opening in the eight-foot-high solid wall which was topped with barbed wire and chunks of broken glass imbedded in the concrete. He stopped the car just inside the driveway and the five of them sat there and stared, each of them thinking they couldn't possibly be the people who would live in *that* place. It was just so massive and grand — and pristine white.

They parked under the *porte cochere* which was supported by four towering Corinthian columns rising two floors above them to the portico. They gazed out at the freshly-sodded front lawn, which was bordered by finely-manicured beds of flowers and shrubs. There was a round pond in the middle where lotuses bloomed, colored fish swam, and a small fountain spurted a stream of water; in the west corner was the traditional spirit house that would be dedicated when Rattana and Little Jim arrived.

Once inside the front door they gaped in awe at the entry hall, where a grand staircase, not-surprisingly, swept up one side to the second floor landing. The entry floors were of white marble patterned in a sunburst design, which continued on throughout most of the rooms on the ground level. After his stay at the Oriental Pompam had ordered marble for all of the bathrooms as well. The buffalo boys proceeded to tour their new domicile like a museum, going from room to room examining the fine furnishings and finishing details, never having been inside a place anything like it before.

After inspecting the main building they took a look at the guest house in the back, sitting next to the forty-foot swimming pool. "The guest house is Kitti's, Nuu's, and Att's 'bachelor pad'; they can keep their wild parties contained out here. Toy, you'll sleep in the main house with me and Rattana and Little Jim." The youngest boy looked relieved when Pompam made this announcement.

The garage was built to hold four cars and the carport by the guest house could hold three. The maids' quarters near the kitchen were fitted out for four girls: one would be the cook, two would clean the house, do the laundry, ironing, and gardening; the fourth would be the nanny for Little Jim. Rattana hired them herself in Buriram, and they had arrived by bus the day before.

"What do you think?" Pompam asked his speechless group.

"Don't you think it's a little pretentious?" asked Toy, the humble one. "It's just that there are so many poor people — and I feel sorry for them — and guilty," Toy added, hanging his head, visibly upset. Kitti laughed.

"I want the very best for my family, Toy," replied Pompam, hurt by his brother's remark, and irritated at him for putting a damper on the happy occasion. "There will be no more living in staff quarters and (he caught himself) other places — for us. You'll get used to it, Toy," Pompam added, trying to smile and recover the mood.

"When do we get to move in, Pompam?" inquired Nuu, eager to change *his* lifestyle.

"Today if you like. Rattana and Little Jim will be arriving on the train day after tomorrow, and the Brahmin priest will come on Saturday to set up the spirit house." Pompam was cheerful again.

"Won't we be having a Buddhist blessing ceremony, too, and have the monks come?" asked Toy, expectantly.

"Yes, of course, but not right away. We'll get settled in first," Pompam replied, knowing it had to be done, feeling bad for not having thought of it himself.

Kitti, Nuu, and Att were eager to get settled in, so they got started almost immediately. Toy went off by himself for a while to think about all the changes; so many things were happening so fast, he could hardly absorb it all.

"What's the matter, Toy? Aren't you happy?" asked Pompam, sitting down next to his brother on one of the pool chaises.

"Why do you want to live this way, Pompam? Why do you think you need all of this? I don't understand you any more; this isn't who we are," and he swept his arm towards the giant white mansion.

"I've worked hard to be able to provide this new life for my family, Toy, and I'm proud of it. We're just as good as the rich Chinese, so why shouldn't we have it?"

"So that's what you're doing: proving you're as good as other people. Didn't you learn *anything* in all your years at the temple?" and he got up and walked away, leaving Pompam in an even more sour mood than before.

"Try your best not to feel lonely when I'm not here, Joy," Pompam said later that evening, trying his best to console the tearful young girl who had just turned seventeen.

"It's easy for you to say that, Pompam, but not so easy for me to do. You'll have your whole family around you while mine is still up in Chiang Mai. I've never been alone my whole life except when you went away on trips; I've always had someone with me," she said, pouting, trying to make Pompam feel sorry for moving out on her.

"I'll try to visit you every day, Joy, and I'll stay here with you at least two or three nights a week," Pompam promised optimistically, knowing he would rarely be able to spend a whole night with his mistress since his first obligation was to his family.

"I know you're enjoying your studies, Joy, and one day when you finish design school I'll open a shop for you and you can become a famous fashion designer. Think about how much you'll enjoy that." He tried his best to make her calm down and stop giving him so much grief. "I've badly spoiled the girl," he said to himself with regret, but at the same time acknowledged that he still had strong feelings for her.

In spite of her sadness, their sex that night was passionate and robust, and Pompam clung to Joy just as he had their first time together in Chiang Mai. She no longer minded his healthy sexual appetite; as a matter of fact, Joy had become, as Pompam had early on predicted, a most adept lover with tastes of her own.

Kitti came to the apartment the next morning and helped Pompam load up both of their cars with the belongings he would take to the new house. Pompam kept a few changes of clothes and some personal items in the flat so Joy wouldn't feel like he had totally abandoned her. Throughout the entire moving process Joy sat on the sofa and wept, not caring at all about Kitti seeing her behave that way. Pompam could say nothing to calm her down.

She really was in love with Pompam in spite of his other life which always came first; that he had purchased her virginity was merely a circumstantial fact, nothing she ever held against him. For months, she had secretly prayed to the Lord Buddha in hopes that she, too, would become pregnant with Pompam's child; then she would have something of him to keep with her always and make him want to be with her more; but now, somehow, she sensed that those prayers would never be answered.

When Pompam was leaving the apartment with a final armful of belongings, Joy did her best to get hold of herself and dry her tears; then she presented him with a special gift that she had been saving for this inevitable moment; it was wrapped in beautiful rose-patterned silk cloth.

"It's really nothing, Pompam, just a small housewarming present; you can open it later when you get home." Her eyes were swollen and red from crying.

Pompam was touched by the sweetness of her gesture and said, "Thank you, Joy, for the gift — and for being so understanding."

On the way to the new house, Kitti was curious about Joy's present and asked Pompam to open up the silk cloth and see what it was. With one hand on the steering wheel Pompam slowly untied the wrapping, which contained a small wooden box. He opened it and turned it upside down on the leather seat. To his amazement, a small golden Buddha statue was staring up at him. Pompam recognized it at once as the same evil, mischievous, grinning face belonging to the Golden Buddha image that had haunted him in his youth; he hadn't seen it in his nightmares or his day-dreaming imaginings for years. For a brief moment Pompam thought he was going to be sick and he shuddered in horror, almost driving the car onto a crowded sidewalk.

"What's wrong with you Pompam, are you crazy?" Kitti screamed at him. "Watch out or you're going to kill us!"

Pompam struggled to get control of the car; he had a look of sheer panic on his face. All of a sudden he reached down to the console and tried frantically to find the button so he could get the window open. When it was lowered he picked up the Golden Buddha and threw it out into the street as if it were a live coal burning a hole in his hand.

When the object was out of the car Pompam slowly recovered his composure, but he looked as pale as a ghost; he kept silent all the way back to the new house.

"Pompam, what happened? Why did you throw the Buddha out the window? What does all this mean?" Kitti was badly shaken by Pompam's insane, uncharacteristic behavior.

Pompam ignored Kitti's questions. After a while he merely

said, "*Mai pen rai.* Let's drink ourselves a bottle of 'Black,'" which they did, never again mentioning Joy's gift and Pompam's bizarre reaction.

When Rattana and Little Jim got off the train the following afternoon Pompam was pleased to see that his wife had, in fact, lost most of the weight she had put on during her pregnancy. She was still very beautiful, he noticed; after all, she was only twenty two years old. Pompam carried his young son to the car while Rattana followed along beside him.

She took one look at the new BMW and practically screamed, "Are you going to teach me how to drive, Pompam?"

"I'll teach you if you like, Rattana, but I would rather hire you a driver so you could be like the other *hi-so* ladies," Pompam answered with a grin.

"If I'm going to have a driver, does that mean that you're going to buy me my own car?" she asked in disbelief.

"Of course, my dear. I'll take you to look at the new Volvos tomorrow and you can choose the one you like; they're supposed to be the safest cars for babies." Rattana found it hard to imagine that she would actually have her own car and driver — a Volvo even!

The photographs Pompam had showed Rattana of the unfinished house in no way prepared her for what she saw when they pulled into the driveway, past the iron gates.

"Oh my God, Pompam. I just left our family 'hut' in Buriram this morning and you expect me to live in this castle tonight?" she asked in a very low voice.

"This is our home, Rattana; you'll get used to it," Pompam exclaimed proudly.

Pompam carried the baby around in his arms as he gave Rattana the grand tour. "I could never have decorated a house like this by myself, Pompam. I'm glad you found someone who could," she remarked, although she really thought it was terribly unfair of Pompam to have had the whole thing done-up without any input whatsoever from her. The interior designer had literally selected everything for the house including the china, glassware, flatware and bed linens.

"Here's a toast to all of us being together in our new home.

May good luck and prosperity continue to be ours," Pompam proposed during their first dinner that night, everyone seated around the dining room table that could expand to seat eighteen. They all raised their glasses and said a cheering "*Chai-oh!*"

After dinner all the boys sat under the Thai-style *sala* by the pool and drank whiskey, all except for Toy who stuck to his Pepsi. They talked about their origins in Isan and acknowledged that, thanks to the Lord Buddha, all their dreams were now being realized.

"Who would ever have thought that we would get to live in a place like this, Pompam?" Kitti remarked.

"Do you remember our first room at Ramkampheng? We considered ourselves lucky just to have an outside window for some air," Pompam replied, laughing.

After a while the three bachelors adjourned to their posh quarters in the guest house and Pompam and Toy walked together towards the main building. "Do you really think you can make all of this last, Pompam?"

"Of course it will last, Toy. What makes you think it might not?" Pompam answered, still hurt by his conversation with Toy two days before.

Toy thought for a while before answering and then replied, "A great philosopher once said that the higher a man climbs the ladder of success, the more people will be there to look up his ass. I am putting it in my own words, of course."

Pompam was once again startled by the boy's precocious insights and said, "Then I guess I'd better watch my ass real closely, right? It's like *Phra* Prateep and *Phra* Asoka were always telling me to be 'mindful.' That's a good thing for all of us to remember, Toy."

"I saw quite a bit of what goes on in your world by living at Isan Sweetheart, Pompam, but I don't know how you make *all* your money, and you don't have to tell me. *But,* if you get it by doing anything illegal, or by doing things that hurt others, then I would be worried for you; it's dangerous to play around with your karma," said Toy, the devout Buddhist.

Pompam was stunned. His first reaction was to get angry at his brother's impertinence, but the look in the boy's eyes told him that his feelings only came out of love for him. "Thanks for caring about me,

Toy. *Mai pen rai.* Sleep good in your new bed and have a good day at school tomorrow." He gave the young man a hug and sent him off to his room.

Pompam, by then in a self-conscious mood, sat down by the pool for a while, alone. "Just look at all I have," he said to himself. "My karma is good because I'm a good person and I take care of my family." In the back of his mind, however, he knew that he might have done wrong from time to time. Toy's remark had unsettled him, and, for a while, made him feel the way he had when he saw Joy's Golden Buddha: sick and disoriented.

Pompam and Rattana were happy to be together again that night. The insecurities and troubles during her pregnancy were forgotten as they joined in love-making. Pompam thought for a moment about Joy having to stay by herself in her small apartment, but he put her out of his mind when he buried himself deep in Rattana and she cried out, wrapping her entire body around him. He knew quite well that this was the woman he had married for his whole life, and that Joy was only an amusement that he could keep or not keep; it was totally up to him.

"Do you still love me, Pompam?"

"Yes, of course, I still love you, Rattana. Why do you ask me that?"

"Because I've been worried that you might have grown tired of me, or that you already have another woman here in Bangkok," she answered candidly.

"You have nothing to worry about, my dear wife. You and I and our children will always be together," Pompam answered, surprised by her remark. He felt a small ripple of guilt, but then thought to himself, such is the complicated life of rich Thai men in today's world: we're always having to please someone. He slept well that night.

The next morning he took Rattana to the Volvo dealership and bought the new car he had promised her. "I want the gold one, Pompam, because it reminds me of your first gift to me: the golden Buddha amulet and gold chain," she said sweetly after making her selection, thinking for a moment about how long it had been since she had worn it; ever since Pompam had given her the diamond pendant she had worn it all the time instead.

Pompam wrote out a check for the full amount of the new car, and the dealer promised it would be serviced and delivered to the Tonglor house that afternoon.

"So, how's it going out there in the world of girl-trading, Chai?"

"Better than ever, Pompam. As you know, our first batch of girls to the southern provinces went off without a hitch, and we cleared a profit of five million *baht*. We've since done two more shipments and we raised our profit from 10,000 to 15,000 per girl. Nopadon has never screwed up once, and he's also maintained a consistent quality product; I would say that now it's time to go into the export market." Chai seemed very confident about his new operation which, Pompam knew, had already put two million more *baht* in Chai's bulging pockets.

"Do you have anyone in mind from overseas that we might start with?" Pompam asked, interested.

"I talked with a friend from my old tour company and found out there's a Japanese big-shot coming into town next week — to relax and play golf — and his company owns several of the major hostess clubs in Tokyo. My friend will discreetly find out if he might be interested in importing Thai girls; if he is, he'll set up a meeting for us."

"That look on your face tells me that you have some reservations," Pompam observed.

"It could be terrific business for us, Pompam; the profits would be enormous. The main thing bothering me is that my friend thinks this guy could be connected to the Japanese mafia, they're called '*yakuza*,' and he could be dangerous. Another thing is the problem of how we would get the girls visas to Japan," Chai replied cautiously.

"As long as we live up to our part of the bargain there shouldn't be any trouble with the Japanese, even if they *are* gangsters. The visa question is another story. It used to be easy for single girls to get visas to go to Japan, but I've read in the newspaper that they've made it quite difficult. Anyway, let's hope we can get a meeting with the guy and get some orders, and in the meantime we can figure out how to solve the visa problem."

"Okay, Pompam, we'll leave it at that for now. By the way,

tomorrow night we're opening a new show at Paradise City and all the media people will be there. It might be something Rattana would enjoy," he suggested thoughtfully.

Pompam considered this for a moment. "Rattana has never been to Paradise City, Chai. She knows about it, for sure, but I don't know how she would react to going there — or how *I* would feel about bringing her there, for that matter," Pompam answered honestly.

"I myself can see no harm in it since the massage department is a separate operation; but check first with Ott to get his input; he's our image specialist," Chai laughed.

"Speaking of Rattana," Pompam began, "I just bought her a new Volvo and I need to find her a driver. Do you know anyone we could hire from your tour company connections? I don't mind paying him a very good salary if he could double as her bodyguard. With the baby I worry sometimes about kidnappers."

"I think I might know just the right person. His name is Vinun, and he's a driver for the Sheraton. He's also an ex-boxer from Suphanburi, and he has a real mean streak in him when he gets angry or threatened."

"He sounds perfect, Chai. Pay him what you need to and see if he can start right away; the car's being sent over this afternoon."

Pompam spoke to Ott about bringing Rattana to the opening of the new show at Paradise City. "After those boy bar accusations it might not hurt for the public to see some up-dated images of you and your lovely wife, Pompam." Ott's answer decided the question immediately.

Rattana was thrilled to be included in the party, and to have the opportunity to buy herself an expensive new outfit. The couple looked like celebrities when they made their entrance.

Pompam and Rattana hosted a table that Ott quickly assembled with Pompam's input. It included *Khun* Apisit from "Dichan Magazine," *Khun* Surapong from the police department, his banker, Nuu and Att, a young movie star and his wife, and *Khun* Arun from the Thailand Pavilion Hotel and his handsome young guest, a well-known model. Pompam had also invited Toy, but the boy declined, claiming too much schoolwork; but Pompam knew by then that Toy preferred to stay as far away as possible from places where sex was for sale — even if it was in the safety of its coffee shop. In fact, Toy never passed up a chance to comment on the negative effects the sex industry was having on Thailand, a habit that sometimes nearly drove Pompam to total distraction.

Khun Arun had been delighted when Pompam called and invited him. Even though they hadn't seen one another in a very long time, Pompam liked and felt comfortable with the royally-connected gentleman, and felt certain he could trust him to keep his secrets.

Pompam wasn't really surprised that *Khun* Arun already knew almost everyone at the table, with the exception of the banker and his brothers. Nuu and Att *waied* very low when introduced, as Pompam had earlier instructed them to do. It was obvious that *Khun* Arun and *Khun* Surapong had known each other for many years and had many stories to trade. *Khun* Apisit had once done a feature story on *Khun* Arun for his magazine, so they, too, were acquainted. *Khun* Arun later whispered to Pompam that the young movie star at their table had started his career as a bar boy, and had been another of the rare, fortunate ones that had gone on to be successful and marry well. Pompam looked at the handsome, familiar face from the movies and was shocked to think that they both shared such shameful, shrouded beginnings.

It pleased him to see Rattana enjoy playing the role of hostess. "You must all come and visit us at our new house," Rattana said to those at her table. "We'll be giving a house-warming party soon, and I'll send you invitations." She was, by now, very proud of her grand new house, and had only just that moment come up with the house-warming idea. Pompam, surprised, looked at her sideways, but made no comment.

Ott had booked two of the hottest groups in Thailand to perform at Paradise City for the next two weeks. Both of the bands had popular cassettes out at the moment, and the audience knew most of the songs by heart. Everyone got up and danced from time to time, and the room vibrated with the loud and lively pop music.

Khun Arun completely surprised Pompam when he walked up onto the stage and told the band he wanted to sing. The audience cheered him on as he discussed his program with the group's lead singer, while fondly patting him on the bum in plain view of everyone.

"This song is for the lovely group of friends at my table — especially *Khun* Vichai and his beautiful wife, *Khun* Rattana."

His first two songs were in English, very sweet, from Rogers & Hamerstein musicals. The third song was in Thai, called "To the Host," which was usually sung at New Years' time. Everyone in the room stood up and sang along, all eyes focused on Pompam, who blushed with embarrassment, his proud wife smiling at him.

At the close of the evening *Khun* Arun took Pompam aside and said, "I'm so proud of you, Pompam, to see what you have done with your life. Thank you so much for not forgetting me, and for not being afraid to invite me tonight."

"I would be honored if you came to all my parties, *Khun* Arun. You were a big hit this evening, and what you did on stage brought everyone closer together; you really helped me out. Next time bring *Khun* Somchai and Ek," he offered.

"I think they would like that," the older gentleman graciously replied.

Rattana walked over and said, "Pompam, you never told me you had such a charming friend. *Khun* Arun, please come to our house one night soon and join us for dinner; I want you to meet our son, Little Jim."

"I would be delighted," *Khun* Arun said as he gave Pompam a wink on the side.

"I hope you didn't mind my suddenly creating a housewarming party and inviting people without discussing it with you first," she said, hoping she hadn't made him mad.

"I must admit that it took me aback for a moment, my dear, but it really is a good idea." Pompam realized that Rattana obviously had natural talents with people, and with the exception of that one nasty incident in Buriram, she demonstrated that she had matured since their marriage. Pompam knew she would soon begin receiving invitations to all sorts of things, and the exposure would help her become the society wife he wanted her to be.

The Brahmin priest and his crew arrived early Saturday morning and the whole family gathered for the dedication of the traditional spirit house. This was not a Buddhist tradition, but an obscure form of Hinduism, with a bit of home-grown animism thrown in. All Thai homes and work places had one of the ornate, miniature houses somewhere on their premises, and were the focus of daily offerings of *puangmalai*, incense and even food. Pompam held Little Jim in his arms and went up close to the shrine, pointing, "You see those tiny plastic people in there? and all those little wooden elephants? They're here to protect you."

At the end of the small ceremony Pompam said to the group, "I suppose we'll all sleep better tonight knowing the spirit has moved in."

"I'd feel far better if I knew the spirit of the Lord Buddha had been welcomed here today," Toy responded bluntly.

Pompam and the others had absolutely no idea what to say to the rude, outspoken one who had become the conscience of their family.

Chapter 15

Chai phoned Pompam about a week later to tell him his friend at the tour company had been able to set up a meeting with the Japanese man, who apparently was very interested in talking about doing business.

"He wants to meet us tomorrow afternoon in his suite at the Shangri-La," Chai reported. "All he has been told is that we're major players in the local entertainment industry, and that we have unlimited sources for beautiful females."

Pompam and Chai showed up at their appointed time at the luxurious Shangri-La Hotel, which was located not far from the Oriental on the *Chao Phya* River. Chai's friend, Mori, met them in the lobby and called upstairs on the house phone; then they waited by the elevators until two of the big-shot's beefy underlings came down to meet them. Mr. Mori spoke in Japanese to the two men, pointed to Pompam and Chai, and said, "I'll say good-bye to you here; Mr. Aoyama wants to meet you alone. Good luck."

In a suite on the top floor they were shown into a vast living room; it had a view of the river Pompam thought was even more spectacular than at the Oriental, where he and Rattana had spent their honeymoon. Before too long a Japanese man in his early forties briskly entered the room; he wore a dark green sports jacket, open shirt, casual slacks and loafers.

"My name is Aoyama. Please sit down and be comfortable. May I offer you something to drink? In Japan we always have refreshments before we discuss business." He offered his engraved name card with both hands, as is the Asian custom; Chai and Pompam did the same with theirs in return.

Pompam and Chai asked the attending butler for Black Label and soda, as did their host, Mr. Aoyama.

"Are you enjoying yourself in Thailand?" Pompam asked. He suddenly felt like he was a *nene* back at *Wat* Po, practicing his English on foreigners.

"Oh yes, Mr. Vichai, very much. I always have a good time in Thailand. You have good golf courses. I can find acceptable Japanese food. And you have beautiful ladies," he answered smiling.

Pompam thought, this guy really gets to the point fast. "I've never played golf and I've never tasted Japanese food, but, yes, we definitely have many beautiful ladies," Pompam answered, playing the game.

"You must learn to play golf, Mr. Vichai. It's very good for business. Here in Thailand it is cheap to play golf. In Japan it is only for millionaires," Aoyama replied, implying that he was very wealthy.

"Will you be in Bangkok very long, Mr. Aoyama?" Chai asked a question this time.

"I never come here for more than four or five days; I can't be away from my businesses in Tokyo too long. If I don't come to Thailand, I go to Hawaii. They have good golf and good Japanese food in Hawaii, too," he answered.

Pompam was beginning to get a feel for the preliminary small-talk he had heard Japanese businessmen were noted for.

"I understand the ladies are very beautiful in Hawaii," Pompam continued, keeping the conversation rolling.

"They are indeed very beautiful, but they spend too much time in the sun. Their skin gets dark."

Now we know he only likes fair-skinned girls; at least this is a start, thought Pompam.

"Many of the girls here in Thailand have dark skin. But the girls in the north are very fair — almost like Europeans," Pompam added.

"I have met a few fair-skinned girls from Chiang Mai. They were most beautiful. Their features were very delicate and refined. Are they all like that in the north?" Aoyama was getting his desired product message through loud and clear.

"Not all of them, Mr. Aoyama. The same as anywhere else, I imagine. There are beautiful girls and not-so-beautiful girls. Some have fair skin and delicate features, and some have dark skin and coarser features." Pompam thought he was being real clever.

"Please have another drink, Mr. Vichai and Mr. Chai," Aoyama insisted.

"Thank you," accepted Pompam for both of them.

"The young man from the tour company tells me that you are involved in the entertainment industry here in Bangkok. Please tell me about it," requested the Japanese.

"We have a medium-size massage parlor on Petchburi Road that employs about seventy-five lovely ladies. In that same facility we have a coffee shop with live entertainment; many of the top acts in Thailand perform there. We also own a combination nightclub/restaurant that features food, music and dance from the Northeast region of Thailand. Near that location we operate a small hotel that provides intimate female entertainment for Thai men. We also have a placement service for Thai females who wish to re-locate to other regions of the country and want to obtain employment. All of our operations are very successful." Pompam thought he had given a very discreet and tactful summation of their various enterprises.

"Very interesting, Mr. Vichai. I would like to visit your entertainment establishments while I am here," Aoyama requested.

"We would be delighted to have you as our guest, Mr. Aoyama. Would this evening be convenient?" Pompam asked pointedly.

"Actually, tomorrow evening would be better; this evening I already have an appointment — with a lovely young lady," he said with a broad grin.

"Then we will look forward to seeing you tomorrow evening for dinner and entertainment at Paradise City; say, around eight o'clock?"

"That will be fine, Mr. Vichai. I shall look forward to it. Before you leave, please tell me, are you interested in expanding your female placement service — perhaps overseas?"

"That would be of very great interest to us, Mr. Aoyama. My colleagues and I have already discussed this possibility. It seems there is an over-supply of fair-skinned, delicate-featured young ladies in Thailand who would like to move to a place where they would be more fully appreciated. We would be ideally suited to assist them in the tiresome process of re-locating," Pompam explained with a flourish.

"How very nice. My organization in Japan might be interested in providing new homes and new places of employment for young ladies such as you are describing. Perhaps tomorrow evening when we meet again you could give me more details, and introduce me to a few candidates," replied Mr. Aoyama.

"Mr. Chai and I will work on gathering some information, Mr. Aoyama, and we would be most happy to make some appropriate introductions for you after our dinner," Pompam concluded. He couldn't believe how cool he was playing it.

"Excellent, Mr. Vichai. It seems that our two organizations may be able to come to an arrangement that would be acceptable and beneficial to us both, pending tomorrow evening's details and introductions. I look forward to seeing you then."

"Good-bye, Mr. Aoyama."

"Good-bye, Mr. Vichai and Mr. Chai." Aoyama then left the room and the two other "gentlemen" escorted Pompam and Chai down to the lobby. Once on the ground floor the two Japanese bowed and got back on the lift.

"You are the smoothest operator I've ever seen, Pompam. You handled that meeting brilliantly," Chai said on the way back to the office.

"Thanks; I seem to have a knack for getting along with foreigners," Pompam replied modestly. In reality he had been quite nervous during the meeting; he was grateful for his temple training in breathing and mindfulness which had kept him from showing it.

"Do you have any ideas on how to solve the Japanese visa problem?" Pompam inquired.

"I've been thinking about it quite a bit since last week. I think we'll have to recruit mostly resident *farangs* and Thai men with good jobs who would like to earn some extra money," Chai replied.

"How do you mean?" Pompam asked, puzzled.

"I'll put together a small team who can discreetly approach *farangs* and respectable Thais in bars and other public places, and offer them money to pose as the boyfriends or fiancees of the Thai girls we want to send to Japan. First, we create fake job backgrounds, and letters from phony employers for the girls. Then these "boyfriends" and "fiancees" go with them to the Japanese Embassy and tell the official they want to take their girls to Japan for a holiday. All they really need are tourist visas. Once the girls are in Japan they're no longer our problem; they'll simply disappear into the big city and Japanese immigration authorities won't even know they're there."

"It sounds like it might work, Chai, but it also sounds very expensive," Pompam replied.

"It will be expensive, Pompam. We'll have to get the girl her passport and pay something to the 'boyfriend.' We'll also have to pay a commission to the recruiter, buy the girl a real round-trip air ticket, pay for the Japanese visa, and perhaps some other expenses I haven't thought of yet," Chai explained.

"We still need to make a sizable profit for ourselves with all the work we'll be putting into it. Do you think the Japanese would be willing to pay so much?"

"We'll find out tomorrow night, Pompam, I suppose. But my feeling is, they would pay a great deal of money when you consider how expensive things are in Japan, and how rich they are right now. Also, they could probably charge enough to make at least a hundred times as much as we could on each girl."

"The girls we send to Japan would have to be top-grade, Chai. They couldn't be any of the village girls Nopadon buys for us up in the north or in Burma. Could he find us enough in the top category to make such an operation worthwhile?"

"Pompam, I seriously don't think that finding the right girls will be a problem. We have several in our own Paradise City that I know would jump at the chance to go to Japan, for starters," Chai answered confidently.

"How do you think it would work out for the girls on the Tokyo end?" Pompam asked.

"I imagine that whatever the Japanese have to pay to get the girl to Japan would be treated as a debt she would have to work off; I believe we're familiar with that system. It's just that the debt would be so much greater, and the girls will have to work a lot longer, before they start making any money for their own pockets. I've heard stories that girls who work in Japan aren't treated very well, but those that choose to go there ought to know in advance what they're getting themselves into," explained Chai.

"I've read that the mamasans can be very cruel, take away their passports, and treat the girls like slaves," Pompam continued.

"Whatever... Let's just talk to Mr. Aoyama tomorrow night and find out what he wants. We can take it from there," Chai replied. There were no further conversations about the plight of exported working girls.

That same day after classes Toy battled the ever-worsening traffic all the way to *Wat* Mahathat to see *Phra* Asoka, who had become his close friend and adviser.

"I'm very worried about Pompam, *Ajarn*. I have these horrible feelings that he's getting involved in things he shouldn't be; and I fear for him. It's like nothing is ever enough, no matter how much he has! What's wrong with him?" an anguished Toy asked the Indian monk.

"Your brother Vichai struggled hard to rise from nothing to where he is today. He is enjoying the rewards of his efforts, Chatree; and he has reached a plateau. Hopefully he will learn that there are other goals and move on."

"But what if he doesn't?"

"Then he will live out his karma, the same as everyone else; and eventually he will realize his true nature. Give him some time, Chatree, and help him by continuing to remind him."

Toy pondered the monk's words and wondered what he could possibly do to shake Pompam awake.

The following night Mr. Aoyama and his two underlings arrived at Paradise City in a Shangri-La hotel limousine, which they kept waiting.

"Good evening, Mr. Vichai; good evening, Mr. Chai," the dapper Japanese greeted them both as he stepped forward. He looked extremely elegant in his tailored suit, expensive European shoes, and subdued, claret-colored silk necktie. His two "shadows" were also dressed in suits and ties this time, but looked a little uncomfortable in them.

"Welcome to Paradise City, Mr. Aoyama," Pompam said as he politely bowed and *waied*.

Chai led them over to a table that had been prepared for them earlier. "My two companions will not be joining us, gentlemen; they prefer to sit at the bar, if you don't mind."

"Of course," replied Pompam. Chai escorted their guest's two colleagues over to the bar and told the bartender to look after them. Pompam didn't realize that they had such class distinctions in Japan, too.

When they were seated at the table, quickly re-configured for three, Pompam asked, "Do you like Thai food, Mr. Aoyama? I fear it may be too spicy for you, but unfortunately it's all we serve here. I apologize. We have no Japanese food or European food to offer you."

"As a matter of fact, gentlemen, my stomach cannot tolerate chilis, so I took the precaution of having a light dinner before I left the hotel. If you don't mind, I will just have some spring rolls with my drink, while you have your dinner."

"Of course, Mr. Aoyama, we understand. Black Label and soda?"

"That will be fine, thank you." Pompam ordered the drinks and snacks for Mr. Aoyama. Chai ordered rice and a few Thai dishes for himself and Pompam.

"Did you have a chance to play golf today?" Pompam asked.

"Yes I did, but I didn't play very well; and I seem to have strained a muscle in my shoulder," Mr. Aoyama said, giving them a wry smile.

"After dinner I think we can help take care of your shoulder, Mr. Aoyama," replied Pompam, and returned the smile with a wink.

Through dinner Mr. Aoyama seemed to enjoy the musical entertainment. He remarked on the loveliness of one or two of the singers, and said he wished he could understand the Thai language. He continued to drink Black Label and soda one after the other, and Pompam and Chai, being the hosts, had no choice but to keep up with him.

When the table was finally cleared Pompam suggested, "Why don't you let us show you the other part of this establishment, and find you some relief for your shoulder pain."

"That idea sounds delightful. I am most anxious to see some of your female employees, and possibly receive an 'introduction' as you mentioned yesterday," he replied with a grin, loosening up from the drinks.

Pompam and Chai led Mr. Aoyama into the lobby. When they walked up to the glass partition to view the girls in the "display" room,

Pompam once again felt quite satisfied that Paradise City truly deserved its reputation for having the most beautiful masseuses in town.

Mr. Aoyama obviously thought so too, judging by the look on his face. "Mr. Vichai, never have I seen such a lovely collection of young girls! I wish I had discovered Paradise City long ago; I feel that I've been wasting my time in all the other places!"

"How nice of you to say so, Mr. Aoyama. Do you see any young ladies that you would like us to introduce to you? or would you like Mr. Chai to do the selecting? We really must get your painful shoulder taken care of," Pompam said with mock concern.

"Since this is your establishment I would prefer that Mr. Chai does me the honor, if he wouldn't mind. Your hospitality is really just *too* gracious," replied Mr. Aoyama who was practically drooling, although both Pompam and Chai could see that he was doing his best to keep a straight face.

"Anticipating your preference for allowing me to do the choosing, Mr. Aoyama, I have already reserved two of our loveliest girls for you. They are waiting for you now in our special VIP room on the third floor. Please let me escort you up there," Chai said to their Japanese guest.

"We'll meet later in my office, Mr. Aoyama. Please take your time and enjoy yourself," said Pompam as he politely *waied* to his guest, not surprised that the two underlings also followed along.

At the bar Chai said to Pompam, "You should have seen Aoyama's eyes pop out when he saw Num and Nut sitting there naked on the massage table when he walked in the room. I explained to the girls that he's a very important customer, so I'm sure right now he's getting the workout of his life. Who knows, his shoulder might be *worse* when they're finished with him." They both laughed out loud, mentally picturing the scene in progress upstairs.

"I can't wait to talk to Nut and Num afterwards and find out what gets Mr. Aoyama turned on," Pompam joked.

About an hour and a half later Pompam and Chai were informed by the captain that Mr. Aoyama had finished his massage and was being escorted with his two "friends" to Pompam's office. The two Thais went up to welcome him and begin the business discussion they had been waiting for.

"How is your shoulder, Mr. Aoyama?" Pompam asked the rather dazed-looking Japanese as he entered the office. "I trust it is much improved?"

"Oh yes...my shoulder," Mr. Aoyama floundered. "Yes, it is indeed much better. *Everything* is much improved as a matter of fact," he said as he laughed out loud.

"Shall we have a drink?" Chai asked.

"Yes, please, a drink would be very useful at the moment," the already red-faced Japanese replied. Chai fixed drinks and brought them over to the seating area. The two "friends" bowed and went outside.

"Would you like to visit our other establishment, Isan Sweetheart, Mr. Aoyama?" Pompam asked smiling.

"I don't think that will be necessary, Mr. Vichai. I am quite content to stay here and discuss business with you. I must say that so far I am most impressed. If the two young ladies I just met are representative of the sort of girls you might be able to re-locate to Japan, then I think we can do business."

"If you approve of Nut and Num as a standard for those whom you would like to employ, then we don't foresee any problem in providing you with a steady supply in the same category," Pompam put forward.

"Excellent. If we can agree on some terms, then I see no reason why we can't place a standing order with you for ten or twenty per month."

"It will be much easier to find suitable girls, Mr. Aoyama, than it will be to get them visas for Japan. We think we've worked out a system for doing this, but we haven't tried it out yet, and it is not going to be inexpensive. You must know about the difficulties with the visa situation, and you also know it's impossible to bribe your embassy officials. These obstacles will have to be worked out using our ingenuity and a ton of cash," Pompam said as he moved towards the "close."

"Yes, Mr. Vichai, I am aware of the visa problems and I have no doubt that the methods you will need to use to get them will not be inexpensive. Please give me a figure per girl and we'll go from there," he requested nicely.

Pompam and Chai had discussed this subject at length, adding up all of the expenses they thought they would incur for each girl, including numerous "commissions" and "finders' fees."

"We feel that 250,000 *baht* per girl would be a reasonable figure, Mr. Aoyama," Pompam offered, his palms sweating the whole time.

"250,000 *baht* is ten thousand US dollars, Mr. Vichai. That is *very* expensive," he replied. At the same time, Aoyama was calculating in his head that it wasn't *really* that great an amount. When he considered the fact that his customers would be paying several hundred dollars every evening for the company of each girl, it was practically a bargain. The girls would, of course, take on this amount as a debt to the company and would have to work very hard to pay it off.

"Yes, Mr. Aoyama, it *is* expensive, but it would be difficult for us to do it for much less," Pompam answered. To give the Japanese room for a "face-saving" compromise he added, "What if we make this figure *inclusive* of the girl's round-trip air ticket? Please don't forget about the tremendous risk that we will be exposed to; should the operation be discovered it would be a *very* big problem for us."

"I fully appreciate your position, Mr. Vichai. But what if we were to modify your figure just slightly to 200,000 *baht* per girl?"

"I don't really think that would be possible, Mr. Aoyama. If we watch our expenses carefully I think our minimum offering would be 225,000 *baht*. I think that's more than a fair price."

Mr. Aoyama paused, sipped his drink, and seemed to be considering the offer. He finally replied, "All right, Mr. Vichai. I will agree to 225,000 *baht* per girl. That's nine thousand US dollars — and you buy the air ticket." He knew the Thais were making a huge profit out of the deal, but he really didn't care. Nine thousand dollars was nothing compared to what each Thai girl would earn his company, and the up-front money would come out of the girl's own hide anyway.

"Very good," Pompam answered, relieved. "Let's have another drink to celebrate our new relationship."

"Thank you very much, Mr. Vichai. You are an excellent host. While we're having that drink we can discuss payment transfers and other things," Aoyama offered.

They actually had three more drinks, but in the meantime they covered all the details regarding logistics, communication between the two countries, money transfers, bank account numbers, and numerous other related items. There would be no written contract for obvious reasons; the two parties would have to simply act on good faith and hope for the best.

"I truly hope you will be able to deliver the girls as you have promised, Mr. Vichai. As we will be advancing you considerable sums of money with no written agreement, you would find yourself in a most-unfortunate situation if you failed," Mr. Aoyama said as he closed the discussion with a thinly-concealed threat.

"We will do our best not to disappoint you," Pompam replied.

"I believe you will. I must return to my hotel now; I am very relaxed after my experience with the young ladies, and I think a good sleep is in order. If all goes well in our business relationship, Mr. Vichai, in a few months we will invite you to Japan so you can see our *own* entertainment establishments. I think it would be interesting for you to see how we do business in Tokyo. I have no doubt that the leader of our organization would very much like to meet you as well," Mr. Aoyama smiled ironically as he said this last sentence.

"I have not yet been abroad, Mr. Aoyama, and would very much like to visit your country — and try some Japanese food," Pompam replied politely.

"I will transfer the money we discussed to your account as soon as I return to Japan," Mr. Aoyama promised, "and I hope we can receive our first shipment very soon."

"Do you realize that just this first shipment of ten girls will net us a profit of 1.25 million *baht*? That's 125,000 per girl after expenses!" Chai exclaimed, looking as if he could practically *taste* the money.

"That's definitely a nice-size profit, Chai. Do you have any doubt we'll be able to deliver?" Pompam asked with true concern in his voice.

"I'll contact Nopadon right away and have him get moving; and I'll speak to three or four girls who work here that have already said they want to go to Japan. I'll work on getting their fake paperwork and letters together while they wait for their passports," said Chai.

"If you don't mind, Pompam, I'd like to put my brother, Suphan, in charge of recruiting and dealing with the *farang* and Thai 'boyfriends and fiancées.' You met Suphan once before, Pompam, when he came by one day to see me here; he was 'salesman of the year' for the Toyota dealership he works for. He's not afraid to take a risk or two and put himself on the line — and his English is near perfect. I think he'll jump at the chance to earn 20,000 *baht* commission for each visa he can get for a girl. And besides, I trust the guy to make sure none of this business could ever get traced back to us."

"He sounds like a perfect choice, Chai."

"I was also thinking that maybe I should locate a similar-type customer in Taiwan. It would be the same exact system, and it would increase our chances of getting visas if we spread them out between two embassies."

"I know Mr. Aoyama wants an exclusive from us for Japan, but there's nothing to stop us from shipping girls to someone in Taipei," replied Pompam.

"Oh! I almost forgot. I want to hear about Num and Nut's experience with Mr. Aoyama!" exclaimed Chai, reaching for the house phone.

It didn't take but a few minutes for Num and Nut to join them in Pompam's private office. They, of course, had never been in the boss's inner sanctum before, so they were shy when they walked in, both of them wearing their pink chiffon "shorty" uniforms, looking none the worse for wear, as far as Pompam could see.

"The Japanese man? You wouldn't believe what he looked like without any clothes on! You tell them, Nut."

"Well, he was completely covered from his neck down to his ankles in *tattoos*! He even had them on his *cock*! These weren't just little line drawings like I've seen before, but great big full-color *pictures*! Dragons, tigers, naked women, snakes; you name it — they were all over his body."

Num jumped in and interrupted. "The tattoos were scary enough, but after we gave him his bath and started to massage him he pushed us off. He didn't want a massage at all! First of all he made us tie him to the bed with the silk stocking he had with him in his suit pocket. Then he wanted us to spank him as hard as we could on his butt. After that we untied him and he laid down in the bathtub and wanted us to *pee* on him! Nut did it, but I refused," confessed Num, self-righteously drawing the line somewhere.

Pompam and Chai did their best to control themselves as they listened to these highly amusing revelations. Nothing could really shock Pompam as far as sex was concerned; but the man begging the girls to pee on him was simply too much!

"Anything else?" Chai asked, trying to look concerned.

"After getting peed on he took a shower then wanted to watch Num and me act like two lesbians. We had both done that before so it was no big deal. Then he wanted to tie *us* up with his stockings. We were afraid to let him tie us both up at the same time in case one of us had to run out for help, so first he tied up Num and put his cock in her. Then he untied Num and tied me up and put his tattooed cock in *me* — if you can actually call it a 'cock' and not a *cartoon!*" Both girls were laughing out loud by then.

"Well, it sounds like you two really had quite a night," Pompam responded, trying to be dignified.

"Did he give you a tip?" asked Chai.

"He gave us 5,000 *baht* each, can you believe it? I've never been given more than 2,000 before, and that was because the guy was drunk and paid me 1,000 *baht* twice!" Num admitted.

"Thanks girls, you can go back to work now," Chai said, smiling.

As soon as the girls left the room Pompam and Chai doubled over in a fit of laughter they thought would never stop.

"Mr. Aoyama revealed his true colors, I would say. And they're all in his tattoos!" Pompam shrieked out loud.

"Pompam, the tattoos, that's a sure sign the guy's a *yakuza*," Chai said seriously, trying not to laugh any more. "My friend, the Japanese tour guide, said they usually had massive tattoos everywhere on their bodies."

"I would actually like to see something like that, Chai. Wouldn't that be something?" Pompam said, feeling a stir of excitement. "Can you imagine how much pain they have to endure, and how long it must take them? I bet it takes years! Aoyama even has them on his cock! Ouch!" Pompam said and started laughing all over again.

"I'll get hold of my brother, Suphan, right away, Pompam, and get started on all this. There's a lot of work to do and I'm anxious to get going."

"Good night, Chai. Thanks for an evening I'll never forget!"

Chai's brother, Suphan, worked very hard that first month and succeeded in getting visas for twelve girls. Six others got turned down by the embassy, however, which statistically made it a one-third chance for failure. For the six that were turned down there was actually no money lost, however; the "boyfriends" and "fiancees" didn't get paid anything, and the air ticket could be cashed in. Suphan was disappointed, though, because of his lost commission. "*Mai pen rai*," Suphan said to himself, "With twelve successes, I've already made 240,000 *baht!*"

Pompam's profit was 1.5 million *baht*, and he nearly swooned when he considered that he could make that much each month from an operation he didn't even have to personally touch. He hadn't taken the time in recent months to total up his income from all of his sources, but Pompam realized then that he was getting seriously rich. He thought for a few moments about *how* he was getting rich, and admitted to himself that so far almost all of the money had come from the paid sex acts of a huge number of other, less-fortunate people.

"*Mai pen rai*. Everyone needs money to survive," he said to himself. "I am only helping others earn their livelihoods and take care of their families; we're all in the same boat."

"Kitti, I think we had better start investing in more land, as you suggested more than a year ago," Pompam said one night while having drinks in the *sala* by the pool.

"The money is piling up, Pompam, and land prices aren't getting any cheaper," Kitti replied, reflecting.

As a result of their discussion that evening, during the next year they bought bits and pieces of land in many areas of Bangkok. They bought a number of vacant parcels in the Sukhumvit area, and a really good piece on Sathorn Road, the next major thoroughfare to the west of Silom in the central business district.

They also bought less-expensive land out in the suburbs, which at that time were spreading far into the surrounding rice farms like the tentacles of an octopus. Pompam thought they could let the cheap suburban land sit vacant and appreciate in value; eventually they might build housing estates when the sprawling city caught up with it. "Kitti is right," Pompam said to himself on a number of occasions, "Land *is* our future, and our way to expand beyond the entertainment business."

"We've been in our new house for four months already and we still haven't had our housewarming party, Pompam; I don't understand why you keep putting it off," Rattana insisted one day.

"You know how busy I've been, Rattana; I just haven't wanted to think about it." Pompam then considered for a moment and said, "You're right, though; if we're going to have a housewarming party at all we had better do it soon or there's no point in having one." Again he remembered they still hadn't had the monks come and bless the house. Toy had mentioned it three or four times at the beginning, but must have given up, Pompam thought, feeling momentarily ashamed.

"So when did you have in mind?" he asked.

"I was thinking about two weeks from Saturday. It will be our second wedding anniversary," she replied, grinning.

"That's right it will be, won't it? Okay, two weeks from Saturday it is. Do you need my help, or do you want to try your hand at throwing a party by yourself?" he asked, knowing beforehand what her answer would be. Lately she had been stretching her boundaries and seemed to be feeling increasingly more confident socially. Hardly a single day passed that she didn't go out on her own to attend at least one function.

"If you don't mind my calling on your brothers and your managers for some assistance, Pompam, I would like to do this party myself," she replied.

"You know that anything you need from Kitti, Ott, Chai, or my brothers is yours. If you want to raid the liquor and food supplies at Paradise City or Isan Sweetheart, go ahead. In fact, it would be cheaper for us if you did. Ott can arrange the entertainment if you want it, and he can help you with the guest list, too, my dear Rattana," Pompam said and gave her a kiss.

"Don't forget, Pompam," Rattana added, "tonight is the night you invited *Khun* Arun to dinner; he'll be here at seven o'clock."

"I hadn't forgotten, Rattana." Though, in fact, he had.

"Welcome to our home, *Khun* Arun," Rattana said warmly as she greeted the stately gentleman with a gracious *wai*. "We're so glad you could join us here at last."

"I'm so sorry I had to turn down your last two invitations, Rattana, but the first time we had clients in town I had to entertain, and the second time I had to attend a convention down on the coast in Cha Am. Thank you so much for not being angry and giving me another chance," he replied with charm.

"*Mai pen rai.* We're just glad you're here now. Please come in; Pompam's waiting for you in the back by the pool," she said.

"This is quite a place you've got here, Rattana. It's truly beautiful. Very impressive. Did you do the decorating yourself?" *Khun* Arun asked, taking it all in as he turned around in a complete circle.

"I'm afraid not. I would like to have, but I was busy at the time having the baby out in the countryside. Pompam hired someone else to do it and all I had to do was move in," replied Rattana with a smile, but annoyed that she had told the truth about not having done the house herself.

"Well, some things are more important than others, and I'm sure having a baby is one of them. I'll be able to meet Little Jim this evening?"

"Of course you will. I'll bring him down in a few minutes after you've seen Pompam. I'm sure you and my husband have a great deal to catch up on, so I'll leave you alone for a while." Rattana escorted *Khun* Arun out to Pompam and then disappeared back inside.

"Well, Pompam, it looks like you're living the way I would be if my father hadn't lost all his money after World War Two," *Khun* Arun said in greeting, admiring the underwater lights in the pool.

"It's so nice to see you again. What can I get you to drink?"

"I'll have English tea, if it's not too much trouble," *Khun* Arun answered, as he rarely, if ever, touched alcohol. Pompam gave the order to the maid and asked for his usual Black Label and soda.

"Did you go back to Buriram for *Loy Kratong*?" *Khun* Arun asked, the holiday having passed only the previous month.

"Rattana begged me to take her, but I just didn't have the time. We wound up putting our *kratongs* in the pool right here."

"My goodness, Pompam, how things have changed for you. This house is quite a step up from your flat on Ramkampheng, isn't it?"

"Yes, it is quite different. But I'm still the same person; just a little older and hopefully a bit wiser," Pompam answered modestly.

"And richer," *Khun* Arun added, laughing. "*Khun* Somchai sends you his best regards. He has your famous poster hanging on the wall in his office. I think he wishes it had been he who had bought you out of the bar that night — and not Hans!" They laughed.

"By the way, how is *Khun* Hans? I haven't heard any news of him for years," Pompam asked, genuinely wanting to know.

"Not too well, apparently. He hasn't been out to Thailand for over a year, but his tour groups keep coming through the hotel. He seems to have become quite ill," *Khun* Arun added sadly.

"I hope it's nothing serious. Please give him my regards the next time you talk to him. But don't encourage him to try to see me the next time he comes to Bangkok, if you know what I mean," Pompam grinned.

"I'm sure he'll be fine and will return to Thailand before too long. I'll tell him you said 'hello.'"

"How's your handsome friend, the one that came with you to Paradise City that night?" asked Pompam.

"He's doing fine, I suppose, but I don't see much of him any more. I try so hard to find myself a good one to love, but it never comes to anything. Maybe it's because I'm too old and they're too young; or maybe it's because I'm too much of a 'butterfly.'"

"You're such a kind person, *Khun* Arun; you deserve to be happy. I think I'll phone Pop and ask him to be on the look-out for someone good. Last I heard he still gets at least ten or fifteen new boys in every day looking for work. Maybe he can find you a fresh young virgin right out of the countryside. Would you like that?"

"It's very kind of you to offer, Pompam. Tell Pop not to go to too much trouble, but if he notices a nice one..."

"I'll call him tomorrow," Pompam volunteered. He could see that the gesture had pleased the older man.

Rattana joined them holding Little Jim in her arms. "Here he is, *Khun* Arun: Pompam's baby boy."

Khun Arun admired the child and told Pompam he looked just like him. "No, Rattana, I would love to hold him, but I can't. Wait until he's a little older," he protested.

"He's already nearly a year and a half; he can't hurt you,"

Rattana joked. "I don't want to let him down on the ground because he'll head straight for the pool."

"I know he won't hurt me, but I just don't do well with babies. He'll start to cry if he sits on my lap." *Khun* Arun looked terrified and smiled helplessly at Pompam.

"*Mai pen rai.* Dinner is ready; you gentlemen please follow me. It's just going to be the three of us and Toy tonight; Nuu and Att are at work," said Rattana.

"I see you're still keeping your brothers working hard as ever, Pompam. Shame on you," teased *Khun* Arun.

Toy was only mildly interested in their distinguished guest. Pompam had explained a little about him to Toy before he arrived, and the young boy *waied* to him very politely. "Toy is the smart one in the family — so far. In another year he'll graduate from the International School. You're still number one in your class?" Pompam asked, knowing all along the answer.

"Yes, Pompam. I really shouldn't be since everyone else had such a big head start with English. But so many of the students are spoiled and too lazy to study," Toy replied.

"That's the way I was when I was in school," volunteered *Khun* Arun, laughing. "I was more spoiled than any child you have ever seen. And now look what it did to me! I'm absolutely helpless." He meant it as a joke, but Pompam knew that it was true. *Khun* Arun had once told him that he was so spoiled when he was young that he still didn't even know how to wash his own hair. Like many of his class and generation he was sent away to boarding school in England when he was twelve years old — with a valet!

"I heard you can sing," Toy said to him, "and that's not being helpless." Not helpless, perhaps, but definitely *worthless*, he thought to himself, not in the least bit impressed by the old man's privileged, high-class up-bringing. The social small talk was making him bored; he could never take very much of it in one dose without losing his patience.

"But singing is *useless*, except to amuse myself," he answered, chuckling.

"And to amuse *others*," Rattana added, reminding him of the party at Paradise City.

"You are very kind, but my talent, if any, is a small one," *Khun* Arun answered modestly.

"Rattana, sorry to change the subject, but do you know where Kitti is tonight? I thought he would be joining us for dinner," Pompam asked.

"He called to say that he had to meet someone about some property purchase. Sorry I forgot to tell you. He says to give you his best regards, *Khun* Arun," answered Rattana.

"You're into buying property these days, are you?" asked *Khun* Arun, somewhat surprised at the possibility that Pompam was making *that* much money.

"We've been buying bits and pieces here and there, nothing major."

"Speaking of property, who owns that big piece next door to your house on the corner? It certainly would be a splendid location for some sort of first-class restaurant or night club," *Khun* Arun inquired.

"Actually, *we* own it. We bought that parcel and this one at the same time, but we just left it vacant. We'll probably sell it off in a few years," Pompam replied.

"You should at least consider my idea before you sell it. *Soi* Tonglor is becoming one of the most desirable addresses in Bangkok — not only for residences, but for night places and shops."

"I think you should build a homeless shelter on the land, Pompam, or maybe a place where your faded prostitutes can take their babies for medical treatment — or to get themselves treated for diseases. I agree with *Khun* Arun; there are all sorts of *fashionable* uses for the land," remarked Toy sarcastically, and then excused himself from the table, *waiing* exaggeratedly to their guest.

Pompam, Rattana and *Khun* Arun sat there in shock for a few moments until *Khun* Arun broke the ice and said, "*Mai pen rai*. Your young brother has a conscience, Pompam, that's all; some people are like that. But just remember what I said about the land..."

Chapter 16

"It's so nice to have you with me again for more than just a few hours, Pompam. I miss you so much, you know. Even though you *do* come by to see me every few days I still get very lonely," she complained.

"*Mai pen rai*, Joy; I'm here now." While Rattana was busy organizing her big party Pompam told everyone a lie and said he had to go to Chiang Mai on business for three days. He did it so he could spend the time with Joy, whom he had badly neglected.

"So, now that you've passed your high school equivalency test do you want to go to a university — or stay in your design school?" Pompam asked, thinking about the possibility of yet another university education to finance.

"I don't really want to go to college, Pompam. I love designing clothes and I want to keep learning as much as I can about fashion. I'm going to hold you to your promise about opening a shop for me."

"Is the dress you're wearing one of your designs, Joy?" Pompam asked admiringly.

"Yes it is, Pompam; do you like it?" she asked as she pivoted from side to side, looking sexy and charming as ever.

"It's beautiful, Joy; very nicely cut. I think you have a good chance of being a successful designer," Pompam said, trying his best to encourage her.

Later, while he was getting dressed to take Joy out for a quiet dinner, he noticed it was raining so he grabbed a windbreaker he had left in the closet. When he put it on he felt something in the pocket and reached in and pulled out a package of Thai cigarettes. Pompam had tried smoking in his teens as did most young boys, but he hadn't liked it, and quit before it became a habit. Upon closer examination of the jacket he detected a very faint scent he didn't recognize. It wasn't from any of the colognes or personal products he used; and it didn't smell like anything Joy wore either.

"Joy, I found these cigarettes in the pocket of my jacket. Have you taken up smoking now?" he asked her crossly.

"You know I don't smoke, Pompam. Those must be Noi's, a friend of mine from the design school. She was here a few days ago and borrowed your jacket; she had forgotten hers, and it started raining just as we were going out for noodles," she answered without missing a beat.

Pompam dropped the subject and made no further mention of it. He made a mental note, however, to have Joy's apartment watched for a week or so, and check on who came and went in his absence.

During the next two days Pompam's *mia noi* was loving and affectionate, and seemed genuinely appreciative of the valuable time her "husband" was spending with her. They made love often, and the feeling was good between them.

A few days afterwards, realizing he hadn't yet bought Rattana an anniversary present, Pompam made a trip to the Peninsula Plaza, near the Erawan intersection, and paid a visit to the most exclusive jewelry shop in Bangkok, the one frequented by Elizabeth Taylor whenever she was in town. He selected a "major" sapphire and diamond set that he knew would look sensational with the dark blue silk dress she would be wearing to her big party. It consisted of a necklace, bracelet, earrings, and cocktail ring. The huge blue sapphires on each piece were perfectly matched, and dozens of large round diamonds encircled every one. It cost Pompam a fortune, but he knew it would please Rattana to show off a bit as she played hostess to her *hi-so* friends.

Pompam presented the extravagant gift to Rattana at breakfast the morning of the event. She opened the velvet box, saw the dazzling display, and immediately closed it, not wanting any of the maids to see what was inside.

"Come here, Pompam; come with me," she implored frantically.

Pompam followed her upstairs into their bedroom; she closed the door and opened the box again. "I've never seen anything like this, Pompam, except in magazines. Are you sure you want me to have it?" she asked him.

"Yes, my dear wife. This *is* our anniversary and I want everyone tonight to see how much I love you. But tomorrow I want you to put it in the safety box at the bank — and let the maids and the boys know you have done so. I don't want it to be known that we keep such things here in the house, Rattana. It might be dangerous," Pompam replied.

"Thank you so very much for the beautiful gift, my husband. I love it, and will be so proud to wear it for you." Then she put her arms around him, closed her eyes, and kissed him deeply, allowing one hand to drift down and unzip his fly; before too long they were back in bed.

"She could have been telling me the truth, Chai, that her girl-friend borrowed the jacket and left her cigarettes in the pocket. I just need to know for sure for my own peace of mind. Can you hire someone to watch the apartment for about a week and report back to you?"

"Sure, Pompam. I don't blame you for feeling uncomfortable. I would do the same if it was me," Chai replied.

"It really looks like Rattana has out-done herself for the party tonight. There were people all over the place when I left the house this morning: putting up tents, covering the pool with a dance floor, setting up a stage, catering people everywhere. I suppose you know that Rattana hired the Oriental Hotel to cater the food. I guess the kitchen at Paradise City isn't good enough for her any more," he joked.

"I'm actually the one responsible for that, Pompam. I told Rattana it would be best if she got a hotel to cater for her; our crew just isn't sophisticated enough to put on the kind of party she wanted," Chai replied. "But *she* was the one that picked the Oriental out of all the hotels — not me!"

"*Mai pen rai.* I told her she could do whatever she wanted," Pompam said resignedly, knowing how expensive it was.

"Kitti," Pompam asked later in the day, "who are you bringing to the party tonight? We're still waiting for you to find a special girl and get married."

"Why? You want me out of your house that bad?" Kitti answered defensively. "As a matter of fact, I'm bringing a girl I met at the bank. She's in charge of the department that receives money from overseas, so you can figure out for yourself how I got to know her."

Pompam could indeed figure that one out: it was obviously from keeping track of the money from Japan that was steadily pouring in. "What is her name and what's she like?" he asked with great interest.

"Her name is Sudar, she comes from a good family in Ayuddhya, she's had an excellent education, and she's very pretty. I think you will like her," Kitti answered, looking pleased with himself.

"I can't wait to meet her, Kitti." Pompam was genuinely happy that his old buddy had finally taken an interest in some nice girl.

That evening Pompam was already dressed and waiting in the entry hall when *Khun* Arun arrived, the first guest, with his new boyfriend in tow. Pompam could instantly see the change in *Khun* Arun's state of happiness since their dinner that first night. His face literally glowed every time he looked at the shy, handsome, fair-skinned boy from Chiang Mai. Pompam thought Pop had done really well in selecting this one for his remarkable old friend. Pop said that unlike most others, the boy was definitely gay, and since he obviously cared for *Khun* Arun, Pompam hoped he wouldn't run out on him any time soon.

"*Sawasdee-khrap!*" Pompam *waied Khun* Arun, then returned the *wai* from the boy whose name was Pet. A perfect name for him, Pompam thought to himself.

"The house looks lovely, Pompam; and you don't look too shabby yourself," he said as he presented the host with a bouquet of flowers.

"Thank you, *Khun* Arun. You seem to be in a good mood tonight."

"How could I not be? Thanks to you and Pop," he said as he glanced towards Pet.

"I'm just glad you two are getting along so well. Can I get you something to drink?"

"*Mai pen rai*, Pompam. We'll just wander around and take a look and find something for ourselves; then I'll be back here shortly and help you and Rattana greet your guests." Pompam was grateful for his help with the greetings; *Khun* Arun perhaps knew more of the guests than Pompam did, since he had assisted Rattana with the list; he had even added many of his own personal friends and acquaintances so he could make introductions that would help Rattana further her social ambitions.

Rattana floated down the staircase into the entry hall looking like the queen herself, making a grand theatrical entrance just for Pompam. Her brilliant smile truly did justice to the diamonds and sapphires, Pompam reflected. She dramatically glided over to her husband, put her arm through his, and gave him a small Thai-style kiss on the cheek, making him laugh.

"Pompam," Rattana began, "I haven't given you *your* anniversary present yet, but I'll give it to you now, if you like," she smiled.

"You have already given me your present, Rattana, by looking so beautiful, and for doing such a good job getting everything ready for the party," he replied.

"I'm going to have another baby, Pompam. That's your present," she whispered to him softly.

Pompam was thrilled. He dearly loved and adored Little Jim, and the thought of another child truly pleased him. "Thank you, my dear wife. It's the most wonderful present you could have given me," he said, kissing her.

Rattana's driver, Vinun, was the *major domo* at the gate, checking off names on the invitation list as people arrived. He had turned out to be not only the perfect driver, but also a sensitive and loyal protector for Rattana and the baby.

Pompam, Rattana, and *Khun* Arun were soon caught up in the excitement of what would turn out to be one of the top parties that year for Bangkok's *hi-so*. Everyone was duly impressed by the house and Rattana's jewelry, and said so with many flowery words of praise. The smiles on most of the guests were genuine, but a few of them concealed feelings of envy and bitterness beneath — no matter how rich they themselves were. Everyone was primarily concerned with both showing and giving "face," and determining where they — and all the others — ranked in the hierarchy so they would know how to communicate.

The majority of the three hundred guests brought flowers or other gifts to warm the house, and the entry hall was soon filled to the brim with floral displays and brightly wrapped packages — all the way up the grand staircase.

"Pompam, sorry I'm late, but I got stuck in a horrible traffic jam on Sukhumvit. This is my friend, *Khun* Sudar," Kitti said as he introduced his date to Pompam.

"Rattana and I are so delighted that you came, Sudar. We'll have plenty of time to talk since we're seated at the same table at dinner." Pompam knew that this gesture would please his old friend, and give him big "face" with his girlfriend.

Pompam could see *Khun* Arun showing off his new Pet to *Khun* Surapong from the police department. They passed all their communications using only their eyes, however, as *Khun* Surapong had attended the party that evening with his haughty and matronly wife.

Nuu, Att, and Toy had each brought dates. Nuu's girl was a model he had met through Ott, Att's was a young lady from Ramkampheng, and Toy's was a fellow senior from the International School, the daughter of an English couple who worked in Bangkok. Pompam was proud of all three of them, but more so of Toy than the others since he actually had the nerve to bring a *farang* girl to the party. Pompam reflected on the fact that Toy never failed to surprise him, sometimes even pleasantly.

"Pompam, this is Pamela Hastings; we're in the same social services club at school and we're working on a project together in the slums at Khlong Toey," Toy said as he introduced the tall, attractive blonde.

"We're happy you could join us this evening, Pamela. I must say, though, I can hardly imagine you going anywhere near a Bangkok slum," Pompam responded with good humor.

"Your brother and I are much alike, Mr. Vichai; we can go anywhere we please, but we generally prefer the company of the less fortunate," she replied, looking her host directly in the eye, and then scanning the opulent scene around her.

Pompam, completely at a loss for words, simply excused himself, not believing he had just been spoken to that way by some do-gooder, *farang* bitch of Toy's. "What is my younger brother turning into?" he asked himself, alarmed; perhaps he's taking his Buddhist social thing too far, he thought.

When Pompam recovered his composure and his mood, he walked up onto the stage and gave his welcome speech. He made all of the expected acknowledgments, introduced the high-ranking guests, and then told the group that, "My wife has just presented me with the most wonderful anniversary present she could give me: news that we're going to have another child."

Cheers and applause came up everywhere, and then *Khun* Arun joined Pompam on the stage. He made a toast to "Two of my very closest friends in this world, to whom I owe all my happiness; may they live long, and warm this new house with the love of many babies." Pompam walked over to where Rattana stood, and together they accepted a thousand good wishes.

Then *Khun* Arun sang "If I Loved You" from "Carrousel," and from time to time looked unabashedly at his friend, Pet, who did his best not to blush from all the attention. *Khun* Arun had never really tried to hide his sexual preference. He felt comfortable enough in his social position, for one thing, and for another, such relationships were quite common. Everyone of *Khun* Arun's class and high social rank (or pretended they were) simply accepted him as he was, and gave him the "face" that, according to their culture, he was due.

Several other guests followed *Khun* Arun's lead and took the microphone to sing their own favorite songs. Pompam nearly fainted when he looked up and saw Rattana enter the spotlight and dedicate a song to him. "This is for my wonderful husband, Vichai," she announced, and then she was suddenly joined by the most famous pop singer in all of Thailand, *Khun* Bee. His appearance was a complete surprise, and everyone spontaneously jumped to their feet. The singer took Rattana's hand, and together they sang a simple love duet in Thai that everyone knew.

The duet ended, Rattana took a small bow, *waied* very low, and left the stage, leaving Bee to perform four more songs. Three female and three male dancers magically appeared behind him, and together they put on a show fit for one of Bangkok's big music halls. At the end of the last song fireworks went off over their heads and filled the sky with bursts of colored lights. The *hi-so* guests, caught up in the moment, forgot who they were and screamed and whistled like teenagers at a rock concert, having a wonderful time.

Towards the end Ott came over to Pompam with Kim. "You're really becoming a famous person, Pompam. Do you realize that?"

"I guess all it takes is a little luck and a lot of money, Ott; which is what it's going to take to pay Bee. How are you doing these days,

Kim? Are you enjoying married life as much as I am?" Pompam asked the new bride.

"There were many times when I never thought it would happen, Pompam. You know how set against Ott my parents were. But everyone seems to have adjusted now, and they even have us over for Sunday night dinner every week; Ott is almost beginning to like Chinese food," she replied warmly, laughing.

Khun Arun and Pet were the last to leave. "*You* really made the party, *Khun* Arun. I can't thank you enough for all you did to make tonight a success," Pompam told him, meaning it whole-heartedly. Rattana joined him at that moment and said the same thing.

"*Mai pen rai*. You've given me so much to be happy for," and turned to Pet. "I would do anything for you and Rattana, Pompam," he said sincerely, tears brimming in his eyes.

When they were undressing for bed Pompam said, "Rattana, you are the most amazing woman in Thailand, you know that? How you ever got up the nerve to sing a duet with Bee — right up there in front of everybody — I just don't know..."

"You are my inspiration, Pompam. But I haven't made love to you since this morning, so come to bed." They both laughed, and then took their moment of closeness and pleasure.

About two weeks later Pompam got a very distressing telegram from his mother informing him that his father was very ill. Maa hadn't said what was wrong with Paw, but she would never have sent the cable if it wasn't very serious. Pompam knew he had to go to Buriram to find out for himself. He would probably have to drag his father by force to the doctor since Maa could never convince him to go.

Immediately, Pompam, Rattana, Little Jim and Toy set out in one car; Nuu and Att followed in another. None of them wanted to waste any time getting there, each one intuitively knowing the situation was bad.

When they arrived at the house Maa came out to meet them wearing the most terrified, worried look Pompam had ever seen. "What's wrong, Maa?" Pompam asked, frightened.

"He just has no energy any more. He can't work. He won't eat. He just lays there in the bed. I *know* he's in pain, but he won't let me call the doctor. He's also lost a lot of weight, Pompam..." she answered distractedly.

The whole group followed Pompam upstairs to the master bedroom. They all drew in a quick breath when they saw the frail and emaciated figure laying on the bed in his *sarong* and T-shirt. He glanced up at them and tried to smile. He didn't, however, try to sit up, or even raise his head, which was propped up on some pillows.

"Paw, we're taking you to the hospital right now," Pompam announced, not intending to argue with him about it. He bent down and motioned to Nuu to help pick him up. Paw raised his hand in a gesture meant to stop them, but Pompam and Nuu paid no attention. It felt to them like lifting a small child, he weighed so little.

"Maa, why didn't you let me know sooner he was so bad," Pompam scolded as they carried Paw down the stairs. She began to whimper, caught between her husband's instruction to keep the news from Pompam, and the anxiety she had felt, knowing how angry her son would be by not being told.

Since it was Saturday all of the younger brothers were around. They looked scared, but kept quiet amidst all the commotion. Pompam mentally calculated they must be thirteen, nine, seven and six by then. He experienced a flash of anger when he thought about all the money he sent them, and yet the youngest was filthy, barefoot, and wearing only a pair of old, torn underpants.

"Nuu, you drive Rattana and Little Jim to *Khun* Direk's house, then come back and load up all the boys and meet me at the hospital in Buriram. Toy, you ride up front with me, and Maa can ride in the back with Paw."

Rattana started to protest being left behind, but realized it wasn't the time to argue. "I'll be back as soon as I can, Rattana," Pompam reassured her.

At the hospital Pompam and Toy carried Paw into the Emergency Room. Maa followed behind. "Get the doctor, quick!" Pompam shouted at the nurses behind the counter.

"Put him in that room over there, Sir," one of them pointed.

In a few minutes the other boys arrived, and all eight of them crowded into the small examining room with Maa. The doctor came in and told the children to go outside, so Toy took the younger ones to the waiting lounge. The six and seven year-olds looked panic-stricken and on the verge of tears.

The doctor looked Paw over and said, "He's in really bad shape. Why didn't you come here sooner?" Maa hung her head and Pompam answered, "We were all in Bangkok and he wouldn't let Maa bring him."

"Your father has a very weak pulse and his blood pressure is way down. I want to get some X-rays immediately. He seems to be having most of his pain in his stomach and abdomen," the doctor said.

They all waited anxiously for the doctor to come back with the results. Finally he motioned Pompam, Maa, and Nuu to follow him into his office.

"I'm afraid I don't have very good news for you. In fact, it's very bad news. Your father is dying of cancer. It seems to have started in his stomach and has spread all through his body," the doctor explained to them gravely.

"Is there anything you can do for him?" Pompam asked, his face white.

"It's far too late to operate. That should have been done months ago. All I can do for him is give him morphine so he can go in peace. I don't know how he has endured the pain for so long without any medication. Didn't he give you any indication he was suffering?" he asked Maa.

"I could tell his stomach hurt him, but he never complained. He just stopped eating and laid there on the bed getting weaker every day. But he wouldn't listen to me — or let me send for my sons in Bangkok," Maa answered, starting to cry.

Pompam was thinking that his father was only fifty three years old. He was still young by modern standards, but had already become an old man from the constant work and unending hardship he had suffered since birth in cruel Isan. Maa was only forty five, he recalled, but she looked well past sixty. People get old quickly out here, he thought to himself.

"What should we do about him, doctor?" Pompam asked.

"I suggest you take him home and keep him as comfortable as you can. Give him the morphine regularly and try to ease his pain. *Khun* Vichai, he could go at any moment. Maybe it will be tonight or maybe in a week, but I don't think he can last much longer. He can't," the doctor replied with finality, trying to show compassion.

Pompam took this news very hard, as did Maa and Nuu. Maa started crying again; Pompam and Nuu wanted to cry very badly, but they held back. Pompam thanked the doctor, and the nurses wheeled Paw out to the hospital entrance while Pompam paid the bill. Nuu brought up one car and Att the other. "Nuu, you explain everything to the younger ones on the way back to the village," Pompam said. He looked to the side at Toy who immediately understood everything, and shuddered as if himself in pain.

Maa wouldn't leave Paw's side for more than a moment, and for the next four days Pompam and the other boys sat with her, taking turns every few hours. After the second day Paw was continuously delirious from the combination of pain and morphine, but he managed to hang on for another forty eight hours. At the end he just closed his eyes and quietly drifted away. There were no words, no parting statements or blessings. Just gone.

Pompam wept openly for a while, but finally pulled himself together and did his best to comfort Maa and his younger brothers, who were in worse shape than he was. All except for Toy, that is, who had lit a candle and some incense at the family shrine, and was sitting serenely in front of the Buddha image in meditation. Pompam envied the boy's self-discipline and control.

He walked over to *Khun* Direk's house to inform Rattana, and to ask his father-in-law to help him with the funeral arrangements. Being the village headman, *Khun* Direk was used to being asked to help in this same regard. Rattana did her best to console Pompam, but he told her he just wanted to be alone for a while and go to see *Phra* Prateep at the temple. By this time Rattana was also in tears, and seeing both of his parents so upset for the first time in his life, Little Jim began to wail.

At the *wat* Pompam sat in front of the Buddha statue totally absorbed in his grief. Before too long the old Abbot came over to him and said, "Vichai, my son; do not be too disturbed by your father's death. Remember your training. Think about the words of the Lord Buddha. Death is only *one* part of life, a very small part. It's all an endless cycle, Vichai, you know that. Birth, life, death. Over and over again. It is the same for everything in nature. Each form of life just keeps living out its karma until finally there is a return to the original Divine state of being.

"Now is an important time for you to be mindful, Vichai. You are the head of the family now, and they will all depend on you even more from this time on. Yes, you think you have already been taking care of your family for years, and this event will make it no different. But it *will* be different, and you *are* up to it." The old Abbot reached over and gripped Pompam by the shoulder. He truly was like a son to him; but as much as he loved him, he knew that only Pompam could heal his own grief.

"Thank you, *Ajarn*. Thank you for reminding me," he said, thinking of the weight of his new responsibilities.

With those words he got up, straightened his posture, and walked back home. *Khun* Direk had already brought over the village coffin in which to place Paw's body. In a poor village like theirs, there was only one coffin, used over and over again; after each occupant's funeral was over, the remains were removed and put into the oven at the temple crematorium; then the coffin was put away to await the next person who died. Pompam would have liked to have provided his father with his own new coffin, but there had been no warning of his death, and now there was no time. Since Paw had been part of the older generation it was probably best that way; just let him leave this world the same way his ancestors have for hundreds of years, Pompam thought.

Pompam, Nuu, and Att washed Paw's body and dressed it in clean clothes. They tied his favorite red, green and blue *pakomah* around his waist and combed his hair which was already gray and thin. They brought the body downstairs and placed it inside the ornately-carved wooden coffin that had been drawn up in an ox-cart outside the front door. Then they pulled the cart over to their old, abandoned, wooden home and stopped it to rest under the house where the farm animals used to be kept. It would be in the old house, the home that Paw and his father had built with their own hands, where they would have his wake.

Early in the evening Toy took Pompam aside and said, "On the day after tomorrow I will shave my head and become a *nene* to make merit for our father. I will stay here at the temple for three weeks. Please inform my school when you return to Bangkok."

Pompam was not surprised by Toy's decision; he had almost expected it. At the same time he felt guilty for not becoming a monk himself, and make some merit so his dead Paw could be re-born with better karma. But he knew there was no way he would interrupt his life like that; everything had become too complicated to afford him that luxury.

That night the family ate their meal quietly, and then one by one walked over to sit on rush mats that had been spread out on the ground near the coffin. Friends and village neighbors stopped by throughout the night to offer their condolences and have a glass or two of Thai whiskey with the older boys. Paw's two brothers and his sister had been notified where they lived in neighboring villages, and they also came to keep vigil overnight.

Maa remained calm, and efficiently went about her duty of providing food and drink for the visitors. She was exhausted from the four days she had stayed awake at Paw's bedside, and now she was numb from grief. By custom the family would only be allowed this one night of mourning; the following day was the funeral, and in Isan, a funeral was expected to be a farewell party.

Just after dawn *Phra* Prateep and eight other monks sat near the coffin and began to chant. Several friends and neighbors had come to the house even earlier to begin food preparations. The night before Pompam gave *Khun* Direk 25,000 *baht* which he figured would be more than enough to cover all of the expenses, and Pompam was grateful to his father-in-law for taking care of the arrangements.

Two whole pigs were killed and butchered, and various pork dishes were prepared to feed the mourners. The first dish was raw minced pork mixed with strong chilies, garlic, shallots and herbs; a generous portion of fresh pig's blood was added, as was the Isan custom. Later on there would be several other pork dishes, some prepared with vegetables or herbs, and some roasted, barbecued or deep-fried in peanut oil. Cooking smells permeated the entire village.

Bottles of Thai whiskey started opening up as soon as the monks finished chanting and returned to the temple. Two hours later, when everyone was sufficiently filled with food and alcohol, the entire party gathered to pull the ox-cart bearing the coffin. A long rope was attached to the front of the cart so everyone could put their hands on it and help pull, at least symbolically.

When they got to the temple gate they continued pulling the cart all the way around the compound three full times before finally stopping in front of the crematorium, its tall brick smokestack silently pointing toward the sky. The brothers, friends, and relatives helped carry the coffin up the steps, and laid it to rest on a bier, level with the oven door. At the rear of the crematorium was an iron hatch that opened at the base, where firewood and kindling had already been stacked and lay waiting.

The monks gathered and began their chanting once more, as the top and sides of the village coffin were removed and the boys rolled the body of their father into the oven. Toy handed each of the mourners a ceremonial match made out of the dried spines of palm leaves, bent and twisted into the shape of a small bird.

With the drone of chanting in his ears, Pompam put a torch to the kindling near the open door of the oven. Afterwards, each man, woman and child marched up the crematorium steps and reverently dropped their bird-shaped lighter into the flames. When the last mourner said his good-bye the oven door was closed and locked.

Some people went back to their homes while others waited at the temple for the black billows of smoke to cease. Then they waited a while longer for the oven to cool enough so the ashes could be removed.

Under the bright sunshine, *Khun* Direk cleared the weeds and debris from a small patch of ground behind the crematorium — about six feet long by three feet wide. Around this patch he drove sticks into the ground and then stretched white string from stick to stick, making a fence. Then he unwound the string all the way to the temple *viharn* and placed the remaining ball into the hand of the Buddha image, sitting there serenely, watching the age-old scene with impersonal, half-closed eyes.

Finally, a temple boy brought over to the cleared patch a bucket containing the ashes and small, unconsumed pieces of bone. *Khun* Direk, being the headman, emptied this bucket of life's final reduction into the center of the small enclosure and then, with his hands, molded it into the shape of a man: head, arms, torso, and legs. The villagers and the family of the deceased stood close by and watched with great interest to see how the likeness would come out. *Khun* Direk then chanted in the ancient local dialect the verses that ordered the dead man to "Depart!" When he stopped chanting he suddenly clapped his hands together, and everyone smiled and relaxed and seemed quite happy again, knowing that Paw's soul had been sent off to the spirit world to await re-birth; he was free from this earth and all its suffering once again.

Khun Direk then reached behind him for a small urn in which to place the bones and ashes. This urn would eventually wind up in a nine-foot-high memorial *chedi* that Pompam would have built on the temple grounds. It would have Paw's name on it, his birth and death dates, as well as a photograph taken of him in his youth.

Khun Direk picked out a piece of bone from the man-like shape on the ground and dropped it into the urn. Then the family members, followed by all the other mourners, formed a line and did the same thing. Everyone, in turn, picked up a piece of bone or some ashes and deposited them in their eternal resting place.

When this was complete, *Khun* Direk used a few swift strokes of his hands to obliterate what was left of the image made of Paw's remains. He scattered the loose material that was left over, and it was as if the likeness had never been there; only a few small, black pieces of charcoal were still visible in the dirt. He wound up the ball of white string and picked up the sticks that had held it, and threw them away to the side. The funeral was officially over, and Paw was now history, if even that.

Weddings, funerals, and *thamboons* were generally the only celebrations the village people of the Northeast ever attended during the course of their limited lives. The families who hosted all three of these events were expected to provide a good time for the whole community.

Pompam and his brothers had, by this time, already moved through the worst part of their grief, and they were ready to move on. Thanks to their Buddhist up-bringing they, like most Thai people, were able to accept death as just another of life's inevitable realities, and recover remarkably quickly. The *mai pen rai* attitude once again prevailed, and the survivors kept going.

Feasting, drinking, and merriment continued late into the evening at the family home. After sundown the former mourners were given a choice: they could either stay with the drinking and the music, or watch outdoor movies at the temple where a large fabric screen had been set up. The movies were mostly for the children and teenagers, so they had been chosen especially for their tastes: a bloody kung-fu movie from Hong Kong, and then a B-class, Thai, romantic police drama with lots of killing and violence.

Pompam's younger brothers thoroughly enjoyed themselves at the movies, while Pompam and the older ones, except for Toy, continued on drinking with the village men. Maa and the other women allowed themselves to have quite a bit to drink, but since they also had to concentrate on the food and cleaning up, they made sure they didn't go overboard.

"Rattana, I think you'd better go back to your father's house with Little Jim and go to bed; this has been a long day and you need your rest," Pompam told his pregnant wife after a while.

"Are you sure you're all right, Pompam?" she asked, concerned.

"Of course, dear. You run along and I'll come for you in the morning for Toy's ceremony."

Pompam, Nuu and Att stayed up late and got completely drunk that night. The next younger brother after Toy, nicknamed 'Black,' tried all night to get close to Pompam. He was now thirteen and Pompam knew it was probably the right time to take him to Bangkok and get him started at the International School. But he also knew that this was not the appropriate moment to take any more of her men away from Maa, so he decided he would wait another year before bringing this next one back to raise.

He seemed like a bright enough kid, Pompam thought. He was skinny, growing tall, and coping with the awkwardness all boys go through at that difficult age. "Don't worry, Black. You behave yourself and study hard. In another year I'll take you to Bangkok," Pompam told him.

Black looked disappointed, and his head drooped dejectedly when he heard this. Apparently he was really counting on going to Bangkok this time, Pompam realized.

"You're the oldest one still at home now, Black. You have to look after Maa and the young ones. Don't you get depressed on me. You have to set an example for the others," Pompam said, doing his best to cheer up the long-faced thirteen-year-old.

Black finally looked his brother in the eye and said, "Okay, Pompam. You're the boss now that Paw's gone. I'll do what you ask, but I won't forget about your promise next year," he grinned.

Pompam drew the boy over close to him and gave him a big hug.

The next morning after breakfast the whole family gathered at the temple for Toy's ordination ceremony. Since Paw was gone it was now Pompam's responsibility to shave off the young man's hair. As he did this he couldn't help but remember the day he himself had sat in that same chair, having his own hair painfully shaved off by his poor dead father. It had been a sacrifice to help the near-starving family survive through the drought, and he had done it willingly with no complaints. "How different things are now," Pompam said to himself, "I could never have imagined then what I have done since that day."

Pompam, Nuu, Att, and even 13-year-old Black, all felt guilty that they, themselves, weren't joining Toy in the monkhood for their father. As they listened to *Phra* Prateep chant the ancient *Pali* sutra, they watched as Toy knelt barefoot in his yellow robes, his posture straight, clear eyes focused on the Buddha image on the altar, the same one Pompam had years before brought as a gift from *Phra* Asoka.

When the ceremony was over Toy walked over to Pompam and said, "Don't feel bad, *Pi-chai*, I am doing this for all of us. It is easier for me than for you and the others." Pompam could feel the love flowing from the boy, and almost started to cry. How can I go back to Bangkok and do what I do, he thought, when my brother is becoming a holy man?

Chapter 17

Back in Bangkok after the long drive, Pompam and Rattana were touched by the scores of telephone messages and letters they found waiting from friends and staff members expressing sympathy for their loss of Paw.

"Rattana, now that *my* father is dead I want to look after *your* father more closely. I don't want the same thing to happen to him. What does he need? What would he like? He helped me so much at Paw's funeral and I'm grateful. I want to do something for him," Pompam said emphatically.

Rattana knew how close Pompam had always felt to her father, and she was deeply touched by his feelings. "I think he would like to come to Bangkok and see our new house, for starters," she replied cheerfully.

"That's a great idea, Rattana. You can wire them money for train tickets and we'll pick them up at Hua Lampong," Pompam said, eagerly embracing the idea.

"You're such a good husband. What can I do to show you my appreciation?"

"To begin with, let's go upstairs and have a nice hot bath together; all that driving has put me in the mood," he teased, and up they went, laughing.

"I have some rather bad news for you, Pompam," Chai said the next day. "I had one of our security guards — out of uniform, of course — watch Joy's apartment for an entire week as you had asked. It seems she has another romantic interest."

"Are you sure, Chai?" he asked in disbelief, stunned.

"More than sure, Pompam. A young man on a motorcycle slept there four nights out of the past seven. Last week Joy called here at the office looking for you and I told her about your father. It looks like she took advantage of your being away."

"That fucking little slut! After all I've done for her. I'll kill her!"

Pompam was enraged. At that moment all his training about mind-fulness and compassion flew out the window and he became the embodiment of raw male ego. His anger astonished even him, but any man would feel this way, he told himself.

"You do what you want to with her, Pompam, but what I've told you is the truth. The security guard even followed the guy home on his motorcycle and found out his name and where he lives. He's a student at Joy's fashion school, twenty years old, and lives near Pratunam."

"What would you do if you were me, Chai?" Pompam asked through his teeth.

"I don't think I would kill the girl," he answered slowly and carefully, "or the boy either, for that matter; it's really not *his* fault. I don't think I could forgive her, so I'd probably throw her out on her ass."

"Give me the boy's name and address, Chai; I have to think about it," Pompam said, trying his best to calm down.

In a moment he was able to switch off and change the subject. "Anything else new? business-wise, that is?" he asked, now more in control, but still feeling bitterly hurt and betrayed.

"I found a possible contact for Taiwan, Pompam. Do you want to go to the meeting or do you want me to handle it? I actually think you should stay pretty quiet right now; your father's funeral was just three days ago."

"Thanks, Chai. You already know the formula and have all the answers; I'm sure you'll do fine without me."

Pompam could not get Joy's cheating on him out of his mind. "How dare she do something like this to me! I've given her everything!" Pompam said to himself over and over as he dialed the number.

"Just calling to let you know I'm home from Buriram, Joy," he said very sweetly, mindfully keeping any emotion out of his voice.

"Oh, Pompam! I'm so sorry about your father. How are you doing?" she asked lovingly.

"I'm doing okay, Joy; how are *you* doing?"

"I'm fine, Pompam, except I've missed you terribly. It's been so lonely here without you," she purred into the phone.

"I've missed you very much, too, Joy, but this has been a very difficult time for me."

"Are you coming over tonight? I promise to take very good care of you if you have the time."

"I'm going to be busy for the next three or four nights, Joy. So much has happened while I was away, and I need to work. You be a good girl and study hard. I'll call you in a couple of days."

"I'll be thinking of you," she whispered, and Pompam quickly hung up before he betrayed his anger.

That night Pompam parked his car a little ways down the street from the apartment and waited to see if the boy would show up. The building had an open balcony hallway so he could see her front door on the fifth floor clearly. Pompam only had to wait about half an hour before the motorcycle roared in, and the boy went directly up to the flat. He was very handsome, Pompam could see that; at least Joy had good taste, he thought cynically.

Pompam drove over to Isan Sweetheart for a bite to eat. He wanted to let the staff know he was fine, and check on Nuu and Att to see how they were doing back at work.

Around midnight he took the lift up to Joy's flat. Very quietly he unlocked the door, and stealthily he entered the living room and closed the door behind him. He walked towards the bedroom and by the light in the bathroom he could see the two of them naked on the bed. Joy was straddling his mid-section, while the young man was lying on his back, gripping her firm buttocks with both hands. She was vigorously riding up and down on the swollen phallus inside her, grinding away, totally ecstatic, and oblivious to the fact that her "husband" and benefactor had just walked into the apartment.

Pompam watched them for a while, completely detached, and became aroused by the erotic exhibition — until he reminded himself just who it was he was watching. He had even gotten an erection, he noticed with surprise, feeling his anger intensify.

Just as he could tell the boy was about to come, Pompam quietly stepped up behind Joy and grabbed her long hair, violently yanking her off the penetrating object that was so obsessing her. She screamed with all the power of her lungs as she fell back on the bed. The boy spilled his seed in mid-air and he sprang to his feet, thinking they were being attacked by a burglar. Pompam swung his arm up smashing the naked youth in the jaw, and he flew backwards in agony.

Then Pompam flicked on the ceiling light and Joy turned to see who it was, the look of rage and fear on her face quickly being replaced with shock and horror. "Oh my God, Pompam! I'm sorry!" she screamed.

The boy got up off the bed and Pompam kicked him fiercely in his unprotected groin. Then Pompam walked over and grabbed him by the neck with one hand and struck him repeatedly in the face with the other. Joy came up behind Pompam and tried to pull him off the unfortunate young man who was doubling over in pain, choking with blood.

"Put your clothes on, Joy!" he screamed. "You get up and put your clothes on too, you little fuck, and get out of here before I cut your dick off! If you ever come near her again — or if you tell anybody about this — I'll have you killed! Do you understand me?" Pompam shouted at the unlucky boyfriend who was struggling to get to his feet, fumbling for his clothes.

"I was so lonely, Pompam. I missed you so much. This is the first time this has ever happened. I promise," she pleaded with him.

"You lying whore! He was here four times last week! You were fucking him while my poor father was dying and I was giving him his funeral!" Pompam went over to her closet and started ripping some of her expensive clothes to shreds. Joy wailed and pleaded.

"Shut up you filthy cunt!" he yelled at her.

The boy finally succeeded in getting his clothes on and, without a backward glance, fled from the apartment. "Remember what I told you, you fucking maggot!" Pompam screamed after him.

"Pompam, Pompam, I'm sorry. Please forgive me. I'll never do this again," she continued to plead, sounding wounded and pitiful as she begged through her tears, but Pompam was not to be moved.

"I told you to shut up. Finish getting dressed. We're going for a ride."

"Where are you taking me, Pompam? Please don't be mad at me. I told you I'll never do it again. Hit me, if you want to, beat me up, but please don't throw me away!"

"Come with me, Joy, right now! I'm getting bored with this whole mess," he muttered angrily.

He finally got her into the car. It was all he could do to keep from beating her to death he was so angry. "After all I've given you, Joy, you give me this! You'll be sorry, that's for sure, but you'll never see me again."

Joy continued sobbing uncontrollably. Pompam turned on the stereo in the BMW and jacked up the volume to keep from hearing her screams and pleas for mercy.

Pompam drove down Petchburi Road and turned into the *soi* next to Isan Sweetheart. He continued on towards the *khlong*, then pulled into his curtain motel. The surprised security guard recognized him at once and motioned him inside a curtained stall and closed it behind the car.

Pompam took the handkerchief out of his pocket and made a gag with it to stifle her screams. He ordered the security guard to help him drag her into the room. Then he ripped her clothes off and threw her down on the bed, her body shaking with fear. She looked up at the ceiling and saw her own terrified face in the mirror. Oh my God I'm sorry, she thought. What is he going to do to me? I was so lonely...

He told the security guard, "I want you to take off your uniform and fuck her for me. She's beautiful, yes? Do you like her? Then do what I say. I'll be back in a few minutes. Joy, you show this nice young man a good time, okay? Just like your other little friend."

The security guard, who looked like he had just gotten out of the army, was a strong and muscular, dark-skinned Isan boy. He did as he was ordered and in no more than one minute he was completely naked and hard. He approached Joy on the bed, and even though she was scared to death she thought she had better obey Pompam and do as he ordered. She opened to the man, still moist from her boyfriend, and let him inside her to take his pleasure. He helped her remove the handkerchief Pompam had stuffed in her mouth, and afterwards she made no further sound other than the small groaning of sex.

Pompam came back with the mamasan. They stood at the door and watched Pompam's *mia noi* and the security guard in the final heated moments of their act together. Not wanting to spoil the young man's enjoyment, Pompam kept silent and watched his own lover being defiled for the second time that night.

"Put your clothes on now, young man, and go back to work,"

he ordered when the security guard had finished. He quickly got dressed without saying a word, or even looking at the girl again. Pompam gave the boy 1,000 baht and thanked him. The guard gave Pompam a respectful *wai* and headed towards the door.

When he had left the room Pompam told the mamasan, "I want you to keep this bitch drugged up and filled with every man she can take for the next two weeks. And I *do* mean as many men as you can drag in here. Do you understand?"

The mamasan fully understood, but she had never seen *Khun* Vichai, her boss's boss, behave this way before. The girl must have really pissed him off for him to do something this bad to her, the old woman thought. But she probably deserves it, she reasoned, or kind *Khun* Vichai would never be so cruel.

"Pompam, you can't do this to me. I love you," Joy continued to scream long after Pompam left the room and closed the door. The mamasan locked it behind her as she followed him out.

"I'll tell you what to do with her in two weeks." Then he left.

"*Mai pen rai*," Pompam told himself. "She deserves what she's getting for doing this to me. She was becoming too much of a problem anyway; I don't want any more *mia nois*. If I want sex I'll have sex, but no more kept whores," he resolved in his mind as he drove away. Pompam hated himself for being so much out of control but he couldn't stop himself now: he was obsessed with venting his overwhelming rage on Joy.

"Are you sure you want her kept at the brothel for two whole weeks? It might destroy her for good," Chai asked the next day, feeling a small amount of sympathy for the unfortunate girl.

"Absolutely. And after the two weeks is over I want you to send her up to Nopadon in Chiang Mai and let him sell her to someone else — as *used* merchandise, of course, since she's hardly a virgin any more. Tell him he can keep the money he gets for her."

"Do you want him to look for another cute young thing for you?" Chai asked him almost sarcastically.

"Definitely *not*. I don't want another *mia noi* for a long, long time, Chai, if ever," Pompam responded, his anger still not fully spent.

Pompam's heart reeled between violent fits of anger and

remorse all the next day. He locked himself in his office and drank one drink after another, his thinking distorted by conflicting emotions. By early evening he was afraid to let anyone see him in such a miserable condition. He got in his car and drove at dangerous speeds far into the sprawling suburbs. All the while he screamed and yelled at Joy, at the Lord Buddha, and at himself. He truly was nearly out of his mind, and at one point he came close to ramming a stone embankment head-on.

At 4:00 a.m. he finally pulled up to the big iron gates in front of his home. He sat there for about half an hour, cold and lifeless, with his chin resting on the steering wheel — staring at the big white house and all it represented.

In spite of his success, Pompam knew that there was something terribly wrong with his life; at the same time he felt powerless to change it — whatever it was.

The following afternoon Kitti nervously approached his old friend and said, "Chai told me what happened, Pompam. I'm sorry to hear it. What should we do with her clothes and her things?"

"I could care less, Kitti. Burn what's left of them — or give them to the girls at Paradise City; perhaps that's a better idea." A good sleep had enabled Pompam to forget about the tormented place his soul had visited just hours before.

"Sure, Pompam, I'd be more than happy to," he answered calmly, not wanting to risk asking more.

"How's everything working out with your girlfriend, *Khun* Sudar?"

"Everything's working out very well, actually. In fact, I'll let you be the first to know that we're getting married in about two months; so you'll finally get rid of me at last," Kitti answered and smiled broadly.

"That's wonderful, Kitti. Congratulations! Shall we build you a new house to live in? Not too far from *Soi* Tonglor?"

"As a matter of fact, Pompam, I bought a house last month just off Ekamai, *Soi* 63. So we won't be too far away at all. It needs quite a bit of fixing up before we move in, but I'll have it ready by the wedding."

"You are a secretive one, aren't you, Kitti? You're getting married and bought a house and you didn't even tell me." Pompam felt hurt.

"You were really busy at the time, Pompam. So many things were going on. You were just getting settled in at *your* new house, and then your father passed away. I thought it could wait to tell you."

Pompam suddenly realized that he had been drifting apart from Kitti for quite some time. He would make a point of spending more time with him from then on, he promised himself.

"Have you decided on a place for your honeymoon yet?" Pompam asked as an idea suddenly occurred to him.

"Not yet, Pompam. That's the last thing on my list. First it's the wedding, and then getting the house ready," he replied.

"Would you do me the honor of letting me give you the honeymoon as a wedding present?" Pompam offered, enjoying a diversion from his dark thoughts.

Kitti smiled. "That would take one thing off my shoulders, Pompam. I would appreciate very much such a nice gift," he said as he smiled warmly.

"Just give me your wedding date and I'll set the whole thing up," he said with enthusiasm.

"I've got everything arranged with the Taiwanese, Pompam. The prices and terms are exactly the same as for Aoyama, and they would also like a standing minimum order of ten girls a month. I've already spoken to my brother, Suphan, and told him to start expanding his visa operation to include the Taiwan consulate," Chai reported.

"What's the Taiwanese guy like? Did you make some 'introductions' for him at Paradise City? Was he kinky like the Japanese?" Pompam was suddenly eager to know.

"He was totally different than Aoyama, Pompam. He smiled and joked all through our meeting, and at Paradise City he took only one girl up to the room and actually *had the massage*. The girl told me later — it was Num again — that when they made sex he was on and off of her in about three minutes and then tipped her 2,500 *baht*. Even though that's a lot of money for her she was still disappointed it hadn't been 5,000 like Aoyama had given her," he said as he laughed out loud.

"It sounds to me like she only had to do half as much work for it," shot back Pompam.

Since the 'Joy' incident Pompam tried to spend as much time as possible at home with Rattana. He had, at least for the moment, developed a new appreciation for his wife and their marriage. Taking care of Little Jim was still the primary activity in her life, but even so, she had appointments nearly every day for lunch, and there were many invitations from one *hi-so* lady or another, as Pompam had predicted. As a result, she became involved in at least a dozen charity projects. Many of these ultimately culminated in large dinners or receptions, and Rattana was constantly up-dating Pompam's calendar with these night-time events for both of them to attend.

Pompam didn't mind Rattana's social life. He was delighted to see her continue to grow, and be able to handle herself in a broad spectrum of situations, with an ever-wider variety of people. Her progress was remarkable when he thought that just a few years before she had known nothing but the rice fields of Buriram. The way she looked and acted now, one would think she had been educated in Europe, he thought, pleased.

When Toy's three weeks were finished at the village temple he came home to Bangkok wearing the inevitable baseball cap over his stubbly shaved head. Pompam had missed him terribly, and personally drove to the train station to meet him and give him a ride home.

They embraced each other in a flood of tears as the memory of Paw's death re-surfaced, and Toy said, "Life is so short, Pompam, and there is so much suffering. Please try not to add to it any more."

Pompam didn't respond; he suddenly found himself immersed in so much conflict he didn't know what to say.

"I spoke to Nopadon earlier today, Pompam. He told me he sold Joy to an old Chinese man in Chiang Rai to be his *mia noi*. He thanks you for letting him keep the money," Chai reported.

"I'm glad the extra money made Nopadon happy. How are we doing on the Taiwanese visa operation?" he asked, not wanting to think about Joy — or feel the desperate pain the memory of her image evoked within him.

"Suphan tells me that his success ratio for the Taiwanese Consul is three-to-one, which is quite a bit better now than the Japanese.

He shipped out thirteen girls to Taiwan his first month and thinks he can hit twenty this time. The money keeps rolling in, Pompam. Don't you ever get tired of making it?" he asked, grinning.

"I haven't even begun to make *serious* money yet, Chai. Just give me a couple more years of practice," Pompam replied.

Pompam bought *Khun* Direk a new pick-up truck during his and his wife's visit to Bangkok. He knew it would be useful to him back on the rice farm. He also bestowed upon him a stipend of 10,000 *baht* that Rattana would transfer to him every month; she was grateful Pompam had such caring feelings for her father.

"Don't be like *my* father, *Khun* Direk. When you get sick you have to promise me that you'll go to the doctor. You're the only father we have left and we want you to be around to enjoy your grandchildren," Pompam admonished him in a loving way.

"You are really too good to me, Pompam. How lucky we are that you and our daughter fell in love and married," he replied, silently reminding himself that he must make a donation to the temple as soon as he returned home.

Rattana was delighted to have her parents around for their month-long visit. She had hoped that they would come to Bangkok more often and save her from having to go all the way to Buriram to see them. She felt more and more removed from her roots as time passed, and knew she no longer had anything in common with her former schoolgirl friends in the village.

After a while, with Joy out of his life, Pompam began to feel a strong need again for extracurricular female stimulation. In this regard he started leading a "secret life," not telling Kitti or Ott or anyone what he did or where he went for amusement from time to time. He didn't want anyone to know about it because he didn't want to be judged; it was bad enough just *thinking* about how Toy would feel about the things he did, much less have to confront him if he found out.

When he was in the mood he would drive down to Patpong and visit the sleazy, darkly-lit bars where mostly tourist customers watched the male/female live sex shows, the lively naked go-go dancers, and the girls who performed solo sex acts with a variety of inanimate objects.

The girls would see well-known *Khun* Vichai from the stage and flock to where he sat to flirt with him and fondle him, trying their best to get him to buy them off for the night. He would usually take two or three at once to an anonymous curtain motel and make them perform for him in private while he lay nude on the bed, becoming aroused watching them.

Then he would have sex with them. Unlike anything he had ever done before, he would often experiment with the bodies of these girls, sometimes causing pain, and indulge himself in his most unorthodox sexual fantasies. He would do things with them that he would never think of doing with Rattana, and never even dared to experience with ever-willing Joy.

Then he would go home, have his shower, and sleep with his wife; sometimes he would have sex with her if his lust was still not satisfied.

He never attempted to set any of those commercial girls up in apartments, and he never bought them any presents. He tipped them well, of course, but after sex he wanted nothing further to do with them, and he would never "off" the same girl twice. After Joy, he wanted everything on his terms and at his convenience; in Bangkok he could have anything, and as much as he wanted — and he did.

Sudar's family was very gracious and traditional, and gave their daughter a beautiful wedding. They had the reception under tents set up amidst the ruins of the ancient capital city of Ayuddhya, which had been sacked and destroyed by the Burmese in 1767. It was a lovely evening outdoors, under the trees and stars. Special lighting had been rigged up on two or three of the mysterious old temples, and Pompam and Rattana went off on their own exploring, hand in hand, very happy. They talked lovingly of their first night together under the full moon at Phanom Rung in Buriram.

Pompam gave a moving speech when he toasted the bridal couple after dinner, a testament to his life-long friendship with Kitti. Sudar felt happy with her welcome into the extended family, and began her own friendship that evening with Rattana.

"Do you remember that new hotel I told you about when I

came back from my first trip to Chiang Mai? The one I told you I would take you to one day?" he asked Kitti, who said he vaguely remembered.

"Well that's where you're going on your honeymoon — just to prove I always keep my word," he exclaimed with a laugh.

Kitti and Sudar were deeply touched by Pompam's thoughtfulness, and they shed some tears when they waved good-bye.

"Pompam is pretty wonderful, isn't he?" Kitti said to no one in particular on the plane the next morning. He knew very well that if it weren't for his friend he wouldn't have even a semblance of the life he now lived, and not a chance in hell of marrying an upper class girl like Sudar. He thought for a moment about what Pompam had done to get them started, and it seemed impossible that things had turned out as well as they had. He remembered one of Pompam's birthdays a few years back and his remark about "reaping our rewards." I guess that's what we're doing now, he thought to himself, and silently thanked the Lord Buddha for his good karma.

Chapter 18

A few months passed and Pompam's second child was born, a daughter whom they named Somporn, after Rattana's mother. The child truly delighted the entire household, Little Jim included.

A few weeks after the baby was born Pompam received his long-ago promised invitation to visit Japan. With the invitation was a round-trip first-class ticket to Tokyo on Japan Airlines. Mr. Aoyama was most gracious in his invitation letter, and said he hoped that Pompam could come soon, as the weather was perfect that time of the year.

Mr. Aoyama's letter also said that his boss, Mr. Yamamoto, wanted to meet him personally to discuss some other possible business opportunities they might develop together. This intrigued the youthful entrepreneur, in spite of the alleged *yakuza* associations that still made him feel somewhat uncomfortable.

Since Pompam and Chai had begun working with Mr. Aoyama's organization, they had sent nearly three hundred girls to Japan; this represented an incredibly huge amount of profit for Pompam and he didn't feel that he could very easily refuse an invitation from such an important client. Disturbing thoughts, however, kept creeping into the back of his mind that kept telling him *not* to go to Japan, *not* to get more involved with Aoyama and Yamamoto; but he pushed these inner warnings aside, confident, as usual, that he could handle anything.

Pompam notified Mr. Aoyama in Tokyo that he would arrive the following week. He immediately received a return fax saying that he would meet him personally at the airport in Narita.

Before he left for Japan he sent Att and Toy to Buriram to collect Black, the next youngest brother. Enough time had passed so that Maa wouldn't feel too bad about losing another son to Bangkok, even though it left her with only three more at home. Pompam enrolled Black at the International School, thanks again to *Khun* Surapong who pulled strings; Toy had already begun his studies at Chulalongkorn University.

By this time Nuu had moved out of the guest house into a lovely condominium Pompam leased for him on Sukhumvit. He lived there with his girlfriend, another beautiful model that he had met through Ott. They were supposedly engaged, but Nuu and the girl wanted to do it the American way and live together for a while before they got married.

This left Att, who was about to graduate from Ramkampheng, Toy, and now Black in the bachelors' quarters by the pool. Toy had been reluctant to leave the main house. He and Pompam had gotten used to living down the hall from one another, and at first — in spite of their regular conflicts — both of them were afraid of losing the closeness of their relationship.

Pompam finally said to Toy, "You're only moving to the back yard; we'll meet every night by the pool." Toy smiled at his *pi-chai* and agreed, knowing Black would need him to help adjust to his new environment.

Pompam dearly loved complex, often recalcitrant, and even rude, Toy. The young brother had grown into a truly remarkable young man and Pompam was proud of him, admiring the way he was always getting involved in projects that benefited the poor and unfortunate. Even though he couldn't always understand him, Pompam realized that Toy's character was born out of his spirituality and his Buddhist faith; otherwise Pompam would never have put up with his outbursts and opposition.

"What can I bring you from Japan, Rattana?" Pompam asked as he was about to leave for the airport.

"If you have time, Pompam, maybe an outfit by one of those really far-out Japanese designers," she answered after a moment of thought, "and a Japanese robot toy for Little Jim — he'll love that."

"I'll do the best I can," he said. "I'll be at the Akasaka Prince Hotel if you need to reach me; Kitti has the number."

"Don't worry about us, we'll be fine; I have lunches and charity meetings almost every day while you're gone," Rattana continued, now more self-confident than ever.

Mr. Aoyama was waiting for him when he stepped out through Customs, just as he had promised. The two underlings were still with him, and Pompam supposed he probably wasn't even allowed to go to the toilet without them; not allowed — or didn't dare — Pompam wasn't sure.

"Good afternoon, Mr. Vichai. Welcome to Japan. I hope your flight was enjoyable."

"So nice to see you again, Mr. Aoyama," Pompam said as he *waied*. "The flight was terrific, thank you. You look well," Pompam told him, and was glad he had decided to wear a tailored business suit on the flight instead of something more comfortable as he would have preferred. Mr. Aoyama was dressed in elegant business attire, as he had been when Pompam last saw him at Paradise City.

"I am very well indeed, Mr. Vichai. You look like a Thai movie star, as usual," he said, giving an honest compliment to his foreign guest.

"I do my best," Pompam replied modestly.

One of the underlings bowed, and without saying anything, took Pompam's bag and led off in the direction of the car, a stretched Mercedes Benz limousine. Pompam was impressed, as he was meant to be.

They made small talk during the fifty mile ride into the city, and since there was a bar in the back seat with a bottle of Black Label, Pompam and Mr. Aoyama had a few drinks and pleasantly passed the time.

The hotel was a giant, soaring skyscraper that overlooked the Imperial Palace. They had put Pompam in one of the best suites, and he thanked Mr. Aoyama profusely for his over-generous hospitality.

"Never mind, Mr. Vichai. You are an important guest. Mr. Yamamoto has been wanting to meet you for a long time and personally thank you for the perfect job you have done for us in Thailand. He is looking forward to entertaining you tomorrow evening for dinner. It is most rare, I think you should know, for him to meet business associates from abroad," Aoyama said to Pompam with emphasis. "The last time I was in Bangkok I secured a copy of your famous travel poster and presented it to him as a gift. He has it hanging in his retreat house."

"I am quite honored, Mr. Aoyama, that Mr. Yamamoto would

care to spend some of his very valuable time with me, and I'm flattered that he likes my poster. I am, after all, just a country boy from Thailand," Pompam said as he tried once again to sound simple and modest.

"You under-estimate yourself, Mr. Vichai. You are quite a remarkable young man. Not many from your country — or from any country, for that matter — have accomplished as much as you have at your age. Mr. Yamamoto is very interested in meeting the talented young man he has heard so much about." Mr. Aoyama really piled it on, Pompam thought to himself.

"Now you must refresh yourself, have a nice bath, and relax. If you aren't too tired I would like you to have dinner with me this evening, and then I will take you to one of our nightclubs. I am sure you would like to see where the beautiful young ladies you send us from Thailand spend their working hours."

"I would enjoy that very much, Mr. Aoyama. Are we going to have Japanese food? You promised me Japanese food when I visited you here in Tokyo," Pompam reminded his host, smiling.

"One of the best Japanese restaurants in Tokyo is right here in this hotel. I have made reservations for eight-thirty. I trust that will give you enough time to rest and work up an appetite, Mr. Vichai," he responded politely.

Pompam took a long, hot bath in the huge tub in the corner of the bathroom, sipped another Black Label and soda, and relaxed, thinking about the evening ahead. He was excited to be in Japan, but he wished that Mr. Aoyama had invited Chai as well. It would have been nice to have some company along from home, he thought to himself.

Pompam took a thirty-minute nap, woke up feeling refreshed, and dressed in his best business suit for the evening.

At precisely eight-thirty Mr. Aoyama and his two "associates" called for Pompam at his suite. "You look wonderfully restored, Mr. Vichai. Shall we go downstairs?"

They entered the tastefully-appointed Japanese restaurant and were greeted by politely-bowing hostesses dressed in rich-looking embroidered kimonos; they were led through several rooms of diners to a hallway with private dining rooms on both sides. *Shoji* screens opened to reveal the small room where they would have their dinner.

"We remove our shoes here, Mr. Vichai. Perhaps you would also like to give the hostess your jacket; you will be far more comfortable since we'll be sitting on the floor," Aoyama suggested.

Pompam was more than happy to remove his shoes and jacket, then he sat down on the cushion the hostess indicated and loosened his necktie. "We also eat on the floor in my native village," Pompam commented.

He absorbed the simple elegance of the room. There were tatami mats, *shoji* walls, a lovely flower arrangement with only three crimson blooms, and a highly polished rosewood table.

"Is there anything that you don't eat, Mr. Vichai? They prepare just about everything in the entire Japanese cuisine at this restaurant, with a few special exceptions. Have you ever tried raw seafood?" he asked.

"I like seafood very much, but I've never tasted it raw. Is that something Japanese?"

"Yes, Mr. Vichai, it most definitely is. I'll order a general selection of dishes that will not be offensive to you — and a small order of *nigiri sushi* for you to try. If we discover that you like *sushi*, then we will have a great deal of enjoyment to look forward to together during the next few days of your visit."

Several interesting-looking dishes arrived and Pompam sampled each one. For the most part he liked the food, and he said so to his host; but he really missed the chilies and spices he had been brought up on, and found the Japanese food to be too bland for his taste.

The *sushi*, however, was another story. Pompam went crazy over it, which truly amazed and pleased Mr. Aoyama. Pompam was not in the least bit squeamish about trying the raw seafood. He loved the combination of the vinegared rice and wasabe, the Japanese horseradish that was so hot and pungent it cleared his sinuses just like Thai chili. At last, some food with taste, Pompam thought. "This *sushi* is terrific, Mr. Aoyama. I could eat this every meal while I am here."

After dinner, the big Mercedes limousine was waiting at the hotel entrance and Pompam and his host climbed inside. The two underlings rode up front with the driver as before.

"While you are here, we want you to see the best of the night-clubs we operate. Tonight we will be going to our second best hostess bar, and perhaps tomorrow Mr. Yamamoto will accompany you to the number one," Aoyama announced proudly.

They soon arrived at the celebrated establishment which was located in the fashionable Roppongi district. Their limousine pulled up under the *porte cochère* and uniformed doormen bowed and opened the car's rear doors.

Several Japanese wearing dark business suits stood both outside, and in the entry foyer; Pompam assumed correctly that they were security guards. Everyone bowed low to Mr. Aoyama and Pompam as they were escorted to their table, a sumptuous banquette in a secluded corner that afforded them a good view of the complete environment.

"I told the manager to have a few of the Thai girls come by our table to say 'hello.' They will sit down briefly with us and then excuse themselves as they have been instructed. I only want you to meet them, speak briefly to them, and see for yourself how they comport themselves here," he explained.

Mr. Aoyama ordered their usual drinks, and very shortly the first two girls appeared. They bowed to Mr. Aoyama and then smiled and *waied* politely to Pompam before they sat down. Pompam could immediately see that the girls had been well-trained in the arts of personal grooming. To Pompam, they looked fabulous — quite different from the way they might have looked in their shocking-pink "shorty" negligees back home at Paradise City. They spoke to Mr. Aoyama in Japanese, and to Pompam in Thai; they understood no English.

"Their Japanese sounds pretty good, Mr. Aoyama," Pompam commented, impressed.

"These two girls were from one of the earliest groups that arrived here, Mr. Vichai. In the beginning they were taught enough Japanese to be able to pleasantly engage the customers, and to flatter them to some degree. From then on, they learned on their own."

Several more pairs of Thai girls came to the table as the two men continued talking over their drinks. The scenario for the others was much the same as it had been with the first two, but Pompam couldn't get over how stunning and "international" they all looked. Their clothes, their hair and make-up, their posture, and their manners were impeccable. "The girls don't seem to be mistreated by some evil mamasan," Pompam said to himself, "they look happy for the chance to be working here; we have truly helped them!" Pompam convinced himself that this was the case, but if the girls had been free to tell him the truth, he would have heard a completely different story; but as it was, he would never know.

"Now that you've seen your Thai girls, Mr. Vichai, I thought it might be nice for you to meet some exceptional ladies from right here in Japan," offered Mr. Aoyama.

Two Japanese girls soon joined them and Pompam could tell at once that these were of a different, higher class than the other Japanese escorts that were seated at various tables around the room, even without Mr. Aoyama telling him. They were especially beautiful, but the restrained manner in which they comported themselves was much more refined and elegant than anything he had ever experienced in a female. They almost seemed to Pompam as if they were from an age long since past.

As Pompam admired them Aoyama explained, "These two girls have been particularly trained, Pompam, by '*geisha*' masters. The *geishas* were the courtesans for rich patrons in Japan during several hundred years of our history. They have an ancient tradition that still goes on today, and it requires many years of apprenticeship and instruction for them to achieve perfection. Their training includes music, calligraphy, etiquette, polite conversation, the tea ceremony, and love-making — among other things. We bought the contracts of these two girls from one of the few remaining *geisha* schools, and brought them here to serve our most discerning customers. They are very hard to find these days," the Japanese gentleman continued in detail.

"They are truly lovely, Mr. Aoyama. I could see the difference immediately between these and all the others I see moving about the room," Pompam replied as he looked closely at the two beautiful girls.

"One of them will meet you later at your hotel, Mr. Vichai. You choose the one you wish, and I will communicate the arrangement to her. This will be my 'introduction' to you for the evening. It is my way of returning the favor you did for me when we first met in Bangkok." Pompam and his host exchanged looks, and Pompam knew that he couldn't refuse — even if he had wanted to.

After a pause Pompam made his choice. "I would very much enjoy spending the evening with the girl sitting next to you, Mr. Aoyama, if you don't mind."

"You have chosen wisely, Mr. Vichai, and it proves that you have excellent taste. But then again I should have known that you would choose well, seeing the way you took to the *sushi* at dinner," he laughed good-naturedly as he said this, and Pompam smiled back at him warmly.

"By the way, Mr. Vichai, her name is Yuki." Mr. Aoyama then turned and spoke softly to the beautiful girl next to him who listened silently and nodded her head from time to time in the distinctively Japanese manner.

After a few minutes the two girls gracefully excused themselves, bowing to both the Japanese and his Thai guest.

"I think that now it's time we got you back to your hotel, Mr. Vichai, as you may want to relax for a short while before your appointment with Yuki." Pompam nodded to Aoyama in acquiescence, then the two men got up and made their way through the crowded nightclub to the limousine that waited outside.

"I will phone you in your room tomorrow morning and come by around lunchtime to take you for more *sushi* and a little sightseeing," the Japanese gentleman said as he bade goodnight to Pompam in front of the hotel.

Upstairs in his suite Pompam removed his clothes and changed into one of the soft, cotton, navy blue and white robes, called *"yukata,"* that he found in the dressing room.

A few minutes later, when Pompam answered the doorbell, he found Yuki standing there wearing a simple, elegantly-tailored dark gray suit and white silk blouse. She had changed from her emerald green cocktail dress which wouldn't have been appropriate for entering the hotel so late at night.

She smiled warmly at Pompam as he silently ushered her into the suite using sign language; then she walked confidently over to the seating area Pompam indicated and made herself comfortable on the sofa. Pompam pointed to the bottle of champagne he had discovered when he got back to his room, already chilling on ice. Yuki looked up at him and smiled, nodding her head, and said, "Yes, that would be delightful; thank you."

Pompam, shocked, said, "You can speak English! I had no idea; at the club you only spoke to Mr. Aoyama in Japanese."

"They feel it would spoil my image as a Japanese courtesan if I spoke English at work; so I never do," she answered.

Pompam opened the bottle and Yuki took it from him and filled their two long-stemmed flutes. They clinked them together, smiled, then Yuki removed her high-heeled shoes and gracefully arranged herself with one leg tucked under the other. After another glass or two of champagne Pompam found that he was enjoying himself with this first non-Thai girl he had ever known; she turned out to be an excellent, well-educated, conversationalist, and provided Pompam with a great deal of information about Japan.

After a while Yuki excused herself and went into the bathroom. Pompam soon heard water running in the big bathtub. The girl re-appeared wearing a *yukata* like his own, and after another glass of champagne she went back into the bathroom, turned off the water, then returned and motioned for Pompam to follow her.

Pompam would never forget that night of love-making for the rest of his life. He soon learned that Yuki was a master in the art of sex. Pompam began to think of her as a completely new gender, so different she was from all of the other human beings Pompam had experienced sexually. She engaged him in a duel of the bodies that required connecting everything they had to some energy source known only to her. She brought him to the brink of exploding time and again, while she herself fluttered back and forth over the abyss. She manipulated his manhood into a heightened level of stimulation beyond the limits of control, delaying the ultimate conclusion until he almost felt pain. It seemed to Pompam that hours passed in this state until he could endure it no more or lose consciousness — or worse. She cruelly made him wait even longer before finally allowing him to dive off the edge into an orgasm that he hoped would never end.

After a while Yuki got up from the bed, showered and dressed. Pompam didn't want her to leave, but he didn't feel he could politely protest her departure. She simply bowed, smiled, and without another word walked through the door that Pompam held open for her.

He poured himself a drink and sat there naked for a while, looking out at the city below him, not believing that he had actually been a participant in a near-spiritual experience — and that he had attained it through sex. He thought about the meditation practices he had studied as a boy, and realized they had never elevated him to the high state where Yuki had just taken him.

The experience made his frequent forays into the dark world of Patpong and curtain motels seem crude and amateurish, which in fact they were. Yuki had opened his awareness to a level of sensuality he had never known existed. But now, what to do with that awareness? That was the question he was left with as he got up and walked to the bedroom and fell into a deep sleep almost at once.

Late the next morning Mr. Aoyama called, as he had promised, and said he would be by at noon to pick up Pompam for lunch and sightseeing.

"I trust you had an entertaining evening and a good rest, Mr. Vichai?" Aoyama said to him in the back of the limousine. It wasn't so much a question as a statement, but Pompam responded, "It was a most amazing evening, Mr. Aoyama, and a very good rest, indeed," and the two men smiled at one another. Pompam, amused, suddenly wondered if Mr. Aoyama had interviewed Yuki about *his* performance, as he and Chai had once interviewed Num and Nut about Aoyama's.

After another meal of *sushi* Pompam told Mr. Aoyama that he wished to buy some robot toys for Little Jim, something for his baby girl, and a few Japanese designer outfits for Rattana, so they went to the appropriate stores so he could make his purchases. Pompam was surprised at how expensive the clothes were and Mr. Aoyama explained that the designer was the most famous one in Japan, an internationally-recognized celebrity. Pompam just hoped that Rattana and her *hi-so* girlfriends would appreciate them.

Mr. Aoyama showed Pompam the vast city, made stops at a few places he thought would be of interest to a visiting foreign businessman, then returned him to his hotel. "I will come back for you at eight o'clock, Mr. Vichai. Mr. Yamamoto will be entertaining you privately at his retreat house this evening. It is quite an exceptional honor."

Pompam was happy to have some time to relax in his room and

reflect on his Japan experience so far. For the first time since he had arrived he was glad that he was alone on this trip. If Chai had come along, Pompam thought, everything would have been completely different.

They arrived at a small walled-in house in the Roppongi district and Mr. Aoyama informed a rather surprised Pompam that he would not be joining him and Mr. Yamamoto for dinner. "The two of you will have much to discuss in private. Mr. Yamamoto's driver will see you back to the hotel later, and I will phone you in the morning. Please enjoy your evening, Mr. Vichai."

One of Aoyama's underlings had already rung the bell for Pompam at the unpretentious gate, and a servant opened it, bowing silently as Pompam passed through. He entered the unexpected world of an exquisite Japanese garden, well-ordered with rocks, small plants, trees and trickling water falling into a pool of colorful fish. Pompam followed the servant into the foyer.

A handsome Japanese gentleman in his early forties entered the room. His feet were bare and he was wearing a long, dark-blue *yukata*, much like the ones Pompam had found in his hotel dressing room. "I am Yamamoto, Mr. Vichai. Welcome to my retreat house. I am delighted that you could join me," he said as he extended his hand American-style.

Pompam shook his hand and then said, "Thank you very much for inviting me, Mr. Yamamoto. And thank you also for your tremendous hospitality, and for the opportunity to visit Japan. I am particularly grateful for the experience you provided for me last evening," he said, referring to Yuki.

"It is our pleasure, Mr. Vichai, to take good care of you while you are here as our guest," he replied with a discreet smile.

Pompam then removed his shoes as was the custom both in Japan and in Thailand.

"This is a very Japanese house, Mr. Vichai, and you can see that I am dressed in a *yukata*, which is both very Japanese and very comfortable. Why don't you change into one yourself; it will be more relaxing than the suit and tie you are wearing, and more suitable for the environment," he said and pointed to a room off the hall.

"Thank you very much, Mr. Yamamoto. I'm more than happy

to get rid of the business suit," Pompam replied and went off to change.

"That's much better, Mr. Vichai," Yamamoto said when Pompam reappeared, barefoot as well. "Let's go into the sitting room where we can talk and have a few drinks before dinner. Aoyama-san tells me that you like Black Label and soda. Would you like that? or would you like to try some '*sake*,' our famous Japanese rice wine?"

"If you are having *sake*, I would like to try some. If I like it as much as I like *sushi* then I'll like it very much indeed," Pompam laughed.

"Aoyama-san tells me that you have really developed a taste for *sushi*" Yamamoto replied, laughing. "It's very rare for a foreigner to take so quickly to our favorite food like that."

Mr. Yamamoto called to the servant and had many specialty dishes served that were totally unlike the ones Aoyama had ordered the night before in the restaurant. For the next hour or so, more and more tiny dishes continued to arrive, and Pompam's *sake* cup was always full. He felt relaxed in this polite man's company, and was genuinely enjoying the food and serene atmosphere of the Japanese house.

"If I might, I would like to tell you how much we appreciate the fine business relationship we have developed with your organization. From our perspective, it has worked perfectly since the beginning," Pompam began his rehearsed speech of thanks.

"I, too, am most happy with the way things have worked out between us, Mr. Vichai. I think we could possibly expand our business activities in Thailand by helping you to expand yours. I am prepared to begin an undertaking with you that will make you wealthier than you have ever dreamed; but let's save this business discussion for another time, if you don't mind; this is a 'social' evening."

"As you wish, Mr. Yamamoto," Pompam responded, his mind racing, trying to guess what his host had in mind. "I look forward to hearing your ideas whenever it is convenient for you."

"Come with me, Mr. Vichai, and I'll show you my *dojo*," said the Japanese man, standing to his feet. "We can relax, have a massage, and a nice hot soak in my Japanese bath, as is our custom. Afterwards I'll take you out and show you the number one members' club in Japan."

Pompam followed Mr. Yamamoto through the sparsely-furnished

and yet extremely elegant Japanese house. The *dojo* had nothing in it at all except Japanese swords, fencing equipment, and a few pieces of black and white calligraphy hanging on the walls. *Shoji* doors opened onto the beautifully-proportioned garden, bordered by a wooden deck which is called in Japanese, the *"ongawa."* Pompam stepped outside and enjoyed the tranquil scene for a moment, a virtual oasis in the heart of downtown Tokyo.

"Come this way, Mr. Vichai. You can change in here; two of the best masseurs in Japan are in the next room waiting for us."

Pompam removed his *yukata* and his underwear and wrapped a large bath towel around his waist. He went into the next room and laid face down on the massage table the burly masseur indicated to him in sign language. Mr. Yamamoto, now also dressed in a towel, came into the room and laid down on the table next to Pompam's.

Pompam was nearly shocked out of his wits to see that Yamamoto's body was covered from his neck to just above his knees in massive, colorful tattoos. Up until then they had been completely covered by the long *yukata*. Yamamoto's body was strong and muscular, and each time he moved the tattoos seemed to take on a life of their own. Pompam couldn't help but stare, completely fascinated.

When Nut and Num described Aoyama's tattoos Pompam had been curious, perhaps even a bit excited. This time he could hardly relax and enjoy the excellent massage, distracted as he was by the strange sight of the body across from him that both repelled and intrigued him. The tattoo-covered Japanese laid motionless with his eyes closed while the masseur worked him over. He was seemingly oblivious to Pompam's stares and agitated feelings.

The masseurs finished after about an hour and Mr. Yamamoto sat up and pointed to the wall. "Did you notice that I have your poster up there?" Pompam hadn't noticed, and said so, very shyly.

He still couldn't stop staring at Yamamoto's skin. "You look surprised, Mr. Vichai. Surely you've seen tattoos before?"

"Yes," Pompam replied tentatively, "but not quite like yours..."

Mr. Yamamoto dismissed the masseurs and indicated that Pompam should follow him. "Now you can experience the famous Japanese '*furo*,' or hot tub, something no visitor to Japan should ever miss."

They entered a humid, window-less room containing a large, dark pool of steaming water. The spa was lit by only a few candles in sconces on the wall, which made Yamamoto's magnificent tattoos seem to glow in the dark. He dropped his towel onto a bench and stepped slowly into the scalding water. Without the covering of his towel Pompam could see for the first time the splendid tattoos to their full extent. He found the snakes, dragons, female goddesses and other images strangely beautiful as their shapes changed with every movement of Yamamoto's naked body. "Come on in, Mr. Vichai. But enter slowly; the water is very, very hot."

Pompam left his towel next to Mr. Yamamoto's and tentatively stepped into the pool. This time it was Yamamoto's turn to look at Pompam's perfect body and his golden, unblemished skin, illuminated by the candles.

"I don't think I can get in, Mr. Yamamoto. It's too hot for me," Pompam said as he winced in pain from the scalding water burning his feet and ankles.

"Just take it slowly, one inch at a time, Mr. Vichai," he instructed, narrow eyes widening.

Yamamoto was submerged up to the neck by now and he watched an awkward, embarrassed Pompam as he gradually sunk into the water. Pompam finally got all the way in and found that he could endure it if he didn't move around too much. It eventually began to feel quite good to him; a nice finish to the strenuous massage he had just taken, he reflected.

The two men remained silent and motionless for a while until Pompam felt Yamamoto's hand reach for his thigh, moving slowly towards his private area. "So this is what he really wants," Pompam said to himself, totally surprised. Pompam didn't know how to react to this unforeseen situation, and he struggled in his mind to find a polite way out.

Meanwhile, Mr. Yamamoto continued his advances on Pompam who, caught in his indecision, remained frozen, and made no move to resist. After a few moments and without speaking, he took Pompam's hand in his and led him up the steps out of the hot water. He spread their towels on the deck next to the pool, sat down, and pulled passive Pompam towards him.

Pompam averted his eyes but still did not protest the advances. He felt like he was in some kind of a dream, being led, he knew not why, into something he knew he didn't want to do, but was unable to stop. He was already quite erect, he noticed, and as he glanced up he saw that Yamamoto had seen it too.

Pompam finally told himself that he had waited too long to protest, and realized at that point that he no longer had a choice. Just relax and let whatever happens simply happen, he thought to himself. After all, he had done this many times in the almost-forgotten past. As if expecting no resistance, Mr. Yamamoto confidently began giving Pompam another well-practiced sexual experience; it was almost like Yuki's energy the previous night, Pompam reflected. "Why should I resist?" Pompam finally said to himself. "The most I ever got from doing this was 200,000 *baht* from *Khun* James; I'm likely to get millions from this one."

He decided to let Yamamoto do whatever he wanted with his body. He simply closed his eyes and treated the Japanese like one of his old customers and in the end, did his best to give him his money's worth, allowing no thoughts to enter his mind that might make him think less of himself.

Later on, after a cold shower, Pompam re-joined Mr. Yamamoto in the sitting room. They both now had on their business suits and Yamamoto said very formally, "Shall we go?" They rose to their feet and in moments were cruising down the streets of Tokyo in the back of another limousine.

If Pompam thought the reception he and Mr. Aoyama had received the evening before was grand, it was nothing compared to what he and Mr. Yamamoto got when they arrived at The Imperial Club, as it was called.

Everyone stood and bowed as Mr. Yamamoto and Pompam made their way across the most splendid room Pompam had ever seen. It's unrestrained opulence made the club the night before look almost simple and middle-class by comparison.

When they were seated at their table Pompam gazed out over the high-ceilinged space, trying to absorb as many details as possible. Yamamoto, enjoying the look on his companion's face, said, "What do you think?"

"We have nothing even remotely like this in Thailand," he replied with not a small amount of awe in his voice.

Mr. Yamamoto ordered drinks from a trembling waiter and then turned to Pompam and said, "No one will ever know or suspect our relationship, Mr. Vichai. You know what I mean..." Pompam only nodded his head in acknowledgment.

"When we are in private you may call me by my first name, which is 'Kenji,'" Yamamoto told his guest, "otherwise we must maintain a formal appearance, which is our custom."

"Then in private you must call me 'Pompam,' which is my nickname," the young Thai replied, trying to be friendly.

The two of them conversed quietly for a while about neutral topics, and no one approached the table except for the nervous waiter to refresh their glasses when necessary. Finally Yamamoto said, "Tomorrow, Pompam, Aoyama will call you and arrange for some sightseeing. I'm afraid I won't be able to be with you in the evening; it's my oldest son's birthday and my wife has planned a special party for him. What can I say?" he explained.

"I have children too, Kenji; I understand completely," Pompam responded politely, feeling somewhat relieved.

Mr. Yamamoto dropped Pompam off at the hotel about an hour later. They agreed to meet again the day after the next to discuss business. Pompam, exhausted, fell asleep easily that night and did his best to think no more about what he had done with Kenji in the *dojo*.

"Good morning, Mr. Vichai. I trust your evening with Mr. Yamamoto was pleasant?" asked Aoyama when he phoned about ten o'clock the next morning.

"Just fine, thank you. The Imperial Club makes my little places in Bangkok look like slums," replied Pompam, just out of the shower.

"I've arranged for Yuki to come by for you in about an hour. She'll meet you in the lobby and show you around today. I hope that will be all right with you?"

Pompam, thrilled, couldn't believe his good fortune. "That will be more than all right, Mr. Aoyama; I couldn't imagine anything better!" he effused, then remembered he might be offending Aoyama and said,

"But I will miss seeing you today — and our sushi."

"*Mai pen rai*, as you say in your country, Mr. Vichai; you'll have a better time with Yuki than you would with me. Enjoy yourself."

It was already the following morning and Pompam sat in front of the television, unable to sleep. The clock said 4:00 a.m. As hard as he tried to hold onto it, the day before was already slipping between his fingers, fading into memory, even though it had been one of the most delightful Pompam had ever spent with anyone. Before the images disappeared, however, he made sure they were permanently affixed in his mind, and he went over each detail again and again. On the other hand, it would take no effort at all to recall the beautiful, talented Yuki: the one who had given him the day like a precious gift — wrapped in silk — and sex.

She would haunt him always, and he knew it — just as he knew he would never see her again. Yuki had once again slipped out of his bed and left him in a spiritual limbo — hanging somewhere between ecstasy and despair. "If only I could have spent more time with her," he lamented longingly. Even though he was sated, he wasn't satisfied; he knew then that perhaps he never would be.

In only a few hours he would meet Yamamoto, a thought that made him depressed, and somehow carried with it a sense of foreboding. Finally, as the sky over the Imperial Palace turned pink, he fell asleep.

"You look a bit tired today, Pompam. Didn't you sleep well?" Yamamoto asked when Pompam entered the back of the limousine.

"It must be jet-lag, Kenji," he answered, knowing that Yamamoto undoubtedly knew all about his day — and night — with Yuki; he had, after all, paid for it.

"Don't worry, you'll get over it soon. I've not yet had the time to take you touring, so today we're going for a drive in the countryside, to a small inn we own. It is a very scenic spot, and the food is excellent," he replied.

The view of snow-capped Mt. Fuji in the distance was lovely, and crowded Tokyo seemed far away. They were seated on the tatami floor of a small dining room, being served *sake* and fragrant, artful delicacies in hand-made ceramic bowls. It appeared that they were the only patrons, and the rest of the inn looked deserted.

"I think it's time for us to begin a new business together, Pompam. You have proven yourself to be not only trustworthy, but talented and imaginative as well. For our new business you must have all three of these qualities. Some more *sake*?" Kenji asked, and signaled the kimono-clad waitress who silently served them.

Pompam had no idea what Kenji had in mind, and he waited patiently for him to begin, a small smile traced his lips.

"I want you to start supplying us with heroin from your Golden Triangle," the Japanese said bluntly.

Pompam, stunned, couldn't believe what he had just heard. He hated drugs. He had only used opium that one time up in Burma with Chai, and it made him sick. His face betrayed his feelings at once.

"Do you have anything to say, Pompam?" Kenji asked after giving his order time to sink in.

"Why should we go into the drug business, Kenji? That isn't my field, as you know very well. I don't *like* drugs," he finally replied.

"Liking drugs or not liking them is not the issue. It is a very good business, Pompam, and one that our organization has been involved in for quite some time. The profits are enormous — far greater than from the entertainment industry — or anything else we do. We were formerly working with an agent in Yunan Province, in southern China, but he was recently captured and executed by the Chinese government. We have learned of your good connections over the Burmese border — where you buy so many of your young girls. I think it's time to see if they don't also have this other product to sell," his tone was not quite as friendly as it had been only minutes before.

"Trading in girls, Kenji, is very different from trading in opium and heroin. With the girls the greedy Thai police are willing to take their bribes, look the other way, and let us go on operating. With drugs from the Golden Triangle the American DEA is involved! They can't be bought — you know that," Pompam said, almost feeling ill.

"That's where your talent and imagination comes in, Pompam. You have to be very clever in order to avoid getting caught."

"Where will the drugs go?" Pompam asked, still reeling from Yamamoto's bombshell.

"Some will go to Japan, but most will eventually wind up in

America where demand is the highest, and they will pay almost any-thing to get it. Actually, Pompam, there is so much heroin making its way to America *already* from the Golden Triangle that you couldn't even begin to imagine the amounts. Some goes through China and Hong Kong, some goes through Europe via the Nigerian connection; there are three or four routes. We see no reason why we shouldn't take advantage of such a splendid opportunity — you and me both, that is. You will, of course, make your share; I'll even split it with you equally — 'fifty-fifty' as they say in the States," Kenji announced as he looked at Pompam with a cruel smile.

"I'm afraid I will have to say 'no,' Kenji. The risk involved will put everything I've worked for — *and* my family — in grave danger. I just can't do it," said Pompam, beginning to get angry.

"Then I suppose you won't mind if ten or twenty of the three-hundred girls you've sent us go to the Thai Embassy and make some headlines for you? Or, perhaps Mr. Suphan, and his brother Mr. Chai, won't mind so much their lengthy prison sentence for visa fraud and trafficking in illegal girls over the border? If you are very, very lucky, you might escape going to jail yourself!"

Pompam, realizing Yamamoto knew everything, figured he was trapped. His mind raced from one scenario to the next and he could see no way out of his deplorable, perilous predicament.

"Then let's hear your plan, *Kenji*," Pompam sneered, not caring that Yamamoto noticed.

Yamamoto, who only the night before had ordered the murders of two men who had failed to give him the deference he felt he was owed, ignored Pompam's disrespectful tone and began to explain his plan. Pompam listened, and grudgingly admitted to himself that it was quite a good scheme; he finally accepted the fact that he had better learn to work with it if he was going to survive.

By the time Kenji was finished describing the proposed heroin-smuggling operation it was already nearly evening. Kenji said he wished to rest and avoid the traffic before setting off for Tokyo.

"We will retire to a room where we can relax and take a short nap."

Pompam, of course, could see it coming, but there was nothing he could do but go along with Kenji's program. He was miles away from Tokyo with a dangerous *yakuza* godfather who had two armed bodyguards just outside the door. He couldn't make a scene or he would lose his "face" — or worse, his *life*. His mind searched desperately for something that could save him. He still had the businesses in Thailand to consider — and his friends and family to think about; he had to protect them as best he could. He realized he was in way over his head — and he became furious with himself for letting his greed get him in such deep shit.

They entered a small, pleasant room, and a futon was already spread out on the floor. Yamamoto began removing his clothes and told Pompam to take off his.

Yamamoto lay down naked on the futon, and shortly afterwards Pompam did the same. Kenji immediately began to make strong advances on Pompam, but the Thai brushed him off and said, "I would really just prefer to rest, if you don't mind; I'm tired." Pompam covered himself with the silk blanket and turned over on his side.

Yamamoto became furious. "How dare you turn your back on me, you little whore!" he hissed through his teeth and pulled Pompam roughly toward him, continuing his assault.

Even though he was in good shape, after a few moments Pompam realized it would be futile to try to resist Kenji's powerful, martial arts-trained body; so once again he gave in without a real struggle. Yamamoto, however, was suddenly in the mood to be cruel, so he treated Pompam not with the gentleness of two nights before, but with brutality and unrestrained force. He even grabbed Pompam by the neck and started to strangle him with both hands.

Pompam flailed his arms and legs about, gasping for breath; he tried to scream out, but there was no voice in his constricted throat. The last thing he remembered before he passed out was Kenji's snarling face above him — and the certain knowledge that he was about to die.

He came back to consciousness a few moments later only to find that Kenji had started to rape him. He had his arms pinned to the ground with his much stronger, tattooed upper body and fists. Pompam wanted to cry out in pain and horror as the rough penetration began tearing him apart. Never before had one of his customers tried to force his way inside him as Kenji was doing, and Pompam became momentarily disoriented, not fully comprehending what was happening.

Even though he was convinced Kenji was going to kill him, he finally made himself relax and allow it to be done, feeling more shame than he had ever known in his life. Not even during his final encounter with *Khun* James and the two street boys had he felt as miserable and defiled; he almost *wanted* to die.

On their way back to Tokyo a few hours later, neither Yamamoto nor Pompam spoke. Pompam, still in pain, had several strong drinks of whiskey and tried to keep his eyes averted out the window, gazing without interest at the endless stream of gray, lifeless suburbs.

Finally Yamamoto said, "Pompam, I am sorry for the rough treatment back at the inn. I hadn't intended to hurt you, but your refusal, and your lack of respect made me angry. You should know that no one treats me that way."

Pompam still said nothing, and Kenji continued, "You may keep silent now if you wish, but listen carefully: you *will* do the heroin trading business as we discussed, and we will both become very rich. You and I will continue to be civil to one another, and from time to time you will come to Japan to see me. You really have no choice. Do you understand?" he said, in a way that was meant to make Pompam feel demeaned and humiliated, and he succeeded.

"Yes, Kenji, I understand. I will do the drug business for you and we will make a pile of money. Please don't hurt me like that again," he said in a mock-pleading, whimpering tone; but inside he seethed with hatred and rage, wanting to strike out and ruin him like he had ruined others in the past. He knew, though, that he was powerless to do anything, and for the first time he could understand how his mistress, Joy, had probably felt that last night at the curtain motel.

As the limousine pulled into the *porte cochere* of the hotel Yamamoto looked with cold, black eyes at Pompam and said, "No, I will not hurt you that way again; not if you obey me and do as I say. I am glad we now understand each other completely. Aoyama will give you further instructions and I will call you from time to time. We will see each other again, Pompam. *Sayonara.*"

"*Sayonara*, Kenji," he said without smiling. He stood up straight and entered the lobby of the hotel, looking confident and elegant, as usual. No one observing him at that moment could ever have imagined what had happened to him only a few hours earlier — or perceive the depth of the anger and self loathing the young man felt.

Sayonara is right, Pompam thought. And he was determined to never come back to Japan again, under any circumstances, no matter how much Yamamoto threatened.

The next morning when Mr. Aoyama came to take Pompam to the airport he brought with him a shopping bag containing a beautifully-wrapped package. "Mr. Yamamoto wants your wife to have this gift," he said.

What an unbelievable son of a bitch, Pompam thought; to send my *wife* a present! He only smiled at the older gentleman and nodded his head, doing his best to control his temper.

They spoke very little in the back of the limousine on the long drive to the airport. Pompam wondered if Aoyama knew all the details of what had happened between him and Yamamoto at the country inn; he had to admit to himself that he would have been surprised if the man *didn't* already know everything.

As if reading Pompam's thoughts, Aoyama said, "You and I will be in touch soon about the new business, Mr. Vichai. I know that this is something you do not want to do, but I believe in your abilities and your cleverness, and I am sure it will go well."

"It has to go well, Mr. Aoyama, or else everything I've been building since I was twenty three years old will go down the drain," Pompam replied grimly.

"I have had experience in this kind of operation before, so I will do my best to protect you and help you avoid making mistakes. I promise you this," Mr. Aoyama answered, feeling deeply sorry for his young Thai friend.

Chapter 19

Pompam caught a bad cold on the return flight to Bangkok. By the time he landed at Don Muang Airport he had a fever and chills, and fell asleep in the back of the taxi on the way home.

The maid carried his luggage upstairs and told him that everyone was out. Pompam took a hot shower and went to bed, feeling miserable.

He woke up to see Rattana sitting beside him, looking worried and anxious. "Are you okay, Pompam? Should I call the doctor?"

"I'll be fine, Rattana; I came down with some kind of bug on the airplane, that's all. How are the kids?"

As if on cue Little Jim bounded into the room. "Don't get too close to Daddy — he's sick!" Pompam warned, raising his hand to stop him from climbing up on the bed. Then he said, "Open up my suitcase over there; I have presents for you."

Rattana opened the big leather valise and Pompam told her which packages belonged to whom.

"None of my friends have anything like these, Pompam. I can't wait to see the faces of the ladies I'm meeting for lunch tomorrow when I show up in this one," cooed Rattana, holding up one dress that had cost Pompam US$1,500. Then she unwrapped another package that contained an ornately-crafted Japanese doll for baby Somporn's future enjoyment: authentic down to the last detail of its blue and pink silk kimono.

"Thank you, Paw," cried Little Jim over his robot toys, and almost immediately ran off to play with them.

"There's another one for you over there in that shopping bag, Rattana. Mr. Yamamoto, the big boss in Japan, sent it to you," said Pompam, careful to keep his voice in neutral.

Rattana got up and went over to the shopping bag and pulled out the elegant-looking gift box. The Japanese, for centuries, have made an art form out of wrapping packages, and she hated to spoil this one. After carefully undoing the hand-made paper, she opened the box and removed a lovely ceramic tea set, piece by piece. "Look at this! It's beautiful, Pompam. Here's a note," and she read a brief description of the gift that informed her it was three-hundred years old, and had been made by a famous ceramics master of the Tokugawa Shogunate.

"My goodness, Pompam; this tea set belongs in a museum," she said with awe, examining it carefully. "It must be very valuable."

Kenji was obviously trying to apologize with the gift to Rattana, and make up to me for his vicious brutality, thought Pompam. But he knew that nothing could ever soften his heart towards the *yakuza* monster who had trapped him into trafficking in drugs — not to mention humiliating and raping him.

Later on, Toy came in to see Pompam who had just awakened from a long nap. "I've been waiting for you to wake up, *Pi-chai*, is there anything I can get for you? You look terrible." Toy wore a worried, anguished expression.

"*Mai pen rai*, Toy. I'll be fine by tomorrow," he replied, happy to see his obdurate brother again.

"The whole time you were gone I kept having the most horrible dreams about you, Pompam. They made me so frightened — I thought you were going to die! Why did you have to go to Japan in the first place? You never did tell me."

Pompam was greatly moved, seeing that Toy was so upset and worried about him. He reached out his arm and grabbed his brother's hand and said, "No need to be concerned about me, Toy, I was fine. I went to Japan on business, that's all. Just let me rest now, okay?" Toy wasn't at all satisfied with that explanation, but he kept quiet and left Pompam alone.

That evening Pompam phoned Kitti to let him know he had returned safely, but was under the weather. "Any important news that can't wait until tomorrow?"

"There's really nothing, Pompam; everything's been pretty quiet. Oh, one of the girls at the brothel — a fifteen-year-old from Burma — hanged herself yesterday. She was the same one who tried to escape twice before, remember? Our police friends handled it and took the body far away from here. Nothing to worry about. *Mai pen rai*."

The tragic news disturbed Pompam. He could, for the first

time, understand how the poor girl must have felt. She had been trapped and abused the same as he had been; her only way out was to die, but he had money and could fight back in other ways, he reasoned; but at the moment he had no idea whatsoever how to combat Kenji; he could only do as he was told, and pray to the Lord Buddha for the best.

By the following afternoon he felt he was well enough to go to the office, so he dragged himself out of bed and got ready. Rattana protested, as did Toy, but Pompam insisted he was fine. He missed his friends and was anxious to see them — in spite of the bad news he had to share.

"We'd better not let you go away again if you're going to come back sick, Pompam," Kitti said jokingly, but, like Chai and Ott, he was genuinely concerned.

Pompam thought they would never get tired of asking endless questions about Japan, the hostess bars, the *yakuza,* and even the long plane ride; they were curious about everything. Let them ask it all, he thought to himself, before I drop my bomb on them.

"Are you ready boys? I have some news that I hate like hell to give you, but it's news we have to deal with, all the same." He paused, watching his good friends, all of them suddenly becoming very uncomfortable.

"Go ahead, Pompam; we've faced hard news before," remarked Ott, "so you might as well spill it."

"The Japanese want us to go into the drug business in the Golden Triangle," Pompam answered directly, and carefully observed their reactions. All three of them stood there with their jaws open.

"We could have gone into that business ourselves long ago, but we agreed we wouldn't touch it," Kitti stated vehemently after he recovered from the shock.

"This time I'm afraid we have no choice," Pompam responded firmly, and explained all the ways they could be ruined by the Japanese *yakuza,* including being murdered. Chai winced when Pompam said Yamamoto even knew the name of his brother, Suphan, and all about the entire girl-buying and brokering scheme.

"Let's just set it up the way they want it done, try to keep ourselves out of trouble, and wait for the time when we can get out of it without getting ourselves killed," said Pompam, sick and exhausted.

Pompam went over the whole plan with a very troubled Kitti, Chai, and Ott. It involved setting up a refinery that would turn raw opium into high-grade heroin; this would be up in Burma, just across the border. The Japanese would be sending them a chemist who would oversee the refinery; Pompam told them the chemist would be arriving in Thailand in about two weeks, so they had to move fast.

"You had better call Nopadon today, Chai, and set up a meeting for us as soon as possible. We'll have to get him to take us up to Burma again and meet with his friend in the jungle. I don't like the thought of repeating that awful trek, but I'm afraid it can't be avoided."

"You're still sick, Pompam; you could never make that hike through the mountains in your condition — and I won't let you. I'll go by myself and that's final!" Chai declared.

"Are you sure, Chai?" asked Pompam, knowing Chai was right about his health; at that very moment he could feel his temperature going up again.

"Yes I'm sure, Pompam. *Mai pen rai.* You just take care of yourself, and I'll tell you what you missed when I get back."

"Thanks, Chai; I really appreciate it," and he meant it.

"Once we get the refinery set up and they make the heroin for us, what happens then?" Chai asked the next logical question.

"We'll have to get Nopadon to arrange to smuggle it over the border into Thailand. Then we'll have it trucked down to Bangkok and hopefully not get caught by the DEA inspectors along the way; this is where we have to be the most careful," Pompam answered, deadly serious.

"I don't even know if Nopadon would want to get involved in this, Pompam," Chai said, looking worried. "It's full of so many risks for him. He's a rich man now, thanks to the girl business, and I don't know if he would be willing to take any more big chances at this point."

"That's why you're going up to Chaing Mai: to convince him. Hopefully he's greedy enough, and still wants to keep helping his friends up in the Shan State," Pompam replied.

"Once we get the stuff to Bangkok, what then?" Kitti asked, still not believing the news.

"Yamamoto explained that they have a connection in Bangkok

— someone that owes them many favors. That 'connection' has a fruit exporting company, and the heroin will be smuggled into Japan in air shipments of Thai fruit." Japan was a huge market for the exotic fruits grown in Thailand; each season produced new varieties that were high in demand in the markets of Tokyo.

"So are you saying that once the drugs get to Bangkok and we turn them over to the fruit exporter, our job is finished?" Kitti asked, looking almost hopeful.

"Yes, Kitti; that's where it ends for us," Pompam answered, and Kitti seemed relieved.

Pompam suddenly had a flash of inspiration. "To get this meeting on to a happier subject I want to tell you about another business we're going to start."

"After your last announcement, this had better be damned good," Ott remarked, looking dour and depressed, unable to stop thinking about the danger he and his wife were about to be exposed to, wishing there was some way out.

"I want to build the most spectacular, exclusive member club in Thailand — even better than the Imperial Club in Tokyo!" announced Pompam, seeing a way to best Kenji, *and* repair his damaged ego.

"Where do you have in mind to build your new high-class temple of luxury, Pompam? And where will you get the money?" asked Kitti, astonished by this latest of Pompam's grand ideas.

"Right next door to my own house on *Soi* Tonglor, that's where. And the funds will come from the enormous profits we're going to make from the heroin business. We'll have to do something with all the money," he answered, laughing now.

Chai, Kitti and Ott looked at Pompam in total disbelief, and slowly let it all sink in.

"And Kitti, enroll Nuu in one of those fancy hotel schools — the Dusit Thani's or the Oriental's — so he can learn how to be the manager when we open; he'll need that level of skill, so tell him I want no arguments."

That night at dinner Pompam announced to Rattana and Toy that he would be building a new "high-class temple of luxury," as Kitti had called it, on the vacant lot next door to their house. "I have decided

315

to name it The Regents' Club. How does that sound?"

"The name is not so important, Pompam, but I don't see how opening up yet another place with female hostesses will improve our community image one bit! I'm totally opposed to it — especially since you want to put it right over there," Rattana pointed in the direction of the street corner.

"You heard what *Khun* Arun said about that location, Rattana; it's perfect. And besides, the type of club I have in mind will only *enhance* our image in society, and give us access to all the top people in Thailand. I have the idea to get *Khun* Arun to help with PR and recruit members; you know he can get all the best ones," responded Pompam, unruffled by Rattana's objections.

Up until then Toy had been sitting quietly, eating his dinner, listening to the exchange between Pompam and his wife. He finally could hold his peace no longer and he stood up, shaking uncontrollably, spilling his orange juice all over the table. He had moved so suddenly that Little Jim and Somporn, startled, began to scream.

"You would have the nerve to open up another whorehouse right next door to your own home? Where your wife and your two young children live? Do you have no shame? Where will you stop, Pompam? In your grave?" He knocked his chair over as he rushed out of the room.

Pompam, totally deflated, leaned over and put his face in his hands, feeling even more sick than when he returned from Japan. "Why do I have to take this from him, Rattana?" he asked his wife. She only looked at him, deeply concerned, and turned to calm down her two children.

Four days later Pompam, Kitti, and Ott gathered to hear Chai's report about his trip to Chiang Mai and the Golden Triangle.

"Nopadon is more than happy to work with us and coordinate the whole operation with *Khun* Ahm and the Shan rebels up in Burma," Chai began. "You could never have made the hike, Pompam, it was dreadful — the hottest and most humid time of the year — I thought I would die. *Mai pen rai.* Ahm can supply the refinery with as much opium as it can process. And no problem about the Japanese chemist, except that he'll have to live in the same primitive conditions as the rest of the people up there. Ahm wants all of the workers to be hand-picked by him for security reasons; we have to pay them, of course; and there will be lots of guards — all with automatic assault rifles; we pay them too.

"Bottom line: I gave him one million *baht* in cash and Ahm will have the building for the refinery ready in ten days. He said the chemist will need to buy his own equipment in Bangkok, and he'll provide porters and mules to have it hauled overland to the site. The one million will also include 500 kilos of raw opium for start-up, and the first-month's wages for everyone involved. After that it will be 50,000 per month for wages, and Nopadon will negotiate the opium price on a monthly basis. I'm sure Nopadon will make a fortune as middle-man for all of this, but it can't be helped."

"Good work, Chai. Thanks for putting yourself to all that trouble. It will be worth your while, you'll see," Pompam promised.

After the meeting Pompam took Chai aside and said, "Did you happen to ask him about Joy?"

"I did, Pompam, and he said she still lives as the *mia noi* of the old Chinese man who bought her from him. She's given him a son, and he bought her a house to raise him in. Apparently she's become an opium addict, so she rarely leaves her village," he replied.

Pompam suddenly felt terribly sorry for the girl, but said nothing; he had more important things on his mind.

That afternoon Pompam called a meeting with the architect who had designed his grand home. "You did such a good job on our house, *Khun* Jod, that I want you to come up with a design for The Regents' Club, a new member club I want to build next door. I want you to design something that will blend nicely with the house."

He then proceeded to give the architect a very long list of amenities he wanted, which included: VIP suites, karaoke rooms, a complete gym, massage rooms, card-playing lounges, a Thai *and* a Western restaurant, a coffee shop, two cocktail lounges, and a big stage in the main entertainment hall with an area that would accommodate a fifty-piece orchestra.

Of course there would be a girl "pen" where male-only members and their male-only guests could circulate among the selection of pretty ladies and companionably choose their young sex partners for the evening.

"There will be several more things I want, too, but I just haven't thought of them yet. So be prepared for changes," Pompam concluded.

Khun Jod, stunned by the scope of the project said, "Where did you ever come up with this idea, *Khun* Vichai? And what, pray Buddha, is your estimated budget?"

"I recently visited Tokyo and was a guest at the two best member clubs in Japan. They were amazing places and I was very impressed; but I don't see any reason why I can't do better here in Bangkok. Don't you agree? And don't worry about the budget. I estimate that it will cost around 200 million *baht*, but I could be wrong. If we go over, then *mai pen rai*." Pompam enjoyed fantasizing about opening a member club of his own that was even more sumptuous than Kenji's.

After he dismissed the architect he phoned *Khun* Arun and said, "How would you like to retire in a year? If not retire, then work two or three hours a day as it suited you?" Pompam knew that in spite of *Khun* Arun's high rank and social position he was penniless except for the salary he earned at the Thailand Pavilion Hotel. He thought about how nice it would be to see his elderly friend fixed for life.

"Surely you are joking with me, Pompam. You know my situation; and you know I have to work, unfortunately. The Japanese took all my father's money during the war, remember?"

"I'm about to build the most fantastic member club ever seen in Asia — on that vacant lot next to my home. You said the first night you came over for dinner that it would be a perfect location for a high-class restaurant or nightclub. Well, I just made a trip to Japan and came home inspired. I met with the architect earlier today and it's a 'go.' But I need you to help Ott with the public relations — especially at the beginning on the membership drive. Each man will have to pay 100,000 *baht* to join; so for every member you sign up, I'll give you 10% commission. That means that for every ten members you'll get to keep 100,000 *baht* for yourself. What do you think?"

"Pompam, my dear boy, what can I say? I'm already sixty-five years old and I'm tired. Of course I'll do it; I'm bored here anyway; when do you want me to start?"

"Give *Khun* Somchai your notice immediately; I'll advance you

100,000 *baht* to keep you going until you sell some memberships — and I'll have it delivered to you by messenger in the morning. Meet me next Wednesday at my office at Paradise City and I'll show you some sketches the architect has promised to have ready. We can make a plan then."

After he hung up the phone *Khun* Arun just sat at his desk and cried like a baby.

Late that night Toy came to his brother's bedroom and made an unusual request: he asked Pompam if he had time to meet at *Wat* Mahathat the following afternoon. He said he and *Phra* Asoka had something they wanted to discuss with him.

"Well, can you at least give me some idea what it's all about? I mean, am I going to go all the way down there so I can get a scolding from both of you about my evil ways? If that's the case, then I can get that from you here at home and spare myself the traffic," Pompam whined, annoyed. He hadn't been to see *Phra* Asoka for months — or *Phra* Voravut at *Wat* Chalaw for *years*, and he suddenly felt like a third grader who had put chalk in the erasers.

"No, Pompam, it's nothing like that. I promise. Please just meet me there at three o'clock — in the *mondop*." He smiled so sweetly when he said this last, and Pompam agreed. He was still fearful, however, of what they might have in store for him — not forgetting Toy's dramatic reaction to his announcement about the new member club.

The next afternoon Pompam gazed up at the red, yellow, and green-tiled roof of the magnificent *mondop*, which never failed to inspire him; he could faintly hear the sound of chanting monks somewhere deep in the compound. He took off his shoes at the threshold and tentatively approached the Indian *ajarn*, slightly crouched over as was the custom. Then he kneeled down and touched his forehead to the floor three times, as he had done so often in the past.

Toy broke the silence when he said, "Thanks for coming, *Pichai*. *Phra* Asoka and I had a wager whether or not you would show up — and here you are!"

"Who won the wager?" Pompam asked with a smirk on his face, wanting to know who had bet against him.

"We *both* won, Vichai," answered the monk ambiguously, and

laughed. "Now come over here and get comfortable; your brother has a proposal for you, and it's something he's been thinking about for weeks; please listen to him."

Pompam turned towards Toy and said, "Well, you have my complete attention — something you would never have gotten anywhere else. Good for you for being so crafty to get me here."

Toy tentatively began his rehearsed speech. "I've told you many times before, Pompam, that I am worried for you; it's those people looking up the ladder at your ass, remember?" He suddenly remembered where he was and blushed bright red; Pompam laughed.

"Excuse me for being impolite, *Phra* Asoka," begged Toy.

"*Mai pen rai*, Chatree. Proceed," replied the monk, undisturbed.

"I feel that the businesses you are in make you more vulnerable than most people, Pompam; it has to do with karma and those sorts of things — we've talked about it before. Even though Rattana works hard for charity projects and donates lots of your money to her causes, you haven't yet begun to make merit on your own, except for taking care of your brothers — and providing for our educations." He paused for a moment, wanting to sense his elder brother's reaction before going any further.

Pompam just sat there staring at him unemotionally, so the young man ventured to proceed. "I think you should set up a foundation that benefits the young and the poor of this country. Call it the Thailand Youth Foundation, if you like. Give a percentage of all your profits to the Foundation and make social programs that help others. With your high public profile you can also get other rich people to contribute money and your projects can become even bigger. What do you think?" Toy looked up at *Phra* Asoka, whose face remained pleasantly smiling.

Pompam, still showing no emotion, thought about Toy's idea for a few moments, and then suddenly realized the tremendous public relations value in what his brother had just proposed. With the membership roster of the future Regents' Club he would have entree to everyone in the country who mattered; since he was confident the top leaders in government, business, and high society would join, he could tap all of them for contributions. He also realized that it would give him a chance to make merit, feel better about himself, and get Toy back on his side again — all at the same time. How could he refuse such a proposal?

And then the words of *Phra* Asoka came back to him, from the time he had brought Dr. Jim to see him when he graduated from Ramkampheng: "Pay back your debt to Dr. Jim, or to another; it's all the same, Vichai".

Pompam reflected how Toy's interests in social issues had increased over the years; he was always running off to meetings for university and community projects involving things like slum redevelopment, drugs, pro-democracy, the environment, and the poor people of Isan. Pompam was amazed at how different he was from all the rest of his brothers who were content just to live for the moment, do their jobs, act like playboys, and have a good time. Toy didn't like to drink and party — or take advantage of the massage girls, leading Pompam to suspect that he was still a virgin; and the boy didn't seem to care if he had any money or not. Pompam could easily see how Toy would come up with the foundation idea — and try to get his rich brother to open up his wallet for the poor; maybe he saw it as the first step in getting him to mend his immoral ways.

"I'll set up the Thailand Youth Foundation and give it as much time and attention as I can, Toy; but only on one condition."

Toy, a big smile appearing on his face, said, "What's that, Pompam? What condition could you possibly have?"

"*You* must promise me to be the Executive Director and run the whole show. I know you're still in college, but you'll be graduating soon. This is what you've been preparing yourself for, Toy, and I'm beginning to think the whole idea is to just make yourself a job!" answered Pompam, laughing. Toy blushed again, deeply ashamed, never thinking his idea might be interpreted this way.

"Did you think I wanted it for these reasons, *Ajarn*?" he cautiously asked the Indian monk.

"Of course not, Toy. Your brother is just taking advantage of your good nature, that's all. Don't be a bully, Vichai," he scolded.

Pompam had never been spoken to that way by *Phra* Asoka before; he winced hearing the crackling tone, and immediately *waied* and bowed three times. "I was only joking. If we're going to be working closely together you have to get used to it, Toy."

"I suppose I'll have to get used to a lot more than that Pompam," he returned, getting even. Pompam got his message loud and clear.

It was Kitti and Sudar's turn to come to dinner that evening. Rattana and Sudar had become almost inseparable friends, and they all had dinner together at least once a week, at one or the other's house. Pompam and Kitti were happy with this arrangement since it gave them time to be together again like "the old days." When the girls went off to gossip, Kitti and Pompam usually sat in the *sala* by the pool, drinking whiskey and talking.

Since his meeting with *Phra* Asoka and Toy that afternoon Pompam had done some hard thinking, *creative* thinking — most of it while stuck in the traffic crossing town. He decided it was time for some changes.

The four of them were gathered back at the dining table when Pompam said, "Here's a toast to the new Managing Director of the VP Group!" Pompam said with enthusiasm as he raised his glass to Kitti.

Kitti, Sudar and Rattana looked back and forth at one another, not having a clue what Pompam was talking about. "How many drinks did you have before dinner, Pompam?" Rattana asked suspiciously.

"Enough. How come no one is joining me in my toast. I expected to hear some *chai-oh's*!," he declared.

"We're always happy to join you in a drink, Pompam, especially if it's to celebrate good news; but first we have to know what we're drinking to," responded Kitti, baffled.

"Okay. It's a long list of things, so I'll try my best to summarize. One: this afternoon Toy and *Phra* Asoka convinced me to found the Thailand Youth Foundation, a new charity for the young people of our country. Two: *Khun* Arun has agreed to do PR for The Regents' Club and spearhead the membership drive. Three: I want to consolidate all our operations under one corporate banner, and I have chosen 'The VP Group' as the name. Four: I want new offices almost immediately since working out of Paradise City is no longer appropriate — especially for a foundation where Toy will be working. Five: I still haven't forgotten the idea of one day becoming a land developer, thanks to Kitti's advice.

And Six: Kitti will be the new Managing Director." Pompam finished the last and raised his glass again.

"You want me to be the MD of the whole company? What will you be, Pompam?" Kitti asked in disbelief; Sudar and Rattana sitting with their jaws open.

"You already take care of all the money, Kitti, so what else is new? I'm going to become the Chairman of the Board and change my image. What do you say?"

Sudar, usually shy, said, "I think I'll say, *'chai-oh'*!" and they all joined her, laughing. Their laughter, however, soon dissolved into animated, creative chatter as they discussed Pompam's new plans until the small hours of the morning.

Three weeks later the corporate headquarters of the newly-registered VP Group moved into rented office space on the 19th floor of a new tower on Thanon Asoke, that section of Ratchidapisek Road that runs between Sukhumvit and Petchburi. Pompam wanted Asoke because it was near his Petchburi operations, and was connected by back roads to Tonglor which was several miles to the south. The merciless traffic had become a primary consideration in decision-making processes everywhere in Bangkok — especially the relationship between where one lived and worked.

Phra Asoka, *Phra* Voravut and *Phra* Prateep — along with six other monks — blessed the offices with a traditional ceremony before they opened their doors for business. "If I'm going to work there then we have to do it right — *not* like the house, Pompam. I won't let you get away with it this time!" stated an emphatic Toy. And so it was done. It turned out to be a happy, warm occasion for everyone.

The day after the blessing ceremony Chai walked into Pompam's office and closed the door. "The first shipment of heroin was processed at the new refinery, Pompam, and made it safely to Bangkok, buried deeply in four truckloads of mangoes," he explained. "The drivers of the trucks never knew what they were carrying. The fruit exporter in Bangkok hid the drugs in three air shipments to Japan, and Aoyama called to tell me there were no problems on that end. Everything went smoothly, Pompam; we should be able to do a shipment every two months or so."

Pompam, relieved to hear the news, knew that he would have to live with tension and worry every time a shipment came down from the Golden Triangle. "Goddamn that Yamamoto!" Pompam said bitterly, banging his hand on the desk. "I don't care how much money we make, Chai, this is going to take its toll on me."

"I know, Pompam, it will affect all of us — never knowing what will happen each time — if we'll make it safely or not. But try to console yourself by the fact that we just made thirty million *baht* — more than enough to take care of your new foundation for at least a year."

"God forbid Toy should ever find out where the money comes from. He would be the first one to call the police," Pompam responded; and for the first time, Chai could see a few gray hairs appearing just over his friend's ears.

PART IV
GRAND DESIGNS

Chapter 20

"Please sit down, *Khun* Vichai; I want you to meet my friend, *Khun* Darunee," exclaimed Police General Surapong as he pulled out a chair for Pompam. They were at the Verandah Restaurant in the Oriental Hotel, and Pompam had just finished a lunch-meeting with his contractor when he ran into the General and his guest.

"I've heard so much about you, *Khun* Vichai. It's hard to pick up a magazine these days and not see your name or your picture," *Khun* Darunee gushed, her round, perky face beaming almost as brightly as the big diamonds on her fingers, wrists and ears.

"I'm afraid it's the price one has to pay if one hopes to raise money for a foundation, *Khun* Darunee," Pompam replied modestly.

"You were a favorite of the press long before you started your Foundation, Pompam," *Khun* Surapong reminded him. "Don't forget about that poster you did for the TAT campaign. I still see them in every travel agency window in town."

"And how old are you now, *Khun* Vichai, if you don't mind my asking?" Darunee probed as she fluttered her heavily made-up eyelids.

"I'll be thirty years old on my next birthday. I'm an old man already."

Darunee laughed a bit too loudly, covering her obviously capped teeth with her right hand as she did so. "An old man already? Bullshit! You're still a baby!" she almost screamed, herself only thirty-five.

"I'm hardly a baby, *Khun* Darunee. I have two small children and the responsibility of a business to run. *And* a foundation." Since Pompam had set up his Thailand Youth Foundation nearly a year before, he tried to slip a mention of it into all the conversations he had with people who had money. By doing so, he had managed to collect several large donations.

"I, too, have a business to run, *Khun* Vichai, and three beastly children to raise with no husband," she said, trying to look victimized. "I still have time for charity work, so please feel free to call me if I can help you."

"I will call you for sure, *Khun* Darunee. I can always use help with the Foundation — or rather my brother, Toy, can, since he runs it. I might also need some advice about real estate, and I understand you are the expert," he flattered her. He knew that she had started from nothing, but through some lucky breaks had been able to amass a fortune by buying and selling land, and eventually building of residential housing in Bangkok and Pattaya.

"I'm hardly the expert, *Khun* Vichai; I'm just fortunate. I also like money, a true Chinese to the core," she cackled, sounding like the dirt-poor daughter of immigrants she was.

"*Khun* Vichai likes money, too. And money likes him back — much more than it does most people," *Khun* Surapong joked. Pompam found this statement ironic as he had rarely met anyone in his life more avaricious than the old police official.

"Seriously, *Khun* Darunee. I'm about to start a new project, and if you don't mind, I will call you for a lunch appointment to talk about it."

"I could think of nothing more exciting than to have lunch with the most talked-about man in Bangkok. Here's my name card; I'll be expecting to hear from you soon," she said with a big white smile, not in the least bit betraying what a bitch she could turn into when the mood struck her, or how tough she was reputed to be in business.

Pompam got up and excused himself, giving both *Khun* Darunee and *Khun* Surapong an overly-polite *wai*.

The following week Pompam met *Khun* Darunee for lunch at the Thai restaurant in the Regent Hotel. He had reserved a quiet table in the corner where they could talk in private, and ordered himself a Black Label and soda while he waited for her. He would soon find out that one of Darunee's greatest faults was that she could never be on time for anything. She always apologized and produced wonderful and oftentimes believable excuses, but nonetheless, she turned up late every time; her daily morning visits to the hairdresser usually got her off to a bad start, causing a reaction like dominos as her day progressed.

"I'm so sorry I'm late, *Khun* Vichai. Traffic! Every day it gets worse," she groaned in apology, her over-dressed five-foot frame landing at the table in a cloud of perfume. "Waiter! Bring me a glass of red wine."

"*Mai pen rai, Khun* Darunee." Pompam tried to be gracious, but he truly hated for anyone to be late for appointments and waste his time. "How is your week going so far?"

"Terrible! On Monday I thought this would be an easy, slow week. Then Bang! All hell broke loose. One of my daughters got sick, I found out my buffalo son is about to get kicked out of school, a deposit check I received from a client buying some land from me bounced and I had to call the police — you name it. Terrible!" She was definitely distraught.

"How about your week, *Khun* Vichai? I hope it's better than mine," she asked him sympathetically.

"Not bad, actually. My new member club is coming along right on schedule. I got my son accepted a good school, I received a two-million *baht* donation for my Foundation from a big insurance company, *and* my wife's been in a pleasant mood," he answered in good humor.

"Your wife *should* be in a good mood. I don't know her, but I saw her at a charity luncheon the other day and she was wearing a pair of ruby earrings I would have killed for. The lady sitting next to me said her husband--you--had just given them to her. All my useless former husband ever gave me was a black eye!"

"Giving my wife jewelry is something I enjoy; besides, she's been a big help lately with my foundation," he replied, trying to figure out how this woman had managed to cultivate so many friends in high places. *Khun* Surapong had told him she knew *everyone* — and entertained dozens of people every week at restaurant parties, discotheques, and after hours clubs.

"Your wife is lucky; I've had to buy myself every little trinket I own," replied Darunee, trying to look waif-like.

"How about another glass of wine? It might put you in a receptive mood." Pompam ordered more drinks.

"Well, what did you have in mind, *Khun* Vichai?" she asked, eyes fluttering. "I'm always in a receptive mood; except when it comes to people wanting to borrow money from me. Then I become a thick-skinned Chinese." They both laughed at this little joke, having shared that same tricky problem from time to time.

"I'm about to start my first land development project and I need a mentor. I was thinking that if I offered you a 'piece of the action,' as they say in America, you might join me in this one. It's a small project, but I want to use it to learn from. The big ones will come later," he explained.

"Well, my new friend, *Khun* Vichai, it just so happens that I have a wee bit of spare cash right now — and some time to spend. Tell me all about your project and I'll give you my honest opinion," she responded in a surprisingly business-like tone.

Pompam told her about the project he had in mind. It was a relatively simple one, he thought. He had twenty *rai* (about eight acres) of land in Bangkapi in a good location. It was close to schools, roads and shopping, and he wanted to build a small townhouse development of about two hundred units. He told her how much he thought he could sell them for, and how much profit he thought could be made.

"Your basic idea is a good one, *Khun* Vichai, and the area you describe isn't bad. But I'll need to see the land before I can tell you any more. I haven't been out in that area in about six or eight months, and at the rate things are changing right now that's a long time. The thing you'll have the most trouble with, if you haven't gone through it before is the putting in the infrastructure — and, of course, the dear *permits*," she practically hissed when she said the last word.

"Do you have time for me to take you there after lunch," Pompam asked.

"You mean *today*, *Khun* Vichai?" she replied in amazement.

"Yes, today, if it is convenient. I had a meeting this afternoon that was canceled so I'm free. I hope you are too," Pompam pleaded with his eyes. He knew he had this woman's attention, and he didn't want to lose it. It might be several days — or weeks — before he could get her to commit to a long ride out to the suburbs.

"This afternoon I'm supposed to go over to Thonburi for a conference with the principal of my son's school. What a bore! I'll call and cancel it," she said before taking another bite of curry.

Pompam was pleasantly surprised to discover that he was beginning to like this rather crude and aggressive female. He took a big bite of his *"nam prik batoo,"* a chili paste made with mashed up fresh water fish.

"How's the membership drive going for your new club, *Khun* Vichai?" she asked with a full mouth.

"It's coming along. We haven't hit our target yet of five hundred, though," Pompam replied, and remembered the dozens of personal calls he still had to make to be able to realize this goal.

"I might be able to help you with that. Your memberships are 100,000 *baht* each, right? If I sell them for you will you give me a commission?" she asked him brazenly.

Pompam thought a moment. "Sure. I'll give you ten percent, the same as I give my other recruiters."

"I'm Chinese, don't forget. They can *never* be too rich, and I would never turn down a few easy 10,000 *baht* commissions. It's a deal. Give me some applications and I'll get you members. I know a lot of people," she said confidently.

Pompam knew that she did, in fact, know a *lot* of people, some very powerful people at that. He was beginning to like her more and more.

"I'm sure you know *Khun* Arun, our PR director? I'll have him send some over to your office."

"I'm not exactly in *Khun* Arun's social set, but yes, I have met him. You were lucky to get him to join you. He'll get you all the aristocrats I can't reach; I'll just get you some rich Chinese businessmen."

They finished lunch and were heading out towards the lobby when she asked, "Do you mind if we both go in my car? You can leave yours here and my driver will bring you back later."

"I'd be happy not to have to face the traffic on my own, for once; thank you," Pompam answered, wishing then that he, too, had his own driver.

"You mean you drive yourself? How can you stand it? You'd be surprised at how much work you can get done in the car while it sits in traffic. You just need to be in the back seat with a mobile telephone or two, that's all." Pompam could see the logic to this and decided that it was time for him to get himself a driver — immediately.

Khun Darunee's driver pulled up in front of the Regent in a brand-new, 500-series Mercedes Benz in a metallic pinkish-gold color. "Nice car, *Khun* Darunee. You'd need to make an awful lot of 10,000 *baht* commissions to pay for this," Pompam joked with her.

"You'd be very surprised, *Khun* Vichai, by what I had to do to buy this car!" she laughed and winked at him.

It was about an hour's drive out to Bangkapi, and Pompam relaxed in the back seat amidst the clutter of brief cases, files, notebooks, make-up cases, clothes, shoes and telephone wires.

"You can see my car is both my home *and* my office when I'm on the road. One can never tell about the traffic," she said, as if she was telling him something new. "The only thing missing in here that I need when I get stuck in a traffic jam is a *toilet*," she said laughing.

They didn't talk much on the way to Bangkapi — at least not to each other. She spent most of the time on the mobile phone: first to her son's school, then to her dinner guests about meeting at Lemongrass Restaurant at eight o'clock, then to her "consultant" as she called him, and finally to one of her maids at the townhouse where she lived.

"Sorry about all that, *Khun* Vichai; but I had to make those calls. I don't know what I would do without a phone in the car." Pompam decided he would buy one the next day, not believing he didn't already have one.

They finally reached their destination and Pompam told the driver where to go to show the property's boundaries. He, himself, hadn't been out to that part of the suburbs in quite a while and was surprised at all of the construction activity going on in the area.

After ten minutes, *Khun* Darunee said, "The location is excellent, *Khun* Vichai. With this size project you should be able to sell out in about six weeks the way things are going in this part of town. But you know what? It's too *small* — for both of us. Why should you spend your time on something that's only going to make you a few million *baht*? The headaches are the same for a small project as they are for a big one — like the damned permits I mentioned at lunch — and they basically take the same amount of time. I have something in mind that I *know* is worth our time, and right now I'm looking for just the right partner; it's too big for me to handle alone, and I don't have a big enough profile."

"I'm certainly willing to listen, *Khun* Darunee," Pompam replied, surprised, disappointed, and intrigued by what she had said. How clever of her, he thought, when he realized that she had turned the tables on him and was recruiting *him* for *her* project.

"You're so formal. Why don't you call me 'Nee,' okay?"

"And you can call me 'Pompam'; all my friends call me that."

"*I* think we can be friends, Pompam; don't you think?"

"I hope so, Nee; especially if you're going to be my mentor," Pompam replied good-naturedly.

"Maybe even your partner! I'll teach you everything you need to know about putting in an infrastructure for a project and how to get the damned permits. I'll introduce you to all the right government people we'll have to pay off to get things done; otherwise we'll be buried in paperwork and waste at least a year. These days the people in all those government departments won't do anything without under-the-table money up front. It's a sad fact, Pompam, but very true. Knowing how the system works helps, though, and I'll teach you," she volunteered.

"I really appreciate the opportunity to be your student, Nee," Pompam said, trying to sound meek, letting her inflate her own good-sized ego.

"Why don't you call me around eleven tomorrow morning and we'll make a plan for the afternoon if you're free; I'll tell you all about my project idea then. Come to my townhouse on *Soi* Ruam Rudee and don't forget to send me the applications for your new club. I think I can get you at least two members tonight at dinner!"

They dropped off *Khun* Darunee at the hairdressers and the driver continued on to the Regent where Pompam had left his car. What an interesting woman, Pompam thought to himself.

The next morning Pompam called up Chai and asked him to find a driver/bodyguard for himself like he had found Vinun for Rattana. Then he decided that the BMW he was driving was too small for riding in the back seat with a driver in front. So his first stop on his way to the office that day was to the Mercedes-Benz dealership on Rama IX Road where he bought himself a big new 500-series model like Darunee's. He chose a dark navy blue exterior with camel-colored leather inside. He told them to install a telephone in it before they delivered it that afternoon to his office.

Later he went through the game of passing down the cars again: Nuu would get the most recent BMW and Nuu would give Att

Pompam's previous one. Toy didn't want either Nuu's or Att's used car; he wanted to keep driving Pompam's old Honda.

Nuu had spent nine months in the hotel school operated by the Dusit Thani Group. He resisted going at first, but Pompam had prevailed, and finally Nuu realized how much he had learned, and how valuable his training would be when they opened The Regents' Club with him as General Manager.

Att had long-since graduated from Ramkampheng University with a degree in business. He was now the General Manager at Isan Sweetheart and Pompam was proud of him for the excellent job he did.

Toy was in his final year at Chulalongkorn, and was ranked in the top five percent of his class. His majors in social welfare, public health, and education had made him highly qualified to be the Executive Director of the Thailand Youth Foundation.

Pompam was impressed with Toy's performance in both the university *and* the Foundation. He got along well with the Board members Pompam had chosen, who were some of the most prominent business and government figures in Bangkok. They almost always voted along with Toy's well-thought-out proposals for the creation and funding of new programs he continually dreamed up.

Black was in his last year at the International School. He was also a bright young man, but no match intellectually for Toy. He was even more handsome than Pompam had been at that age, and was popular with all his classmates — especially the young girls. His main interests were music and the performing arts, so Pompam figured he would one day go into show business — especially since his "uncle" Ott had so many connections in that field.

That left three brothers still at home in Buriram, aged thirteen, eleven and ten. Pompam sometimes felt he should bring all three to Bangkok and give them an earlier start than he and their other brothers had had. But he knew that Maa would miss them terribly, for one thing; he also felt that they should have the full "benefit" of the same country up-bringing as the rest of them. It would make them just too *different* from he and the other older ones if they came to the capital at their present ages, Pompam decided. *Mai pen rai*, Pompam thought; the three left at home could just wait their turns.

Maa was healthy, but had very little to occupy her time since

Pompam had persuaded her to stop planting the rice when Paw died. "It's just not necessary for you to work that hard, Maa. You have everything you need now without breaking your back, day after day stooping in the fields."

All of the provinces in the countryside were full of old people who were literally "bent" at right angles from the waist — permanently. A lifetime of working the rice fields had taken away their ability to stand up straight, which was just another indignity imposed upon them by their hard life of toil and poverty. Pompam didn't want this for his aging mother.

Pompam encouraged her to stay busy by weaving silk fabric, but it was lonely for her at home when the three boys were at school; she needed company, she said.

Pompam phoned *Khun* Darunee at eleven o'clock the next morning, and when her secretary put the call through he could tell that she had just gotten out of bed, "Dinner last night was excellent for business, Pompam. I told you yesterday I thought I might get you *two* members for your new club; but you should be real proud of me, I got you *three*!" she shrieked.

"Congratulations, Nee, you made yourself 30,000 *baht*!"

"There were six of us for dinner and the bill was 5,000 *baht*, so I netted 25,000 for doing practically nothing. I think I like working with you, Pompam."

"What time should I come by this afternoon for our meeting?" he asked, laughing.

"Why don't you come at two o'clock — and don't forget to remind *Khun* Arun to send me those membership applications for Regents'!"

He arrived promptly at her townhouse at two o'clock. Even though she was in her own home she still kept him cooling his heels for almost thirty minutes. He waited in the living room, drank coffee, and took in the "interesting" decor. The furniture was massive, intricately-carved imitation Louis Quatorze, with bright floral brocade upholstery. There were several built-in, glass-fronted cabinets that displayed Nee's rather impressive jade collection, and Chinese ceramic statues, some as high as five feet tall, inhabited every corner, like sentries on guard duty.

Pictures of Their Majesties the King and Queen in wide gilt frames were hung high on the wall above the sofa; and the biggest television screen Pompam had ever seen stood against the opposite wall, flanked by speakers almost as tall as Darunee. The floor was entirely gray marble, with an intricately-patterned Chinese carpet under the "Louie" seating arrangement. The effect was overwhelming, even to Pompam, especially when considering that the owner was a short, slightly-plump Chinese working mother. Obviously "scale" was not one of her considerations, Pompam observed.

The secretary came to let Pompam know he could go upstairs to *Khun* Darunee's office. With the secretary was an elderly lady she was escorting to the front door. The stately-looking matron had the mandatory dyed, jet-black coifed hair; Pompam *waied* and smiled politely, and she returned the same to him.

Pompam entered *Khun* Darunee's private office and was again struck by the size of the furnishings. She sat behind a huge, black-lacquered desk that would have been suitable for the president of the United States.

"Come in Pompam; sorry to keep you waiting. A lady stopped by unexpectedly who sometimes sells me jewelry. Look what I just bought!" She held out a hand with her signature brightly-painted nails and displayed a gigantic marquis-shaped diamond ring that nearly reached past her knuckle.

"It's a *pink* diamond, Pompam. I've always wanted one. And it's ten carats."

"I don't think I've ever seen a diamond that big, Nee!" Pompam exclaimed, feeling quite impressed. "That must have cost nearly as much as your car."

"It was only two million *baht*," she replied as if it was nothing. "I could sell it for double that if I wanted to. The old lady needed the cash."

Pompam simply shook his head in disbelief. "You'll be happy to know that first thing this morning I phoned my manager and told him to find me a driver. I also went to the Benz store and bought a car like yours — *with* a telephone! My BMW was too small in the back seat to spread out my portable office," he teased her.

"Good for you, Pompam. I'm glad to see you're a fast learner.

If we work together it will make things so much easier."

Pompam opened up his briefcase and said, "Rather than calling *Khun* Arun I brought you the Regents' Club membership applications myself. Will twenty-five be enough for today?" he asked her sarcastically.

"For today, yes, but I'm going to try to get you a hundred. That will make me one million in commissions — and I never like to do anything for less than a million *baht* if I can avoid it. It's just not worth my time. You see! That will pay for half my new diamond," she said with a laugh.

Pompam's admiration for the little Chinese ball of fire was growing by the minute.

"So what is this big project you wanted to talk to me about?" he asked, unable to contain his curiosity any longer.

"I feel like I can trust you, Pompam, even though we haven't known each other very long. You must keep this information top secret. Okay?" she asked, dead serious.

"I have many secrets I'll take to my grave, Nee, so don't worry about me; I promise," he replied, thinking momentarily about the drug business and Kenji's rape, for starters.

"You may or may not know about the thousands of military contracts that routinely come up for bid — for everything from fighter jets to frying pans; it's the law that every purchase be put out to tender. We both know, of course, that 99% of all bids in this country are rigged by bribes — and the same thing applies to the military ones."

"What do military bids have to do with us? I don't see the connection," asked Pompam, wondering where she was leading.

"The military, under the office of the Supreme Commander, is putting out a contract for bid on a huge housing estate for military personnel — to be built somewhere in the outskirts of Bangkok. The military banks will guarantee low-interest financing so the soldiers can afford to buy the units — making it risk-free for the developer. The profits for the lucky party that wins the bid will be absolutely enormous." She rolled her eyes around in her head when she said the word "enormous," practically going into an ecstatic swoon.

"So you think you can get this contract, Nee? Is that the idea?" Pompam asked, suddenly very interested.

"I've been lining up my 'ducks' with the military boys for a long, long time, Pompam. I know exactly who will be making the decisions when the bids come in, and I've already begun laying the groundwork for setting up the payoffs. But I can't do this whole thing alone; because I'm a woman, for one thing, and I simply don't have enough "face" for another. But I think you and I can do it *together!*"

Pompam listened closely as she told him about the scope of the project — as well as the identity of some of the "ducks" that were involved. He was both shocked and not-shocked at the same time, knowing quite well how business deals were made in his country. By the time she finished explaining the whole thing, he knew he wanted to play this game with Darunee.

"What better place to throw my hat into the ring as a land developer?" he asked himself, smiling. The little townhouse project he wanted to build on his suburban land was already forgotten.

"Toy, I've been thinking a lot about Maa lately, and I want you to think of something for the old ladies in our village in Buriram *to do*; Maa needs company, and some kind of an activity," he said to his younger brother that night at home. "She's going to go bad in the mind if we don't come up with something soon; and you know she won't come to Bangkok to live."

Toy put his mind to work on this assignment, and after a few days he came to the conclusion that the weaving of silk was the common denominator shared by most of the village women. So he produced a plan to build a weaving factory right on the grounds of the village temple, and make the Abbot, *Phra* Prateep, the "boss" of the operation.

The village women were used to making silk by the *piece* using their traditional Isan patterns and designs. The problem was this: a very limited market existed for the "ethnic" look they made. The interior design company Pompam had used for his house said they would buy *un*limited quantities of hand-woven silk by the *yard* in plain, simple colors. They could even sell it for export if they could be guaranteed a steady supply. So Toy persuaded the village women, including Maa and Rattana's mother, to convert their production to conform with what the market wanted, and a new industry was born in the small village in Buriram, thanks to his idea.

All of the women were paid a daily wage, meals were provided for them twice a day, and profits were split between the temple and the temple school for the village youngsters. All of this was accomplished with the Foundation's initial investment of only 150,000 *baht* that went for the construction of the open-sided factory (a thatched roof supported by wooden poles), looms for thirty workers, and start-up supplies. They manufactured the silk every step of the way: raising the worms, cultivating the mulberry leaves to feed the worms, spinning the thread, making the dyes out of plants and bark from the area, and finally weaving the fabric.

The benefits to the village from that one project were incredible. There was work for nearly fifty women, their native craft was preserved, they maintained their community social structure, the temple made money, and the children were provided a better education and free lunches every day.

One day about a week before The Regents' Club grand opening Pompam got a call from *Khun* Darunee from her car. "I just got confirmation from three big-shot *phuyais* from the military, and I'm going to be entertaining them for dinner. I think tonight's the night for you to get to know them; they're on our list of 'ducks.'" Pompam could tell she really wanted him to be there.

"Okay, Nee, where should I meet you and what time?"

She quickly told him and then said, "Sorry, Pompam, I've got to go; I'm late for a meeting and I have calls to make," and hung up.

That evening at eight o'clock, Pompam's new driver, whose name was Chaiya, dropped him off at the Dusit Thani Hotel. They would be meeting for dinner at the elegant Thai restaurant on the ground level that served artfully-decorated "royal cuisine." Every time Pompam walked into the Dusit Thani he couldn't help but remember the first time he ever stepped through the doors: he was a poor *nene* in worn-out rubber slippers, and about to be Dr. Jim's tour guide to Isan.

During the past few years since his graduation he still heard from Dr. Jim occasionally, and Pompam wrote to him not nearly as often as he felt he should have. "One day I'll see him again," he said to himself that evening, which was what he always said whenever he thought about his kind benefactor.

He entered the restaurant, the pleasant sound of classical Thai music greeting him, and the attractive hostess, dressed in a costume of pink and silver Thai silk, showed him to *Khun* Darunee's table. "I can't believe it, Nee, you are actually already here!" Pompam exclaimed in surprise.

"I may be late most of the time, Pompam, but I'm never late when I'm entertaining generals. In fact, I asked you to be here at eight o'clock so we would both be early; the three big-shots won't be here until eight-fifteen," she replied. "I wanted to be able to tell you who they were and give you some background before they arrived."

Khun Darunee then proceeded to give Pompam a briefing on the three men who would be joining them. One of the generals was the senior *aide de camp* of the Supreme Commander of all of the military in Thailand: army, navy *and* air force. "Pompam, he's the key to getting to his boss, whose vote on the contract carries the most weight. The other two aren't on the selection committee, but they're personally very close to the Supreme Commander; they're all from the same class at the military academy — and that really counts with these boys; they take care of each other. Here they come, I'll tell you more later..."

She rose from her chair and *waied* low to the three uniformed men approaching their table. They all *waied* back, smiled, then turned towards Pompam as Darunee introduced him. Pompam *waied* low and tried to act as meek and subservient as he thought the situation demanded. He knew that self-effacing behavior around Thai generals was more or less expected — no matter who one was.

Pompam was amazed at how well Darunee handled the generals. She teased them, flirted with them, joked with them, and, best of all, knew how to flatter them and feed their general-size egos. They all seemed very happy to meet the well-known *Khun* Vichai, and they enjoyed the attention they were getting from other tables because they were with him.

"*Khun* Vichai and I are forming a land development company together; he needs to get himself a day job," she chuckled, giving Pompam a poke in the ribs.

Pompam laughed and said, "I have to find a way to keep up with my wife's shopping bills; besides, *Khun* Darunee has agreed to become my mentor; I couldn't do without her." Darunee looked pleased, and smiled, signaling the waiter to pour more drinks. A bottle of Black Label sat on a cart next to her.

"You couldn't possibly have a better teacher. She always finds a way to knock down all her barriers — which are usually *people* in her way. But she does it with such charm the victim doesn't even know what hit him. She would make an excellent army officer," one of the generals commented, making them all laugh.

"I hear you are opening a new members-only club in the Tonglor area, *Khun* Vichai," the Supreme Commander's *aide de camp* commented, changing the subject.

"That's right, I am; just next week. Please be my guest for the grand opening — all three of you," Pompam replied graciously.

"We would be delighted to attend, *Khun* Vichai; it may be the first and only time we ever get to see it, being just poor army men." Pompam picked up the obvious hint.

"Nonsense. I would like you to come often." Pompam looked over at Darunee who gave him a "go on" look. "In fact, I would like to make all three of you honorary members," Pompam said, only that second having thought of the new category. Darunee looked at him and beamed, thinking this will be a favor we can draw on later...

"We couldn't possibly accept such a gift, *Khun* Vichai," he lamely protested.

"I insist, General Chamnan. It will be a great honor to have you all as members. In fact, if you were *not*, our membership roster would be grossly incomplete," Pompam ingratiatingly replied.

"Well, then, in that case, we accept. It seems like it would be an appropriate place for us to entertain visiting military elite from our neighboring countries, which we have to do from time to time. Has the Supreme Commander already joined?" he asked, knowing full-well that he had *not*.

"I'm sorry to say that he hasn't, General Chamnan; however, I would like to offer him an honorary membership as well. I'll be most grateful if you would inform him for me and I will follow up with a letter to him tomorrow." General Chamnan seemed *very* pleased. He had just scored something of major value for his boss, *and* for his two former classmates as well. *Khun* Darunee winked at Pompam and tried not to smile too broadly. She clearly knew the value of what Pompam had just done for their "cause."

From then on throughout the dinner it was as if the generals had known Pompam all his life. They immediately took him in and made him "one of the boys." Pompam knew *Khun* Darunee had already been accepted as "one of the boys" quite some time ago; they were all so familiar with her.

When dinner was over the three tipsy generals departed with many *wais* and "thank yous." Pompam promised to follow up on the club memberships while he and Darunee escorted them up to the *porte cochere* where their car and driver was waiting.

"Now that business is over for the day, you must go out with me," Darunee said as the generals' car was pulling away, more than just suggesting.

During dinner he thought he might indulge himself in a visit to the "sexotic" Patpong area since it was practically across the street from The Dusit Thani; but he suddenly changed his mind and accepted her invitation instead. "Just for a little while, Nee; I don't want to get to bed too late tonight."

"Good. Then we'll take my car and drop you off here later so you can get yours."

Comfortably ensconced in the back seat of Darunee's cluttered Benz, Pompam asked where they were going.

"Why don't we go to NASA; I love it there," she replied.

"NASA? You want to go to NASA tonight?" he asked in total disbelief.

"Yes, Pompam. I feel like having a lot of energy around me tonight, if you don't mind. The generals were boring."

This Chinese working mother never ceased to amaze Pompam. NASA Spacedrome was an enormous, extremely popular, multilevel discotheque and concert hall up in Klongtan near Ramkampheng. Pompam had been there a few times several years before as the guest of *Khun* James, and had enjoyed himself. So, he thought, why not? He, himself, was also in the mood to be entertained; the dinner had been stressful.

Khun Darunee's driver let them off at the entrance where hundreds of young people were loitering around, waiting to go inside. All heads turned when the big Benz pulled up and Darunee and

Pompam emerged from the back seat. Nearly everyone instantly recognized Pompam and began calling out his name, approaching him with *wais*, reaching out to touch him. They followed him and Darunee up the big staircase and through the glass doors to the lobby, creating a stir of excitement as they moved along. The assistant manager at the entrance gate stepped aside to greet them, *waied*, and ushered them past the long queue of young people waiting their turn to get in.

When the attendant opened the doors for them the music hit with cyclone-force, pushing against them with a blast. The manager led them through the dark, cavernous room upstairs to the second level, and a special table that was always reserved in case someone famous showed up. The table was against the chrome railing overlooking the giant dance floor below. People began to notice Pompam's presence and started to drift by, oftentimes stopping to get a closer look, sometimes even approaching to say "hello."

"It's so much fun going out with a well-known celebrity, Pompam. Now you can really see how popular you are for an old man of thirty," Darunee said as she fluttered her hands around, the big ten-carat pink diamond sparkling on her finger as the laser lights flashed randomly across the huge room.

"I already have a bottle of whiskey stashed here, and they'll be bringing it over shortly," she said with confidence, having been there many times.

The bottle and mixers came, the captain made them drinks, and Darunee said, "I would like to propose a toast to the fastest, most adaptable learner in Bangkok. You had those generals drooling all over you tonight, Pompam; you handled them perfectly. Giving them honorary memberships in your club — which costs you nothing — was a stroke of genius! You really made some points for us tonight, Pompam. Congratulations."

"You really think I did all right?" Pompam asked sheepishly, knowing full-well he had.

"Yes, of course! You were brilliant! I know you're busy with your opening right now, but once that's out of the way we need to concentrate on getting that housing contract. After tonight — and past years of my own conniving — we're already on our way." Darunee was very enthusiastic.

"Do you really think we can win the bid?" Pompam wasn't yet totally convinced.

"I'm not kidding when I say that it's well within our reach. And it's definitely worth the sacrifice of spending some time with those stupid old military boys. They'll have to be taken care of — it'll cost us plenty — and a whole lot more besides those three, but the rewards for us will be huge. I guarantee it," was her solid answer.

A popular rock group was performing live on stage that night, and Pompam, to his surprise, found that he was enjoying himself. He had met the rock star about a year before when Ott had signed him to perform at the Paradise City; a nice chap, Pompam remembered, and since he was not yet a bit star at that time, he was grateful to be given the chance to perform in their coffee shop.

After the group performed two numbers the lead singer made the announcement that, "All of us at NASA wish to welcome *Khun* Vichai Polcharoen here tonight! He gave me a big break when I was just starting out, and I will never forget him. In my book, *he's* the greatest star in Thailand!"

Pompam was thoroughly embarrassed by the rock star's over-generous acknowledgment, and wished he could have just slipped through the cracks in the floor. The crowd went crazy with applause for Pompam when the spotlights searched out his table. Pompam, caught, got up and waved to the crowd like a Caesar in Rome.

"I don't think I can take too much more of this, Nee. Do you mind if we go when this group finishes their act?" he pleaded.

"Don't you want to dance a little bit first?" she asked him with begging eyes.

"Are you kidding? I wouldn't make it out of there alive," Pompam said, looking down at the gyrating mass of bodies.

"Come on, Pompam, just for a short one. You'll be all right; Dragon Lady is here to protect you!" she shrieked. She had *loved* the spotlight on them, and she would gladly sacrifice Pompam's security on the dance floor for a few more moments of such spectacular attention.

Pompam could hardly believe that he was allowing himself to be led down the stairs towards the completely packed dance floor. NASA's capacity was 5,000 souls and that night it must have been pushing that number, he thought with fear.

Darunee pushed and shoved her way out into the gigantic arena, dragging Pompam behind her by the hand. He was grabbed at from every direction, and almost felt afraid for his life. "Don't worry, Pompam; enjoy yourself!" Darunee screamed in his ear.

Darunee finally reached a point on the dance floor that she estimated was its exact center. Then she stopped and turned to Pompam and started to dance with him. She began to move back and forth and wave her arms around with abandon — at least to the extent that she could, given the crowd's crushing in on her.

The rock star noticed Pompam and screamed into the microphone, "Go, *Khun* Vichai; show us how to do it!" The spotlights shone down on him again — and onto the flashing, capped-toothed smile of Darunee who was absolutely in heaven. After a few intense minutes Pompam felt he was on the verge of passing out from claustrophobia. He reached for Darunee and pulled her along, struggling to make it to the edge of the vast floor, flashing colored lights coming up from underneath, and lasers going wild up above.

"Please don't ever make me do that again, Nee," Pompam said as they finally reached the relative safety of their table upstairs. "I nearly died out there!" he groaned with relief.

"Don't worry, Pompam. I told you you'd be safe with the Dragon Lady; you made it back in one piece," she yelled closely in his ear over the loud music and started laughing with abandon.

Then she ordered champagne for the two of them, knowing that the ceremony of the cork-popping would attract even more attention to their table. Pompam didn't care any more by this time. He had planned on an early night at home, but since it was already 1:00 a.m., he thought, what the hell?

They wound up having *two* bottles of champagne, and finally stumbled out to the car at three o'clock, waving good-bye to the remaining revelers who sent them off with cheers.

"Rattana is going to kill me for getting home this late. You'd better drop me off at my house, which is on the way, and I'll phone my driver on the cellular to go on home," he said when at last he was able to relax in the back seat.

"Wasn't that fun, Pompam? I know you enjoyed yourself. You're not even a movie actor or a rock star, but everyone loves you!"

Darunee cooed admiringly while thanking her lucky stars that fate had brought her such an exciting partner. She would exploit their relationship to the moon, she calculated, just as she had done that evening at NASA.

When they finally reached Pompam's gate she quietly said, "Call me tomorrow, but not too early."

"Good night, Nee. Be sure to be a good girl now and go straight home," answered Pompam with a slight slur in his voice.

"I will, Pompam. Good night to you, too." But to her driver she gave the order to go to her ladies' member club where well-trained young men danced with — and sold their bodies to — rich, single professional women like Darunee. There were four such places in Bangkok at the time, each of them doing quite well. These clubs provided their female members what their male counterparts had openly been enjoying since the beginning of time. Darunee was suddenly in the mood to have sex with a handsome young boy after all the excitement at NASA. And so she did.

"You got home awfully late last night," Rattana said the next morning while looking down at her bleary-eyed, obviously hung-over husband lying next to her.

"Darunee dragged me out to NASA after our dinner meeting with the generals. Can you believe it?"

"I believe everything you tell me, Pompam; but I'm surprised you did it. I'd better watch out for your new friend, Darunee. I don't think she's a very good influence on you." She tried not to sound peeved or jealous, but she was indeed furious.

"*Mai pen rai*, Rattana; just let me sleep one more hour." Then he drifted off.

Chapter 21

The day of the grand opening for The Regents' Club finally arrived and Pompam and his group spent the entire day attending to final preparations. Even Rattana volunteered her time to help where she might be needed.

Only Toy refused to participate, claiming he had Foundation work to do. But everyone in the family knew that Toy wouldn't help out because he didn't approve of anything that had to do with the sex industry. Of late he had begun to make his feelings more and more known — even to journalists — which made Pompam look almost foolish. Pompam didn't know how to handle him most of the time.

The final count for memberships was 630, which was even higher than Pompam's goal; *Khun* Arun had sold 285, and Darunee had managed to sell 110. The member RSVPs for that evening had totaled 520, so they knew it would be a full house when they included the wives, girlfriends and other guests.

Pompam wanted the evening to be very low-key: quiet music, cocktails, and a light buffet supper. There would be no floor show or speeches.

Pompam invited Mr. Aoyama to attend, as he happened to be in town for some amusement. Pompam kept an open dialogue going with the Japanese man, partially because of their business relationship, of course, but also because he genuinely liked him. A third reason was because he needed a buffer between himself and Kenji, who called him every few weeks and demanded that he go to Japan. Pompam knew Yamamoto only wanted him there so he could humiliate him, make him pay homage, and demonstrate his power over him. But each time Pompam refused, he knew it made Kenji angry, and there was always some kind of a threat. So far they had been lucky with their heroin operation, no one had gotten busted, and it was still a well-guarded secret known only to Pompam and his three lieutenants.

"You have done a magnificent job on The Regents' Club, Mr. Vichai," Aoyama said to him as he looked about the sumptuous room.

"Thank you very much, Mr. Aoyama. Do you think it is as beautiful as The Imperial Club in Tokyo?"

"To tell you the truth, I think it is even *more* beautiful," he said, meaning it, but he knew he would never say this to Yamamoto back in Japan; the boss would be livid, and might be tempted to harm the Thai man, whom Aoyama had grown to like and respect.

From the street The Regents' Club looked like a marble palace that might once have stood in Rome at the height of the empire. The exterior was decorated with soaring Corinthian columns over the *porte cochere* (the same as Pompam's house, but bigger and more of them), elaborate plaster work, arched windows, and thousands of tiny white lights strung up everywhere. The small lights delineated the walls and the roof line of the building, the windows, the columns, and were stretched from the pinnacle of the *porte cochere* to the wall in front like rays of the sun. It was indeed quite a spectacle on the outside, which was all the general public would ever get to see.

On the inside it was even more elaborate, if that could be imagined. The designers, at Pompam's insistence, had indulged their imaginations to the limits, making sure nobody in Bangkok, perhaps in all of Asia, had ever seen anything like it. A lighting designer had been brought in from New York who worked with the architects to create special built-in effects. A technician sat up in the rafters at an electronic board and continually altered, dimmed, and brightened the hundreds of interior lights throughout the evening to coordinate with the music and changing moods. The entire building became a theater.

Nuu had done an excellent job assuming the role as General Manager, and Pompam was enormously proud of him. He had grown and matured and learned his trade well at the Dusit Thani's hotel school.

Pompam, Rattana, Ott, and the now financially-secure *Khun* Arun were the official hosts, and greeted everyone personally as they entered and signed the guest book. Darunee, who had never before met Rattana, instantly felt daggers from her, in spite of the big smiles and complimentary remarks they exchanged about each other's hair and outfits. They managed to keep a proper "face" on for everyone, but Darunee also kept her distance, and stood off to one side as she greeted the members she had sold.

"After all, Pompam, they're *my* contacts, and I'll greet them as I please; fuck your bitch wife!" she hissed at him in private. Pompam wasn't at all happy about Darunee's remark, but he knew better than to upset this outrageous firecracker that was his new business partner.

The Supreme Commander and his *khunying* wife showed up, as did the other three generals to whom Pompam had given the honorary memberships. Darunee, Pompam, and Rattana together approached the Supreme Commander, General Prasart, as he entered the building, and *waied* deeply, the two men introducing their wives. After a few pleasantries were passed back and forth the General said, "If you have a moment to spare later on, I would like to speak with you privately, *Khun* Vichai and *Khun* Darunee; I have an idea I would like to discuss with you."

"At your convenience, Sir; we'll be waiting," Pompam answered, Darunee smiling obsequiously. The peaks of Rattana's cheeks reddened slightly, but she quickly joined the team and turned to the General's elaborately-coifed wife and said cheerfully, "Don't worry; I'll keep you company when they go off for their talk."

The princes of Bangkok's business and social worlds had all purchased memberships, thanks to everyone's combined efforts, and were there that night en masse. Even the Prime Minister, several cabinet members, and Members of Parliament showed up for the event. Pompam had, of course, given Police General Surapong an honorary membership, and he arrived with an entourage of his fellow high-ranking officers.

Members of the press weren't allowed inside the walled compound that evening — or on any night thereafter. That didn't stop them from camping out on the sidewalk in front, trying to photograph guests as they came in and out through the tall iron gates in their chauffeur-driven automobiles. Protecting the privacy of members was the first rule at The Regents' Club, and Nuu would rigidly enforce it for Pompam.

The fifty lovely hostesses who would be working at the club were nowhere to be seen that evening. Everyone — including the Prime Minister — knew perfectly well that high-priced prostitutes would be employed there, but in order to keep up appearances in front of wives and other female guests, the working girls wouldn't start their jobs until the following night.

Shortly after cruising through the magnificent buffet, General Prasert drew Darunee and Pompam aside and Rattana, observing, moved in to take care of the wife, as if on cue.

In the privacy of a sumptuous, unoccupied karaoke room the General said, "Perhaps we could get your Thailand Youth Foundation to set up some programs for the children of military personnel, *Khun* Vichai." The old boy definitely knew what he was up to; how could the review committee possibly turn down someone for a contract who had generously contributed to the welfare of military offspring? Brilliant, Pompam thought; it would smartly eliminate any chance of accusations about anyone giving or receiving bribes.

"My brother, Toy, who is in charge of the Foundation spoke to me just the other day about such an idea. I think it is excellent, and I'll tell him to pursue it at once," Pompam answered quickly. The idea would, of course, be news to Toy.

"If you don't mind, I will go over some thoughts I have on the subject with General Chamnan and he can contact you next week to review them. You see, I know where the most help is needed and would be most appreciated," he said directly, giving Pompam no opportunity to misunderstand him.

"Then that will save us a lot of time with research, General," Pompam answered and smiled, thinking that this man isn't the single most powerful man in Thailand for nothing.

"Good. Then if you'll excuse me I had better be getting back to my wife," he responded, announcing the end of their private interview. Pompam noticed the rather portly man wore a huge jade ring encircled by diamonds; it curiously reminded him of the unscrupulous flesh trader he had encountered that time in Phayao.

Just as they were leaving the private room Darunee said, "Thank you so much for coming tonight, General Prasart; my fortune teller said it was going to be a lucky year for *all* of us," letting things unsaid dangle in the air. She and Pompam looked at one another and winked at the same time, sensing they were one step closer to victory.

"Another big hit, Pompam. Congratulations," Rattana said to Pompam later when they walked back to their home next door. They had stayed until the last guest departed, of course, and were completely exhausted.

"Let's just hope they go on and on, my dear," he said, and silently begged the Lord Buddha for continued protection against misfortune — and Kenji.

Pompam and Darunee had just spent the day again out in the suburbs, battling the traffic, looking unsuccessfully for the right piece of land for the military housing project. Their meeting with the Supreme Commander at the Regents' Club opening had given them confidence to start putting their proposal together, but finding the right piece of real estate had become an annoying, unforeseen obstacle.

Pompam declared to Darunee that he was exhausted beyond words. Darunee didn't even answer him; she simply kicked off her shoes in the back seat of the Benz and curled up in a ball in the corner and went to sleep.

Pompam dozed for a while, too, as they inched their way through the rush-hour congestion on their way back to Darunee's townhouse. It took them nearly two hours to travel no more than ten miles.

"Wake up, Nee; we're back. If you don't invite me in for a drink right now I'll never speak to you again," Pompam said to her as he gathered up his documents and stuffed them back into his briefcase.

"I could use a few strong drinks, myself, partner," she replied as she tried to force her high heels back onto her tiny, swollen feet. Finally she gave up and walked into the house in her stockings, throwing the expensive shoes on the sidewalk for one of her maids to pick up later.

When they were comfortable with their first drink, downstairs in the amazing sitting room, Darunee asked, "What do you want to talk about, Pompam? Do you want to see our picture at NASA?" then began fumbling for a magazine on the end table. "I think we both look terrific."

Pompam looked at the two glossy photos in the *hi-so* party page of "Dichan Magazine" and sarcastically said, "My wife is going to *love* this, Nee." But he smiled as he thought back on that night at NASA. He *did* have a good time, but it was sad he couldn't go out any more without getting himself photographed and put in print, he realized glumly. "When did this magazine come out?"

"I just picked it up yesterday," she answered as she fixed them another drink.

"I'll have this last drink and then head on home; I hate to face that traffic again, but I hate the thought of facing Rattana even worse; she's bound to have seen those pictures by now."

Darunee merely shrugged her shoulders.

It took Pompam a little over an hour to get to the house. The maid told him that Rattana was out shopping and would be going to dinner with friends afterwards. A small reprieve, Pompam thought.

He went out to the guest house and only Toy was home. As usual, he was sitting at his desk doing some work for the Foundation. The austerity of Toy's room and the dozens of Buddha images on the shrine in one corner always took Pompam aback.

"Where's Black?" Pompam asked.

"He's rehearsing with his new band, Pompam; they're going to be in a concert at NASA next month. Speaking of NASA, I saw the photos of you and *Khun* Darunee: not bad, but I don't think they pleased your wife too much," he added solemnly. Pompam could tell at once that Toy did *not* approve; one more thing about my life he doesn't like, Pompam thought despondently.

"I just saw them myself a couple of hours ago. I'm expecting Rattana to be just a little bit pissed off," he replied with resignation. "*Mai pen rai.* Come over and have some dinner with me; I'll order something with cook. Just give me a few minutes to shower, change, and see Little Jim and Somporn before they go to bed."

He felt much better after his bath. The children were delighted to see him, as usual. The little girl was a miniature version of her mother, and seeing Little Jim was like looking in a mirror for Pompam.

The kids soon ran off to watch a little pre-bedtime television and Pompam went downstairs to the kitchen where he could smell his dinner being prepared. Toy was sitting at the table waiting for him.

"That silk project in Buriram is running really well, Pompam. I'm going to propose to the Board that we set up similar programs in other Isan provinces. I think we can help a lot of people. *Phra* Prateep wrote to me to say that all the village women are happy, the children in school are happy, and he is happy, too, with his job as 'boss,' and the money it's bringing into the temple," Toy remarked.

Pompam was proud of Toy for following through and creating something truly meaningful for his mother and her village friends. He had everything else running smoothly at the Foundation as well. "It was a brilliant idea, Toy, and I agree with you about expanding it to other villages." He observed his brother for a few moments and then said, "It seems like something's bothering you, Toy; what's the matter?"

"It's really nothing, Pompam. You already know I'm the family worrier. When I see you taking on more and more work I can't help but worry about your health, and worry about all those people looking up the ladder at your ass," he answered honestly. "I'm also worried about all those poor girls who work for you — including the fifty you've got at your new club next door," he added, not wasting an opportunity to scold.

Pompam ignored the remark about the girls and answered, "I'm fine, Toy, so don't worry about me. I've got my ass well-guarded. I just dread the thought of facing Rattana when she comes home," he said, knowing he had no sympathy from Toy.

Pompam was already in bed when Rattana came up to their bedroom about eleven o'clock. "How was your evening with the girls, Rattana?"

"Fine, Pompam. Just fine." Pompam could tell he was in big trouble by her staccato delivery.

"That's good. I had dinner with Toy and put the kids to bed. It was nice to have a quiet evening here at home after fighting the traffic all day."

"I thought you might be out at NASA tonight with your girl-friend," she replied in a haughty tone.

"Don't be mad at me, sweetheart. I've had a long hard day out looking for property — which isn't so easy to find these days."

"So you spent the whole day with Darunee, didn't you?" she was getting angry now.

"As a matter of fact I did, Rattana, and so what? She's only a business associate. And she is definitely *not* my girlfriend; you should know that. Calm yourself down," he said, trying to remain calm himself.

"Everyone in Bangkok, including all my friends, have seen

those two pictures of the two of you at NASA, and you both looked completely drunk! I am so embarrassed I could die," she began to cry as she sat down at her dressing table and began removing her jewelry.

"It's nothing to be upset about, Rattana; I told you the morning after we went to NASA that we had gone. I can't help it if those magazine people were there. Please stop carrying on!"

"That woman has such a bad reputation, Pompam. Why did you have to pick her to get involved with?"

"I'm only involved with her in a business deal, and I'm doing it because she's a real professional," Pompam was beginning to get angry himself now. He didn't like the idea of having to defend his actions to anyone — much less his own wife.

"A professional what? She's a slut!" Rattana screamed.

"Shut up, you bitch! How I conduct my business — and with whom — is up to me. You had better learn to be more respectful, Rattana, or one day you might be in for a big surprise. I give you everything I can to make you happy, and you give me this shit attitude in return."

Pompam stormed out of the room and went off to sleep in one of the guest suites. He spoke not one syllable to Rattana for two entire days. This time, Pompam's emotional withdrawal was just fine with Rattana. She couldn't remember ever being more angry with him, and she had no intention of letting his moodiness upset her or distract her from the children and her social activities. She had her own "face" now and she found she had increasingly less patience for Pompam's short-comings.

The argument about Darunee and NASA was still seething, but a trip to the doctor quickly confirmed that Rattana was pregnant again. Two weeks after their blowup Pompam, Rattana, Toy and the children were sitting down to Sunday night dinner. Since the maids were off on Sundays Rattana had cooked the meal herself. Toy had just returned from Chiang Mai that afternoon where he had gone on a survey trip for the Youth Foundation.

"How was Chiang Mai?" asked Rattana, while placing a tureen of *tom yam ghoong* on the table. The dish, a fragrant hot/sour, spicy soup with lemongrass and prawns, was a favorite with the whole family.

Toy, rarely one for small talk, and oftentimes out of synch, answered, "Just wonderful, Rattana; filthy and polluted like everywhere else in this country!"

The answer surprised Pompam and Rattana, but they said nothing. Then Toy started talking about getting the Foundation involved in environmental issues. He said, "I know it's supposed to be for the youth of Thailand, Pompam, but if we don't start protecting the environment, there won't be anything left for the young people — even ten or twenty years from now!"

He went on to mention a whole host of problems such as shrimp farming in the south which was destroying the mangroves, illegal logging, salt mining in Isan, new golf courses that stole water from the farmers, and over-building in Bangkok, which was slowly sinking into the muck. "All of these destructive things, Pompam, and dozens more like them, are because of one thing: greed. One generation is getting rich now — while all the rest that follow will suffer and be poor. Something has to be done about all those Regents' Club members of yours who are raping Thailand!"

Pompam and Rattana, putting aside their differences, sensed that Toy was striking pretty close to their mutual interests; they looked across the table at one another in alarm.

Pompam said, "Why are you so serious, Toy? The economy of Thailand is strong because of the businessmen who belong to The Regents' Club. This family wouldn't have anything at all if it weren't for their patronage. Please remember that."

Toy made no response, and it was only the noisy children that saved them from sitting uncomfortably in silence until the end of the meal. Pompam had a feeling they hadn't finished hearing from Toy on the subject of greed and the environment; he dreaded what might come next.

The following week Pompam, himself, made a day-trip to Chiang Mai; he and Chai had to attend one of their periodic meetings with *Khun* Nopadon about the girl business and heroin. About an hour after lunch Pompam became violently ill and started running a high temperature. Chai decided to get him home to Bangkok as quickly as possible, so they jumped on the next flight.

"It's probably food poisoning, *Khun* Vichai," announced the doctor who had been summoned to the house. He gave him an injection for the vomiting and diarrhea, and said, "Just stay in bed and you'll be fine soon; there's no sense in running tests to find out which bacteria it was that attacked you; it will just have to run its course for a couple of days."

Toy brought Pompam special fruits from the market, and encouraged him to drink his liquids to recover from the dehydration he had suffered. Rattana was touched by how much Toy obviously loved his *pi-chai*, in spite of the philosophical disparity between them.

Toy was worried, and kept pestering Pompam about his trip up north, wanting to find out why he had gone to Chiang Mai in the first place. "You're not going to open another exclusive, members-only whorehouse up there are you?"

"I was looking at property Chai's friend, *Khun* Nopadon, had for sale in the countryside: an investment," was his repeated excuse, and it made him feel terrible to lie to his brother — to have yet another thing to hide from him. But what can I do? he thought, I can't allow Toy to find out the truth.

"I want to go to Los Angeles next month for a World Health Organization conference on AIDS, Pompam. Do you have any objections?" Toy asked, frowning, somehow not believing Pompam's explanation.

Toy rarely asked Pompam for anything, so he agreed to let him go and said that he would pay for his plane ticket and expenses. Pompam assumed that AIDS would become Toy's new "cause," and he foresaw an eventual conflict because of the consequences it would have on his "entertainment" businesses. The thought of being at odds with Toy on yet another issue caused his head to start to ache.

Rattana, who happened to be in the room, overheard the conversation and said, "Are you sure you want to get involved with AIDS, Toy? That's not exactly a popular subject, you know." She was thinking about her *hi-so* friends, and the attitude they all shared about the terrible shame the disease brought to the families of victims; everyone she knew did their best to ignore its existence, and avoid even mentioning the low-class plague.

Toy answered, "Yes, Rattana, I'm going to get involved. It's becoming a big problem here, and I have to try to do what I can. Somebody's got to do something before it's too late!"

Rattana just shook her head, already thinking about the embarrassment she would have to endure when her social circle found out about the inevitable AIDS programs Toy would start up.

Pompam, already feeling miserable, felt even worse after *Khun* Arun visited him later that same day and told him that his old friend, Hans, from Amsterdam was dead after suffering a long and terrible illness.

Pompam got well enough to attend Black's debut concert at NASA three days later. He decided to make a big party out of the event and booked the private, glassed-in VIP room overlooking the stage. He invited the whole family — and even Little Jim and Somporn were allowed to come, after begging him and Rattana beyond endurance. Kitti and Sudar were there, Nuu and Att and their girlfriends, Toy, Ott and Kim, Chai and his wife, and *Khun* Arun and Pet. Pompam had wanted to invite Darunee, but Rattana threw a fit in protest.

NASA was absolutely packed to the rafters that night. Not everyone had come to see Black, however, as he was not the main attraction. The headliner was the number one act of the season: a tall, skinny, androgynous young man who tried hard to be an Asian clone of Prince, but unfortunately had none of the American performer's genius.

The opening act and the headliner both gave terrific performances, and the build-up of energy at NASA was so intense the walls were pounding; everyone was high on enjoyment — including the party in Pompam's VIP enclosure. When Black finally came on it quickly became apparent to all that he was a natural, brilliant entertainer; he sang and danced to his own music, and the audience loved him, screaming. No one except Ott, who managed him, had any idea the young man was so talented. Seeing the way the crowd reacted to Black caused Ott to declare with enthusiasm, "I'll make him the biggest thing to happen to Thailand since Bee."

Pompam, feeling excited and happy, ordered a case of champagne when Black joined them afterwards in the VIP room, followed by a trail of reporters and photographers. Pompam, of course, felt proud of his little brother, but suddenly realized that he didn't really know him — even though they lived in the same house. He knew the brothers younger than Black, still back in the village, even less, he thought sadly.

Toy walked over and congratulated Black and said, "You were great, *nong chai*, just don't let it go to your head and forget who you are; we have enough of those in our family already." Pompam overheard the remark and knew that Toy was referring to him; he was deeply hurt, but said nothing.

"*Mai pen rai*," he said to himself, "he has no idea of the sacrifices I've made for this family. He'll appreciate me one day."

"How could you have a big party at NASA and not invite me, you bastard!" Darunee screamed at Pompam in fury, not faking it one bit. The two of them were meeting to discuss the military housing contract, but Darunee couldn't talk about business until she let Pompam know how hurt she was.

"I'm sorry, Nee, but it was just family. You know how angry Rattana was when I went to NASA with you and our pictures got in the magazine," he said trying to reason with her.

"So what, Pompam? Is your wife jealous?" she continued, her temples were now red and pulsing. "I have *yet* to make a pass at you, you know!"

"I don't think she's jealous any more, Nee, but I told you she's pregnant, and when she's pregnant she gets moody and weird. I thought it might be nice to avoid a scene at NASA between the two of you."

"Do you really think that Rattana and I would fight over you? My God, you're even more conceited than I thought you were!" she hissed, but Pompam could see that she was on the verge of calming down, her anger almost spent.

"Come on, Nee. Relax. It was just a small party for my brother. You and I can make another party sometime. I promise," he said soothingly. Why do I have to spend so much time trying to get women to calm down and stop being angry with me? Pompam wondered. What do I ever do but try to please them?

"As long as you promise there will be another time, I'll behave." Then she abruptly changed into her business mode.

"Are you ready to do a little more military brass-licking?" she asked.

"If you mean, would I like to help you entertain some more generals? I would be happy to; just say the word," was his reply, relieved she had changed her tune.

"We have to give a dinner for General Chamnan, the Supreme Commander's chief *aide de camp*. Remember him? The purpose of the dinner is to get him together with my 'consultant,' *Khun* Somsak. Have I told you about him before?" she asked, not sure if she had.

"No, Nee, you haven't, although you have spoken about your 'consultant' many times," Pompam responded; he had always been curious about the identity of this mystery person, but out of politeness had never asked.

"*Khun* Somsak is the Vice Chairman of the Board of the Industrial Bank of Bangkok, one of the big five, as you know. He's been a close friend of mine for many years, and I would have married him if he didn't already have a stupid wife. He and I had an affair about six years ago. I was just starting out on my first big development project and a friend of mine introduced us at some charity reception; I knew he could help me so I went to bed with him a few times. Very simple. But that's been over for a long time and we're still good friends. He was a big-shot back then, Pompam, but now he's a *super* big shot — a major player in the circles that make Thailand's economic policies and control the local banks."

"So what does *Khun* Somsak have to do with General Chamnan and our strategy for ultimately winning the military housing project?" Pompam asked, not seeing a connection; he was also a bit surprised by her confession of having had sex with him for personal gain.

"*Khun* Somsak has agreed to be our figurehead, the Chairman of the Board, of our development corporation; so we can bid on the housing contract, Pompam. We need someone who is older, very powerful, and has a respected, clean reputation that goes back many years. It will give our presentation big 'face,' and make it look even more legitimate — no matter how much money we've paid under the table," she said cynically. "That's just the way it's done in this country, Pompam."

"So you want the general and your 'consultant' to meet so they can assure each other they are serious about supporting our cause, is that it?"

"Very good, Pompam; you catch on fast," she answered with a big smile.

"So what does *Khun* Somsak get out of all of this, Nee?"

"Bigger 'face,' Pompam: with the military, the politicians, the bankers and the public. He will also get a ton of money from us, of course," she replied caustically.

"I've been spending quite a bit of time with General Chamnan while you were being sick and giving parties at NASA without me," she continued. "We've more or less worked out a payment plan for all the military brass we'll need to take care of. General Prasert will be retiring from service next October, and he wants to make sure his nest egg is big enough to last him 'till the end of his days. He's milking every opportunity he can until then to increase his private assets. His part of the pot will be 25 million *baht*, while General Chamnan will get ten million. Others down the line will get five million, some two million, some one million, and the lowest on the food chain will get four or five hundred thousand. As I've told you, there's a whole 'committee' that has to give their approval. Ten million for Chamnan is a lot of money to him, and I don't think he could get that much from any of our competitors. He's pushing very hard for us," she explained.

Pompam remembered when he and Kitti had paid the local Buriram military official 10,000 *baht* each to get them out of their required military service. The price for favors certainly gets bigger the higher these guys move up in rank, Pompam thought to himself.

A few days later Pompam and Darunee hosted the dinner for *Khun* Somsak, the illustrious banker who had agreed to be their Board Chairman, and General Chamnan, the Supreme Commander's right hand man; it was one of the last strategic exercises involved in lining up all their 'ducks' to get the housing contract.

During the evening they succeeded in getting the General to spill the beans regarding the contract's parameters. Chamnan also reminded Pompam about the Supreme Commander's "suggestions" for the Youth Foundation, and Pompam assured him they were working hard to implement them. Pompam couldn't believe the acting games that were going on at the table. Everybody knew the whole deal was a con game involving big time corruption, but the proper words simply had to be said at the right time to the right people in order for everyone to have "face." It was a complete charade and they all played their parts to the hilt; after all, there was a great deal of money at stake — for everyone.

Back in the car on their way home Darunee smiled to Pompam and said, "I think we've just pulled off a coup on the military. How's that for turning the tables on them?" and laughed. She was referring to the numerous coups the military had pulled on various elected governments over the years — usually claiming they had to seize power because of "corruption in the highest places." Pompam and Darunee got a kick out of the irony.

"It seems that all the key points were handled tonight: we have the cash, we have the experience, we have the figurehead, and we have the Foundation which will put everyone beyond suspicion," Pompam commented.

"It looks like it's in the bag, Pompam," she yawned, and then curled up to one side and fell asleep.

Chapter 22

Pompam's thirtieth birthday passed with very little fanfare —
just a small family dinner at home. The next few months were fright-
fully busy for all of the Polcharoens: each person going off in his or her
own direction with very little time to interact with one another except
at scheduled meetings.

Toy came up with plans and timetables for implementing
General Prasert's ideas for the Foundation. As a result, they built
libraries and gymnasiums in ten major military installations scattered
around Thailand. Ott made sure the press was very well-informed
about these donations, and Pompam and Toy's pictures often appeared
in every newspaper in the country — usually in the company of the
Supreme Commander himself. General Prasert praised the Foundation
publicly for its generous contributions to Thailand's youth.

Toy came back from the World Health Organization conference
on AIDS in Los Angeles. He had his eyes completely opened regarding
the rest of the world's perception of Thailand as the "sex capital of the
world." He was crushed by the revelation, and more angry than ever
that the country of his birth had moved so far away from its traditional
Buddhist roots and values. He was disgusted by the fact that poor
country peasants commonly sold their teenage daughters into sexual
slavery for a few thousand *baht*. It tormented him to know that his own
family's wealth was founded on the *legalized* sex trade — and that
Pompam also employed under-age girls.

Rattana's pregnancy was progressing and Pompam was
relieved that her emotional state remained relatively stable this time.

Pompam's younger brother, Black, continued to rise as a pop
star. Ott had produced a cassette for him, and it was selling like hot
bowls of noodles in Chinatown; a concert tour around Thailand was
about to start that would keep him outside Bangkok for nearly a month.

Nuu finally married his beautiful live-in girlfriend and
Pompam and Rattana gave them a beautiful wedding reception in their
garden on Tonglor. Nuu managed The Regents' Club with the skill of a

Swiss-trained hotelier, and Att never failed to fulfill his managerial duties at Isan Sweetheart.

The VP Group empire was running smoothly on all fronts and they were perfectly poised to take another big leap forward. Pompam was riding the crest of a wave, but he still had a constant feeling of desires and passions not yet satisfied. He wondered from time to time where it all would lead.

"The military housing contract will be put out for bid next month, Darunee, and we still don't have the land. I'm getting worried that all the 'ducks' we've already lined up will end up hanging in the window of some goddamned Chinese restaurant if we don't find the right piece of real estate soon." Pompam vented his concern on Darunee.

They had learned from General Chamnan that the military preferred the new housing estate be built in Bangkapi district, because of its close proximity to several military installations. The problem was that there were hardly any pieces of available land that were large enough for the scope of the project. Pompam and Darunee had been trying desperately for months to solve the problem, but so far with no luck.

One day Pompam and Darunee were in the back seat of Pompam's car, and Chaiya, the driver, overheard their conversation about the land problem. He said, "*Khun* Vichai, you know that I was brought up in Bangkapi. My father and grandfather were also born there; we were all rice farmers. They sold off our land when I was a young man, but I know one family who kept theirs — and it's a big piece."

"Do you mean that you had someone here all the time that might have the answer to our problem and you didn't even know it?" Darunee scowled at Pompam.

"If I had known you wanted land in Bangkapi I would have taken you to see *Khun* Rossakorn a long time ago, boss!" Chaiya spoke up. "Do you want to see the land now?"

"Yes, Chaiya, please show us," he replied as he tried to remain calm. "While you're driving us there maybe you can tell *Khun* Darunee and me a little bit about this *Khun* Rossakorn and her land," Pompam added, trying not to sound impatient with his gentle, loyal employee.

Chaiya told them the property was located on Sukhapiban 3, a relatively new road that had become a main connector for some of the suburbs in the eastern sector of Bangkok. He thought they still had about 300 to 400 *rai*, although he knew that the family had been selling off bits and pieces over the years to pay bills and keep afloat. Chaiya had grown up with the oldest son in the family, *Khun* Prayuth, and they were the same age. Prayuth, himself, had tried to develop parts of their land, but with no experience, his attempts failed miserably. When they reached the property Chaiya drove Pompam and Darunee around the perimeter and showed them a sub-division of townhouses and single family homes that *Khun* Prayuth had started, but had left half-finished to crumble and decay. They had simply run out of money and had to stop building.

Pompam and Darunee realized immediately that this land would be absolutely perfect for their needs. They looked at each other and smiled.

Pompam told Chaiya to telephone *Khun* Rossakorn at her home, find out if she had any interest in selling her land for a good price, and see if he could set up a meeting — immediately.

The next afternoon Pompam couldn't help but feel sorry for the wrinkled old woman sitting next to him on the sofa; she had visibly arthritic hands, gnarled up toes on her bare feet, pure white hair, and a permanently-bent waist from many years of back-breaking work in the rice fields.

"My father always taught us to love the land and to treat it with respect. We have lived here for many generations, and always planted the rice to keep us alive. It is good land, there *was* plenty of water, and it has always taken care of us. Now I am too old to plant rice; the old canals have been drained so they could build houses, so there's no water anyway. My son and daughter here don't feel the way I do, and they don't want the land. They only want the money they'll get from it if I sell. The only reason you're here today is because they can't wait until I die and they can sell it themselves. I am a very unhappy old woman, *Khun* Vichai and *Khun* Darunee. Over the years I have sold off parts of the land trying to help my children, but they have always failed. Tell me what I should do," she finally ended in a cracked, reproachful voice; her son and daughter, Prayuth and Simporn, looked angry and embarrassed enough to be able to kill her right there on the spot.

"I also come from a family of rice farmers, Maa (Pompam called her 'mother' out of respect), in a small village in Isan. I understand how you feel about the land. My father is dead and my mother is now too old to plant rice on our farm. There are eight boys in my family and now five of us live in Bangkok; the youngest three will eventually come here to get an education, too. Our farm lies dried up and untended because the times have changed in Thailand, and the young people don't want to plant rice any more. Please sell us your land, Maa, and let us use it to build homes for people who no longer grow rice, and have been driven into the city so they can find work and survive." Pompam's moving speech sounded so sincere it caused Darunee's eyebrows to rise. His words came across as genuine because he could vividly imagine how his *own* mother would feel if faced with having to make the same decision.

The old mother looked at Pompam eye to eye; what he had said to her seemed to have struck home, and she sensed he was sincere. Then she looked up at her son, and then her daughter, and said, "I have lived through the reigns of four kings. I have seen this country change from Siam to Thailand; I have seen many, many things, and have lived through hardship after hardship. I have done my best to provide for you, but I can see now that it doesn't mean anything. Go ahead and sell the land — do whatever you want with it. It doesn't matter to me any more since I will be dead soon anyway. At least with the money you will have your last chance to do something with your lives. I am tired now and I want to go to bed. When you are ready for me to sign papers, just bring them to me," she said as she painfully rose from the sofa and crossed the room without saying another word to anyone.

Everyone was silent for a while until Prayuth finally said, "Well, *Khun* Vichai and *Khun* Darunee, I guess we can do business." He seemed so elated by his mother's decision that he could hardly contain himself. A look of new-found power appeared on his face that thoroughly disgusted Pompam and Nee; even Chaiya turned his face away and stared at the floor.

Once the property was secure, Pompam and Darunee met with the architects so they could get started on the site plan. The architects told them it would be easy, and they could have it finished in about ten days. Builders and architects were quite used to turning fertile rice fields into concrete by then; they had been doing it for years. By this time Bangkok had become a hungry, land-eating monster, already devouring over three hundred square miles.

The project's plans were finalized, the military sent out its official bid notice to the public, and Pompam and Darunee turned in their proposal.

There were a total of five contract submissions to the "committee" of assorted military personnel — each of whom was a "duck" already lined up by Pompam and Darunee. Even though the committee's collective mind was made up long before proposals were submitted, they waited a month to reveal their decision to make it look fair and carefully considered.

The decision was finally announced, and all of the daily papers — both Thai and English — carried the news that Pompam's and Darunee's development company had won the contract. As expected, no one in the general public found fault with the decision or suspected any hanky-panky. Pompam's reputation as a reputable businessman was unblemished — and his philanthropic gestures towards the children of military personnel and his Foundation's other charitable projects stood him above reproach.

Before too long construction started on the new complex which they had named "Royal Hills," even though there wasn't a hill anywhere near the project for at least a hundred miles.

It was now time to pay off the military brass, and General Chamnan was particularly eager to get that matter out of the way. He and Pompam and Darunee met for lunch to agree on how this could most-efficiently be done in secret. Pompam, who had given the matter some serious thought, said, "I think it would be best for all concerned if we paid the moneys into individual off-shore accounts." For quite some time Kitti had been having payments from Japan, for both heroin and girls, go directly into an account at the headquarters of the Hong Kong and Shanghai Bank; he had wisely decided it was best to be paid that way for both security and tax-evasion reasons. As a result there were several million Hong Kong dollars readily available in their current account.

"My company has an account at the Hong Kong Bank in Hong Kong. If everyone who will be receiving payments from us would open personal accounts there, the three of us can fly up to Hong Kong and witness the transfer of the moneys. That way, no one but *Khun* Darunee, me, and you, General Chamnan, will know anything about this — except for my Managing Director and closest friend, *Khun* Kittipong. How would that work for you, General?" Pompam asked after giving him a moment to let the idea sink in.

Chamnan thought for a second before answering, "Yes, *Khun* Vichai, I think that would be excellent. If the money is paid in Hong Kong there would be no record of it, or any way to trace it to Bangkok. Whenever the individual account-holders wanted all or part of the money they could have it wired to them here in Bangkok through the local branch of the Hong Kong Bank on Silom Road. Perfect," he speedily agreed.

Rattana was absolutely enraged when Pompam told her he was going to Hong Kong for three days with General Chamnan and Darunee. "You're taking that slut to Hong Kong and you have never once taken me abroad! In fact, you've never taken me anywhere. I got my passport years ago thinking we would go traveling, but all you ever do is work. How dare you go with that Chinese bitch!"

Pompam reminded himself that his wife always got jealous and insecure during her pregnancies, and this time she had been very good about controlling herself — except for that one incident over the untimely NASA pictures. He remained calm and said as sweetly as he could, "Rattana, this is a business trip. I absolutely have to go — and Darunee does too. I'll only be gone for three days. Right after I come back, you and I and the kids will go somewhere on holiday for a few days; you just pick the place."

"You would really promise to do that, Pompam?" she asked, starting to calm down.

"Of course I would. Would you like to take the kids with us — or would you like to just go alone with me?" he asked softly, giving her the option.

"We have never had a family vacation before, so I would really like to bring the children along. Maybe we can go to Singapore; that's a good, clean family place. What do you think?" she smiled, beginning to like the idea more and more.

"I've never been to Singapore either, Rattana; it sounds fine to me. I'll have my secretary book everything and we'll go just as soon as I get back from Hong Kong. Okay?" his voice was almost pleading, trying hard to avoid any more arguing.

"All right, Pompam. But you just make sure you don't let that bitch make any passes at you; I know how she is," was her final admonition, not in the least bit joking.

The following week Pompam, Darunee, and General Chamnan boarded the first-class cabin of a Cathay Pacific flight to Hong Kong. It was an enjoyable but short flight, and Darunee was already studying the catalog for in-flight duty-free items she would buy on the return trip. "Pompam, you know I never go shopping in Bangkok; even though I have the money I don't have the time. I'm always running around from one appointment to the next — always late — and never do anything for myself," she complained.

When they arrived at Kai Tak Airport they were met by one of the Peninsula Hotel's dark green Rolls Royces. After the short ride they entered the lobby of the grand old hotel of Hong Kong and were blatantly ogled by the dozens of patrons enjoying the Peninsula's legendary, gossipy, afternoon tea. It was Pompam's first trip to Hong Kong, but General Chamnan and Darunee had been there several times before; neither of them, however, had ever stayed at the Peninsula. Pompam chose the hotel because an old customer of his at Number Ten had often praised it, and ever since he had dreamed about staying there one day.

Their banking transaction was scheduled for the following morning, and as there were still a couple of hours before dinnertime, Darunee suggested they hit the shops in the Peninsula Arcade downstairs. "Come on, you guys, they'll be closing soon. Don't waste time," she urged them emphatically. The two men followed along behind her from one designer store to the next, getting somewhat shocked by the outrageous prices.

Pompam knew that he had better not return to Bangkok empty-handed or he would really be in hot water with Rattana. There was an absolutely dazzling fire opal and diamond ring in the window of one of the jewelry stores that caught Pompam's eye. I might as well get Rattana's present out of the way now, he thought, then I won't have to think about it again. General Chamnan went into the store with Pompam to have a look while Darunee darted off to the Gucci shop next door. She had no interest whatsoever in wasting her precious shopping time on buying a gift for Pompam's wife. Pompam examined the ring, paid for it with his credit card, and told the shopkeeper to gift-wrap it.

They caught up with a smiling Darunee whose arms were already full of packages and shopping bags. "I think that's enough for today, boys. Please help me get these up to my room and then we can go out for dinner," she said with excitement. "By the way, Pompam, I hope you didn't buy that ring," she said.

"Why not, Nee? It's the finest opal I've ever seen," he answered, surprised.

"Because everyone knows opals are bad luck; and even though I know she doesn't like me, I don't want Rattana to become unlucky."

"Really, Nee! I had no idea you were so superstitious," he exclaimed.

"You'd be superstitious too, Pompam, if you had started out your life selling flowers at Sanam Luang," she replied, and gave him a look he didn't understand.

The three of them went out and had Chinese food at a restaurant Darunee had been to before. Pompam tried a number of unusual Cantonese delicacies, but nothing was ever spicy enough, or satisfied him the way Thai food did. They consumed nearly a whole bottle of Black Label with dinner, and Darunee boldly announced that she was taking them to a nightclub in the Tsimshachui District of Kowloon. "Don't worry, guys, it's not very far from our hotel and we can walk back later. Tell the driver he can go home after he drops us off," she ordered.

In spite of their better judgment, the two men followed Darunee not only to the first club, but afterwards to the disco at the Shangri-La as well, where she forced them to dance with her. All three of them had become quite intoxicated, and Pompam finally put his foot down, "No more, Darunee! We're going back to the Peninsula!" The General looked at him with round, glassy eyes and vigorously nodded in agreement.

Instead of walking back to the hotel they decided it was more prudent to take a taxi the short distance. Darunee made quite a bit of unnecessary noise as they wove their way across the opulent, high-ceilinged, gilded lobby which was nearly deserted at that late hour. "*Mai pen rai*," she screamed to her embarrassed companions, "We're paying guests in this fucking place and we can do anything we like!"

They got upstairs to their rooms, said goodnight, and stumbled off to bed. About thirty minutes later when Pompam was just about to turn off the light he heard a knock at his door. When he opened it Darunee was standing there in her lace and chiffon dressing gown with a bottle of champagne in one hand. "Do you mind if I come in, Pompam?" she asked with a very prominent slur in her voice.

"It's okay, Nee, but we have the bank in the morning and I want to get some sleep," he said with exasperation and tiredness in his voice.

"It's too early for me to sleep, Pompam; you know how I am in Bangkok. I never go to bed before four or five in the morning. Have some champagne," she said, popping the cork.

Pompam had already taken off his clothes and was wearing one of the big, monogrammed, terry cloth robes from the bathroom. "Okay, Nee, just *one* glass," he reluctantly consented.

"Here's a toast to the best friend and best partner in the whole world," reaching out to clink glasses, but she missed and had to try again.

Pompam aimed and clinked back and said, "To you, too, Nee. You've brought me lots of good luck and I am grateful to you for many things."

"I'm grateful to you, too, Pompam, my dear. And I'm going to show you just exactly how much." In one swift motion she put down her champagne glass and lunged for Pompam's crotch where she spread open the robe and grabbed his sleeping manhood.

"Come on, Nee, stop it!" he protested, trying to extricate himself from his embarrassing, awkward predicament by sliding upwards on the sofa. It was like trying to free himself from an angry ferret, so tight was her hold on him with both fist and jaw. Trying to escape was more painful than his usual path of non-resistance, so he finally just sat back and let her go for it, suddenly remembering Rattana's prophetic warning.

Even in those circumstances it didn't take him too long to get aroused, and he closed his eyes and imagined he was with Yuki again in Japan; how he would love to be with her once more and experience the absolute perfection of her love-making.

In another swift move, faster than drowsy, dreaming Pompam could comprehend, Darunee hiked her dressing gown up around her waist and impaled herself on Pompam's stiff organ; she began gyrating on it as if possessed by some bewitching, Chinese demon. Pompam, shocked, sat there and watched the delirious contortions on her face; the heavy, smeared make-up causing her to look like some kind of rabid animal, and strange, low noises rose up from her throat as she used Pompam's sex to bring herself to a climax. She kept going until Pompam, too, had finished, and he immediately felt ashamed and guilty for not doing a better job of trying to throw her off of him at the beginning.

Darunee fell back on the sofa and passed out before she might experience any shame or guilt of her own. Pompam pulled her dressing gown over her chubby, fair-skinned body and showered before collapsing in his own bed.

When Pompam woke up the next morning there was no sign of Darunee anywhere, and he realized she must have awakened sometime during the night and gone back to her own room. Embarrassed, he slowly recalled what had happened between them, although it seemed unreal, like a dream that makes no sense. *Mai pen rai*, Pompam thought, it's not important; and he let it go at that.

Their meeting with the bank was scheduled for eleven o'clock. The night before the three of them had agreed to meet downstairs for breakfast at half past nine. Pompam thought about giving Darunee a wake-up call just to be safe, but he decided against it. "Let's just see if she can be on time..."

Pompam went down to the coffee shop early, thinking that he would be the first one there. To his great surprise, Darunee was already sitting at the table with a spoon in her hand and a big bowl of Chinese rice soup with octopus in front of her. She smiled up at him with clear eyes and said, "Good morning, Pompam; did you sleep well?" as if nothing had happened the night before.

"I slept fine, Nee, but I'm feeling a little bit hung over this morning; we really over-did it," he replied, playing along with the charade.

The General arrived and the three of them ate their breakfast and made small talk. Darunee commented that she hoped the bank meeting would be over quickly so they could hit the discount shops on Nathan Road.

They arrived at the Hong Kong & Shanghai Bank's magnificent headquarters building in Central District on Hong Kong Island promptly at eleven o'clock and were immediately ushered into the office of the manager in charge. Pompam produced the fifteen account numbers on a list with the appropriate amounts to be credited written out next to them. He showed them his passport and bank identification card so the money could be withdrawn from his account. The bank manager disappeared with the list and in a very short time he returned with fifteen receipts. The entire transaction took less than twenty minutes.

"Banking matters are certainly faster here in Hong Kong than they are in Bangkok," was Darunee's comment as they were back inside the Rolls Royce on their way to Nathan Road.

"They've had a lot more practice with money here than we've had in Thailand, Darunee," was Pompam's accurate reply. "Just give us a few more years..."

"Now that you have an extra ten million *baht*, General Chamnan, are you going to buy some nice presents for yourself and your wife?" Darunee asked and smiled.

"A few small things, perhaps; nothing along the scale of yours and *Khun* Vichai's, of course." Pompam had noticed over time that the General was more than just a bit *"kee neo,"* or stingy with his money. He had never once even taken one *baht* out of his pocket in Pompam's presence. Chamnan's wife would probably get a cheap silk scarf from the Chinese Friendship Store, he mused to himself.

At some point mid-day they stopped for a *dim sum* lunch, but otherwise they kept on shopping until nearly sunset. The Rolls Royce followed them from shop to shop while the driver loaded up the trunk with each purchase. At one point he informed the Thai trio that he had to go back to the hotel to unload and return for more. Darunee bought three empty suitcases in which to pack all her loot; Pompam bought one. He liked playing Santa Claus with his staff and family, so he bought everyone several gifts.

That night they had dinner in Aberdeen Harbor aboard Jumbo, the giant, ornate, multi-level barge-restaurant, a major tourist attraction. They almost polished off another bottle of Black Label, but Pompam was determined not to allow himself to get drunk again; he didn't want a reprise of the episode the night before. Despite loud, belligerent protests from Darunee, he insisted they go directly back to the hotel after a circle island trip around Hong Kong to see the lights.

"Tomorrow we go back to Bangkok, and all of us have to work," he said, pretending to be tired.

Darunee never said a word other than a pert "good night" when they returned to the Peninsula. He didn't see her again until they met in the lobby the following morning for their transfer to the airport. This time it took *two* dark green Rolls Royces to get them to Kai Tak: one for them — and one for their luggage.

Chapter 23

The afternoon of his return, Rattana continued to act cool towards Pompam until he gave her the opal and diamond ring. Then she warmed to him considerably, and declined to mention his trip to Hong Kong with Darunee.

After a while, she went over and put her arms around him and thanked him for the gift as graciously as she always had. "I'm sorry for being so mean, Pompam; please promise me you won't throw me away," she said, suddenly worried that her fits of anger and jealousy about Darunee might push him past his patience. Pompam remembered hearing Joy use those exact same words the night he dumped her in the brothel.

"*Mai pen rai*, Rattana. I know you do the best you can," he responded, "and before we go to Singapore tomorrow I have some things to do at the office; I'll be home late."

He paid Chaiya, his driver, a commission of five million *baht* for his introduction to *Khun* Rossakorn. "If it hadn't been for you, Chaiya, we might not have been able to find the right land for the military project, and the whole deal would have gone down the drain."

Pompam thought Chaiya would immediately resign his position, but he said, "What would I do if I didn't work, *Khun* Vichai? My wife would drive me crazy. I'll stay with you to the end." Pompam was pleased by Chaiya's loyalty, and the obvious affection he felt for him.

He met with Chai, who reported that the latest shipment of heroin from the Golden Triangle had gotten through to Bangkok intact, but that one of the trucks had had an accident en route and had run off the road. Part of the load of lychee fruit it was carrying had spilled out, but not enough to uncover the heroin buried underneath.

"That is really too close, Chai," Pompam said, truly worried. "I hate this fucking business!"

When he met with Kitti he was informed for the hundredth time that they needed new offices. "I can't cope with the lack of space too much longer," whined the Managing Director.

"Why don't we build our own office, Kitti?" Pompam suggested out of the blue. "Don't we have land somewhere that might be suitable for a big commercial building?"

"The best place would be over on Sathorn, Pompam. We own a perfect parcel of land right on the main road," Kitti replied. "But building an office tower isn't the same as building a housing estate, you know; you'll have to find an architect that can properly design it."

"The office tower was invented in America, Kitti. I think I'll look for an American architect — or at least a Thai architect that was trained over there. I'll speak to *Khun* Somsak at the Bank," he replied, thinking that Darunee's "consultant" would know just the right person to speak to.

"While you were in Hong Kong you got a phone call from a *Khun* Wharavut, the Secretary General for some political party. He said he had met you years ago at the opening of Isan Sweetheart; he was a Member of Parliament from Korat at that time," Kitti informed him.

"Why in the world would he want to speak to me?" Pompam asked.

"He said it was confidential and to please call him back when you got back from your trip," Kitti answered, handing Pompam the phone number.

After his meeting with Kitti, Pompam phoned *Khun* Wharavut who requested a private meeting with him. Pompam told him he was going out of town again and would call him when he returned. When Pompam asked what he wanted to see him about, *Khun* Wharavut replied that it could wait until they met in person.

Pompam's last meeting that day was with Toy who gave him an up-to-date report on the Thailand Youth Foundation. When they went over the financials, Pompam was surprised to see how much donations had increased from organizations other than his own, and he wondered why. "You know, Pompam, Rattana has worked harder to raise money for the Foundation than you realize. She is an excellent campaigner, and you should acknowledge her more for it since she thinks you don't notice," Toy informed him. Pompam made a mental note to praise her efforts while they were on holiday. That woman never ceases to amaze me, Pompam thought to himself.

"Thanks for letting me know, Toy; I'll do that. Are you still expanding your military bases program?"

"In another six months we'll have either a gymnasium or a library — or both — in every military base in Thailand where there are resident families," Toy replied.

"The latest program I'm working on is a prototype for providing job training for hilltribe girls to help keep them from going into prostitution. This is a growing problem up in the North, Pompam. But then, you probably already know about this," he dropped the words like a grenade.

This announcement took Pompam completely by surprise. He managed to hold his temper and said, "What do you mean by that, Toy?"

"You have to keep your places supplied with girls from somewhere; I'm assuming you probably get them from up north, too, that's all. A journalist friend of mine says there's a guy up in Chiang Mai named Nopadon who appears to be the biggest dealer of hilltribe girls. He supposedly brokers all kinds of young girls from the north to places all over Thailand, and even up to Japan and Taiwan. He said the guy was suspected of being in the drug business, too."

Toy hadn't actually accused Pompam of being connected with Nopadon, but he was suddenly sick to his stomach with fear; Toy was far too near to the mark this time. Damn that reporter! he thought to himself. He needs to be stopped; and Nopadon warned.

He considered for a moment the irony that he, himself, had encouraged hundreds — if not *thousands* — of girls to go into prostitution (not to mention *buying* a good percentage of them outright), and now his saintly brother was developing training programs to keep them *in* the villages and *out* of the brothels.

"The new program sounds like a good one, Toy. For your information I don't know anything about hilltribe girls. Chai is in charge of staffing, and I don't know where he gets his female employees. I'm sure it's not through some broker as you describe." God, how he hated to tell his brother such lies. He had rarely in his life felt worse than at that very moment, but he knew he had to tighten his guard to make sure Toy wouldn't get any closer to the truth.

Pompam and his family enjoyed their holiday in Singapore. They were all impressed by how clean, beautifully landscaped, and orderly the island republic was; even the children couldn't help but remark on the contrast to the conditions of dirt, congestion, and chaos they had to live with every day in Bangkok.

They stayed in a large suite at the Shangri-La, which was close to the shopping district on Orchard Road, the main attraction for Rattana. They enjoyed sampling the rich Malaysian food and found it to be almost spicy enough for their Thai palates.

Pompam delighted in playing the role of the good father, and he took Little Jim and Somporn to the various theme parks and tourist venues on the island. Rattana was too far along in her pregnancy to go along on most of their excursions, and instead spent most of her time shopping in the near-by mega-malls.

They crossed the causeway over the Straits into Malaysia and spent two days and nights at a luxurious beach resort. Pompam horsed around with his two youngsters in the pool, and they treated themselves sailboat rides and snorkeling while Rattana sat covered up under an umbrella, shading herself from the intense sun. She wanted no suntan for herself, and scolded Pompam for letting himself and the children get so brown. Pompam was reminded of his first time ever at the beach — in Pattaya with *Khun* Hans, the deceased Dutchman.

They returned to Bangkok in harmony as a family for the first time in years. Rattana was satisfied that she had finally gone abroad, and could brag and compare notes on Singapore and Malaysia with her *hi-so* lady friends.

The day after their return Pompam phoned *Khun* Wharavut and set up a lunch meeting. He was curious why some political party boss would want to meet with him.

When they were seated at The Regents' Club the former MP said, "I'm sure you don't remember meeting me at Isan Sweetheart the night of the opening, *Khun* Vichai; you were busy being host, and there were so many guests; but I felt very proud of what you did for the people of Isan that night, and decided to keep my eye on you in the future."

"I am very flattered, *Khun* Wharavut. We've tried our best to show that people from Isan are every bit as good as people from other regions of Thailand, and certainly the Chinese. We don't have to be only the slaves of the rich," Pompam replied, thinking that he, himself, was a good example.

"Indeed we don't, *Khun* Vichai. And I believe you could help get that message across even better if you were in politics. Have you ever thought about it?"

Pompam was taken by surprise by the question, and admitted that he had never thought of such a thing.

"Many of the leaders of our party are in the military, as you know. Several high-ranking officers, with whom you are acquainted, have lately commented that we should recruit you into our party. We not only have the backing of powerful members of the armed forces, but we have a strong popular base in Isan as well, and we intend to be a major part of the next government coalition. Would you be interested in working with us, *Khun* Vichai?" the sixty-something year-old party official smiled as he made the overture.

"It's something I would have to think about very seriously, *Khun* Wharavut. I'm in the middle of some big projects right now, including the military housing development in Bangkapi. I don't think I would have time — at least not at the moment."

"It doesn't have to be right now, *Khun* Vichai. You can wait a year or two until you are ready. I just wanted to meet with you and let you know that we are interested in having you join us at some point in the future. We feel that you could add a great deal of strength to our party, and help us raise our Isan people out of the mud. We also feel certain that we could get you elected quite easily — in Buriram. Please think about it," was his reply.

"I am honored that you have approached me, *Khun* Wharavut. I promise I will indeed think about it, and, perhaps in a year or two..." Pompam politely concluded, the seed now planted in his mind about the possibility of becoming a regional — if not national — political figure. Perhaps he could, in fact, help his people — while helping himself as well.

"Darunee, I want you to set up a lunch meeting with *Khun* Somsak from the Bank, I need to talk with him about something important,"

Pompam asked when he phoned her that afternoon.

"I'll set it up, Pompam, but I think I should tell you now that I don't want to start any new projects for a while," she said. "I'm getting tired of working so hard, and there other things I want to do before I get too old."

Pompam liked having lunch at the Thai restaurant at the Regent Hotel where he had first met with Darunee. She arranged the meeting with *Khun* Somsak there and, of course, arrived an hour late.

Pompam used the time to tell *Khun* Somsak about the tower he wanted to build on Sathorn Road. He explained his need for a good architect who could design a state-of-the-art high-rise office building.

"I know just the right firm, *Khun* Vichai; all of the principals were trained in America; and they usually have one or two Americans working in their office in Bangkok to provide fresh input from the States. I would be happy to make the introduction," *Khun* Somsak offered.

"I would be most grateful for that, *Khun* Somsak, as I am for all the help you have given me with the military housing project," Pompam answered, thinking about the many millions *Khun* Somsak was raking in from the project in Bangkapi.

An over-dressed, bejeweled Darunee finally arrived and made her usual apologies for being late. "I'm going into semi-retirement, gentlemen. I'll see this Bangkapi thing through to the end, but I don't want to take on anything new — ever. I don't want to work so hard any more, and I hardly ever see my derelict children," she complained.

The two men were surprised by her announcement and *Khun* Somsak said, "What on earth will you do, Darunee, without your beloved business deals to keep you active?"

"I'm going to be like Pompam's wife and concentrate on charity projects. I want to be a *khunying*," she declared. A *"khunying"* was a title given to hard-working *hi-so* ladies by His Majesty the King for long histories of raising money and doing charitable works.

"I think that's a worthy pursuit for a wealthy retiree with good connections," Pompam replied. "Rattana would like the same thing, but she thinks she's still too young to even hope for it any time soon."

"Well, I'm *not* too young, thank you very much; and that's what I want," she said emphatically.

When Pompam entered the reception area of the architectural firm overlooking Silom Road sixteen floors below, he immediately felt pleased by the sense of space and the tasteful decor of the room. There were two or three scale models of high-rise buildings in Plexiglas cases near one wall; Pompam examined them while waiting for *Khun* Amnard, the managing partner whom *Khun* Somsak had arranged for him to meet. Pompam was impressed by the models; they were relatively simple, and had clean powerful lines that appealed to him.

They also lacked the unnecessary, arbitrary-looking decorations that had been tacked onto high-rise buildings by ambitious Thai architects during the building frenzy of the preceding five years. One well-known designer even had a signature trademark of putting domes and cupolas on the roofs of all his tall buildings, much like those on the Capitol of the United States. Pompam thought that sort of thing was ridiculous, and wanted nothing of the kind for his own building, which would be his crowning achievement so far. Many of the rich and powerful leaders of Thailand's economy were, at the moment, building such monuments to themselves for their companies, so "Why shouldn't I?" Pompam asked himself; I'll even pay for the whole thing in cash, something he knew very few could do.

A white-haired gentleman in a dark business suit entered the reception room and greeted Pompam. "I am Amnard, *Khun* Vichai; welcome. It is indeed a pleasure to have such a famous Bangkok celebrity visit our office," he said warmly.

Pompam *waied* to him and said, "The pleasure is mine, *Khun* Amnard. I am delighted to meet the man responsible for giving Bangkok's skyline some beauty and refinement," a remark he had rehearsed that obviously pleased the distinguished architect.

Khun Amnard led Pompam to a large meeting room. "I have asked one of our associates from America to join us. This is Miss Jennifer Carlisle," and presented the most beautiful *farang* female Pompam had ever seen.

She confidently reached out and offered Pompam her firm handshake and smiled. She had piercing blue eyes set beneath an aristocratic forehead, fair skin, and thick blonde hair pulled back in a simple ponytail. Her dark blue suit had no ornamentation; and her only jewelry was a gold watch and tasteful gold "shell" earrings. She wore very little make-up, and yet to Pompam she looked just like a cover girl on an American fashion magazine.

"Miss Carlisle has joined us on a temporary basis from a colleague's office in New York. She was trained at the Pratt Institute and comes to us with a great deal of experience in high-rise design. If you choose to hire us as your architectural firm, *Khun* Vichai, I would like to put her in charge of the design team," *Khun* Amnard said, giving praise to the young woman who appeared to be about Pompam's age.

"Perhaps we could start the meeting, Mr. Vichai, with your description of the sort of building you would like and where it will be located," Miss Jennifer began.

Pompam opened his briefcase and took out a site map and some aerial photographs he had ordered for this purpose. "I know there are certain restrictions in the area regarding how high and how much we can build. I will have to leave that study to you. I want the building primarily for my own company's use, but I think two or three floors will be sufficient for us. The rest I will lease out to long-term tenants. I had also thought that we might have a Regents' Club II on the top floor," Pompam explained, not taking his eyes off of Jennifer.

"An excellent idea, *Khun* Vichai," *Khun* Amnard exclaimed. "We can do the research on plot ratio very easily; considering the value of the land I know you will want to maximize the size of the building. Why don't we have a look at some of our recent projects and you can let us know what appeals to you in terms of design and detail."

As they looked through the firm's portfolio Pompam noticed in himself a growing sense of attraction towards Miss Jennifer. He had never before been particularly attracted to Caucasian women, and had never desired or experienced one sexually. He had, quite simply, never really thought about them very much. This was a new feeling for him, and perhaps it was his imagination, but he sensed she might be feeling something for him, too. Perhaps he was just *hoping* she did, he thought to himself.

Pompam made comments as he pointed out various elements he liked and didn't like, and after about forty-five minutes of discussion he surprised *Khun* Amnard by saying that he would definitely like his firm to begin designing his new building, a decision that usually took weeks. Pompam eagerly wanted to discuss fees and schedules, and the formulation of a contract even at this first meeting. Pompam knew instinctively that Amnard's was the perfect architectural company for his project, and that the lovely foreign girl would produce exactly the right design.

"Do you have time to go with me now and look at the site?" Pompam asked the astonished *Khun* Amnard.

"Yes, of course, *Khun* Vichai; if you like," he replied.

Khun Amnard sat in the back seat with Pompam, and Jennifer sat up front with Chaiya, as they slowly crept down Silom Road to the nearest street where they could cross over to Sathorn. Pompam only listened with one ear to *Khun* Amnard's on-going monologue about each building they passed along the way, both old and new. His attention was on Jennifer's lovely neck, and her classic profile when she turned from time to time to listen to the conversation.

Pompam showed them the site, which still contained one of the few remaining wooden mansions that had once graced Sathorn Road. In years past, stately trees had lined both sides of the street and a clean-water canal flowed down the center. The trees had long-since been cut down to widen the roadway, and the *khlong* had eventually been covered over for further widening, although it still flowed unseen, a stinking black sewer beneath the thoroughfare. Most of the old mansions were gone, but every few hundred meters one still stood, a doomed monument to another age, an era of elegance destroyed by Bangkok's unconscious and rapid development boom, rising land prices ruling the day.

"The old house is lovely, Mr. Vichai. I would like to have seen it about fifty years ago," Jennifer commented reflectively.

"It *is* a lovely old home, Miss Jennifer, but unfortunately the land has become too valuable to be able to restore it and keep it as it was," Pompam replied.

"So much of the old Bangkok is already gone, and it sometimes saddens me," she commented. "I came here many years ago with my parents when I was only about ten, on our 'grand tour of the Orient.' I can still remember what this street looked like then."

"What it was *then* is not the point right now, Jennifer, but what it will look like with Mr. Vichai's new building on it *is*," *Khun* Amnard said, bringing them back to focus on the reason they were there.

"Of course it is, Mr. Amnard, and I will do my best to come up with a design that will do the old street justice," she answered with a soft smile.

By the time Pompam dropped off *Khun* Amnard and Jennifer at their office it had been determined that it would take about two weeks to get some preliminary sketches together for Pompam to see, and they would meet again then.

In the meantime, Pompam couldn't keep the image of Jennifer's face from constantly intruding on his thoughts. He could think of no pretext upon which to call her, so he could only bide his time and anxiously await their next meeting.

He knew he still loved his wife, in spite of her "moods," but Rattana was heavy with child at the moment, and could neither inspire nor satisfy him sexually. So he indulged himself in his "secret" life, and every two or three days he prowled the lairs of Patpong, looking for new stimulation. He would always "off" a few girls and take them to a motel for sex, but it frustrated him that he could never duplicate the experience of Yuki in Japan, or eradicate the haunting visage of Jennifer from his mind.

The time for his next meeting with *Khun* Amnard and Jennifer finally arrived, and at the last minute Pompam requested that it be moved to *his* office; he wanted to find out if seeing the girl on his own turf would somehow change his growing feelings for her.

Pompam kept them waiting in the conference room for a few minutes while he pondered how he would act when he saw Jennifer again. He had dressed that morning in his finest charcoal gray suit and a handsome silk tie that Rattana had bought for him at Peninsula Plaza; at least he would look his best, he thought, momentarily feeling insecure.

When he stepped into the room his eyes immediately met Jennifer's. He imagined he saw reciprocal feelings for him, sensing them as only a man who was still much admired by many women could. There was an uncomfortable moment as they stumbled through their greetings, but *Khun* Amnard, not being in the least bit aware of the subtle connection between the other two, noticed nothing.

"Miss Jennifer has come up with a concept for your building, *Khun* Vichai, that I think will please you. It is a totally original design — quite contemporary — but one that we feel will not be dated by time," the architect said as he unrolled the preliminary plans.

Pompam was stunned. The artist's rendering of the exterior of the building, shown in perspective, was like nothing he had ever seen. It was at once both modern and classical. There were no cheap gimmicks, and no embellishments or details that were not an absolute part of its intrinsic form.

"It is stately and grand, to fit your masculine image; and yet it is also elegant and simple, perfectly scaled, to express your restraint and sensitivity." At least that's how Jennifer flatteringly described it to her big new client.

"The building will be twenty-eight stories high, *Khun* Vichai. You can see that it's set back at these two stages to accommodate for the 'shadow effect' in the building code, and yet it doesn't look forced or contrived," *Khun* Amnard pointed out. "The exterior is primarily a skin of blue-gray glass, but it is interspersed by these white columns, reminiscent of the Thai Buddhist temple."

"I tried to make it look like something expressive of Thailand, Mr. Vichai, and not like some building in New York or any other city," Jennifer explained as she smiled slightly to Pompam, once again locking eyes with him, her piercing blue to his penetrating black.

"It is beautiful," was all Pompam could say as he stared at the girl, not at the drawing.

The two architects looked at each other and smiled, secure in the knowledge that they had produced something their client admired, and that they had interpreted exactly what he had wanted as well, achieving two goals.

They took him through the building's sections, one by one, explaining all the details, until Pompam finally said, "Let's do it. It's perfect. I have some additional input regarding a few small items, but if you don't mind I'll go over them later as I have an urgent meeting to attend at my club."

"Just give me a call, Mr. Vichai, and I will come back when it is convenient for you," Jennifer said calmly, delighted that her work had been so well-received. She had given it her best effort, had dared to be imaginative, and the client had loved it. What more could she have asked?

Pompam really didn't have a meeting at his club; he just wanted to delay further talks for a chance to meet with Jennifer *without Khun* Amnard around.

Later he called Kitti and Chai into the meeting room and showed them the plans. They could see the enthusiasm the new project had aroused in Pompam, and even with their unsophisticated eyes they could also see the beauty of the design work Jennifer had done.

"You've been complaining for nearly two years now about not having enough office space here on Asoke, Kitti. How do you like your future home?" Pompam asked as he gave him a big grin.

"I wish we could move in tomorrow, Pompam. It's terrific," he exclaimed.

"We need to do is give the building a name. Any ideas, guys?" Pompam asked, smiling.

"Isn't it obvious?" Chai asked. "The VP Tower."

That evening Toy handed Pompam an article he had received in the mail from a doctor in Atlanta; he had met him at the World Health Conference in Los Angeles.

"I think you should read this, Pompam. AIDS is becoming an epidemic in Thailand, and the majority of Thai people are ignoring it. The statistics in the article will shock you; they don't match at all what the government is telling us here."

Pompam looked at the article and nodded his head at Toy, saying he would read it later.

"Do you at least make sure the girls at your places insist the men wear condoms?" he asked emotionally.

"Of course they have condoms, Toy, and we've explained all about AIDS to the girls," answered Pompam, knowing full-well that the service girls couldn't force their customers to use condoms; most men didn't like wearing them, including him.

"You've got to make condoms the law, Pompam, otherwise you'll be responsible for many deaths," the younger man pleaded.

"I'll do what I can, Toy," responded Pompam, his mood

spoiled.

After a few moments he allowed his thoughts to drift back to Miss Jennifer, and soon he felt much better.

The next day Pompam phoned Jennifer and made an appointment for the following morning. "I'll send my driver to pick you up at nine-thirty and have him bring you to The Regents' Club; I want you to see it so you can be thinking about the new club in the VP Tower," he said.

Pompam greeted Jennifer at the *porte cochere* when she arrived. He thought she looked even more beautiful that day than the other two times he had seen her. "As you know, this is a men's' club; that's why I asked you to meet me here at this hour, before any of the members arrive," he explained with a big smile.

"I've heard about these members' clubs, Mr. Vichai. I'm sure that even though only men can become members, there must be lots of pretty young women working here," she answered with a teasing smile. He was sure *Khun* Amnard had explained about the ubiquitous young hostesses one encountered in places like this.

"The ladies who work here come only at night, so you are in no danger of running into any of them, Miss Jennifer" he laughed.

"I'm very glad for that," she responded cheerfully. "Please call me Jennifer. In America we did away with calling women 'Miss' long ago."

"Then you must call me by my nickname, 'Pompam'; everyone who knows me well does," he answered. And I hope you get to know me very well, Jennifer, he thought to himself.

He led her to the office he maintained for himself on the premises, and on the way she made several mental notes about the interiors of the lounges and dining rooms. Dear God, she thought, totally unimpressed; now I know what a "classy" Bangkok whorehouse looks like.

Pompam explained to Jennifer about how he wanted the Regents' Club II to be even more beautiful and elegant than the present one. He wanted a new approach to the interiors which required a talent he didn't think would be available in Thailand.

"One of my closest friends in New York is one of the most gifted interior designers in the States. Perhaps you should consider hiring her," she suggested. She noticed that she felt oddly uncomfortable in Pompam's presence; he really is gorgeous, she thought to herself, never before having been attracted to an Asian male.

"I would like very much for your talented American friend to design the interiors of the new club, the lobby, public spaces, and my company offices as well, Jennifer. *If* you think she can do a good job," he replied.

"Wow, Pompam, you sure make fast decisions for a man in your position," she laughed.

"I think one of the reasons I'm in my position is because I've always listened to people who know more than I do about things," he replied, "and I know practically nothing about interior design."

"How wise you are, Pompam. I wish all my other clients thought like you do."

"Why don't you send your friend a copy of the plans when they're ready and let her prepare a presentation. Then you can take me to New York and she can give it to us in person," he answered, making his first move.

Surprised at his boldness she said, "Wouldn't it be easier for her to simply *send* it to us out here — or maybe bring it to Bangkok herself?"

"It might be easier that way, but then I've never been to New York."

"We'll see, Pompam; it might be fun to see how you would react to Manhattan," she answered, momentarily amused by the thought.

"It might be fun to see how you would react if you were to come here to this club at night," he retorted, laughing. "By the way, the Regents Club II won't have any female hostesses. I want the members to be able to entertain their wives or lady friends in the finest restaurant in Bangkok with the best view of the city down below."

"Well, Pompam, that will be a novel approach: a members' club *without* female hostesses. I just can't imagine," she said in a mock-southern accent.

They passed a pleasant morning and lunch time together (at the Dusit Thani Hotel, *not* The Regents' Club) going over ideas for The VP Tower, while sparring with one another in the classic man-woman tradition. Pompam dropped her off at her office with the agreement that she would call him when the next set of plans were ready for his review.

"And don't forget about New York, Jennifer," he called out to her from the car.

A couple of weeks later Rattana had the baby. It was another boy whom Pompam named Surapong, after his old friend and customer, the police general who had helped him time and again with matters of protection and self-preservation. General Surapong was pleased by the gesture, appreciated its irony, and continued to enjoy the great wealth that he had accumulated, a good deal of it through his association with Pompam.

The arrival of the baby seemed to be the start in a season of family triumphs, beginning with Black, whose *second* cassette was already in its third pressing.

Att married his long-time girlfriend. She came from a well-known Chinese family that had not in the least objected to their daughter marrying the brother of the famous *Khun* Vichai, even though he was a full-blooded, "original" Thai from Isan.

Toy graduated from Chulalongkorn University, giving Pompam and his family enormous "face." He and Rattana watched proudly as His Majesty The King presented the diploma, and Toy *waied* and bowed low when he accepted it, looking so strong and dignified. Pompam realized then that he loved Toy more than all his other brothers, and he was still extremely proud of him, in spite of their numerous — and growing — differences of opinion. He never knew when to expect the young man to confront him with some new project idea that would be in diametric opposition to his businesses — or hit him with a stinging criticism that would wound him and cause pain.

The number six brother, Suvichai, nicknamed Top, came to Bangkok to begin his studies at the International School. That left just the two "babies" at home in the village with Maa. She was reluctant to let Top go, but Pompam had insisted, and she knew in her heart that it was for the best.

At Toy's insistence Pompam organized a *thamboon* ceremony at the temple in Buriram on the anniversary of their father's death.

Pompam claimed he was too busy to attend himself, so he sent Top, Att, Black, and Nuu, with Toy.

When they were about to depart Toy said to Pompam, "Don't you ever feel that making time for your religion — or your dead father — is just as important as your whoring business?"

The other brothers just stood there looking at Toy, not believing he had spoken so disrespectfully to eldest brother. Pompam felt cut to the quick and replied angrily, "Why should I worry about my religion when I have you to do it for me?"

"Because I won't always be there, Pompam, and then you'll have to deal with your karma yourself."

Pompam turned and walked away before he said something he would regret later; but on the inside he wanted to scream out, knowing that Toy was probably right.

PART V
KARMIC TIES

Chapter 24

Ott organized a press party for the unveiling of The VP Tower scale model and the launching of its leasing program. The event was held at the Grand Hyatt Erawan, Bangkok's newest five-star hotel. It was located right next door to the famous Brahmin shrine where thousands of Thais and tourists went every day to offer incense and fragrant *puangmalai* -- even dances -- to the "god" known as *Phra* Prom, who could grant wishes and bestow riches if it so pleased him. Before the party Pompam and all of his staff went to see *Phra* Prom and make offerings; each one made a silent, private wish as they lit their sticks of incense. It was custom that no one, no matter who they were, ignored the spirit of the Erawan Shrine; even passing motorists never failed to give him a respectful *wai*.

Khun Arun and Kitti had put together a list of Regents' Club members who might be likely candidates for tenanting the new building; many of them were in attendance at the party. "We've already received verbal commitments for nearly 75% of the leasable space; can you believe it?" gushed Khun Arun, drawing Pompam aside for a moment to tell him.

"You're just a one-man leasing dynamo, aren't you?" responded Pompam, pleased. It would make him happy later on to cut his friend a check for a little over a million baht as finder's fee; the older man was becoming increasingly self-sufficient.

"Who's the tall, sexy blonde, Pompam?" whispered Darunee, "Your new *mia noi*?"

"Shame on you, Nee! She's the architect who designed the building!" he exclaimed, unnerved by her remark.

"*Mai pen rai* about the building, you buffalo; I think she likes you. A woman can tell these things about another woman, you know."

Jennifer definitely stood out in the room, Pompam noticed admiringly. She was the only *farang*, and one of only a handful of women in attendance; and Rattana, who said she was busy that day, wasn't one of them. Pompam still couldn't stop thinking about Jennifer.

Ever since meeting her he had tried everything in his power to start an affair; each time he tried she would rebuff him and say, "You're married, Pompam, you have three children, and I'm too old for you!"

"Today I will try for her one last time and then give up," he said to himself. "Life must go on, and I'll finally know once and for all." Chasing the blond *farang* woman had exhausted and frustrated him to the end of his endurance and patience. This day he sought closure, one way or another.

"Congratulations, Jennifer; everyone seems to be admiring your work; I'm sure *Khun* Amnard will be pleased when I tell him that four people have already said they'll be calling him to design their new buildings," Pompam remarked as he sided up to the girl.

"I'm pleased to hear that, Pompam. Why do you look so serious? You should be happy today," she responded, smiling.

Instead of giving her an answer, he discreetly grabbed her hand behind her back and placed a key inside it, closing her fist. "What's this, Pompam?" she asked, surprised, looking at the key.

"Suite fifteen-o-seven. Upstairs. A private party for you and me when this is over. Please join me," he practically begged, looking directly into her blue eyes.

She started to speak but he stopped her and said, "Don't say anything now. Just think about it. I'll be waiting. If you don't come, I won't bother you ever again. I promise."

Two hours later Pompam was upstairs in the suite, feeling like he was dying inside. The party had been over for an hour and she still hadn't come. He decided he would wait a few more minutes and then go home to his wife.

"This is stupid!" he shouted out loud. "How could I have ever let that blonde bitch get to me like this?"

He fixed himself another drink and stood by the window, staring at the four cranes moving from side to side, still working after dark on the World Trade Center across the street.

The key turned in the lock, but he didn't hear it; he was totally absorbed in thought, feeling lost and dejected. Jennifer walked silently up behind him and put her arms around his waist.

"I didn't think you gave up so easily, Pompam."

He swiftly turned around, dropped his glass, and grabbed her with both his hands, violently pressing his mouth against her lips, almost sucking the breath out of her. She responded by tearing at his necktie, ripping the shirttail out of his trousers, jerking his belt loose. They were naked in a few seconds, and he was quickly buried to the hilt inside her, hips thrusting; they dropped to the floor next to his spilled drink, and started drinking from each other, their throats parched from pent-up desire.

After the third time Pompam, finally relieved and satisfied, remembered to thank *Phra* Prom for granting his wish.

Before Jennifer finally decided to get involved with Pompam she had gone out with a handful of men from various private clubs and expatriate social circles she belonged to in Bangkok. None of them were very interesting to her, and they were definitely *not* the kinds of men she would have even considered going with in New York. She only dated them out of boredom. She discovered that being a single man in Bangkok may be paradise, but life for a single woman -- especially a single foreign woman past thirty -- was more often than not very dull and lonesome.

So, she finally gave in to Pompam's charm, courting, and flattery, realizing that day at the party that he was serious about not trying any more. She liked him, and after a while, perhaps even loved him a little; but she knew the barricades that existed between them, and the rules that governed their sort of relationship; not to mention the problems that went along with mixing two disparate cultures such as theirs.

She let Pompam, in effect, become a convenience for her. They never met in public except for an occasional business lunch, usually in the company of *Khun* Amnard or some consultant connected with The VP Tower project. They were very discreet, and being from different worlds as they were, Rattana never found out or even suspected that anything was going on between them.

The relationship worked relatively well for Jennifer, given her circumstances as a healthy, single American woman living in exile for a couple of years. It did not always work well for Pompam, however, who wound up falling hopelessly in love with her.

He tried his best to please her, which he usually did -- especially in bed. They enjoyed being in each other's company, and would often spend the evening in her apartment having a quiet dinner and watching videos. The evening always ended by making love -- at least that was how Pompam thought of it. Jennifer simply used him for sex, which she needed; and Pompam, in his naiveté, had absolutely no comprehension of this notion in a female. To Pompam it was always the man who used the woman; not the other way around.

Their somewhat one-sided, but practical (at least for Jennifer) love affair went on for nearly five months before Jennifer agreed to go with Pompam to New York. Her designer friend had prepared a presentation for the VP Tower and promised Jennifer that if she got the job she would give her a huge commission. That she would secretly be making money off of her lover was of no moral concern to her. She finally decided that it would be to her advantage to take Pompam to New York, to use her influence on him, and make sure he bought her friend's design package. She also knew that having handsome, exotic Pompam in tow would create quite a stir among her chic, artistic social set in Manhattan.

Their plan was to fly to New York together, and for him to stay at the Plaza while she stayed at her parents' apartment on Park Avenue. Jennifer would show him the sights, take him to the theater, introduce him to her friends, and, of course, attend the presentation by her interior designer friend. After four days Pompam would fly out to San Francisco alone, and visit his old sponsor, Dr. Jim. She would join him afterwards, and then fly back to Bangkok together the following day.

If Pompam thought he had seen Rattana throw fits when he had gone out of town before, it was nothing compared to the week-long war she waged with him when she found out he was going to America without her.

"You bastard!" she screamed at him. "How dare you go to America without your wife! I suppose your old girlfriend, Darunee, is going with you, you goddamned prick!"

Pompam couldn't imagine where Rattana had learned such crude language, and was appalled at how vehemently she stormed at him day after day -- sometimes even threatening violence. During the peak episode, she picked up the priceless teapot that Yamamoto had sent to her from Japan and aimed it at Pompam's head, smashing it to pieces against the bedroom wall. That senseless action caused Pompam to completely come apart. The nerve of her destroying something so valuable on purpose! he thought, enraged. He grabbed her by the arm and smacked her as hard as he could in the face, causing blood to pour out of her nose and mouth.

"You're a shallow, fucking bitch, Rattana! No matter how much I give, you still act like the daughter of a fucking rice farmer. I told you I'm going to New York on business with my architect and you accuse me of going with Darunee. Fuck you, Rattana!" he screamed at her and then stormed out. He checked into the Grand Hyatt hotel, refusing to see or speak to her again before his departure for the States.

It didn't really matter to him any more. He was in love with Jennifer and he was going on a business holiday to New York with her. "Fuck Rattana," he said to himself, "I just might send her back to Isan when I return; I've gotten rid of women before."

Despite Pompam's angry self defense, Rattana decided that something was, in fact, going on with Pompam and another woman -- even though she had no hard evidence. It made her desperately ill to be so out of control with unfounded jealousy, but she felt helpless to stop the rivers of rage that her husband -- whom she believed to be lying and cheating -- caused to be released in her soul. She loved Pompam desperately, but she was growing to hate him with equal intensity.

Pompam and Jennifer departed for New York in the first-class cabin of a Northwest jet bound for Tokyo. Pompam was glad to be leaving Thailand -- and Rattana -- for a while; and Jennifer appeared to be happy as well, albeit he could sense there were certain things she was keeping from him. *Mai pen rai*, he thought, it's just the way *farang* women are.

While waiting in the lounge at Narita Airport for their connecting flight to New York, Pompam remembered the telephone conversation he had had with Kenji Yamamoto just two days before. When Pompam refused once again to go back to Japan, to submit to him and allow himself to be humiliated, Yamamoto became angrier than ever before, and told him his extinction was imminent.

This time Pompam was scared to death because Kenji said he would foul up a drug shipment, something Pompam knew would be so easy to do. As a result, he said, "All right, Kenji, I'll come soon; I'll let you know the date when I return from New York." But he was determined to somehow delay the inevitable as long as he could, hoping and praying he could keep coming up with excuses to buy himself time.

Even though he was groggy and irritable when the plane landed at JFK, Jennifer came alive as Pompam had never before seen her, and he couldn't help but catch an energy boost from her contagious high spirits. In the back of the limousine on the way into Manhattan Pompam found himself becoming almost as excited as he had ever been in his life, forgetting all about Kenji and his threats.

They first dropped off Jennifer at her parents' apartment on Park Avenue; they were away at their home in East Hampton, and she planned to visit them after Pompam left for San Francisco. Pompam tried once again to persuade her to stay with him at the Plaza, but she refused.

"How could I explain it to my parents and my friends?" she countered. It's too soon and too unexpected; please give me a little time."

At the Plaza Pompam checked into his suite, took a shower, and slept. Jennifer called him late in the afternoon, and then came over to take him for a walk through Central Park. Before they left his room he teased her and tried to get her into bed with him, but she protested and insisted he go outdoors with her to "clear the cobwebs" as she put it.

She noticed his Rolex, gaudy jade and diamond ring, and his gold chains, and made him take them all off before they went out. "This is *not* Bangkok, Pompam; this is New York City. You simply cannot wear those things out on the street if you want to stay alive."

The weather was sunny and cool, and after an hour of walking around the park Pompam could feel the jet-lag disappearing. "Can we get some Thai food?" he asked her, "I'm really hungry."

"You come all the way to New York from Thailand and you want to eat Thai food?" she asked, disbelieving. "There are restaurants here with food from every country in the world, Pompam; no Thai food for you today!"

She took him instead to one of her favorite Italian restaurants down in Little Italy where she ordered a large meal for both of them. Pompam liberally sprinkled chili peppers on every dish, and eventually made the food spicy enough for his liking. That night she took him to Broadway and they saw the latest revival of "The King and I," which was still banned in Thailand, and Pompam enjoyed himself immensely.

She went back to the hotel with him and told him with a grin that the energy of being back in New York, the Italian food, and the theater had whetted her appetite for sex. This good news brought a big smile to Pompam's face and he practically jumped on her.

This time in bed she claimed the role of aggressor for herself, behaving as though her appetite for his strong, smooth body could never be satisfied. She used him to make herself come again and again until he physically couldn't take it any more.

After his breathing was restored to normal, Pompam thanked the Lord Buddha for Jennifer's love, and he knew that it would always be good between them. She clung to him closely the whole night, and they made love again in the early morning, her needs still not yet satisfied.

She went back to her parents' apartment to change clothes and returned in a short time to take him sightseeing. She proved to be an admirable tour guide in her native city, and she very considerately took Pompam to all the places he wanted to see.

"I want you to be totally rested by tomorrow, Pompam. We have the presentation for The VP Tower in the afternoon, and then I'm giving you a party at my parents' apartment in the evening. You'll get to meet all of my closest friends." Pompam was surprised when he realized how nervous and apprehensive he was at the thought of entering her social world.

The following morning Jennifer said she had some errands to run in preparation for her party. "I can do them faster if I do them alone; I'll come back for you at one thirty," she told him.

He decided to walk around the perimeter of Central Park for some exercise, and then have lunch back at the hotel. He enjoyed being alone in the dazzling city he had so often dreamed of visiting. It was so different from Bangkok -- much more densely packed with people and tall buildings in a smaller space; but he noticed it shared one quality that Bangkok had: it offered a grand feast for his eyes at every moment, every direction he looked. Pompam felt exhilarated.

When he reached Tiffany's at Trump Tower he stopped and

looked in the display windows. Over the years, thanks to experience with Rattana and Darunee, he had developed a good eye for fine jewelry, and he spotted the most beautiful blue diamond he had ever seen. He immediately thought about the color of Jennifer's eyes, and went into the store and bought it for her, hardly paying any attention to the exorbitant price. He used his credit card and told the salesman to have it gift-wrapped and delivered to the concierge at the Plaza; he didn't want to walk around with it, heeding Jennifer's warning of the day before. He thought about how happy the magnificent six-carat stone would make his beautiful, blond *mia noi* when he put it around her neck that evening before the party.

That afternoon he found Jennifer's designer friend, Patricia, a bit too abrasive and flamboyant for his taste, but the work she had done for The VP Tower was indeed superb. They would be like no other interior spaces in Thailand, Pompam thought, and said so to the girl who looked to be about four or five years older than Jennifer.

"That is the most gorgeous man I have ever seen in my life, Jennifer," Patricia said to her later in the privacy of the ladies' room. "I've never been with an Oriental before; what's he like in bed?" she asked as they both laughed, and Jennifer praised Pompam's sexual abilities and the quality of his fine skin.

"He really is cute -- not to mention rich -- and I know I'll miss him," Jennifer said, already feeling nostalgic about their relationship.

That night Pompam took a taxi to Jennifer's parents' apartment early so he could spend some time with her before the other guests arrived. He had guessed correctly that she would wear a simple black cocktail dress, which would show off the diamond to perfection. He handed her the package from Tiffany's and her deep blue eyes suddenly lit up as if some magic switch had been turned on inside. She gave Pompam a big hug and a kiss and then tore open the present.

When she lifted the lid of the velvet box her hand shook so violently she nearly dropped it. So stunned was she by the expensive gift that she almost had second thoughts about her plan; a momentary flicker of guilt tweaked her self-focused consciousness.

"It's absolutely beautiful, Pompam. Thank you, my love, but you really shouldn't give me things like this," and Pompam almost levitated, hearing her call him "my love."

"*Mai pen rai*, Jennifer; the gift is nothing compared to the gift of your heart," Pompam answered, feeling that he had never truly experienced love until that moment. Jennifer smiled at him, and then quickly turned away.

There were about twenty guests that evening, and one by one as they arrived, they nearly fainted when they saw the blue diamond around Jennifer's neck. Their second surprise came only a few seconds later when they were introduced to the handsome Asian man who stood beside her. During the evening when they had a private opportunity, each guest would speak to Jennifer in whispers about how lucky she was, how gorgeous Pompam was, and ask what he was like in bed.

Pompam had one of the major shocks of his life when he was introduced to the last guest to arrive, an obviously gay designer who worked mostly in theater. Pompam immediately recognized him as one of Ott's former customers at Number Ten from many years before. Way back then the man had taken a group of the boys -- including Pompam -- out for drinks after closing time, and wound up taking Ott to Pattaya for three days.

"I've been going to Thailand every year or so for the past fifteen years," he said to Pompam. "I just love your country," he gushed. He seemed to not remember Pompam, so the Thai breathed a sign of relief and made a point of staying out of the man's way throughout the evening. Every now and then, however, Pompam would catch the guy staring in his direction, as if he was trying his best to place a familiar face from the past. This terrifying, "small world" encounter ruined the party for Pompam, and he became quiet and tense, not at all behaving in his usual smiling and charming manner. Jennifer was so pre-occupied with her other guests she didn't even notice.

"If you have a contract prepared for The VP Tower I will sign it tomorrow and give you a deposit check," Pompam said to Patricia, who immediately went ecstatic and threw her arms around him. She ran off to tell Jennifer and the others the good news.

"This deserves a toast," one of the guests declared. "To Patricia's first big contract in the Far East; may there be many more," he nodded in Pompam's direction. Pompam hated being the focus of attention in that unfamiliar social setting, and almost wished that he had never allowed Jennifer to have the party for him in the first place.

He felt terribly out of synch with her trendy New York group, and knew that he was way out of his depth on many levels. He realized that he was a rich, well-known, and powerful man in Thailand, but in New York he was just some wealthy, ornamental object of interest -- sort of like Jennifer's pet.

All through the evening he could sense the whispers behind his back, and Jennifer, caught up in her own excitement, did very little to make him feel more comfortable and at home. He felt that she had become one of them again, and had unconsciously (perhaps on purpose?) kept her distance from him throughout the evening -- in spite of the expensive blue diamond she wore around her neck that he had thought confirmed the seriousness of their relationship to everyone. Pompam suffered through to the end of the party, mostly in silence, generally feeling useless, and like a complete stranger.

After the party Jennifer went back to the Plaza with Pompam and went through the motions of sex, but Pompam sensed a feeling of detachment, so completely different from their first night in New York when she couldn't seem to get enough of him. He kept his feelings to himself, however, thinking that he must have been incorrectly reading things into his experience; this is the *farang* world, he reasoned, and *farangs* are different from Thais.

The next day they went to Patricia's office and Pompam signed the contract she had prepared. He gave her a hefty deposit in the form of a bank draft on his Hong Kong and Shanghai Bank account; he knew she could cash it in the New York branch. The three of them went out to lunch to celebrate, and Jennifer ordered a bottle of champagne. Pompam once again felt left out as the girls gossiped and prattled away while barely acknowledging his presence. He actually got more attention from diners at other tables, and from the passing waiters who couldn't take their admiring eyes off of him.

That evening they went to dinner at the Rainbow Room, high above New York in Rockefeller Center. Pompam's spirits were some- what lifted by being alone with his beloved Jennifer, who once again wore the blue diamond pendant. The sight of New York City spread out below them was one that he knew he would never forget. He thought that they would come back again one day and ask for the same table.

"I wish you would change your mind and fly to San Francisco with me tomorrow, Jennifer. How can I be in your country without you?" he pleaded.

"*Mai pen rai*, Pompam, as you are always saying. You have your Dr. Jim to visit and we'll see each other soon enough," she said as she smiled, but Pompam noticed a cloud pass across her face and wondered what it was.

The next morning she saw him off at the Plaza and he took her in his arms and kissed her -- not caring in the least about the several pairs of eyes that stared at them. This is America, not Thailand, he thought to himself, and for the first time in my life I'll show my love in public if I wish.

"I'll call you tonight from my hotel, Jennifer; I'll miss you," he said softly, and tried as hard as he could not to cry.

"Tonight I'll be at my parents' house out on Long Island. I'll call you when I can," she replied. "Thank you for everything, Pompam; I've had a wonderful time."

That evening at the St. Francis Hotel in San Francisco Pompam called Dr. Jim and they made plans for his visit to Berkeley the following afternoon. "I can't wait to see you, Vichai; this is like a dream," he told him.

Pompam waited anxiously all evening for Jennifer to call, but the phone never rang. The next morning he stayed in his room until it was time for the limousine to take him to Berkeley, but there was still no word from her. He left to see his old friend with a troubled, worried heart.

His concerns about Jennifer vanished with the reception he got from Dr. Jim. Neither of them even attempted to hold back the tears during the first moments of their reunion as they held each other in a long, warm embrace. They stood apart, looked at each other, and thought silently about the many ways they each had changed since their last encounter at Pompam's graduation, nearly nine years before. Pompam was still as handsome as ever, Dr. Jim could see, but good-looking as a grown man -- not as a boy any more; he had put on a little weight, probably from not enough exercise, but it sat on him well and gave him an air of maturity. The Thai man still had the best posture Dr.

Jim had ever seen, his training as a *nene* leaving him with good habits; and he smiled, as usual, with his whole face, and to Dr. Jim, he radiated good health and success.

Pompam thought Dr. Jim was pretty much the same -- except for his hair which had gone totally gray, and he wore it perhaps a bit too unfashionably long. There were a few more crowsfeet around the eyes, and the teeth were not as bright as before, but to Pompam he looked fit and well for a man in his late forties.

Pompam felt completely at home with Dr. Jim's Chinese wife, Lily, and their two young sons, aged two and four. The two boys couldn't keep off of Pompam's lap, not in the least bit shy around him even though they had just met.

"These boys are like Thai children; instant family after only five minutes," he said and laughed. "Remember my brothers when you came to our home in Isan?" And indeed Dr. Jim remembered every moment of that trip with Pompam; it was Dr. Jim's "Ten" in terms of rating experiences, his benchmark for comparing everything he had done since then.

Pompam did his best not to think about Jennifer during that happy evening in Berkeley. But he couldn't help but worry that something awful might have happened to her in New York; it had to have been horrible to have prevented her from calling "her love" who was now far away on the West Coast. New York is dangerous, he recalled, and she could be lying under a bush in Central Park. He feared his worst fears for her.

"I've set up a foundation, Dr. Jim, for the young people of Thailand. I am doing my best to pay back my debt to you," he said with affection.

"I'm so proud of you, Vichai. It's obvious you have done well for yourself, and now you tell me you are using your resources to help others. I couldn't ask for more," he said, and started crying again.

"I could never have become what I am, or achieved what I have without you, Dr. Jim. You gave me the boost and support I needed, when I needed it the most. Ever since then I've been blessed by the Lord Buddha with many lucky breaks and opportunities," Pompam said sincerely, bits of unpleasant memories seeking to disturb him.

They talked for a long time about Pompam's family, his business (at least the parts he could openly discuss), *Phra* Asoka, and the current economic scene in Thailand. "It's not really the same place you visited years ago when we first met. My brother Toy is convinced the whole country will one day self-destruct," said Pompam. "He thinks the 'old boy network' as he calls it will eventually break the economy; I think it will only get stronger."

Dr. Jim was particularly interested in hearing about his name-sake, Little Jim, who was thriving at the International School and playing junior soccer. "Sometimes I think he's missing something by growing up the way he is in Bangkok. He knows nothing about being poor, or not getting everything he wants, or planting rice and being an Isan buffalo boy," Pompam said to the *Ajarn*, but then thought to himself that those things really weren't so important, compared to the "good life" he was giving his children.

Pompam distributed presents from Thailand: Thai puppets for the two boys, silver hilltribe jewelry for Lily, and an antique Buddha image from Sukhothai for Dr. Jim. They were all very happy with their gifts, and Pompam, feeling playful, got down on the floor and animated the puppets for the children, enjoying himself immensely.

Dr. Jim explained that his professional life really hadn't changed that much over the years. "I'm still a professor at Berkeley, teaching the same subjects. I publish articles from time to time in various professional periodicals, and I travel occasionally within the United States to attend seminars and conventions. So you can see what a very dull life I have, Vichai," he remarked, looking around at his rather plain, middle-class home.

Pompam realized for the first time the sacrifices Dr. Jim must have made to be able to sponsor him those four years at Ramkampheng. When Pompam first met Dr. Jim in Bangkok he thought the man was rich because he was able to stay at the Dusit Thani, rent a car to travel through Isan, and spend money on parties and presents for his family. He hadn't known that Dr. Jim had received a research grant from the university that covered most of his expenses.

When the evening came to a close Pompam thanked Dr. Jim and Lily graciously. He had kept the hotel car waiting for him because he didn't want Dr. Jim to go to the trouble of driving him back to San Francisco, knowing that he would insist upon doing so. He had, at the same time, hated for Dr. Jim to see the black, stretched limousine in the first place, but, he thought, this is my life now, and I have far worse things to hide than a big car.

Dr. Jim embraced Pompam and the tears started once again. "I can never in my life thank you enough for stopping off here to see me, Vichai. I am so proud of you; please keep in touch with me always," and he walked back inside his house, overcome with emotion.

On the drive back over the bridge Pompam was also the victim of strong emotions of various kinds. Many were the result of old memories brought back by seeing Dr. Jim again, and some were more recent memories of being with Jennifer in New York. So many changes, Pompam thought to himself; so many people and experiences in my life, both good and bad.

Pompam checked with the reception desk for messages. There were none. He went upstairs to his room, turned on the television, and absently watched whatever filled the screen while he drained the mini-bar.

The next day he forced himself to go out and walk around Union Square, and he picked up some last-minute presents at Saks and Nieman Marcus. Then he decided to hire the limousine again and have the driver take him on a brief city tour. "After all," he said to himself, "this is my first time here, and I refuse to waste it waiting for a bloody phone call." Frustrated, he said "Fuck her!" out loud as he walked back to the hotel, ignoring the stares of passers-by.

He went all the way out to the airport to meet her flight from New York which arrived at 9:00 o'clock, but she wasn't on it. He had no telephone number for Jennifer out on Long Island, and now it was far too late to call Patricia to see if he could find out what had happened to her; Patricia's office was already closed for the weekend.

The next morning, after passing a tortured, restless night, he got up, packed, and left for the airport again. There was still no message for him, and it was Saturday; he could do nothing but go back to Thailand alone and see if there was any word waiting for him there. He was still hopeful, but he could not understand why she hadn't called. After all, she loved him...

The return trip to Bangkok was the most depressing eighteen

hours Pompam had ever spent in his life. When he got to the airport in San Francisco the attendant at the check-in counter informed him that the reservation for Miss Jennifer Carlisle had been canceled two days before.

"What could possibly have happened that would have made her cancel her trip back with me?" he kept asking himself again and again. Scores of scenarios passed through his mind -- except for the obvious one. He had never been dumped before by anyone other than a paying customer, so nothing was farther from his mind. His confidence in his desirability as a man remained completely intact, and he had no doubts whatsoever about himself. Something terrible must have happened to her, he reasoned incorrectly.

He drank whiskey all the way across the Pacific until he finally fell asleep. He had a vivid dream that Kenji would be waiting for him in Japan when they landed, and wouldn't let him board his continuing flight to Thailand. Kenji was dressed in a "*fundoshi*," the traditional Japanese loincloth, and the tattoos were shining on his sweating skin from the light of many fiery torches all around. He brandished a huge Japanese sword and the expression on his face was fierce. He threatened to cut off Pompam's head if he didn't return to his retreat house with him.

It was at this very moment that he was awakened by the flight attendant; he was sweating and shaking. "You must have had a bad dream, Sir; can I get you anything?" Pompam was disoriented by sleep and alcohol, and momentarily didn't know where he was. He finally calmed himself, drank some coffee, and was able to get off the plane at the gate. Fortunately, there was no Kenji waiting to confront him, but Pompam was wary and felt afraid nonetheless; he knew he still had to face him one day, sooner or later.

He stayed awake throughout the next flight to Thailand, and it was late at night when he finally cleared Immigration and Customs at Bangkok International Airport. He was surprised to find Toy in the arrival hall waiting for him, and he immediately feared that something must be wrong at home.

"Toy, why are you here? Didn't Chaiya come to get me?" he asked his younger brother anxiously.

"I came for you, Pompam. I had a daydream about you this

afternoon, and I sensed danger for you in Japan. I just thought I would come out to meet you and make sure you were all right," Toy replied with great concern and affection.

Pompam grabbed him tightly in a desperate hug and started to cry, never happier to see anyone in his life. Toy held him protectively and said, "*Mai pen rai*, Pompam, it's all right. I'm here now. You'll be okay."

Toy was deeply concerned for his *pi-chai*, but he didn't ask any questions or make any negative, confrontational remarks. At least for the moment there were no differences between them.

Chapter 25

On Monday Pompam telephoned Patricia in New York to find out if she had any news of Jennifer. Patricia answered politely, now that Pompam was a big client, that she knew Jennifer was still in New York, she was safe, and nothing was wrong. She did not, however, volunteer any more information in regards to Jennifer's plans or motives. Pompam asked Patricia to please tell Jennifer to call him as soon as possible.

About a week later and still no phone call, Pompam received a letter from New York. In it, Jennifer informed him bluntly that she was not returning to Thailand. Her term with *Khun* Amnard's firm in Bangkok had come to an end, all her work with him was finished, and she would soon begin working in her New York office.

"It's really better that we don't contact one another again, Pompam. We come from two different worlds, you are married, and it would never work out for us long term," she said in the letter. "Thanks so much for everything -- especially the blue diamond. You've been a wonderful friend. I'll make sure Patricia does a good job for you on VP Tower. Good luck."

It took Pompam months to heal from the unceremonious, one-sided break-up. He had never imagined it could be so difficult to recover from a terminated love affair, and it gave him much to think about as he struggled to repair his smashed ego.

In the meantime he tried to mend his tattered relationship with Rattana. They both apologized for the killing words that had spilled out before Pompam left for New York, and tacitly agreed to settle back into the routine of a normal married couple again -- except that they were no longer normal or typical in any way. They were very wealthy, high-profile Thais at the apex of the nouveau riche social ladder; and a great many people looked up at their asses.

In spite of their truce, it wasn't long before they went off in their own directions and followed their own instincts. They joined together only when it was absolutely necessary or whenever it furthered their individual objectives. They still slept in the same bed at night -- at least those nights when Pompam came home. If he didn't, Rattana chose not to complain. She decided, like most wives in her position, not to care about the things she couldn't see. Besides, she had learned the hard way that making a fuss made it even more painful for both of them.

Months passed and Pompam indulged himself more and more in things of the physical realm, believing that material distractions would put him in a better mood. Without Rattana's knowledge he bought himself a huge penthouse condominium in one of the new buildings in the Sukhumvit area. He fitted it out magnificently and used it for purposes of "retreat," much like Kenji used his Japanese-style house in the heart of Tokyo. He bought himself watches, cars, a large motor yacht for cruising the islands in the Gulf of Thailand, and other toys and objects that momentarily held his attention and amused him.

He reconnected with *Khun* Wharavut, the political party boss, and gradually became immersed in the dark, murky world of Thai politics. He found himself surrounded by military brass, *phuyais* from the business world, and ambitious minor characters who hung around like obsequious groupies, trying to catch crumbs from business deals, hoping some of Pompam's glamour and good luck would rub off on them. There were always plenty of sycophants who would take all he would give: parties, presents, connections, information, and women.

When Pompam finally allowed himself to get talked into an involvement in the political arena, he started doing favors for people he didn't know; he also helped put together deals in land speculation, and then generously shared the inevitable profits. He let outside people invest with him knowing they would make out well, and he made political points in the process. He contributed to numerous election campaigns, special political funds, favored charities, and *thamboons* for countless temples throughout the country.

He became quite close to General Prasert, the former Supreme Commander. The statesman had retired some months back and accepted a few Directorships in private corporations, entertaining his own political ambitions. General Prasert took Pompam under his expansive wing and promoted him among his political cronies as a future leader in

Parliament, perhaps even one who could rise to become a Cabinet Minister one day.

All the while Pompam worried about the heroin business and Yamamoto. News of his political involvement had already reached Kenji, and the telephone calls that summoned him to Japan became increasingly more threatening.

"You said you would come after you returned from New York, but it's been months! You're playing a very dangerous game with me, Pompam, and this is your last warning." It felt to Pompam like a massive pile of rocks was being suspended over his head -- secured only by a thin silk thread that could snap at any moment. He finally knew he couldn't put Kenji off any longer, so he started looking over his calendar for a date when he could break from his busy schedule, dreading the inevitable humiliation and degradation.

Pompam spent a great deal of his time with Toy on Youth Foundation work; General Prasert encouraged it, saying it was good for the image. The two brothers traveled around the country inspecting existing programs and laying ground work for future ones. Pompam was called upon frequently to perform public speaking assignments on behalf of the Foundation and its fund-raising activities. Combined with his new involvement in politics, his public persona changed from that of a glamorous entertainment entrepreneur to a philanthropist and standard-bearer for social consciousness and reform. It made him begin to feel better about himself as a person, little by little.

Toy, however, criticized his brother in private for his material-istic indulgences, and up-braided him for not being a good Buddhist. "Have you taken a good look at yourself lately to see how you've changed! All your money has warped your spirit, Pompam. Even Rattana has become superficial and corrupted by your wealth. Think how spoiled your children are, and what they'll be like in a few years. Please save yourself -- and them -- before it's too late!"

Pompam couldn't take it when Toy vented on him like that. "What do you mean by attacking me? My wealth has given you all you have -- and goes to finance any new 'cause' that catches your fancy. I work very hard to support whatever programs you choose -- and put myself on the line even when it's not in my best interest. And your new

AIDS project has caused Rattana and me a great deal of embarrassment."

"What a hypocrite you are, Pompam. You give money and you make speeches about social reform, and yet you still run a massage parlor and a cheap whorehouse. God knows what else you do!" These flare-ups became more and more frequent, and Pompam didn't know where they would eventually lead.

Black's show business career continued to soar, and Pompam used him for political and fund-raising events whenever a need would arise. Black was a good-natured young man and he was always happy to help the causes of his famous *pi-chai* whenever he was asked.

Pompam rarely visited *Phra* Asoka at *Wat* Mahathat, but he had become a large contributor to the revered monk's own foundation whose aim was to spread Buddhism in India. *Phra* Asoka had several times invited Pompam to accompany him on trips to his native land, but he never even really considered it, saying, "*Ajarn*, I can't go anywhere; I'm chained to my work so I can keep the money supply flowing."

Darunee was finally given the title "*khunying*" by His Majesty the King as part of his annual birthday favors list. It had made her exceedingly happy to have at last achieved this goal, and several of her friends gave lavish parties in her honor to celebrate the occasion -- including Rattana, who finally accepted the woman she had once considered her rival.

"*Mai pen rai*, Pompam; Nee is a *khunying* now, and we're good friends," Rattana said to him one day, and all he could think of was the fit she had thrown over those old NASA photos.

The image of Darunee's round, smiling face was routinely seen on the pages of the daily newspapers and monthly *hi-so* magazines. She was so rich that she would never have to work again, but unfortunately problems with her wild, out-of-control children never ceased, and they sucked up all the extra time her retirement was supposed to have given her.

Pompam received a telegram one day informing him that his mother had suddenly died of a heart attack; she was working at her loom in the village temple and just keeled over sideways, dead. There had been no warning, and Pompam and his brothers were completely devastated. The entire family went to the village for the funeral rites in a virtual parade of expensive automobiles.

The morning of the funeral Toy confronted all of his brothers, saying, "I became a *nene* when our father died, and tomorrow morning I will shave my head again and become a monk for our mother. What about you, Pompam? And the rest of you? Are any of you willing to give up some time and make merit for the poor, dead mother who gave you life?"

Each of them looked at the ground, shifted from side to side, and said nothing, feeling ashamed.

"Fine, then; I'll do it by myself -- for all of us -- again! *Mai pen rai.* But it's a tragedy that everyone in Thailand these days cares more about money and having a good time than they do about their souls -- and the souls of their dead parents. Go make some more filthy money -- and I'll see you in three months!" Toy committed himself to ninety days this time; he felt he needed a good long break from his self-absorbed brothers.

This time *Phra* Prateep, himself, shaved the hair from Toy's head. No one in his family had the nerve to face him at his ordination, so no one went.

A few weeks after his mother's death he received a call from Mr. Aoyama in Japan. They spoke occasionally on the telephone and still got together for dinner whenever Aoyama came to Bangkok to play golf, accept "introductions" with young girls, and check up on the fruit exporter who facilitated their drug business. They never discussed Yamamoto and his repeated threats, but Pompam picked up clues from their conversations that indicated Mr. Aoyama was aware of the delicate situation, and he did what he could to protect him.

"How are you today, Mr. Vichai?" Aoyama asked in his familiar polite manner, "I hope all is well with you."

Pompam replied that everything was fine, no problems, and everyone was in good health. "I'm planning a visit to Japan later in the month, Mr. Aoyama; I'm looking forward to having some sushi together, and..."

Aoyama interrupted Pompam and said, "I am afraid I have

some bad news for you today, some rather sad news, Mr. Vichai. Mr. Yamamoto is dead." There was no emotion in his voice.

"Dead? Yamamoto is dead? What happened?" Pompam asked eagerly, experiencing an almost euphoric feeling of freedom and release.

"It appears that an intruder broke into his retreat house last night and murdered him. It may have been a burglary, but I really don't know any more at this time; the police are still investigating. This has caused a major problem in our organization because it is not yet clear who his successor will be. He was still young, as you know, and had made no plans regarding who would take over after him. It will be very sensitive here for quite a while, I am afraid," Aoyama confided.

What he did not tell Pompam was that Yamamoto had been found naked and stabbed to death in his big Japanese hot tub. He was apparently the victim of some attractive young Japanese boy that he had arranged to have sent to him for his pleasure. It seemed that Yamamoto's enemies had used the not-so-innocent boy to get past his heavy security precautions and assassinate him.

"How will this affect us here in Bangkok?" Pompam asked, suddenly very concerned.

"It is very hard to say right now, Mr. Vichai. I suppose that affairs can move along in their normal way for a time, but I suggest that you look out for yourself," was Aoyama's response, being cautious, but he was also implying that Pompam should protect himself.

"I'm concerned about our export programs," Pompam said, knowing that Aoyama would understand what he meant without having to actually use the "heroin" word on the phone.

"Yes, Mr. Vichai, I can understand your concern. I believe you must act in your own best interests; just keep me informed," Aoyama answered, and they ended the conversation shortly.

Pompam couldn't believe his good luck. The bastard Kenji was dead and Pompam was free of him forever. He took a long deep breath and exhaled slowly, feeling deep knotted tensions relax their grip on his strained, over-stressed body. There would be no more threats and no more pleading calls for him to return to Tokyo -- ever again. He suddenly felt better about life than he had in many months.

Pompam immediately got hold of Chai, Kitti, and Ott, and

summoned them to his office. He wanted to act quickly before the *yakuza* struggle in Japan affected them in some negative way in Bangkok.

"The big boss in Japan, Yamamoto, is dead. Mr. Aoyama just called me from Tokyo," Pompam informed his stunned lieutenants. "He was murdered last night, and it looks like there might be a war of succession in his organization. I want to stop the heroin business immediately."

The boys were shocked to hear this astounding news, and pondered Pompam's directive for a few moments before Chai finally responded, "We can kill the business, Pompam, but we have to protect Nopadon."

"I think you'd better phone him in Chiang Mai right away, Chai, and tell him. I know he will want to protect his 'face' with Ahm in Burma, so I think we might have to end it by making it look like a bust by the drug authorities," Pompam replied, his mind racing.

"There's a shipment due to leave for Bangkok from the north two days from now. Maybe we should tip off the Americans at the DEA in Chiang Mai. The fruit trucks can be intercepted en route to Bangkok; the drivers will probably be arrested and go to jail, but that can't be helped. We know they can't be traced to us, but what happens if they're led to the Japanese exporter in Bangkok? Will he inform on us?" Chai asked, worried.

"Aoyama has been their only contact, and the guy here in Bangkok has always taken all his orders directly from him. I don't even know for sure if he knows we're involved in this thing," Pompam answered, frantically trying to envision all possible scenarios.

"I think those *yakuza* guys know they would be executed if they ever turned traitor. But if he should implicate us in any way, I think our friends could handle the police and the media," was Kitti's comment.

"We'll just have to take that chance, I'm afraid," Pompam said. "Chai, call up Nopadon and let him know what's happening. Give me all the details about the shipment: description of trucks, what they're carrying, license tag numbers, place and time of departure -- those sorts of things. I'll make the call to the DEA myself."

Nopadon wasn't at all happy about killing off a business that had made him the wealthiest man in Chiang Mai, but after hearing from

Chai he knew it had to be done. He also realized that he couldn't just walk up into Burma and tell his friend, Ahm, to shut down the refinery and smuggling operations. Their drug business was the most important source of funds for the Shan resistance, and the last thing they wanted was to kill the golden goose.

So Nopadon agreed that it had to be busted, and then he would lay low for a while until he was sure the DEA and the police hadn't linked him to the heroin trade. He also thought it would be better if the bust didn't occur anywhere near Chiang Mai, so he and Chai devised a plan where the drug agents would intercept the trucks just north of Bangkok in Chainat Province.

Pompam made the anonymous call to the DEA headquarters in Chiang Mai. He told the officers about the refinery operation in Burma and its location as best he could. He gave a description of the four trucks that would be coming down to Bangkok, and the approximate time that they would reach the check-point in Chainat. Then he hung up the phone before his number could be traced. "My God, that was scary," Pompam said as he let out a big sigh, his hands shaking almost uncontrollably.

"It will be all over in forty-eight hours," Kitti said. "We'll know by then if we've got a big problem with the law -- or no problem at all." For the next two days Pompam and his inner circle sat tight, drank lots of Black Label, and did their best to remain calm and not let their anxiety show; they knew their lives were at stake.

As it turned out, the boys at the VP Group had no problem at all. The DEA agents didn't intercept the trucks in Chainat, but followed them instead all the way to their final destination in Bangkok, which was the warehouse of the Japanese fruit exporter. Then they sealed off the entire building, made their bust, and arrested the four drivers, the Japanese boss, and six of his staff. They were all hauled into the police station and photographed with the five hundred packages containing pure, uncut heroin spread out on the table in front of them; all the newspapers carried the story the next day and reported that it was the biggest heroin bust that year.

The Japanese exporter kept his mouth shut and suffered the consequences: twenty years in a filthy Thai jail. The DEA couldn't do anything about the refinery in Burma, but they increased their surveillance of the border areas. They were able to make three more large busts when Ahm's people couldn't control their greed, and stupidly tried to smuggle more drugs across the river into Thailand.

Pompam and his three lieutenants went to the nearest temple. They made huge donations, thanking the Lord Buddha for his protection throughout the frightening ordeal, and for their newly-appreciated freedom which was still theirs to enjoy.

After Toy's three months in the monastery he returned to the world, but not completely. He seemed somehow changed -- more spiritual, perhaps -- and at the same time, more openly aggressive in his campaign to rid Thailand of the avarice and corruption he felt was killing off the environment and enslaving the people. Pompam could feel the tension building between him and his crusading brother, and he was convinced that Toy actually knew more about his sordid business activities than he let on.

He soon became worried that Toy might do something that could jeopardize his whole regime. He was already creating waves in the media about certain cases involving the environment that were affecting a few of Pompam's political friends. *Khun* Wharavut approached Pompam and asked him to please try to control the young man.

"Do you realize, *Khun* Vichai, that your brother is helping to attack our MP in the south who owns most of the shrimp farms down there? Who cares about the goddamned mangroves? There are millions of them! We have to protect our man -- who stands to lose a fortune if your brother persists," the party boss complained one day.

"If you knew my brother you would know that it's impossible to stop him from doing something he believes in. Especially now, since he was a monk; it's like he's become a warrior Buddha," Pompam replied, not knowing what to do.

"At least speak to Toy, *Khun* Vichai; our shrimp farmer friend has a very bad temper, and he might try to stop the boy himself."

Pompam knew exactly what *Khun* Wharavut meant, and he was suddenly terrified for his brother's safety. Later, when he tried to speak to Toy about it, he just said, "*Mai pen rai*, Pompam. If they kill me for doing what's right, then it's on their own heads. Their karma will be bad -- not mine."

As the weeks and the months passed by Pompam still thought bitterly about Jennifer; the old wound would temporarily open up and he bled with longing for her. He still found it impossible to accept that their relationship had meant so little to her that she could end it the cruel way she had. He suffered, knowing that her decision to leave him had been totally pre-meditated, and that she had planned the whole thing before they even left for New York.

The pain came to the surface again when the interior designer, Patricia, came out to oversee the installation of her work on The VP Tower. She was in town for nearly three weeks, and Pompam saw her almost every day on the site. He tried to talk with her about Jennifer, but she had no intention of discussing her friend with an old boyfriend she had dumped.

"Mr. Vichai, please forget about Jennifer," she told him. "What she did was not kind, and I think she's sorry for the way she treated you. But she is engaged to be married in about six weeks, so you have to accept that whatever happened between you is over."

Pompam tried to take the shocking news of Jennifer's upcoming marriage in stride, and said, "How wonderful for her; please give her my best wishes," but inside he felt like he had just been stabbed in the stomach.

They gave a lavish party for the grand opening of The VP Tower. The guest list was one of the most impressive ever assembled for such an occasion, and the ribbon-cutting was presided over by the son of the King, whom Pompam had gotten to know personally through his military friends.

After Pompam's opening, the tenants gradually began to move into their leased spaces; the bank opened on the ground level, and The Regents' Club II on the top floor quickly took its place as the social venue of choice for the power brokers of the Kingdom.

About this same time Royal Hills was finally completed and Pompam and Darunee received their final payments from the banks; the profits they made off of the project were enormous. They gave a big dinner to celebrate, and invited all the old military boys they had paid off to get the contract. About half of them, including General Prasert and General Chamnan, were already retired and openly enjoying their fat nest-eggs and ostentatious lifestyles; nobody in Thailand even bothered to wonder how they had managed to save up so much money over the years from their meager army salaries.

The highlight for Pompam much later in that year was the royal decoration he was awarded by His Majesty the King for his philanthropic and charitable works. Royal decorations for men are very much the same as they are for women except that no titles, such as "*khunying*," are bestowed.

During the ceremony at Chitrlada Palace, the royal family's official Bangkok residence, Pompam trembled as he waited in line to approach his beloved Monarch to receive the decoration. When he knelt and received it from the King's own hand his heart nearly burst with strong emotion and pride. Rattana and *Khun* Arun were present at the ceremony, and both wept silently as they witnessed their buffalo boy from Buriram receiving the highest acknowledgment in the Kingdom for service to his country.

When they came home after the ceremony Pompam immediately went out to Toy's room in the guest house; he wanted to show him the royal decoration and share his moment of triumph.

Toy looked down at the silver ornament and it's pink ribbon, pinned to Pompam's lapel, and laughed, saying, "Congratulations! I didn't know they gave those to pimps!"

Pompam, crushed, slapped his brother in the face, leaving bright red finger marks on his cheek. Their eyes met, blazing, but neither one said a word and Pompam fled from the room.

He became more and more involved in his political party's activities nation-wide, and finally the day came when *Khun* Wharavut said, "Now is the time for you to run for elective office, *Khun* Vichai. All of the groundwork has been laid. You have the reputation, the 'face,' the background, and the support. We want you to run in the next election."

"If you feel this is the time, *Khun* Wharavut, then I am ready," was Pompam's response, feeling thrilled. "Since it will be my first campaign, I'm counting on you to guide me through the process."

"I will be there every step of the way, *Khun* Vichai. I feel I must warn you now that when you stand for public office your every action -- both past and present -- will be scrutinized by certain dedicated and very tenacious journalists. These reporters aren't like any of the ones you've known before, that idolize you and print only nice things; they are idealists, *Khun* Vichai, and they feel it's their duty to dig deep and reveal things they think make a candidate unfit to serve; and they can't be bought off. No amount of money can keep them from writing what they might discover in the process of dredging up the past."

He paused to give some time to let this sink into Pompam's brain, then he looked him directly in the eye and said, "We know everything there is to know about your company, *Khun* Vichai. We know who all of your connections are, and everything about all of your operations. I hope you understand, we have to research all of our candidates thoroughly before we give them our complete endorsement. So please look and see if there are any activities going on within your organization that might not make you look good in the newspaper; if there are, then you might want to get rid of them," he suggested solemnly.

Pompam, although shocked to the bone by these statements, immediately understood what *Khun* Wharavuth was referring to, and wondered just exactly how much of his past they had uncovered in their background investigation. He dared not ask.

"I will do what needs to be done," he finally told the friendly, but deadly serious, old party boss, and suddenly remembered Toy's often-repeated remark about climbing up the ladder of success and watching his own ass.

"Thank the Buddha I don't have to worry about the heroin business," he said to himself, "and the boy bars are long gone."

Pompam called a meeting with Kitti, Chai, and Ott that very afternoon. "I have decided to run for political office -- for Member of Parliament from Buriram. I've more or less been told I have to get rid of the brothel on Petchburi and the girl buying and brokering operations, both in Thailand and overseas. I have to do this immediately if I want to avoid being embarrassed, and maybe ruined by the press. I know this will affect your incomes, and that of your brother, Suphan, Chai, as well as Nopadon up in Chiang Mai. But it has to be done as quickly as possible," he announced to his partners.

Kitti and Ott both responded with *"Mai pen rai"*, at the same time, and Chai said, "Don't worry about my income or my brother's, Pompam. We've both made more than enough money from these sources. I'll call Nopadon today and stop the girl business. *Mai pen rai.* He's also made himself a fortune, and it won't hurt him in the least to retire at this point. He still has his little bar in Chiang Mai to keep him busy."

"Thanks to all three of you. Chai, I think you should give all the girls working at the brothel some money and a bus ticket back home. Just close the place down. I don't care if it sits empty until our lease expires. In fact, pay off the lease and get that old motel out of our names. I will call Mr. Aoyama in Japan and tell him there will be no more girls coming from Thailand, and you call the guy in Taipei, Chai, and tell him the same thing. You do what you need to do about all the brothels out in the provinces we've been supplying," Pompam instructed.

He thought momentarily about the thousands of young girls they had led into a life of prostitution. Boys, too, in the past. "Perhaps Toy is right," he said to himself, "and I am a hypocrite." He shrugged his shoulders and turned back to the business at hand, which was politics.

"I've been told that during the campaign there are certain journalists who will do their best to expose everything in my past. We've got to be extremely careful about what we do and say from now on," Pompam said, moving his attention to the important issue of self-preservation.

"What about Paradise City and Isan Sweetheart, Pompam? And the girls who work at The Regents Club? Will owning a massage parlor and a string of taxi dancers affect your image as well?" asked Ott.

"They are all legitimate businesses, and everyone in Bangkok already knows we own them. Since no one cares about massage parlors and such, I don't think it will matter. In reality, as I've said before, our true future is in land development. With my track record, and all the information I'll be getting in Parliament, there's no end to what we can do," he concluded.

As expected, Kitti volunteered to be Pompam's campaign

manager. He had no past experience with elections, but he figured that if he could run the finances and day to day operations of The VP Group, he could manage the affairs of just one candidate running for MP. He wound up spending a lot of time canvassing and organizing in Buriram, going back and forth from Bangkok, but it wasn't so bad since he had long-since acquired his own Mercedes Benz, driver, and car phone.

Khun Wharavut was the one who actually ran the most important activities in the campaign. His many years of experience came in handy to Kitti, who had never dealt with village headmen before. Getting the *tambons* all set up and primed with enough money needed to buy each vote in the district was no small task. Vote-buying was a long-standing tradition in nearly all provinces in rural Thailand, and the village headmen were the key players in the game. It usually boiled down to each vote costing 300 to 600 baht: not expensive at all for someone even a fraction as wealthy as Pompam.

The candidate attended and paid for *thamboons* in every village temple in his District. He was forever hearing the chanting of monks, and eating bowls of *somtam* with masses of villagers who showed up to meet the great man. He was the local hero -- the buffalo boy who had made good in Bangkok. Everywhere he went he was swarmed by barefoot rice farmers in *pakomah* and Isan-plaid *sarongs*; they all wanted to get close to him, to touch him.

Even though Pompam felt uncomfortable in the beginning, eventually he began to enjoy being with the poor and unfortunates of his native land, and in his mind he resolved to do his best for them in Parliament. He convinced himself that he would become the protector of his people, the fixer of the social and economic dilemmas that had kept them down for generations.

A few weeks before the election, rumblings surfaced from one particular journalist who had made it his life's mission to get to the bottom of famous Khun Vichai's roots; he was also determined to discover the exact sources of his great wealth.

The scenario played out just as *Khun* Wharavuth had predicted. The journalist followed Pompam around like a shadow wherever he went. In Bangkok he relentlessly pursued anyone who could give him clues about Pompam's past. He interviewed present and past employees, massage girls and taxi dancers, musicians, entertainers, and neighbors on Tonglor -- even *Khun* Arun, who, of course, said nothing. He did, however, uncover bits of information that linked Pompam to an assortment of unsavory deeds and individuals; but he decided not to go to print until he had a real "clincher."

One night the journalist, a forty-ish, balding man named *Khun* Nimit, was sitting in an open air beer bar on a cul de sac off one of the side *sois* of Patpong's red light district. The majority of the patrons were dissipated foreigners who were filling up on cheap brew before continuing on to the "sexotic" bars in the vicinity where drinks were exorbitantly expensive. Nimit was there to pick up ideas for another article he was working on about foreign sex predators.

A television behind the bar was tuned to one of the Thai language stations, and *Khun* Nimit absently watched the news program that focused on the up-coming parliamentary elections. His attention perked up when an image of Pompam appeared, bowing before an elderly monk in a temple in Buriram during a *thamboon* celebration. It also caught the attention of the bartender who looked up at the screen while rinsing out beer glasses and made the comment, "What a phony asshole that guy is; at least if he still has an asshole after all the buggering he got in the old days."

Since the bartender had said this in the Thai language, only Khun Nimit understood him; the foreigners paid no attention, concentrating on their bottles of Singha beer while leering at the passing parade of gaudy prostitutes and transvestites. Immediately Nimit's interest was acutely aroused.

"You know this *Khun* Vichai?" Nimit asked the bartender, pointing to the TV.

"Not any more I don't, now that he's become so rich and famous and charity-minded. Years ago when he was a poor student at Ramkampheng he used to live down the hall from me and my wife. He certainly led a different life then than he does now," the bartender muttered, betraying his envy of the wealthy, present-day candidate for MP.

"What was he like in those days?" Nimit questioned him, ordering another beer.

"He was like any ordinary student from the countryside: dirt poor, struggling to survive," he said and continued. "He worked for a long time at a Chinese seafood restaurant in the area. I remember he started out as a bus boy and worked his way up to assistant manager. He was hard-working, I have to give him credit for that. Then one day I heard he had quit and started working as a rent-a-boy in a gay bar. I hardly ever saw him again since he was always out. He lived with a roommate who was a friend from his village. The roommate worked as a bookkeeper for the same restaurant part time while he studied, if I remember correctly."

Khun Nimit could hardly contain his excitement upon hearing these first-hand revelations from the bartender. He already knew the stories about Pompam and Kitti living together and working in the Chinese restaurant were true, so he figured the bartender must know something.

Then he suddenly remembered an article in the press some years before about Pompam's alleged connections to boy bars. This had been retracted with apologies by the newspaper's editor and it became a dead story. Nimit had thought at the time that the incident was undoubtedly the result of a slander perpetrated by some jealous competitor, just as *Khun* Vichai had said it was. He hadn't even bothered to research this angle during his present investigations since it had seemed like a ridiculous waste of time. But now...

"Do you remember the name of the gay bar he worked at?" Nimit asked.

The bartender suddenly became suspicious and answered, "Why do you want to know about this?"

"I am a journalist and I'm doing a story on *Khun* Vichai. I will pay you for any information you can give me," he answered eagerly.

The bartender was obviously jealous of Pompam's success, but he was also a fellow countryman from Isan and had no real wish to see Pompam hurt. The offer of money, however, was too tempting to resist, and finally he said, "I don't think it exists any more; I heard it was down on Sukhumvit some place. How much money?" he asked, feeling not at all ashamed.

"I will pay you 10,000 *baht* if anything you tell me leads to information I can use in my story. What else can you remember?" Nimit asked with a crooked smile.

"Why don't you come back here tomorrow night and I'll see what I can find out from my wife when I see her after work," he replied, now as one conspirator to another. Nimit couldn't believe his unexpected good luck with this accidental discovery right there in the bowels of Patpong.

The next day he searched back through the archives at his newspaper and finally found the incriminating article about *Khun* Vichai from years before. The journalist who had written the piece was no longer with the paper, but Nimit tracked him down at a magazine where he worked as editor for their entertainment section. He called the man and tried to get the origin of his old story out of him. The guy refused to divulge his source, but he did say that he had been ordered by his boss to drop the matter immediately and print a retraction.

"Someone put pressure on the paper to kill the story, that much was obvious. We had no choice but to let it drop. The only strange thing about it was that a few days later I learned a gay bar called Number Ten was closed down after its owner was burglarized and beaten up so bad he ended up in the hospital. It was rumored that later he committed suicide. I thought at the time there might have been some connection, given what my source had told me earlier."

Nimit became convinced that there was, in fact, some vital connection between the two events, and he felt he was hot on the trail of linking *Khun* Vichai to the sordid fate of the defunct Number Ten and its deceased owner.

The following night he went back to the beer bar in Patpong to meet the bartender as they had agreed. "My wife said that in those days she was friends with another boy down the hall who worked at the same bar as Vichai. She couldn't remember his name, but she thinks he came from Sukhothai and he liked to take pictures. One day they had a few drinks together while I was out working, and he told her that both he and Vichai worked at a place called Number Ten on Sukhumvit."

The Thai equivalent of the word "Gotcha!" rang out in Nimit's ears. He felt that with this connection made -- combined with the items he had already dug up -- he now had enough information to be able to begin a series of damaging stories on the golden *Khun* Vichai. He paid the grinning bartender the 10,000 baht he had promised, drank another beer, and went off to his news room to compose his piece.

An associate editor saw a copy of the article before it appeared in the newspaper and called up Ott, an old friend, to warn him. Ott phoned Pompam immediately and passed on the information. Pompam was horrified. What to do now? he thought, both worried and angry at the same time.

The next day the article appeared in the newspaper and the VP Group's telephone lines were ablaze with calls. Ott prepared a denial statement for Pompam's office to issue to the press, but in the article *Khun* Nimit had promised that he would expose even more dirt in follow-up stories -- unrelated to the bar-boy accusations -- as his investigations progressed.

Toy burst into Pompam's office and said, "The last time a story like this came out you told me it was a lie; now I'm not sure I believe you. Surely, Pompam, you never went that low for money. What a disgrace!"

Pompam vehemently denied it, of course, but Toy's comments only fanned the flames of his fury.

He had barely finished this confrontation with Toy when *Khun* Wharavut called up and said, "You see what I mean, *Khun* Vichai? This guy Nimit will stay on your ass until he buries you. I don't care if his allegations are true or not, but you can't let him continue to print this kind of shit about you or the party will lose 'face,' and you'll lose the election."

Pompam picked up the telephone and called his old friend *Khun* Surapong from the police department, who had helped him out of all sorts of sticky, unpleasant situations in the past, including the punishment and ultimate destruction of *Khun* Anuwat and Number Ten.

Surapong was sympathetic to Pompam's case, but he politely told him there was nothing he could do about the problem. The fact was, he didn't want to get involved in anything that might jeopardize his own position: an honorable retirement was only months away. Pompam was indeed angry with *Khun* Surapong, but he didn't show it over the telephone. What an ungrateful bastard, he thought to himself after he hung up; he's even my young son's godfather!

Pompam then called up Chai and simply said, "Handle it." Pompam didn't want to know anything more about the matter, or to know in advance what Chai might arrange to remedy the situation.

Chai coldly answered, "Consider it handled, Pompam."

Chai himself drove down to Petchburi Province which was about three hours southwest of Bangkok. Historically, Petchburi was -- and had been for over a hundred years -- a "den of thieves," so to speak. Assassins could be hired there as easily as ordering a bowl of noodles from a sidewalk vendor, if one knew where to look. Chai knew.

The next day a dark-colored motorcycle pulled up beside *Khun* Nimit's red Nissan Sentra at the noisy and perpetually-clogged intersection of Rama IV Road and Asoke. The helmeted driver pulled a hand gun out of the inside pocket of his leather jacket and deftly fired four shots through the window into Nimit's head. Glass, blood and other human matter sprayed the inside of the vehicle and the body slumped against the steering wheel, blaring the horn.

The traffic light changed and the anonymous motorcycle and its driver took off in a cloud of exhaust fumes. It disappeared into the small *sois* near the freeway entrance and literally vanished into thin air. Horns honked at the intersection when Nimit's car failed to move forward, but he was already as dead as the future stories he had promised the public on Pompam's past. By the time the police arrived, the assassin was already well on his way back to Petchburi, and there were no witnesses to give any descriptions.

The assassination had cost Chai 20,000 *baht*, which annoyed him because he thought it was too expensive.

Pompam smiled to himself when he saw the article in the newspaper the following day about the shooting death of the journalist. "Murder in Broad Daylight on Rama IV Road" screamed the headline. Pretty brazen, Pompam thought, but then such events were common occurrences in Thailand those days -- particularly when businessmen had economic motives to eliminate rivals. The last few months Pompam himself had taken to having an armed motorcycle man ride behind his chauffeur-driven Benz at all times, just to prevent a similar incident from happening to him. A wise move, he thought at that moment.

He was relieved knowing that there would be no more damaging newspaper articles about his shady past. Any thoughts of guilt that tried to pry their way into his mind were quickly pushed aside. "What was done had to be done," he said to himself, "for the greater good of the people I will serve."

There wasn't an honest journalist in town who was brave enough to take up the banner *Khun* Nimit had so briefly waved. No one in the media dared to print or broadcast anything that would link the murder to *Khun* Vichai, who, it seemed, was a man to be feared.

Late that afternoon Toy stormed into his private office and said, "You killed that journalist, *Khun* Nimit, didn't you? It's so obvious it was you, Pompam; how could you do it? Aren't you brave enough to allow anyone to stand up to you?"

"I had nothing to do with that man's death, Toy. He must have been investigating many other people -- one of them probably wanted him out of the way." Pompam was shaking, trying hard to gain control of his emotions.

"For your information, I happened to have known *Khun* Nimit. He was a very honest man, Pompam, and we worked together two or three times trying to get to the bottom of some corruption spawned by one of your Regents' Club types. Weren't you surprised the day I mentioned the name, Nopadon, from Chiang Mai? You, yourself, even said it was a Nopadon who took you to look at property in the countryside up there -- when you got sick, remember? I learned all about him from *Khun* Nimit, who was investigating his drug and girl-buying operations across the border in the Shan State. He told me he suspected you might be involved with Nopadon, but I defended you, and swore on my life that you didn't do any of those things. He backed off because of me, Pompam; I tried to save you, and now you've killed him."

"I told you I didn't do it, Toy! You've got to believe me," Pompam screamed.

"Now I know you're a liar as well as all the other things, Pompam, including a whore. May the Lord Buddha forgive you, *pi-chai*. I have always loved you more than anyone, but after this incident I'm leaving -- and you will never see me again."

"Toy, wait, come back and..." he called out as Toy rushed out and slammed the door. Pompam went running through the office after him and Toy turned around and shouted, "Don't! If you ever want me to forgive you, don't try to follow me. Just leave me alone."

Pompam stopped. The entire office stood still; only the whir of the copy machine sounded in another room. He said nothing, and turned around and walked back to his room, closed the door, and wept.

Pompam, although shaken and depressed by the confrontation with Toy and his subsequent disappearance, was never plagued again by adverse media coverage during the election campaign. From that time he was always portrayed as a man of the people -- the shining star of Isan. Dozens of articles were printed about the work of his Foundation, which, without Toy, had no leader and was floundering; but the public knew nothing of that.

Pictures of Pompam and his elegant *hi-so* wife, Rattana, appeared with regularity in the dailies and the tabloids. It seemed to all analysis that he would easily defeat his out-matched and under-financed opponents. Kitti managed the balance of the campaign superbly with the help of *Khun* Wharavuth, who never once made mention of the unfortunate demise of the out-spoken, public-spirited journalist, *Khun* Nimit.

Pompam poised himself for victory. The cloud had passed.

A few days before the election Pompam received a call from *Phra* Asoka at *Wat* Mahathat. "After you and your brother had your confrontation he came to me for refuge, Vichai. He asked to be ordained as a monk for life, and I, myself, performed the ceremony."

He added that Toy was now known as *Phra* Chatree, and that the day after his ordination he had set off on a "*tudong,*" a solitary spiritual journey in the forests, barefoot and penniless. No one knew where he had gone, and no one knew how long his lonely quest would last. He would be one of those invisible, rare ones from an age past, who wandered throughout the country, begged from the poor, and slept under his umbrella: a *true* monk -- desiring nothing but peace and enlightenment.

Pompam's certain victory at the polls felt hollow all of a sudden. The cloud had returned.

Chapter 26

It was the night of the election and Rattana and Pompam were standing side by side in the noisy ballroom of the Grand Hyatt Erawan as photographers snapped away, and reporters held up their microphones for comments from the new MP from Buriram.

"I swear to the Lord Buddha that I will continue the fight to help the young people of our country -- not only through the Thailand Youth Foundation, but by supporting the passage of laws that will protect their rights.

"When I was a boy I was forced to go to Bangkok to continue my education and find work so I could send money home to my parents in the village. It is my pledge that future generations of young Thai men and women will be able to achieve their goals closer to home. I want them to earn wages comparable to those in Bangkok, stay in their native provinces, carry on their cultural traditions, enjoy the uninterrupted companionship of their families, look after their elders, and never have to leave home in order to survive. I want to see the people of the countryside finally get their share of Thailand's new wealth, and enjoy the same benefits as their brothers and sisters in the capital."

Pompam's acceptance speech was impassioned, and to his audience, seemed to be genuinely from his heart. He did, in fact, mean every word he said, identifying, through his own experience, the primary problems faced by the rural poor.

The evening of triumph, however, was marred for Pompam by Toy's absence. Of all the people he wanted to be there with him, he wanted Toy the most; but his dear brother was gone, perhaps for good.

The first few months after Pompam took office, he was often challenged by trying to balance the ideals he expressed in his election-night speech with the commitments he had made to the Party bosses -- *and* satisfy his own self interests. Little by little, however, his backers began to put forward their demands and Pompam was forced to compromise himself and serve their personal -- and usually financial -- interests.

He gradually found himself retreating from the promises he had made to the young and the poor. *Mai pen rai*, he thought to himself, it's my duty to take care of myself and my friends first. I still have time to look after the people.

Rattana found out she was pregnant once again. She told Pompam she was convinced the conception of their fourth child had taken place on the night of the election. That evening after the party she and Pompam had gone home and made love in a away they had not shared in a long time, temporarily closing the chasm between them, recalling feelings from their courtship days in the village. They remained happy for a few weeks until Pompam's various obligations and Rattana's social and charity activities took them once again their separate ways.

Pompam went often to his penthouse retreat and indulged himself in the sensuous and private entertainments he seemingly couldn't do without. After all, he thought to himself, I am a Thai man in my prime; is it not my right? What is my position and my money for, but to enjoy myself when I feel like it?

These days he tried hard never to be alone. Whenever he found himself in his own company he would think about Toy, and become depressed and hate himself for causing him to run away. "Why couldn't Toy just accept me and all the things I had to do to provide for my family?" he would ask over and over again.

"You are the luckiest and most fortunate man in Thailand," *Khun* Arun said to Pompam one evening after dinner as they sat by the pool in Pompam's house. "Is there anything else you want out of this life?" he asked.

"I only want to see my brothers and my children grow up to be happy, and to fulfill their dreams as I have fulfilled mine," he replied, sounding like a politician. "I also want to live long enough to be able to see the young boys and girls from the countryside -- the sons and daughters of rice farmers like myself -- not have to do what I did when I was young in order to care for their families."

"You may have to live to be very old indeed, Pompam, to see the end of suffering children in Thailand. There is no question that the country now has great wealth; there's plenty of it all around us. It's just that it's in the hands of so few people, and the chances of spreading it around so the poor get their share seems slimmer each year," *Khun Arun* replied, sounding uncharacteristically philosophical. "I've heard it said that only one hundred mostly ethnic-Chinese families control the whole economy of the country." Then he added with a chuckle, "It doesn't seem very likely that any of them will get less greedy, does it?"

Pompam said nothing, thinking about the excesses of the new rich in Bangkok, his own included. Then he thought about Toy wandering around in the forest barefoot, and didn't understand why it had to be that way.

The months passed and Pompam took his work as an MP increasingly more seriously, often working twelve to fifteen hours a day. The arduous schedule he kept sometimes made him frustrated and short-tempered. He had always enjoyed perfect robust health and unlimited energy, but he began to tire easily, andhe could gradually feel his body running down.

"I must be getting old," he said to himself, feeling far more than his actual thirty-three -- nearly thirty-four -- years. He sensed that the depression he had suffered ever since the departure of Toy had undoubtedly added to his malaise.

"Rattana, let's take the kids up to Chiang Mai for Songkran vacation. I could use a break from everything -- and some rest, too. What do you think?" he asked one evening.

"It's a great idea, Pompam, but I can't see you'll be getting much rest with the children dragging you all over Chiang Mai and getting water thrown on you," she answered with a laugh. She had noticed the toll Pompam's strenuous routine seemed to be taking on his body, and she knew how much he missed Toy; perhaps Chiang Mai might provide him some relief.

Pompam's office booked a large suite at the Empress Hotel in Chiang Mai for the Songkran holidays. Rattana found herself looking forward to the vacation nearly as much as the kids, even though she was five months pregnant.

When they arrived at the northern capital they weren't surprised to see that the water games were already in full swing throughout the ancient city. The children were eager to dump their luggage in the room and head out with Pompam to join the festivities; the youngest, Surapong, who had just turned three, began whining for fear of being left behind.

Pompam had brought along Chaiya, his loyal driver, and Chaiya's wife to help look after the children. The two ladies stayed in the hotel while the two men ventured forth with the three youngsters, all of them equipped with buckets and squirt guns, and dressed in traditional northern dark-blue shirts and pants, *pakomah* around the waist, and rubber slippers.

Pompam enjoyed himself as he had not been able to for years. No one recognized him in the streets, and he behaved just like a child again, aggressively joining the water fights alongside his two sons and daughter. For a while he was able to forget about his businesses, the government, and Toy. Pompam and the rest of them stayed thoroughly soaked to the skin all day; it was impossible for anyone in Chiang Mai to keep dry for even a moment, since everyone in town was "armed" and on the prowl for victims.

They returned to the hotel in the late afternoon and Rattana immediately ordered the children to their baths, fearing that they would catch cold in the air conditioning. When the children finished bathing, Pompam went in next and stood under the hot water until his chilled flesh felt normal.

Not wanting to risk getting wet again, they stayed in the hotel that evening and dined together in the Thai restaurant on the ground floor. Pompam felt tired, but happy he had taken a break to enjoy the holiday with his family. All through the meal he kept recalling his many memories of Chiang Mai: perhaps the strongest was of the night he took Joy's soft virginity; another was the look in the black eyes of that terrified little hilltribe girl in the forest who had tried to run away. He had to blink to bring himself back to present-time.

They went to bed early, but in the middle of the night Pompam woke up shivering and had Rattana cover him with the spare blankets. "You're coming down with a cold, Pompam; too much water-throwing; I hope the children don't get it, too."

Pompam burned with fever all through the night, and by morning he knew that he was really sick. Rattana called for the hotel doctor, and he reported that Pompam's temperature was one-hundred-three degrees. He gave him aspirin to try to get the fever down, and an injection of antibiotics to fight off infection; but throughout that day and the following night his temperature remained high. Chaiya and his wife took the kids out to play Songkran with worried looks on their faces, and tried their best to keep the overly-excited children calmed down. All the while Rattana stayed next to her husband.

The second day Pompam was still no better, and the doctor said they had to put him in the hospital. Rattana reluctantly let the paramedics put him on a stretcher and take him away in an ambulance; Pompam was too weak and feverish to complain.

His condition continued to get worse. That evening the doctor confirmed that his lungs were filling up with fluid and he had developed pneumonia, so they moved him to intensive care and placed him on oxygen. Rattana had Chaiya and his wife take the children back to Bangkok; she couldn't cope with both her sick husband in the hospital and the children in a hotel during a holiday season gone bad for all of them.

The next morning Kitti and Sudar flew up to Chiang Mai and sat with Rattana until Pompam's condition was stabilized. After three days he became well enough to be transferred back to the hotel, and in another three days the doctor said he could get on the plane and fly back to Bangkok. He realized he had had a close call, and the doctor told him to rest in bed for three full weeks. Pompam protested, but in actuality, he was too weak to do anything but stay in bed.

After his three weeks of rest he gradually started going into the office for an hour or two each day, and to Parliament two or three times a week. "We've been very worried about you, *Khun* Vichai; you mustn't do anything to jeopardize your health. We need you," *Khun* Wharavuth said to him when they finally met.

To Kitti he said, "I just don't seem to be able to get my old energy back. Rattana even brought the Chinese doctor to see me and he's treated me with herbs and acupuncture. I get momentary relief, but then I'm flat on my back again."

One month later he had a relapse and was rushed back to the hospital in the middle of the night: another serious bout with pneumonia. That time he was hospitalized for two entire weeks, and by the time he was released he had lost nearly fifteen pounds.

Darunee came to see him at home and told him that he was shrinking, "You've had too much work and not enough young girls lately, Pompam." He tried to laugh at her joke, but he was too weak to give her more than a smile.

"What's the matter with me, Rattana? Why can't I get well and feel healthy again -- like I've felt all my life?" he complained almost every day.

The following month he felt a bit better and started a routine of going into the office once again. He continued to remain moderately healthy for another two months, and regained hope that his body was on the mend and would soon be back to normal. He started putting on a few pounds, and got back some of his old appetite -- at least for food. His other appetites would have to wait until he had more strength.

Pompam and Rattana's fourth child was born: a daughter, whom they named Khoranee. It was a difficult birth for Rattana, unlike the first three that had been so quick and natural. The baby was sick from the beginning and although the doctors said there was nothing congenitally wrong with her, she wouldn't breast-feed, didn't gain an ounce, and her tiny body couldn't digest the formula they tried to feed her. She seemed to have no strength -- not even to cry.

The doctors began to run a series of tests on the child and finally called a meeting with both parents and announced, "We're sorry to have to tell you this, but your baby is HIV-positive. She is dying of AIDS."

An explosion went off in the ears and minds of Pompam and Rattana. "That's impossible," Rattana screamed, "she's only an infant!"

"Babies can become HIV-positive if one or both of the parents is a carrier," the doctor said slowly and carefully, trying not to upset the already-overwrought parents.

"I don't have AIDS!" Rattana continued screaming. "It must be you, Pompam; you're the one who fucks anything that moves!"

"Shut up, Rattana," Pompam shouted, "you don't know what you're talking about."

"You're the one who's been sick for the past four months, you idiot! You are the carrier that is killing our baby!" Rattana was becoming uncontrollable, creating a scene.

Pompam finally couldn't stand his wife's hysterics any longer and he fled from the room. He left Rattana with the doctors who would finally have to sedate her to calm her down. The two doctors looked sadly at each other and shook their heads. The thought that the handsome, famous *Khun* Vichai had infected his own newborn daughter with AIDS was more than even they, as physicians, could handle. It was depressing and disgraceful beyond words.

Pompam ordered Chaiya to take him to his penthouse retreat on Sukhumvit. He was in a complete state of shock. Thoughts too horrible to think were crowding his brain. "Oh, my God!" he screamed out loud at the top of his lungs. "My new baby has AIDS, which means that I must have AIDS, too!"

He poured himself a glass-full of whiskey and collapsed in a chair, his head suddenly throbbing with pain. He quickly drained his glass and picked up the phone. "Kitti, please come to my apartment now. I must see you immediately." He hung up.

He sat in the chair waiting for his old friend to arrive and drank another glass of Black Label. He began to feel drunk, sick drunk, and ran to the bathroom where he vomited until he didn't have the energy to get up off the floor. After a while the doorbell rang, but he couldn't get up to answer it. After several more rings Kitti finally used the key Pompam had once given him, and burst into the room.

"I'm in here," Pompam called out weakly.

Kitti followed the sound of Pompam's voice to the huge master bedroom where he found him sprawled out on the floor; the stench of whiskey and vomit was overpowering.

"Pompam, what's happening?" Kitti asked frantically as he lifted him to the chair.

"Oh my God, oh my God," was all he could answer, over and over again.

"What's wrong, Pompam?" Kitti screamed, looking down at his friend, not having a clue what was wrong.

"My new baby has AIDS," he finally muttered, "and I'm sure she got it from me. I have killed my own baby daughter..." he whispered with tears streaming down his face, saliva pooling at the corners of his gaping mouth.

Kitti stood there horrified, unable to fully comprehend the

devastating news his life-long friend had just given him. "Pompam, this is impossible; it just can't be true," Kitti uttered in painful disbelief.

"I only wish I was lying, Kitti. I just came from the hospital where the doctors told me. Rattana..." Pompam trailed off, staring out into space at the unimaginably grotesque scene confronting his mind.

Kitti sat down on the floor next to Pompam and gazed at the carpet, unseeing.

Some minutes passed this way and finally Pompam said, "We can't let anyone know about this. We have to keep it to ourselves. Please go and get Rattana at the hospital and take her home. Tell her maid to stay with her in her room and not to let her use the telephone. In fact, take the telephone out of her room," he ordered. "Get some drugs from the doctor to make her sleep."

Kitti nodded and pulled himself up off the floor using the arm of Pompam's chair. He felt like he had been hit by a shotgun blast, and was numb all over from the shock to his brain.

"I feel like I'm getting sick again. Tell my doctor to come here as soon as he can, Kitti. Tell him not to say a word to anyone," Pompam continued.

Kitti was devastated. He couldn't even turn his face to look at Pompam. He kept telling himself that it was all a dream; it wasn't real. His childhood friend, his leader, was surely an immortal, he told himself. He couldn't possibly have AIDS! He was rich and handsome and, up until a few months ago, the healthiest man alive. Only the poor and uneducated get AIDS from going with filthy, infected prostitutes from Burma, he thought to himself; but in reality he knew better.

He knew from articles he had read that Thailand was on the verge of a terrible AIDS epidemic, even though the government still refused to admit it. For far too many years the men of the Land of Smiles had indulged themselves in promiscuous, unprotected sex with prostitutes, their macho self images still not able to accept the use of condoms in spite of the many warnings. A whole generation of working-age men was at risk of being wiped out.

Kitti, reluctant to leave Pompam alone, went out to do what he had been told. Downstairs in the garage he said to Chaiya, "Go up to the apartment and stay with your boss until I come back."

Pompam, wretched, sat in silence as the sun sank behind the

forest of new high-rises that had grown up out of the ground. The doctor arrived about two hours later and put Pompam to bed. He checked his vital signs and drew the blood upon which to perform the dreaded test.

He gave Pompam a sedative and told Chaiya to look after him; he said he would be back in the morning. In the middle of the night the sick man was awakened by horrifying nightmares -- forced to confront demons he was in no way prepared to meet. He wept, wishing that Toy was there with him to comfort him. "Only Toy can help me get through this bad dream -- and say the words I need to hear so I won't lose my mind," he cried to himself.

Just after dawn Kitti arrived, followed by the doctor a few minutes later. The physician discovered that Pompam was running a high fever. Immediately, Kitti and Chaiya carried Pompam to the car in the garage downstairs and rushed him to the hospital.

The doctor and Kitti did not tell Pompam that during the night Rattana had suddenly awakened from the strong sedative she had been given, and her mind snapped in two when she realized she had not dreamed that her innocent new baby had AIDS. She started throwing things and beating herself, and tried to cut herself with broken glass.

The terrified maid telephoned Kitti at 3:00 a.m. Kitti called the doctor, dressed, and sped over to Pompam's big house where lights were ablaze and the entire household in an uproar: children screaming, sobbing servants immobilized by fear, and Rattana shrieking like a banshee in some haunted Irish castle. He and the maids did their best to restrain Rattana, to keep her from hurting herself. They held her pinned down on the bed until the doctor arrived and gave her an injection of thorazine. When she was quiet they bundled her in a blanket and carried her off to the hospital.

Although she would be kept sedated for weeks, she would never completely regain control over her mind. She would drift between states of lucidity and terror, her heart turned to stone by her overwhelming hatred of Pompam. She could never forgive him for what he had done to her baby, and most-likely to her as well.

As much as Kitti and Ott tried to keep the word of Pompam's illness from getting out, it was inevitable that it would. Too many people (doctors, hospital staff, servants, etc.) knew about it, and like anywhere else, bad news about celebrities often travels very fast. It only took two days for the newspaper headline to read: "Vichai Polcharoen Dying of AIDS."

That night Paradise City, Isan Sweetheart and The Regents Club were as silent as tombs. The stigma attached to HIV was so severe that no one wanted to go anywhere near those formerly popular places, much less have sex with one of the girls who worked there. What if *Khun* Vichai had gotten AIDS from one of the girls? What if *Khun* Vichai had *given* it to one of the girls? What if it had spread to all of them? These were the questions that not only kept the customers away in droves, but caused the bulk of the staff to resign -- particularly the "service girls" who figured they had better get out fast, or be tainted and not be able to find work someplace else.

The general public was stunned by the news. Never before had a well-known Thai person been stricken by AIDS and have the sad news wind up on the front page. No one could talk about anything else for several days. The general reaction, unfortunately, was not one of compassion or a calling for prayers for healing; instead it cried unanimously for damning and shunning.

It was almost as if Pompam had *betrayed* the people of Thailand by getting the disease: it just wasn't supposed to happen to someone like him. It made everyone altogether too fearful that the AIDS threat wasn't as remote as they had thought it was, and that they themselves might be just as vulnerable as respectable *Khun* Vichai. They couldn't quite handle these realities psychologically, so they made Pompam an "evil one."

Very quickly stories of Pompam's past began to surface, one by one. Hardly a day passed without the media carrying news of the latest scandal to be uncovered. It seemed like anyone from anywhere who had ever been even remotely connected to Pompam was anxious to come out of the closet and tell their sordid tales.

Within a month it was all out: Pompam's career at Number Ten, the Jamestown Pub, the low-class brothel near Isan Sweetheart, the girl-brokering activities, allegations of *yakuza* connections, *Khun* Nimit's murder, and even suspicions of drug dealings with the Shan State via Nopadon in Chiang Mai. Everything was exposed.

The effects on Pompam's family and business partners was devastating. Paradise City and Isan Sweetheart had to be closed; this put Att and Kitti's parents out of work. Nuu was forced to resign from The Regents Club because the staff lost complete respect for him, and the few members who still frequented the place drove him out. Black's show business career took a dive into oblivion and he couldn't get work anywhere, or even *give* his cassettes away. These three brothers all turned their backs on Pompam -- in spite of all he had done for them -- and ran for cover.

Top and the youngest two brothers were treated like lepers at school and had to drop out, becoming paranoid and neurotic. They withdrew into cocoons back in the village in Buriram where they had escaped; it wasn't quite as bad there, but they were taunted and rejected, just the same.

Kim's Chinese parents forced her to leave her disgraced husband, Ott, with words of, "I told you about marrying those no-good Thais!"

Chai had a whole raft of legal problems when he was named as the primary link between Nopadon and the VP Group, and all that entailed -- including the drugs in the Shan State. In addition to being suspected of hiring the assassin who did-in *Khun* Nimit, he was also looked at by the public as the scum of the *khlongs* when the newspapers started printing estimated figures on the number of young girls he had ushered into prostitution -- not to mention those he had bought out-right. Nopadon was arrested and faced a long jail sentence; Chai expected the same thing would happen to him, as did Kitti and Ott for the various roles they had played.

Khun Wharavut and Pompam's colleagues in the government passed a resolution which effectively kicked him out of Parliament in disgrace. It was hard to find anyone in that sector who would admit to have even *met* Pompam, even though so many of them had enjoyed his favors and entertainments.

The Thailand Youth Foundation's illustrious Board of Directors all resigned and put as much distance between themselves and The VP Group as they could. Toy was nowhere around to run things anyway, so everything was put on hold -- permanently.

Even *Khun* Arun, guilty by association, was no longer treated with his former level of respect -- or found himself welcome in his previous high-level social circles. He began to go downhill health-wise after his boyfriend, Pet, suddenly left him and went back to Chiang Mai seeking a life of obscurity.

Kitti was left with the task of trying to hold as many pieces together as he could for as long as he could -- concentrating on the legal issues which pressed in from all directions. He knew there might not be anything left after the courts got finished with them. They faced heavy fines should they be convicted of charges that ranged from tax evasion to prostitution to child abuse to drug dealing, and the government had frozen their bank accounts. They even started looking for money they suspected Kitti had stashed overseas.

Kitti's wife, Sudar, took their baby back to her parents' house in Ayuddhya and said she would stay there until things got back to normal. In reality, she had no intention of ever getting back together again with her permanently-clouded husband -- even if he managed to escape going to jail, which was doubtful.

Pompam would be constantly in and out of the hospital over the next four months: it was the only thing that kept the authorities from dragging him off to prison. He was never treated for the same malady, and each month, each hospital stay, was for some new disease that attacked Pompam's weakened immune system. He hated it every time he had to stay in the hospital. The staff treated him coldly and with disrespect, and the newspapers inevitably found out he was there, invading his room with cameras and reporters. Each time he was admitted, one more photograph would appear of Pompam's diseased, frail body in his hospital bed, accompanied by headlines that were far less than compassionate.

Pompam couldn't quite fathom the fact that he was ruined, nearly alone, and had plummeted so far from grace to the fantastic, unprecedented, extent that he had. In the beginning he read the newspaper reports, but after a while he refused to look at them. He simply couldn't accept the fact that not only was he dying, but he was leaving this world with no honor, no love, and no "face."

Even the maids deserted, and when he wasn't in the hospital he lived in the big house alone except for his driver, Chaiya, who became his nurse and cared for him. Chaiya remained with his boss because

Pompam had been so generous with him when he had helped find the land in Bangkapi. He also stayed because he was a devout Buddhist: he believed he would make merit for himself if he took care of Pompam until he died.

Towards the end only Kitti visited Pompam regularly, and Darunee came to visit from time to time. Without servants, the big white house began to look dirty and neglected, and things started breaking down, only to be left unrepaired. The gardens began to return to their untamed, natural state, and the fish in the pond died and rotted.

Darunee cried each time she came to see Pompam. "You stupid buffalo," she teased, trying to suppress her tears, "how could you get yourself so fucked up?" She would try to amuse him with malicious, gossipy stories about her new *khunying* friends. She also told him that she had a wonderful new man in her life -- one that she might consider marrying one day. Pompam said he was glad for her.

"I really miss our conspiracies from the old days, Nee. We really pulled off some pretty amazing tricks didn't we?" he reminisced. Darunee kept remembering -- with regret -- that stupid, drunken night in Hong Kong, and worried that she, herself, might be in danger. She couldn't bring herself to be tested, however, and did her best to put it out of her mind.

Pompam, confined to his bed, spent most of his waking hours silently reviewing in his mind his amazing life, going over it scene by scene. He took a great deal of medication for pain and depression, so he often floated in and out of consciousness, one memory blending and flowing into the next in a continuous state of twilight.

One of his great regrets was that he had never become a monk. He wished he could be ordained now -- even though he was sick -- to make merit for his dead mother and father: this was his duty as a son. None of his younger brothers -- except for Toy -- had become monks or *nenes* either, thanks to his lack of encouragement, he realized sadly.

He remembered that he had never had the monks come to the house for the traditional Buddhist blessing ceremony. He felt guilty about the omission, but then reminded himself just how busy he used to be, and let it go.

He sent for *Phra* Asoka from time to time; he knew that he was probably the only person in the world who wouldn't judge him. The revered Indian monk never even seemed to notice Pompam's failing condition, and he always acted the same as the first day Pompam had met him, so many years before.

Conforming to the Buddhist religion, *Phra* Asoka put very little emphasis on death in his personal philosophy; he rarely even spoke about it. Each time Pompam would bring the subject up, the monk would wave his hand and say, "It is nothing, Vichai. It is only a minor event when you consider the whole scenario of your life -- going all the way back through your countless births-and-deaths." He said the universe had its own rhythm, its own speed; every single entity of creation moved through its own cycle in its own time.

"*Mai pen rai*, Vichai. You have all the time in the world -- in the universe, even -- to do what you are ultimately here to do, which is to transcend your karma and realize yourself. Don't be concerned by just one death."

Each time *Phra* Asoka came to visit, Pompam would ask him if he had heard any news from Toy, and each time *Phra* Asoka had to tell him that he had heard nothing; Toy's whereabouts were still unknown. Pompam begged the monk to try to find him, and *Phra* Asoka agreed to put the word out through the Buddhist "grapevine," but so far there was no news. Pompam began to worry that he would die before seeing his beloved brother again.

Earlier on, Pompam telephoned his old friend, *Khun* Surapong from the police department, now retired and enjoying the fruits of his corrupt career. "Please help me find my brother, Toy. I need him," he pleaded.

"I will do my best, Pompam," he assured him; but he did nothing, knowing he would get no "donation" for doing it. He also wanted to keep his distance from Pompam, thanking the Buddha that he, himself, was one of the few lucky ones who so far had escaped being tainted from having been close to him.

Pompam desperately missed and needed Toy -- more than anyone. He knew that Toy could help get rid of his depression, and guide him into the realm of death more cheerfully, and with dignity. As it was now, he was horribly afraid of dying, fearing that he might be doomed to many lifetimes of suffering and pain. Perhaps his saintly brother could make merit for him and help him with his re-birth, he thought. Not a night went by that Pompam didn't cry out for Toy in his sleep, certain that he would hear his call and come home.

He never did.

The baby Khoranee finally died, her frail body never having a chance to fight off its many afflictions. When Pompam heard the news he went even deeper into depression and refused to eat. He often thought about his other three children and missed the sounds of their voices, remembering how happy they had all been at Songkran in Chiang Mai. He also missed Rattana, who could have provided him comfort had her mind survived the disaster that had so suddenly destroyed her life. *Khun* Direk, Pompam's father-in-law, had come to Bangkok and taken Rattana and the children home to the village. He fed his daughter the drugs that would keep her debilitating nightmares at bay, and did his best to pacify his poor grandchildren who were confused and disoriented by the abrupt annihilation of their world.

He refused to visit Pompam, the former pride of his village, such was the degree of the hatred he now felt for him. He even refused to accept any further money from his son-in-law, save those funds that would be used for the care of his fragile daughter and his three bewildered grandchildren. How ironic, Pompam thought one day, that Little Jim, Somporn and Surapong would begin their lives again in the same place where he, himself, had started his own.

Mr. Aoyama, ever the thoughtful Japanese, never asked to see Pompam during this period, but not a week went by without a floral bouquet arriving from him. One week the flowers did not arrive; then a second week, and a third. Kitti finally received a call from Japan informing him that Mr. Aoyama was dead, apparently the victim of another assassination in the power struggle that had arisen after Kenji's death. Kitti kept this sad news from Pompam, knowing that it would only make him feel worse.

Kitti tried to visit Pompam every few days, but it hurt him deeply to see his old friend reduced to such a feeble mass of suffering. In addition to the news of Aoyama's death, Kitti did his best to keep further news of their crumbling empire from reaching Pompam's ears. Kitti, himself, lived in a continual state of shock, never knowing where the next attack would come from. He wanted desperately to escape the horrid, degrading, legal dramas he was forced to deal with every day; he wanted to return to the village and be a simple buffalo boy again, and get drunk on Lao whiskey. But even if he was able to clear his name in the courts, he still had to wait; he owed it to Pompam.

Towards the end, even though Pompam knew he would be prosecuted for many crimes had he not been sick and dying, he felt he had only done what others had done -- and do -- every day. He had merely played the "system" and won, and had ultimately been decorated by the King.

Even after witnessing the crashing down of everything he had built, he still didn't consider himself a bad person. He only thought that he was unlucky for having caught AIDS, and didn't understand why he had to suffer so much, and have to do it alone.

One day Pompam sent his faithful Chaiya to the village in Buriram to fetch *Phra* Prateep, the old Abbot. Pompam felt a desperate need to see him again, feeling that somehow the old man held his last hope for recovery.

When the elderly monk entered Pompam's bedroom and saw his wasted condition, he sucked in his breath and slowly sank into the chair at the invalid's side. By this time Pompam had developed the red, blotchy rash that sometimes accompanies the final stages of his illness, and it was as if Pompam's face and form had been splattered by some careless crimson paintbrush. *Phra* Prateep was deeply shaken by the sight of the once-perfect body, now shrunken, discolored, and diminished. Even though he knew every detail of Pompam's humiliation and downfall, he didn't think he deserved to die like this.

"Tell me what I must do to get well, *Phra* Prateep," Pompam pleaded softly. "I will give any amount of donations, and will build dozens of temples to make merit so the Lord Buddha will heal my body." He had always been able to buy himself out of ugly situations in the past, and he thought, as a last resort, he would try to buy himself out of death.

Phra Prateep looked sadly and lovingly at the still-young man lying in the bed next to him. He thought about all the time they had spent together when Pompam was a *nene* and the Abbot had looked after him like a son.

"Your illness has already sealed your fate, Vichai, and no amount of money in the world can reverse its course. I am sorry to tell you this, but it is true."

"But why, *Phra* Prateep? Why must I die?" he said with anger, his eyes flashing brightly.

"You have created your own condition, Vichai; you should know this already from all your years of training. You also know, in your soul, everything you have done in the past that has caused you to be exactly where you are, and as you are. All you can do now is be mindful, calm your mind, accept your karma, and prepare for your next birth."

Pompam thought with bitterness about the life he could have enjoyed for many more years: his children, his wealth, his future accomplishments, and his pleasures. He had had everything in the world to look forward to, and now there was nothing.

Early in the evening Pompam raised his head and looked around the room as if searching for the faces he loved. But there was only Chaiya, his driver. He called to him and said, "Has Toy come?"

"No, *Khun* Vichai. No one is here right now. *Phra* Prateep left about two hours ago," he answered. Chaiya felt terrible that his boss was so alone. The silent house darkened with the sunset, and Chaiya could almost see death creeping into the room.

Pompam wished that Toy was there to hold his hand. He felt afraid. Then he closed his eyes and went back to sleep, never to wake again in that lifetime.

The following morning the wandering monk, *Phra* Chatree, entered the city of Korat. He had been walking in the jungles for many weeks, and had spent the rainy season in a solitary meditation hut at a remote forest temple in Ubon Ratchathani. He felt cleansed and refreshed, and completely healed from the experiences of his former life. His time away from the world had prepared him to go back into it again, and begin his work as one who serves the people; he had decided to be a teaching monk for the rest of his life and leave his former "causes" to others. He was on his way to the station to catch the train to Bangkok and present himself to *Phra* Asoka for an assignment.

Walking barefoot near the open market, he passed a newsstand and saw the headline announcing that Pompam, his *pi-chai*, was dead. He breathed deeply, and then picked up the paper and tried to read the story calmly. He went into shock, and the world he had left behind suddenly came rushing towards him again.

The train conductor let him ride for free in the third-class compartment, and Toy settled down and tried to digest the awesome, tragic news. From Hua Lampong station in Bangkok he took three changes of public buses and finally arrived at the massive white house on *Soi* Tonglor about nine o'clock that evening. The building looked dark and empty; Toy was surprised to see the garden looking so over-grown. He rang the bell several times and no one came out to open the gate, so he finally used his own key and let himself in.

The electric lights were turned off everywhere, but there were two large orange candles burning in the massive, marble-floored entry hall. They gave off enough light so Toy could see the coffin resting on a table in the middle of the room.

"Is anybody home?" he called out. There was no answer. He walked slowly through the big house all the way to the kitchen and the maids quarters, but still no one answered him. Finally it came to him that Pompam's body had been left alone and unaccompanied its last night on earth. Toy walked from room to room in disbelief.

He took one of the chairs from the dining room and brought it to the entry hall and placed it next to the makeshift bier. Then he opened the lid of the coffin and looked inside at the shadowy face of his elder brother. Toy screamed out loud when he saw the shrunken form, the red paint of death on its hollow cheeks. He closed the box, and then sat down and wept until he ran out of breath.

"Why didn't you listen to me, *pi-chai*? I tried to save you. How could you have let yourself come to this? You see now how right I was to be worried for you?" Toy asked these questions and many more as he waited for the sun to rise.

Chaiya and Kitti came early in the morning with a hired van to take the coffin to *Wat* Mahathat for the funeral. Kitti and Toy had very little to say to one another as they rode together to the temple. *Phra* Asoka and the other monks were already assembled when they arrived, and the chanting began when it became apparent that there would be no more mourners. Toy was shocked that the man who had known and entertained thousands in his lifetime would wind up so alone at the end.

When the ceremony was over and the body was burned, the temple boy came forward with the urn containing Pompam's ashes. Toy reached out and took it from him, tears in his eyes, the reality sinking in that all that was left of his brother was contained in the small jar.

Kitti, choking with emotion, said, "I want to take the urn to the temple in Buriram, Toy. Will you come with me?"

Toy held the urn close to him, embracing it, and only managed to nod his head. *Phra* Asoka came up to him and patted him on the shoulder, knowing it would be a while before the young man could speak.

Chaiya declined to go with them, saying he had done all he could for *Khun* Vichai, so Kitti and Toy drove themselves to Buriram. Together they interred the ashes in the family shrine that Pompam had built. It already held the remains of Maa, Paw, baby Khoranee, and the sister who had died before the seven younger brothers were born.

Toy said to Kitti, "It was only a short time ago that Pompam built The VP Tower as his monument to himself. But this is where he belongs."

Then he reached into his yellow, cloth monk's bag and took out the gold-encased Buddha image and thick gold chain that Pompam had worn for so many years; he himself had removed it from Pompam's body before it was cremated. He placed the object reverently on the *chedi's* base and then he and *Phra* Prateep chanted for three or four minutes.

It was over. Not one person from the village even showed his face.

In the early evening a thin, frail-looking woman accompanied by an elderly man entered the deserted temple grounds. They approached the small *chedi* and she knelt down and placed a small flower garland next to the photograph of Pompam. Then she *waied* and lit three sticks of fragrant incense. Afterwards, she removed the simple, golden Buddha amulet that she wore around her neck on a fine gold chain, and then placed it at the base of the *chedi* next to the other one that was already there. As she did so she couldn't help but think about that special *Loy Kratong* moon so long ago.

Epilogue

"I stood in that very same spot, Little Jim, when your Paw shaved my head after our Paw died," *Phra* Chatree said to the ten-year-old boy. "And many years before that, your father became a *nene* when he was exactly the same age as you -- and our Paw shaved his head." Little Jim winced and whined as *Phra* Chatree nicked his scalp with the ancient, dull safety razor; then he closed his eyes and prayed his uncle wouldn't miss and cut his nose off when he shaved his eyebrows.

It was one year to the day since Pompam's death, and his oldest son, Prakart, was entering the monkhood as a *nene* to make merit for his father's soul. Old *Phra* Prateep died only three months after Pompam, and Toy had taken over as Abbot of the village temple.

"Top, you and the other two come over here and sit by Little Jim during his ordination; help him if he starts to forget his vows," *Phra* Chatree said to his and Pompam's youngest three brothers, now aged sixteen, fourteen and thirteen, all three of them *nenes*. They obeyed *Phra* Chatree immediately, as they always did, ever since he took over as head of their family when Pompam passed away.

Nuu, unshaven and hung-over, shuffled into the *viharn* and slumped onto the floor. "I'm glad to see you made it, Nuu," remarked *Phra* Chatree. "And I'm glad to see you left your whiskey bottle at home."

The monk treated his older brother with compassion, even though he scolded him about his constant drinking. Since Nuu's wife left him, he was living alone in his parents' old wooden house, bringing the fallow rice fields back to life, and living the life of a simple village peasant, just like his father before him. His *pakomah* was tied jauntily around his head like an Isan-style turban -- exactly the way Dr. Jim had worn his so many years before.

Att couldn't come to the ceremony for Little Jim; his Chinese wife had left him also, but he was able to get a job in Bangkok as an accountant for a big export company.

Black, too, wasn't there that day; he was performing his music on the "hotel circuit," going from resort to resort from one end of the country to another, making a living.

The brothers fared far better than Kitti, Chai, and Ott who were all serving long prison sentences in Bangkok; they would be very old men when they were finally released.

"Come, Rattana; you, Somporn, Surapong -- you sit here on my left; you are giving your oldest son to Lord Buddha, remember?"

Rattana did as she was told, and with vacant eyes sat down near the simple altar, her two youngest leaning against her bony arms. She now lived in the house Pompam had built for his parents, the only thing the government had let them keep; and she worked in the weaving factory Toy had built years before for *Phra* Prateep. Her mother taught her the craft of spinning silk yarn, and the clack-clack sound of the looms lulled her mind into a state of relaxation, a big improvement over her previous manic condition. She still didn't say much, but she loved her children, took good care of them, and gave the monks food every morning at dawn when they made their rounds collecting alms.

"*Khun* Direk, you and your wife are the grandparents; you sit here on my right," he said, motioning to the elderly village headman.

Half a dozen emaciated, very sick-looking men and two women were the last to enter the *viharn*, and *Phra* Chatree waved his arm for them to come forward. These were some of the AIDS patients he looked after, those that could still walk; there were a dozen others bedridden in the make-shift clinic *Phra* Chatree had caused to be built in the far corner of the temple grounds.

Their families had disowned these people for getting AIDS and bringing down shame on them. They were left on their own to die, so *Phra* Chatree built his hospice, and depended on a few of his wealthy Bangkok contacts from the Youth Foundation to give him money to buy medicines. He also had the income the temple still received from the weaving factory, and he dipped into that when he needed to. In the year since Pompam's death he had been the last witness to eighty four such persons who had succumbed to the disease. He burned their bodies in the temple crematorium, but nearly all of their bones were still unclaimed, waiting for uncaring relatives in individually-wrapped plastic bags with tags identifying who they belonged to.

Phra Chatree felt that caring for the AIDS people was one "cause" he had to keep since so few others were doing it. The unfortunate men and women came from many parts of the Kingdom to die in his poor country temple; for many, there was no place else to go.

"We will begin the chanting now. Little Jim, are you ready? Do it right so your Paw will be proud of you," instructed *Phra* Chatree. Then he led the other monks in the chant, thinking all the while about the brother he loved more than anyone in the world, the simple buffalo boy from Buriram.

Glossary of Thai Words

ajarn - professor.

baan - house.

baht - Thai unit of currency; before July of 1997, twenty-five baht equaled approximately one dollar.

chai-oh - cheers!

chedi - pagoda-like shrine.

chok dee - good luck.

Dhamma - Teachings of Buddha.

farang - foreigner.

gai yang - marinated, barbecued chicken.

graing jai - "standing on ceremony."

guit dio - noodle soup.

hi-so - slang for "high society."

jai dee - good heart.

jai dum - "black" heart; evil or mean.

jakutee - ticklish.

kamoy - thief.

kee neo - stingy.

khanom - candy or dessert.

khao - rice.

khao neo - sticky, glutinous rice.

khap khun - thank you.

khatote - I'm sorry.

khlong - canal

khroo - teacher.

Khun - polite title for male or female; e.g. "Mr." "Miss" or "Mrs."

khunying - title given to ladies by the King as a reward for services to Thailand.

kratong - small floating vessel made for Loy Kratong holiday.

kuti - monk's room or cell in the temple.

leau hang yao - long-tail boat

Loy Kratong - Thai holiday of "Harvest Moon"; usually late November.

mai pen rai - "never mind."

mali - Chinese jasmine.

mau mak - very drunk.

mia luang - major wife.
mia noi - minor wife.
mondop - building in a temple that contains a shrine.
nak-rong - singer.
nam prik - chili paste.
nene - novice Buddhist monk.
nit noy - just a little bit.
nong-chai - younger brother.
pakomah - long, narrow piece of multi-purpose fabric, worn around
          waist or head.
Pali - Buddhist liturgical language; a derivative of Sanskrit.
pang - expensive.
pee - ghost
Phra - title for Buddhist monk.
phuyai - "bigshot" in government or business.
pi-chai - big brother.
puamgmalai - flower garland.
rai - unit of land measurement; one acre equals approximately 2 1/2 rai.
ram wong - traditional folk dance.
sabai - happy or healthy.
sala - open-sided pavilion.
Sangha - Buddhist clergy.
sanuk - fun.
sarong - wrap-around skirt for men or women.
sawasdee - Thai greeting.
so-co - slang for "soda and cola" mixed.
soi - small street or lane.
somtam - spicy green papaya salad.
Songkran - Thai New Year holiday; usually mid-April.
tambon - village headman or chief.
thamboon - fund-raising ceremony for a Buddhist temple.
tudong - a solitary "walk-about" for a monk.
tuk-tuk - three-wheeled taxi vehicle.
viharn - main sanctuary of a temple compound.
wai - gesture of respect performed by joining hands together as if
        praying.
wat - Buddhist temple.
wat dek - temple boy.

Karmic Ties